NO SAFETY FROM LOVE

Charlotte came back from London to her Lancashire home determined not to repeat the mistakes of the past. Her marriage to idealistic, improvident Toby Longe had plunged her into poverty and insecurity. Now, with his death, Charlotte was free to return to the settled, ordered life she had known as a girl.

But Charlotte soon learned she had left girlhood behind her forever. She was a woman, with a woman's needs, a woman's strength, a woman's determination—and when she met Jack Ackroyd, she was a woman in love.

She would do more than share his bed. She would stand by his side in a struggle that turned the act of love into a supreme act of courage. . . .

AN IMPERFECT JOY

Great Fiction From SIGNET

- [ ] **THE RUNNING MAN** by Richard Bachman.
  (#AE1508—$2.50)*
- [ ] **SLEEPING BEAUTY** by L.L. Greene. (#AE1548—$2.50)*
- [ ] **WIFE FOUND SLAIN** by Caroline Crane. (#AE1614—$2.50)*
- [ ] **DEVIL'S EMBRACE** by Catherine Coulter. (#AE1853—$2.95)*
- [ ] **MINOTAUR** by Benjamin Tammuz. (#AW1582—$1.50)*
- [ ] **THE CURE** by Len Goldberg. (#AE1509—$2.50)*
- [ ] **KINGDOM OF SUMMER** by Gillian Bradshaw.
  (#AE1550—$2.75)*
- [ ] **NEW BLOOD** by Richard Salem. (#AE1615—$2.50)†
- [ ] **ROOFTOPS** by Tom Lewis. (#AE1735—$2.95)*
- [ ] **GAMES OF CHANCE** by Peter Delacourte. (#AE1510—$2.95)*
- [ ] **POSITION OF ULTIMATE TRUST** by William Beechcroft.
  (#AE1551—$2.50)*
- [ ] **LIONHEART!** by Martha Rofheart. (#AE1617—$3.50)*
- [ ] **EYE OF THE MIND** by Lynn Biederstadt. (#AE1736—$2.95)*
- [ ] **MY LADY HOYDEN** by Jane Sheridan. (#AE1511—$2.95)*
- [ ] **TAURUS** by George Wells. (#AE1553—$2.50)*
- [ ] **MIDAS** by Piers Kelaart. (#AE1618—$2.50)†

*Prices slightly higher in Canada
†Not available in Canada

Buy them at your local bookstore or use this convenient coupon for ordering.

THE NEW AMERICAN LIBRARY, INC.,
P.O. Box 999, Bergenfield, New Jersey 07621

Please send me the books I have checked above. I am enclosing $_____
(please add $1.00 to this order to cover postage and handling). Send check
or money order—no cash or C.O.D.'s. Prices and numbers are subject to change
without notice.

Name_____

Address_____

City _____ State _____ Zip Code _____
Allow 4-6 weeks for delivery.
This offer is subject to withdrawal without notice.

An Imperfect Joy

Jean Stubbs

A SIGNET BOOK

NEW AMERICAN LIBRARY

TIMES MIRROR

SIGNET TRADEMARK REG: U.S. PAT. OFF. AND FOREIGN COUNTRIES
REGISTERED TRADEMARK—MARCA REGISTRADA
HECHO EN CHICAGO, U.S.A.

SIGNET, SIGNET CLASSICS, MENTOR, PLUME, MERIDIAN and NAL BOOKS
are published by The New American Library, Inc.,
1633 Broadway, New York, New York 10019

First Signet Printing, July, 1982

1 2 3 4 5 6 7 8 9

PRINTED IN THE UNITED STATES OF AMERICA

To my family

Felix
Mouse, Jonna, Jo & Pickles
Bob, Pat & the Brooklet

Acknowledgements

I thank all those who have in any way helped me with this book: but particularly my editor Teresa Sacco, and sub-editor Honor Burgess, for their creative care; Bob Gilbert of Gilbert's Prints and Books, Truro, Cornwall, D. G. Willcocks of Longs Booksellers, Poulton-Le-Fylde, Lancashire, and the staff of Helston Branch Library, Cornwall, for finding essential books with such enthusiasm; the Ironbridge Gorge Museum Trust for existing; my grand-daughter, Joanna Mathys, for the portrait of Cicely Longe as a child; and my husband, Roy Oliver, who listens to the unfolding tale and cooks the supper when the Howarths have tired me out.

Contents

Part Four
Man of Worth

How far from then forethought of, all thy more
boisterous years,
When thou at the random grim forge, powerful
amidst peers,
Didst fettle for the great grey drayhorse his
bright and battering sandal!

Felix Randall
Gerard Manley Hopkins
1844–1889

Part One

———◆●▸———

Man on His Mettle
1785—1793

ONE

Make Way for the Mail!

November 1785

By midnight there were only two travellers still waiting in the parlour of The Royal Oak at Market Street, Manchester. But a lanky lad made up the fire on the broad hearth, and brought fresh candles, so they were comfortable enough. Both had journeyed some distance already—the threadbare clergyman from Preston and the dandified young giant from Millbridge—and were understandably weary. Still, the landlady had conjured up salt fish, boiled mutton and capers, with apple tart to follow, and they had washed it down with strong beer before finding a quiet place in the chimney corner. There, Parson Peplow ordered brandy and hot water, a clay pipe and tobacco, prepared to smoke and talk until the coach should depart for London. He was a short, cheerful man dressed in dusty black, with a grey bag-wig and pebble glasses. Life had been niggardly in regard to wealth, but he constantly enriched himself by study of his fellow men, and found his unknown companion a delightful mixture of contradictions.

The young fellow was very fine in his plum-coloured suit and plum velvet waistcoat, the white stock fashionably tied, yet he wore his own black hair plainly ribboned at the nape of his neck. When he stepped down from the Yorkshire coach he had greeted the landlady courteously and formally, and then a moment later was chatting to the ostlers about horses as though he were one of themselves. He did not spit on the floor, wipe his nose on his sleeve or make disagreeable noises over his food, but he ate without any of the finicking manners customary in a gentleman. His great shoulders and sturdy limbs, his broad hands and deep chest suggested that he was used to heavy labour. His quick dark glance showed an intelligence above the ordinary, and he was handsome enough to have all the serving-wenches running round for him at supper. Nor did he lack money and some genteel connections, for when he took out his watch to tell the time it was of an older age than this, and beautifully wrought in silver.

A proper conundrum, thought Parson Peplow. Age about six-and-twenty. Son of a small landowner, used to working his father's estate. Good blood on one side and honest ancestors on the other. His mother, or some close female, loves him dearly and sees to his linen and comforts. And the journey to London? Not business, more likely an affair of the heart. He'd rather consult with the fire than with me.

So the clergyman turned his attention to the landlady, who had that moment entered to bring his order herself.

'This is most kind, ma'am,' cried Parson Peplow. 'I thought it wise to warm myself with spirits before the journey, which I understand to be arduous though swift.'

'Well, sir, when you think that twenty year ago the coach used to leave from here regular, Mondays and Thursdays, and take three and a half days to get to London, and now the Mail reckons to do it in less than half the time, I ask you, sir, even allowing for the roads being better, can you stop at all the places as you used to? So best to warm up afore you start, like you say.'

She was moving about the room as she spoke, setting it to rights. Now she stopped by the young man and asked him if he wouldn't take a little something to keep out the cold.

'For it's raining fit to burst outside,' she added, 'and once the Mail gets going it don't stop until Ashbourne, and even then you won't get breakfast, sir. Derby's the breakfast stop, and it'll be a half after ten in the morning, and you'll be clemmed by then.'

'I thank you, ma'am. I'll take brandy and water with this gentleman.'

'That's right,' she said, satisfied. Then raised her voice and called the lanky lad, and addressed herself again to the travellers. 'With the Mail having to be on time,' she continued, 'they don't even stop for a meal if they're late. Which is inconvenient. And you're best advised to carry victuals and drink, so should I be making up something for the journey?'

'I thank you, ma'am,' cried Parson Peplow, beaming upon her kindness, 'but my good wife has seen I shall not want,' and he indicated a stout wicker basket by his side.

'And I also am well provided for, ma'am,' said the young man, 'for my mother has done likewise. I thank you,' and he pointed to a similar basket, and smiled as if at a private joke.

4

'Well then, sirs,' said the landlady, disappointed of her hospitality, 'if there's anything as you want, just call Jack. For the coachman's in the kitchen with me, and I promised the guard as I'd keep an eye on him,' and she nodded significantly. 'Yes, sirs, I've known Jacob Sorrowcole since I was a girl. He's been forty year on the stage-coaches, and he isn't used to being sober and on time. But Mr Walters—that's the guard—begged me, with the tears standing in his eyes, not to let him have another drop afore they started. And I swear I never did, but I think Mr Sorrowcole must have had a flask on him, and he's a-snoring on the settle, fit to wake the dead.'

'Dear me,' said the clergyman, disturbed by the thought, 'and they say the Mail averages ten mile an hour or more! I find that difficult to believe, mind you.'

'Yet the Prince of Wales reckoned to drive a phaeton-and-four faster than that, good sir,' the young man observed pleasantly.

'He was always a boastful fellow. Still, we must move with the times—even though they do progress at ten mile an hour!' And he laughed at his own jest.

The landlady having withdrawn to minister to Mr Sorrowcole, the two men looked into the fire for a while to find the next topic of conversation.

'So we set off at two o'clock sharp, eh?' said Parson Peplow, and studied a watch whose face was as plain as his own. 'And are to be companions as far as Leicester, I believe?'

'Allow me to introduce myself, sir. My name is William Howarth of Garth, near Millbridge, and I am travelling to London.'

'And I am Simon Peplow, Parson of Inglethwaite near Preston, sir. Garth? Garth? I cannot quite recall the place. Millbridge, of course, is a thriving town. Or perhaps Garth is the name of your establishment?'

His evident curiosity both piqued and amused William Howarth, who nevertheless answered patiently.

'Garth is a hamlet, some nine miles from Millbridge, and boasts no more than a hundred poor souls. My father owns a farm on the fells there, called Kit's Hill, sir.'

'Ah! A large farm, Mr Howarth?'

'Large enough to keep them all working from dawn to dark, sir,' said William drily, and to forestall further questions asked, 'And did you say you were going to Leicester, sir?'

5

'Yes, indeed. For my sister has recently lost her husband, poor creature, and I journey to bring her solace—and the offer of a home with us, if so she desire. There is nothing greatly to be gained by travelling faster, but I am something of an adventurer in my humble way, Mr Howarth, and I confess to an interest in this new mail-coach. "Louisa," I said to my good wife, "Louisa, I think I shall try the Mail!" "Do you think that is wise, Simon?" she said. "Why, my love, wise as Solomon and safe as houses!" I replied. But I dare say she will be relieved to know when I have arrived at Leicester, so I shall write to her directly. How long has the Mail been running, Mr Howarth, do you know?'

'Up here, sir? Since the summer. The first essay, I believe, was from Bristol to Bath last August, and beat the ordinary stage-coach by an hour. I, too, confess to an interest—nay, a devouring curiosity—in all new ventures. But that is not why I have chosen to travel this way. . . .'

He appeared to regret the admission, since it brought Parson Peplow's glasses to bear on him immediately, but he was saved by the entrance of his brandy and hot water.

'Old Sorrowcole's well away,' the lanky lad confided, with a solemn shaking of the head. 'The Post Office might lay the law down, sir, but it can't lay down human nature. Mrs Alcock's brewing coffee this minute to fetch him round afore the guard gets back!'

And having disturbed the parson's peace of mind, and amused William, he departed.

'I shall offer my assistance, sir, if you will excuse me for a moment,' said William, escaping his amiable inquisitor. 'The lady should not have to deal with a drunken fellow by herself.'

'I will come with you, Mr Howarth. A commendable thought on your part.'

Mr Sorrowcole's person was large enough to have concealed several flasks, and he must have imbibed them all. In spite of a cold compress on his forehead, and the ungentle attentions of Jack—who was trying to shake him awake, the arms of Morphus held him in a close embrace. For though his snores changed into desperate snorts, and certain movements of his hands and legs suggested that he was reining in a team of horses down a steep hill, he did not rouse himself.

'I dare say they'll be training up new drivers,' said the landlady hopefully, 'but Mr Sorrowcole's an old stager, and they was always heavy drinkers. Well, they've got to keep out

6

the cold somehow, and if it isn't brandy then it's rum, and that's all there is to it.'

'Sober and on time,' mused Parson Peplow. 'When I was a boy the stage-coach had only just been thought of, and folk travelled by wagon. Now this worthy old fellow is seeing the last of his ways and days depart!'

'Well, true as God's my judge, sir, you can set your clock by the Mail, but there's many an ale-house has lost custom through them not stopping. And the bye-letters, and cross-post letters are in a right mess, along of the Mail being so quick. For if you don't catch it on the hour then you wait another day. Whereas the stage-coach don't mind being late, and stops to water the horses and wet everybody's throats, and will turn off the main road, and set folk down and pick them up wherever needful. Oh, it don't matter if folk live in a big town, but little places must take their chance, and I say there's a deal of goodwill being lost. Not to speak of the government putting up the price of postage to pay for it all! And then the staff and the stabling we have to keep, for it's only five minutes to change the horses, and fifteen to feed the travellers, and then off like maniacs with the horn blowing. And no tolls to pay at the turnpikes, and everybody on the road to make way, make way.'

'Let me dash some water down his neck,' Jack suggested, with great relish. 'That'll fetch him to, Mrs Alcock.'

'And wet all his clothes, and him going out on the box for the next twenty-seven hours or more? He'll catch his death!'

'I think that if I hold him upright, ma'am,' said William Howarth, who had been considering the problem, 'you could pour the coffee down his throat, a little at a time. And I think he should be brought away from the fire, which is inducing sleep.'

'It is a half after one o'clock,' Parson Peplow reminded them. 'Let us try to walk him up and down. I feel that his slumbers are largely due to the comfort and warmth in which he finds himself, as my young friend says. Here, I will take one arm, Mr Howarth, if you do but take the other. . . .'

So, unevenly, between a tall man and a short one, Jacob Sorrowcole once more learned to walk, and was making his twentieth turn round the kitchen when a thin harassed fellow entered the room. He did not so much wear his scarlet uniform, gold-frogged and of a military cut, as it wore him. His leather top-boots were glistening with mud and rain. The cockade in his hat seemed wilted. He had been through too much already, and would soon be going through more.

'Oh my Lord!' he whispered, as he saw the coachman.

'No great harm, Mr Walters,' said the landlady, soothing. 'Mr Sorrowcole just fell asleep afore the kitchen fire. He's right as rain, aren't you, Mr Sorrowcole? Here, let me help you into your things.'

Whereupon she began to clothe him with coats and wind him into mufflers, until he looked like an enormous swaddled baby with a crimson face and three chins.

'Don't I keep on telling you as every minute counts?' Mr Walters demanded of the erring driver. 'Haven't I said as we're supposed to set an example? I'm wearing the King's uniform, ain't I. . . ?'

Here Mr Sorrowcole made a diversion by shaking himself free of his supporters, shaking his fist, and crying, 'And where's *my* uniform then? Tell me that!'

'You'll get your uniform,' said the guard, inspired, 'when you behave yourself. Falling asleep afore the kitchen fire, while I've been out in the cold and the wet, chivying the Warrington mail and waiting for the Chester bag, checking my timepiece ready for two o'clock sharp. And you call yourself a King's Messenger!'

Here Mr Sorrowcole drew himself up to his full height, which was not very great but more than redeemed by his width, and announced that he could drive a team blindfold through a blizzard and was ready for owt.

'That's more like it!' said the guard, mollified. 'I'll tell you something else as well, Jacob. There's many a one is saying as the Mail won't keep to time in the winter. An hour late they say, along of the weather. Now be that as it may, Jacob, a drop of rain shan't stop us. I want us to be drawing up at St Martin's-le-Grand by a twenty past five o'clock tomorrow morning. On time, Jacob. On time.'

The old coachman clapped his hat upon his head, reached for his long whip which was propped against a corner of the kitchen dresser, and stood to attention. Relieved, the guard checked that his pistols and blunderbuss were primed, his leather bag full of powder and shot, his watch ticking away in its pouch and his posthorn hanging by his side. Portentously, he locked the iron mail-box, saying under his breath reverently as he did so, 'King's Regulations!'

While this impressive pantomime was being performed, Mr Sorrowcole handed a large flask to the landlady, whispering,

'Fill her up, Doll, with the usual!' Which the landlady, being a woman and weak, did.

William Howarth observed all this with quiet amusement, Parson Peplow with a philosophical shake of the head. Both men then paid their separate reckonings, wrapped their cloaks about them, pulled down their hats, and picked up their wicker baskets.

'The Reverend Simon Peplow for Leicester? Mr William Howarth for London?' the guard asked formally. 'This way, if you please, sirs!'

It was a wild night, and the drop of rain had become a torrent. In the wind and wet two ostlers were securing the wheel horses, before putting the leading horses to, while the coachman made an overall check with his portable lantern. Stout, formidable, unvanquished by forty years of hard work and harder weather, he was in command again.

'Nice and fresh, are they?' Mr Sorrowcole asked of the four bay geldings.

'Fresh?' cried the elder lad, rain running down his neck. 'Why, they'd go to London and back if they was let!'

'If they'll take us as far as Ashbourne that's as good as a bargain,' replied Mr Sorrowcole drily. He lifted a congested face to the night sky. 'It's a deal too light for the time of morning,' he said gloomily, 'I shouldn't wonder if it snowed.'

The guard sighed, for if it did snow it would be he who took the mail through on horseback.

'Come along, if you please, sirs!' he called to the two waiting figures at the door of The Royal Oak.

They hurried forward, each inwardly confounding himself for being a fool, neither able to control that tightening of the throat, that increased throb of the pulse, which the sight of the coach occasioned. They were among the first to try this new mode of transport. They were pioneers.

In the gentle beam of its lamps the Royal Mail coach glistened with fresh paint: a rich maroon below, a richer black above, and the sparkling wheels bright red. A small and compact vehicle, austere in comparison with the present sprawling monsters of the road, and proudly bearing the royal coat of arms upon its door, the royal cipher upon its side panels. Inside, there was room for four passengers, and four leather straps hung ready to be grasped on the tight turns. A little dark lined cavern, at once claustrophobic and comforting.

'I have taken the opportunity of providing myself with a portable lantern and tinder-box,' said William Howarth. 'So if you should need a light at any time, sir, I beg you to say the word.'

'Most opportune. Most kind,' said Parson Peplow.

They settled in their seats, and put their provisions by them.

Outside, Mr Sorrowcole was being hoisted on to his box by the guard and an ostler. He ran the reins lovingly through his fingers and looked along the line of his team's ears. The guard handed up the iron mail-box, a truss of straw and a skin rug. Upon this box, protected only by the straw, his feet would freeze for twenty-seven hours. He pulled himself up beside the coachman and consulted his watch by the wan light of the lamps.

'Get ready, boys!' he warned the ostlers.

They stood by the horses' heads in the pouring rain, a half-grin on their faces, as though they comprehended the immensity of the occasion, and were yet embarrassed by it. Then Harry Walters lifted the chill brass horn to his lips and startled every sleeper in earshot, once, twice, thrice. The ostlers whipped off the cloths, Jacob Sorrowcole flicked the leading horses, the coach moved, the wheels spun, they gathered momentum, they were off. The Royal Mail had started at two o'clock precisely. As they passed the parish church a chime pursued them as if to say, 'On time. On time.'

The first lurch had sent Parson Peplow's basket to the floor. The second lurch sent William Howarth's basket to join it, and flung both men together as they strived to save their refreshments. By the time they had sorted themselves out the coach had settled into a swaying motion, much like an ocean-going ship in a rough swell, interrupted only by a bounce or a drop as they struck stones and splashed through pot-holes.

'We are certainly going at a fair pace,' said Parson Peplow, when he had recovered his breath. 'Shall you sleep, Mr Howarth?'

'I doubt it, sir, but I shall try.'

But the clergyman wanted company in his adventure.

'So the Post Office are seeking to turn us into a punctual nation?' he observed. 'That is ambitious of them! And what matter, sir, if we or our letters reach our destination a day or so sooner? It is not time that counts but how we use it.'

'Why, sir, you are no worldly timekeeper, and that is the answer!' said William pleasantly. 'Your life and works are of a philosophical nature, and so deal with the eternal rather

10

than the temporal. But I was apprenticed to a Quaker businessman, Bartholomew Scholes of Birmingham. A week to send a business letter—sometimes a fortnight—means the difference between profit and loss, labour and idleness. They say now that we shall have letters "by return of Post", meaning that we write today and receive a reply (if our correspondent has been as speedy) the day after tomorrow. Change is misliked, and there will be much prejudice against the higher postage and these new ideas. But I am for them, sir, simply from a practical viewpoint. This is a new age, sir, and we must progress.'

Now the clergyman was roused in truth, and his pebble glasses gleamed, his forefinger pointed protest.

'*Festina lente*, Mr Howarth. Make haste slowly. I fear, like all young men of ardent spirit, that you confuse progress with speed!'

'Forgive me, sir, but are you not being merely a praiser of times past? *Laudator temporis acti?*'

'What would you, sir? That I fall in with the crowd and say that everything unknown must be marvellous? *Omne ignotum pro magnifico?*' cried Parson Peplow, delighted to cross scholastic swords. 'No, my friend, I look into the future with hope but with misgivings also. If we save time so that we can do more business, then what shall become of us when all the world is busy in the same fashion? Shall we not be eaten up by business, slaves to business, slaves to time? Then the clock will be our master, and the need to make more money our taskmaster. The worship of Baal is an old sin, and raises its golden image in every generation; but once we begin to conquer distance and time, Mr Howarth, that image may be multiplied exceedingly. And the people will cast God out, my dear sir, whereas only He can stand between us and our destruction! But there, as my good wife says, I give sermons on weekdays as well as Sundays. And we are basing our surmises upon the Post Office's desire for speed and punctual delivery, now in its infancy!'

'But, sir,' cried William, captivated by surmise of another sort, 'why should we stop there? I am fascinated by the new steam-engines. My friend Caleb Scholes is the son of the ironmaster who has but recently purchased a rotative engine. Now he can work the mechanical hammers, blow the blast furnaces and drive the rolling mills by steam power. Let us go a step further, my dear sir. Suppose it were possible to power this mail-coach by means of steam? What speeds could we accomplish then?'

'Oho, oho, my friend, let us not be fantastical in our speculations. Ten mile an hour is fast enough for our purpose. . . .'

The coach stopped as suddenly as it could, and both men raised their blinds simultaneously and peered through their windows to see what was afoot.

'A highwayman perhaps?' ventured Parson Peplow, losing a little of his colour. 'Well, he will find me but a poor crow for the picking!'

'No highwayman,' said William, 'for I heard no word of command, and see no one but—ah!—Mr Walters.'

'Naught wrong, sirs,' cried the guard sticking a wet hat round the opened door of the carriage. 'I'm just putting the brake on, ready for Hartshead Brow, else the horses'll run away with theirselves down here.'

'Should I hold the lantern for you, Mr Walters?' asked William.

'It's a regular downpour, sir. You'll get wet through.'

'No matter. I shall dry again. Come, give me the lantern.'

Neatly the guard unhooked an iron shoe-skid, and applied it to one of the back wheels. They both returned to their places while the coach lurched and slithered downhill. Once on the straight, he and William repeated the process in reverse, and Mr Sorrowcole prepared to make up for those few lost minutes.

'We thought you were a highwayman, Mr Walters,' cried Parson Peplow pleasantly, as the guard closed the door.

'We shan't see hair nor hide of them this weather,' said the guard. 'They'll be sitting with their feet up the chimbley corner, mark my words, sir! They've got more sense than come robbing in the rain.'

'True. Very true,' said Peplow, comforted.

The coach resumed its jounce and sway.

'We were held up by a highwayman on the road to Birmingham once, when I was a lad,' said William Howarth. 'The fellow was most courteous, and returned my pocket-money to me, saying he was a boy himself once! Whether he would have accorded the same respect to my silver watch, I know not. To save him from temptation I had thrust it into a pie I was eating at the time, and it took no hurt though covered in meat and potato! I was glad, for I set great store by it, since it belonged to my great-grandfather.'

12

Aha, thought Peplow, the genteel side of the family.

'And how shall you protect your property in a similar emergency, may I ask, Mr Howarth?'

'Possibly in the same way. For my mother has packed one of our best pork pies in my basket. Or perhaps I should rely upon Mr Walters shooting the fellow's head off with his blunderbuss!'

'Your mother is a fine cook, I dare say, sir?'

'My mother does not cook at all, sir, but has a gift for finding and supervising those who do.'

'Unusual,' murmured the interested clergyman, 'in a farmer's wife.'

'Well, sir, I see you will have my small history out,' said William, somewhat exasperated. 'My father is a fairly prosperous yeoman, of honest stock. My mother comes of a genteel family, with high churchmen on one side and good businessmen on the other. And I am the product of that most strange and most happy partnership.'

'I did not mean to pry, Mr Howarth.' Conscience-stricken. So the parson was silent for a few moments, and then began again.

'How much do they pay the excellent Mr Walters for his responsibilities, I wonder?'

'Half a guinea a week, I believe. In addition to which he should pocket more than a half-guinea in tips, and be well paid for carrying an illicit parcel or so of game or fish in the boot! It is not bad, sir.'

'Better than I, in my small parish, Mr Howarth!'

'Better than I in my small forge, sir!'

'Forge? You are a farrier? But, of course,' cried Peplow triumphantly, 'the hands, the stature and the strength. Forgive me, sir, I am insatiable in my curiosity, and you have set me a riddle such as I do not solve every day. An elegantly dressed gentleman, with the hands of a craftsman, who lives on a farm and runs a forge, yet discourses with all the art and fire of an educated person, and wears his great-grandfather's silver watch—the which I should be delighted to examine more closely, for I take great pleasure in horology—admit, Mr Howarth, you are a mighty puzzle!'

Then William laughed aloud at the clergyman's innocent enthusiasm, and could no longer be annoyed with him.

'Sir, I am a puzzle even to myself. Know then thyself? *Nosce teipsum?* I fear it may take me a lifetime to decipher William Howarth!'

13

'Where did you learn your Latin, my young friend?'

'My mother taught the three of us: my sister Charlotte, my brother Richard and me. Though I fear young Dick was given up in some disgust before he was twelve. He takes after my father, and will farm Kit's Hill and make a love of labour. Later I studied at Millbridge Grammar School under Mr Tucker, but I do not keep up my Latin and Greek as my mother and sister do. I have enough to serve my purpose, but am no scholar, sir.'

'Well, well, well,' said Parson Peplow, rubbing his knees in satisfaction. 'May I trouble you with a final impertinence, for my guesses so far have been mainly correct...?'

But before he could put his question they were startled by the winding of Mr Walter's horn, closely followed by another, and some note of urgency or apprehension in the sounding brass made William let down the middle window and peer into the night. They were approaching a fork in the road, and rumbling towards them at an angle to the left of the main highway was a huge stage-coach. Both guards were blowing their horns in a frenzy. Both coachmen were lashing their horses on, determined to take the lead. Most powerfully did the stage lumber forward: a mighty pachyderm which could crush the little black and red coach like a beetle. Nimbly spun the vermilion wheels of the Mail, briskly did it rattle through puddles and stones. Neither vehicle gave way, though the distance between them was narrowing rapidly.

'Great heaven!' cried Parson Peplow. 'We shall overturn!' And he sank back in his seat, trembling.

But William put his head and shoulders out of the middle window entirely, regardless of the mire splashing up the sides of the carriage, while Mr Walters shouted into the night, 'Make way for the Royal Mail!'

'Get out of the bloody road!' yelled the other guard, unimpressed. 'We're the Macclesfield Dreadnought, we are!'

Mr Sorrowcole jammed his hat hard down over his eyes, which were pinpoints of battle. He arched over his team, vast and formidable, wheezing, 'Hold on to your seat, Harry, and keep a-winding of that there horn. That old Dreadnought can't take a fast turn, and we're on the crown of the road. But we shall cut it very fine. Hooroar!' and he laid his whip upon the galloping team. They were almost flying now, ears laid back, eyes starting, coats lathered.

'You bloody fools!' yelled the Macclesfield Dreadnought. 'We'll have you in t'ditch!'

14

'Hooroar!' cried Mr Sorrowcole raucously. 'Hooroar, my beauties!'

The leather flourished and cracked.

'Make way for the Mail!' bawled Mr Walters.

His scarlet uniform endowed him with more than mortal courage. He wound his horn fit to wake the dead. While William roared, 'Make way! Make way!' through the funnel of his hands, and Parson Peplow prayed in the corner of the carriage.

Now the two teams were galloping almost neck and neck, and for a flashing moment William feared both gladiators might irrevocably crash. Just for a second he could have touched the leading horse of the stage-coach, then with inches to spare the little Mail was drawing away and the Dreadnought was heeling, wavering, swerving.

'I said,' Mr Sorrowcole growled, 'as it couldn't take a fast corner.'

There was a splintering of wood, a shattering of glass. The coachman hauled on his reins, the lathered team tossed up their heads and whinnied with terror. Too late, too late. With a final lurch, roll and crash, the Dreadnought sank into a ditch and halted: one wheel spinning silently.

Then William whipped off his hat and cried, 'Hurrah! Well done, Mr Walters! Well driven, Mr Sorrowcole! Hurrah for King George and the Mail!'

The stranded pachyderm, its lamps gleaming like reproachful eyes, was already fading into the dark. Night closed about them once more. The Great North Road was their own again. As the Mail bowled along, and Mr Sorrowcole allowed the horses to move back into a steady canter, the guard wound his horn in victory. It was not a crow of delight, or the rude blare of the conqueror, rather was there something elegiac, something poignant in that music of the highway. A victory had been gained, in the name of the King. William drew up the window and sat down, breathless, muddy, and smiling.

He must have fallen asleep, for when he woke it was daylight; and the sound of cobbles under the wheels, and the winding horn, informed him and the drowsy clergyman that Ashbourne was reached. The guard was at their door in a trice, crying, 'Five minutes, sirs, while we change the horses!'

In the courtyard of the inn two ostlers were waiting with a fresh team ready-harnessed, and they set to with a will. The rain had stopped, a wintry sunlight illumined the landscape, and smells of coffee, hot toast and fried chops stole from the kitchen of The Wagon and Horses. While a gentleman and his wife were ushered aboard the Mail, William and Parson Peplow relieved themselves behind a hedge.

'I think I shall partake of a first breakfast,' joked the clergyman, 'and welcome a second one at Derby!'

'I shall join you, sir,' cried William, sniffing the fresh air and the smell of frying.

'If only one could wash and shave,' mourned the parson, 'but there is no time. I shall not care to greet my sister with unshaven cheeks.'

'I dare say I shall breakfast and shave in London tomorrow morning, before I greet my sister,' said William, 'for we shall arrive well before they wake.'

'That is Charlotte, is it not?' enquired Parson Peplow comfortably as they walked briskly back. 'She is young, of course?' Wistfully.

'Nineteen at Lammastide, and expecting her first child shortly, sir.'

The mail-guard was propelling Mr Sorrowcole back on to the box.

'I've got to pass water, haven't I?' the coachman grumbled. 'I'm not a bleeding camel, am I?'

'It ain't what you lets out as bothers me,' said the harassed guard, 'it's what you imbibes, Jacob. We're two minutes late already. Put your mind to Derby, Jacob. Think of the ale at The Cat and Bells! You can wet your whistle there as much as you like, and I'll not gainsay you.'

Introductions once made inside the coach, and the man and his wife busy settling some private matter, Simon Peplow leaned forward confidentially.

'I shall pray that your sister comes through her ordeal safely, and bears a healthy infant, Mr. Howarth.'

'I thank you, sir. We are all praying for that happy outcome.'

'Her mother will be distressed, so far away from her daughter at such a time. Louisa and I were not blessed with children, but have had many at secondhand. Nephews, nieces and cousins. All were fruitful, save ourselves.' And he was silent for a few moments, then brightened again. 'Ah, Mr Howarth, I was about to ask a question when we encountered the Dreadnought. Poor souls, I do hope that none of them suffered injury, and were soon relieved! I was about to ask you whether you were six-and-twenty, which was my estimate of your age when we met at The Royal Oak. But, sir, you need not reply to that, for your youthful exuberance at the triumph of the Mail betrayed you. I struck off a few years instantly, sir. Am I correct?'

'Sir, I am but recently one-and-twenty,' said William, smiling. 'I came home at the end of the summer, as journeyman and man, and celebrated both events royally. This splendid suit'—indicating the tailored broadcloth—'was my mother's gift, made up for me in Millbridge. This waistcoat she sewed with her own hands, and lined with silk from her wedding gown. And at Kit's Hill, in the stables, is a stallion my father gave me—and I wish I were riding him now, in my own stages, to London. But time was pressing, on both sides, and I yielded to my mother's wishes and took the fastest mode of travelling.'

'There I was wrong,' mused Parson Peplow, 'for I believed your journey—forgive an elderly man's sentiments!—I believed it to be an affair of the heart.'

'It is certainly a journey of strong affection and grave concern,' said William, 'for I am the family emissary. My sister married early this year, indeed she eloped, and we know nothing of her circumstances and little more of her husband. I seek to build a bridge between both sides, for my parents are inclined to be hasty in judging the fellow, whereas I shall love her well enough to attempt to love him, and so perhaps heal the hurt he has done.'

'You are wise beyond your years, Mr Howarth. I pray you may succeed. And who cares for your forge while you are away?'

'There lies another tale, sir,' said William ruefully. 'I came home, as I mentioned, intending to take a month's holiday—for I have been away from Kit's Hill for seven years—and then I should have begun work as a journeyman for the ironmaster, Caleb Scholes. . . .'

'Indeed? An ironmaster! Well, well. Goodness me!'

'. . . but I found my friend and first master, Aaron Helm, gravely ill. He had let me work, nay play, at his forge in Flawnes Green when I was but a little fellow and I honoured and loved him exceedingly. What could I do but endeavour to set his business up again, while my mother ministered kindness and medicine? But, as she feared and prophesied, he is mortally ill and like to die at any time. He has neither wife nor child, and wishes to make me his inheritor. And I dread that he may leave this world without me there to comfort

him at the last, and I travel with a heavy heart in consequence.'

'My poor young friend. I grieve for you. I grieve for all of
you.' He pursed his lips reflectively. 'But what of the ironmaster, Mr Howarth? Shall you not work for the ironmaster?'

'No, sir,' said William resolutely. 'I have wrote and
thanked him, and explained myself as well as I could. My
mother has thrown up her hands, and cried that her children
cast away their opportunities. . . .'

'An understandable reaction, Mr Howarth!'

'. . . but I shall become the blacksmith of Flawnes Green.'

'You place your friend's wishes above your own ambition?
That is most laudable, but not, in the world's terms, prudent,
my friend.'

'I have transferred my ambition from Somer Court to
Flawnes Green, sir.'

'Somer Court being. . . ?'

'The ironmaster's residence, and a small domestic heaven
upon earth, sir. Some day, God willing, I shall have a Somer
Court of my own.'

'Well, I hope you do, Mr Howarth, for you seem to be an
excellent young man, and have made a considerable sacrifice
for your friend!'

And he shook his head at the wildness of that gesture.

Mr Sorrowcole made such rapid progress that they arrived at
Derby one minute before time. Again the ostlers were waiting
with a fresh team, and set about their task straightaway;
while the landlady of The Cat and Bells had the table laid
and a hot breakfast before them in moments. The lady traveller then adjourned to find a chamber-pot, and the three
men to a field. At a quarter to eleven o'clock precisely, the
mail and parcels loaded and his timepiece checked, Mr Walters gave the order to start, and they were off again. Now
William dozed fitfully. At the top of every steep hill the
guard applied the iron shoebrake, and took it off again at the
bottom. Fine carriages, rough wagons, and solitary horsemen,
all gave way to the bustling Mail. They flew past turnpikes
with an arrogant snarl of the horn. Occasionally, bogged
down by mud, the passengers dismounted and helped to push
the coach on to drier ground. Once or twice they got out and
walked uphill, while Mr Sorrowcole urged on his patient
team. But on the whole a rattling, jouncing speed was
maintained.

At Leicester Parson Peplow shook hands with William, and gave him final encouragement and advice.

'My dear young friend, I shall be praying for you and all your dear ones. You have made this journey most memorable and most pleasant for me. Permit me, sir, to offer a suggestion. *Festina lente*, my ardent young friend. Make haste slowly. I feel you will go far in life. Go not too far, be not too hasty. And God be with you, sir.'

Then, catching sight of a short stout lady with grey hair, who looked like Parson Peplow in skirts, he cried, 'Dorothy, here I am!' and was enveloped in a tearful embrace.

William dined briefly but well at The Three Tuns, and slept most of the afternoon as they rattled through Leicestershire. Another passenger had been taken on in Parson Peplow's place, but he appeared to find so much in common with the married couple that William was left to his own thoughts. Evening was drawing in, bringing fresh gusts of wind and rain and a cruel coldness to the air, as they crossed Northamptonshire. At six o'clock he swallowed a mouthful of brandy to warm himself, and thought of the two men perched outside on the box. He could not find it in his heart to blame the coachman for an addiction to spirits.

As the weather worsened the roads became quagmires, and at one point were so badly flooded that they seemed forced to find an alternative route. Again, Mr Sorrowcole's experience won the day. He drove his team through the rising waters and safely out to the other side. But these delays cost them their supper at Northampton. Frozen and famished, their appetites sharpened by the smell of hot beefsteak, the passengers had to content themselves with bread and cheese, and William shared what was left in his wicker basket.

The night stretched before them interminably. William drank from his flask, feeling that he would never be warm again. It was impossible to sleep properly, and every bone in his body had a separate ache. He almost welcomed interruptions on the hills: scrambling stiffly out to help Mr Walters, while the coachman sat bulky and imperturbable on his box, and the tired horses hung their heads. But in the last hours he must have dozed off, for he was slowly conscious of a change in sound and motion. He drew up his window-blind and looked out. Houses pressed in upon them, street after street, set close together and higgledy-piggledy built, old and new, overhanging and set back, timber and brick. A rich medley of odours delighted and offended his nostrils: coffee, fried fish, burned toast, dung and soot and sour urine. They were driving into the heart of the metropolis.

William reached for his portable lantern and tinder-box, and with only a little difficulty struck a light. Then the other passengers roused themselves, and all began to smile and talk as though some miracle had been accomplished. They forgot their chagrin at leaving Northampton supperless, and their annoyance at the chivying of the mail-guard. William recounted that early victory over the Macclesfield Dreadnought, and everyone agreed that the mail-men were English to the backbone and worth their salt.

'How much do you reckon we should tip the guard?' one gentleman asked.

'Well, the last time I hired a post-chaise,' said the other, 'I paid a shilling a stage and tipped the postboy each time. So this fellow should be worth as much, and the coachman should have his due.'

In the end they collected six shillings between them, with some amiable joking about the different number of stages they had travelled, and handed it over to William as spokesman.

'Shall we be on time, sirs?' asked the lady traveller, and each man obediently took out his watch and consulted it.

There were discrepancies. William's watch, set by St Mark's church in Millbridge, told him it was a half after four. The Ashbourne watch-owner insisted that it was ten minutes to five, according to the town sundial. Whereas the Leicester gentleman was convinced of six minutes past the same hour.

'There is but one man who has the official time,' said William, 'and he is sitting on the box outside!'

Night was lying on the close streets still, but London was astir. Silent shadows glided from alleyways and joined the host of early workers. Farmers were driving in their wagons full of produce for the markets. Late revellers turned for home in private carriages. But all made way for the Mail without question. Here, in the capital city, where new enterprises began, they were rather proud of it. So over the cobbles dashed the muddy little coach, with Mr Walter's horn heralding its arrival, to draw up at last with a flourish outside the General Post Office in St Martin's-le-Grand. The guard clambered down for the final time on this eventful journey, and opened the door. His face, dirty and unshaven and ex-

hausted, was nevertheless triumphant. In one frozen red hand
he held out his official timepiece for all to see.

'Twenty minutes after five o'clock of the morning, lady
and gentlemen,' he announced. 'The Royal Mail is on time!'

Up on the box, Jacob Sorrowcole emptied the last of his
flask.

T W O

Longe's of Lock-yard

Sustained by his best clothes, his ruddy good looks and a very
fair opinion of his capabilities, William had expected to take
London by storm. After all, he had thought, it is but Birmingham on a greater scale—with the King in his palace. So he
asked for directions to his sister's home at Lock-yard with supreme confidence, almost expecting the stranger to cry, 'What?
Longe's of Lock-yard? Why, my wife drank tea there but yesterday!' and to gain recognition in an instant. But the first
man had not heard of it, and the second hurried away, mut-
tering to himself, 'Why do they come here, these fellows?',
while the third spoke loudly as though William's speech was
that of a foreigner. 'First turn to your right, down past Newgate Prison, along Holborn, turn left down Farringdon Street
and you find yourself on Fleet Street. Keep the dome of St
Paul's at your back, sir, and you will not go wrong!' He set
out obediently, though a little disheartened by this reception,
and was immediately transfixed by the sight of Newgate
Prison: a cruel legend come to life again, rebuilt after Lord
George Gordon's rioters had burned down the jail and released the prisoners, five years since. And as he walked and
reflected upon this recent piece of history, William went too
far, and on turning left found himself in the noise and hustle
of Covent Garden.

Here the onlookers enjoyed themselves at his expense, passing remarks about his dress, his parentage and his intentions.
Here, too, a nobleman somewhat the worse for wine jostled
him into the mire and then, at William's remonstrance,
threatened to draw his sword and show him who should have

precedence. Lost and angry, the young man took refuge in a barber's shop, and while he was divested of a two-day beard listened to a monologue of good advice.

'Keep a grip on your baggage, and button up your watch and purse,' said the barber, trimming William's hair without being asked. 'There's pickpockets a-plenty round here. Stay on the main thoroughfares. The side-lanes is full of murder and wickedness. If you want a nice quiet breakfast take it at Platt's Coffee-house—I'll point it out to you as you leave. If you want a whore to go with your food then find a coffee-house that shows a woman's hand or arm holding the pot, on the sign outside.

'You're a stranger round here, aren't you, sir? Yes, I can always tell. Now that's the reason I'd choose Platt's, rather than a better-known establishment. In London, you see, the coffee-houses have their favourites, as you might say. Actors go to one, wits to another, politicians somewhere else, scholars here, professional men there. But Platt's welcomes everybody, even Scotchmen—you're not a Scotchman, are you, sir? No, I thought not. They speak a sight thicker. You'll feel at home, sir, at Platt's.

'Now, sir, you're looking more like yourself again. Would you be wanting anything else? An aching tooth drawn, sir? A little blood-letting after the journey? Travelling often brings on vile humours, sir. No? There you are then, sir. Ready to meet King George!' Jocularly. 'Oh, thank you, sir!' As William, in embarrassment, tipped him far too much.

But Platt's was an excellent choice, a poultice on the wound of his self-esteem. Though poorly furnished, and dingy with years of smoke, the place was warm and comfortable, and above all it was not jouncing along at ten miles an hour. At this time of morning it was fairly empty, since the bulk of customers arrived between eight and ten o'clock. And the woman who served William was stout and homely, which relieved him very much, for he had been troubled by the notion of whores.

She gave him the choice of chocolate, tea, coffee, wine, punch or ale. He would have preferred ale or tea, as his usual beverage, but feared to seem unsophisticated, so ordered coffee as though he drank it often, and was pleased to find it a hot and agreeable drink with a rich aroma. Since toast was a rare treat, and his stomach felt unsettled, he ordered several slices. And, the morning papers coming in soon after, he found himself in possession of the news of the day

22

for tuppence. Now regular customers and passing strangers began to fill the benches and form into groups. Most of them smoked, and the air became thick. All of them talked freely; for coffee-houses were regarded as the bastions of English liberty, taking pride in the fact that any topic could be discussed, and even the monarchy criticised within their walls.

Listening, while pretending to consult *The Morning Post*, William deduced that the company at the adjoining table was composed of a titled gentleman, a shoe-maker, a wool merchant and a physician. He was accustomed to open debate, having spent seven years in the Scholes's household where any opinion warranted serious consideration—provided it had been formed on serious thought—but this conversation sounded highly seditious, and smacked of revolution, and he was somewhat amazed that nobody went for the constable. By and by he folded his newspaper, paid his reckoning, and wandered out again into Covent Garden feeling braver and better for his breakfast. He buttoned his coat over his waistcoat to protect the silver watch, took a firm grip of his wicker basket and carpet-bag, and headed for the Strand: mindful that he must now keep the dome of St Paul's Church in front of him. Though anxious to heed the barber's warning, he found himself in narrow streets from time to time, which he trod cautiously for a number of reasons. Chamber-pots were being emptied from high windows. Little piles of excrement stood outside the doors, waiting for the farmer's cart to collect on his way back from market. The stench from the open gutter was appalling, but dirty children were floating paper boats down its foul stream and splashing through it in their play. There was nothing childlike about these wretched creatures. Though the poor of Garth village could show ribs as sharp as theirs, and shout abuse as rudely, there was a difference between the city and the country starveling. In London they were unknown members of the army of want, whereas even the feeblest child in Garth belonged to the people and the place.

Morning had come, and the city was wide-awake and hustling. The rumble of iron-clad wheels and iron-shod hooves on the cobbles assaulted him, and against this constant roar of traffic came the piercing cries of street vendors bent on selling a multitude of wares. A Bow Street Runner passed William, looking supercilious in his scarlet uniform; and soon after him an impudent beggar who actually caught hold of William's coat as he pleaded for money, and must be thrust aside before he would desist. Then once more the young man lost his way in the press of people, so busy staring at the splendours in shop windows, and found himself on the Thames bank, all mud and ships and gray water. One stench cast out another, one clamour outdid the other, and everywhere were crowds in a hurry to get somewhere else. In his weariness and excitement William felt the great city like a single bully at his heels, dogging him wherever he went, bent on mindless pursuit. It compelled him to take notice, and was indifferent to his opinion. It showed him extreme poverty and extreme wealth, without caring a fig for either. It was at once the most magnificent place he had ever experienced, and the most arrogant, and the most brutal.

Gathering his wits, he stopped short in his ramblings, checked the progress of an inky printer's boy who was dodging through the throng, and followed him meekly into Fleet Street.

'Third left!' said the lad, and took William's copper without thanking him.

The traveller turned sharply down into an airless court full of overhanging houses. On the wall opposite, a plaque read LOCK-YARD. Close by, a shabby swinging sign bore the familiar name of LONGE & SON, Printers, Publishers, Booksellers. He had arrived at last.

The door stood open, for air or customers, and William stepped inside. A tawny man of middle height and slender build was bending over a press. An apron covered his shirt and breeches. His sleeves were rolled above the elbows, his Cadogan wig hung on a peg, a tankard of ale stood near at hand. He was just past thirty but his movements were those of a youth: eager, supple, blithe. He was humming to himself as he worked, completely absorbed in his task, utterly self-contained. Then, aware of a shadow across his threshold, he looked up in quick good-humoured question.

'Mr Tobias Longe?' William asked, uncertain of his reception (and wondering whether he should shake the seducer's hand or kick him down his own front doorsteps). 'I am Charlotte's elder brother, sir. I am William Howarth.'

Toby Longe straightened himself and wiped his hands upon a piece of rag. His brown eyes were wary. A muscle twitched in his brown face.

'I am come to London upon business, Mr Longe,' said William, dignified and calm as befitted a good liar. 'So I

24

thought to see Charlotte and make your acquaintance. I must be back in Millbridge by the end of the week.'

Toby Longe had reached a rapid conclusion. He held out his hand, smiling.

'Welcome, William. Don't sirrah me, Will, for we are brothers. My name is Toby. Come, Charlotte should be awake by now and will be glad to see you. She is near her time, and lies abed in the morning. She is well, but not over-cheerful. You shall fetch the smile back to her face!' Then he shouted into the dark recesses of the shop, 'Davy, take over for me, will you? I shall be upstairs for a while.' And putting his arm about William's shoulders in the most natural man-ner, he rattled out a volley of questions as they mounted the wooden stairs. 'Have you breakfasted, Will? When did you arrive? Have you tried the new mail-coach? Now there is progress for you. I am solidly behind Tasker in this project, but mind you those damned rogues in Parliament will try to squash it! Watch your step. I meant to move those books an age ago, but there is no more room. We live pretty com-fortably here, Will, like two mice in a great cheese. . . .'

All the while, though charmed by the ease of Toby's man-ner, and amazed to find him very likeable, William could not help noticing the squalor. No. 3, Lock-yard, was a tall, thin, dilapidated house: three storeys, attic and basement. Since it looked upon a courtyard and was bounded by a street at the back, it was dark and damp and smelled of mushrooms. The lower staircase served double duty as a library and a store-room. Piled against the stained walls were parcels of old tomes tied with string, packets of paper, battered manuscripts, bundles of quills, bottles of ink. On the second floor— whose rooms were used as the Longes' sitting and dining quarters—the stair contents changed to lop-sided stacks of unmatched china, bundles of bent cutlery and baskets of table linen. Up again they went, and on the third landing William was not surprised to see the night's chamber-pot, a heap of unwashed clothes, and several pairs of slippers and shoes.

Toby knocked upon the door and called softly, 'Are you awake, love?'

A muffled voice answered that it thought so.

'There is a gentleman come to see you, Lottie!'

The voice said wearily that it would be down very soon, and sighed.

'Very soon?' cried Toby joyously. 'Is that the welcome you

give to your brother William, who has come all the way from Lancashire in the Royal Mail?'

The voice gave first a shriek, and then a sob. Bare feet pattered across bare boards. The door swung open, and Charlotte—great and clumsy with child—was crying and laughing in William's arms, while Toby stood triumphantly to one side as though he had organised the entire reunion.

'Come now, Lottie,' said William, patting her thin shoulders, 'stop all this weeping and wrap up warm. You must take care, so near your time.'

'Aye, so she should,' said Toby heartily. 'You will breakfast with her, Will? Then I shall leave you both to wag your tongues in peace. I have an appointment at the coffee-house. You are staying with us, Will?'

'Nay,' William replied uncertainly, torn between his fear of unknown lodgings and the obvious drawbacks of Lock-yard. 'Nay, I have an address given me by a barber in Covent Garden. I would not trouble you.'

'Oh, fiddle!' cried Toby impatiently. 'You can sleep on the parlour sofa and we shall all be merry. Wine for supper, Lottie, and a feast from the bakehouse to celebrate our meeting!'

Then Charlotte added her entreaties, and looked so pitiful with her swollen belly and childlike face that William agreed and thanked them; while Toby clapped him on the back, and shouted downstairs for the girl to make breakfast; and Charlotte changed her nightshift for a pale blue morning gown, and pinned up her fair hair in a jaunty knot.

It was one of the strangest meals William had ever eaten. The slattern who waited upon them fetched out an old heel of cheese from a side-cupboard, and a misshapen loaf from the basement kitchen. Charlotte discovered the butter in a dish beneath the sofa, and picked out the best of the crockery on the landing. Now the initial delight and surprise were fading she was embarrassed, and kept stealing little looks at William to see what he thought of her ménage. But he tactfully busied himself getting the parlour fire to draw, which it did at last though the chimney clearly needed sweeping. Alone, they sat down at the round table, and Charlotte poured his tea and drank hers, and for a while they were silent. An expression on her face told him that she was about to voice an unpleasant truth. He hoped it did not concern his uninvited presence, for he was now so tired that he could have lain down on the scuffed carpet and slept like a dog. Charlotte began directly.

'You see why I cannot ask Mamma to stay, do you not?' she asked.

'I can see,' replied William, unable to soften the statement without lying, 'that it would be difficult on all sides.'

'Did Mamma send you?'

Revived momentarily by the tea, he said, 'No, Lottie. I came upon some business, but I can tell you of that another time. It is not important, except to me of course.'

She observed him closely, but he ate his second breakfast unmoved.

Suddenly she cried tearfully, 'I am very much afraid I shall die. And I need her. But she and my father were harsh to Toby, and ordered him away from Millbridge when they saw him. And they mislike him.'

'They misliked the secrecy, and the elopement,' said William gently.

'But it was the only way,' said Charlotte, despairing and yet defiant, 'they would never have consented to our marriage else.'

She had always been indifferent even to the dearest opinion, once her mind was made up.

Again there was silence between them.

'Great-aunt Tib, and Aunt Phoebe, and Agnes and Sally all send their love and many gifts for yourself and the infant,' said William cheerfully.

Her expression changed from determination to the utmost tenderness.

'Oh, how is Aunt Tib? Does she still scold Aunt Phoebe? And Agnes, how is her rheumatism? And is Sally courting yet? Oh, and have the Misses Whitehead filled my teaching post at the Academy in Millbridge?'

'The ladies of Thornton House pursue their course in life unchanged, save for your presence, Lottie, which lightened them considerably. I believe the Academy for Young Ladies will contrive to manage without another teacher. One feels your learning was too much for the Misses Whitehead! They would rather their female charges tatted and tattled than studied ancient languages!'

Charlotte laughed, and struck her hands together with pleasure, as she used to do in their childhood.

'How long you were away, Willie,' she said, and then sighed and looked pensively at a hole in the tablecloth.

He failed to conceal a tremendous yawn, and she suddenly saw how weary he was of travelling and emotion.

27

'Come,' she said affectionately, 'there is a bed in the other room upstairs, though the room is not yet furnished. You shall sleep until dinner. Why, you are quite wore out!'

He woke to find the winter afternoon well advanced. The room was dimly lit, due to an old coverlet being hung across the window for a curtain, and bitterly cold. But Charlotte had come softly in while he was asleep, and endeavoured to make it more comfortable for him. Delectably, up the well of the staircase, overcoming the smells of mice and mould, drifted the odours of cooking. He could hear Toby's voice in the parlour, Charlotte's answering laugh, the scolding of the slut in the scullery, and a hollow mewing outside his door. He descried a candlestick in the gloom, with a tinder-box laid conveniently alongside, and struck a light. His suit had been brushed, sponged and laid ready. A clean shirt had been fetched from his bag. On a note pinned to the sleeve Charlotte had written, in that elegant script favoured by Dorcas and herself, *'Dearest Willie, I am so happy you have come to see us, and Toby likes you very much. . . .'*

'Damn his eyes!' William commented, but had to smile.

'. . . We dine at four o'clock, so the girl will bring you hot water at a half after three. Pray join us for a glass of sherry, sir, in the parlour! Y^r loving sister Lottie.'

He flicked open the silver pair-case of his watch and peered at its ivory dial. Five o'clock. For a moment he was dumbfounded to think he had overslept. Then he smiled and shook his head. In the Longe household time would not be held of much account. An hour or so mattered little, and they could have called him if they were ready and waiting. Now the insistent mewing caught his attention. He threw aside the bedcovers and opened his door. Outside stood a copper can of lukewarm water and his top-boots newly polished. And inside one boot, vainly trying to extricate itself, one brave black kitten. He shook it carefully out and watched it negotiate the stairs. Then made a rapid toilet in his fireless room, and joined the company in the parlour.

He was relieved to find his presence obviously beneficial. An attempt had been made to tidy the room. Instead of slipping out to a tavern with his boon companions, Toby had chosen to preside at his dinner-table and honour his brother-in-law. And though the meal was late, even by London reckoning, the food was good and plentiful. But Charlotte and Toby greeted William effusively. The local bakehouse had furnished a veritable banquet, and Charlotte and her cook had also contributed to the feast. There was a jug of home-made pea soup, a dish of soused herrings, a rump of boiled beef with dumplings under it, a roast fowl, a raised pigeon pie, a currant tart and a blanc-mange, and two sorts of over-ripe cheese, with almonds, raisins and apples to follow. Toby had brought in several bottles of claret, a bottle of port and a bottle of rum, plus the ingredients for a hot punch which he planned to mix in William's wash-basin.

'Had it been summer,' said Charlotte wistfully, 'we should have took you to Sadler's Wells, where there is entertainment from afternoon to night. Else sailed down the river and supped at Vauxhall.'

'But as it is not summer,' said Toby, pouring sherry into three large tumblers, none of which matched, 'we shall sit by the fire and talk. Besides, there is a fog outside as thick as Lottie's soup. We are not far from the river, and the Fleet runs just to the east of us. So we suffer at this time of year from mists—and from miasmas.'

'Why, Lottie, you must have worked all the while I slept,' said William tenderly, admiring the preparations as he sipped his sherry. 'I would not for the world you had so tired your-self. But for the soup especially, I thank you.'

She made a pretty fluttered gesture of the hands.

'I hope I have got the receipt aright. But Betty used to make it for us, near Christmastime, when we were children. And I watched her while I conjugated my Latin verbs. Indeed, I marked the ingredients by means of the conjuga-tions!'

'It is a clever head,' said Toby fondly, 'and do not fear, Brother Will, that I shall let it rust for lack of use, nor spend its powers upon the paltry tasks of housekeeping and shirt-sewing!' William could see good evidence of this, and smiled polite agreement. 'No, No. I respect intellect in a woman. So let us drink to the three most important people on this august occasion.' He raised his tumbler. 'First to Brother William who has come to make all well between the two families,' and his tawny eyes gleamed gold, to let William know that he was not impressed by this excuse of London business. 'Second-ly, to my wife, professionally known by the initials C.S.L., whose work will be honoured long after her beauty has gone to dust! Lastly to the infant who is shortly to take its place among us. If he be a son he is right welcome. If a daughter, then thrice welcome, for good women bless the house that they adorn.'

'Amen to that, Toby!' cried William.

'And now to dinner, for it is nigh on six o'clock and I am famished,' said Toby, and helped them all to soup.

There were lengthy pauses between dishes while the servant washed up, but Toby was a fervent conversationalist and a generous wine-pourer, and William well-versed in discussion, so two leisurely hours passed before they reached the stage of tea-drinking. By this time Toby had taken the government apart (which William did not mind very much), attacked the Constitution (a more troublesome idea), and was now espousing open revolution. At this William held up his hand in protest, but spoke less heatedly than he felt because of Charlotte, who was looking anxiously from one man to the other.

'Why, Toby, you had a taste of revolution here but five years since,' said William lightly. 'Did the Gordon riots not cure you of a fondness for civil war?'

'What? An ignorant rabble running after a madman, crying *No Popery?* Religious quibblers? Pox on them! Nay, Will, I do not speak of people's prejudice but of people's rights. The majority of folk are ruled and worked and robbed by a handful of rich and powerful men. And this new age of coal and iron and steam engine—aye, wait a bit, I know your interests! You shall have your turn, by and by—this age of mills and sweated labour will make rich men richer, and poor men poorer still. You must have seen that for yourself in Birmingham. I saw it in Preston. Aye, and took the trouble to look at Manchester where I discovered such a hell of want and misery as I had not seen before. . . .'

'Then take trouble to look but a mile away,' said William angrily, 'and you shall find stews as dirty as any in the north.'

'You are right, Will. And one hellish stew is no better than another. We should wipe them all out. They have hells in the back streets of Paris—but that is another story. The French monarchy is stirring a cauldron that is like to boil over upon them, but we English are content to be exploited. . . .'

'Oh, the French!' cried William scornfully. 'A nation of lick-spittles and time-servers. They snap at our heels like a pack of vicious dogs. I care not whether they have a revolution or no. They are a scrubby nation.'

'So speaks the man who has never—I dare say—so much as crossed the Channel to meet them!'

'My reading is as wide as yours, sir,' cried William, stung by the truth. 'I am no ignoramus, mouthing opinion without a fact to prove it. I dare swear you congratulate yourself upon shocking me with ideas hitherto unknown to me, and would like me to gape with admiration at your daring. But each morning my master, Bartholomew Scholes, would read the papers at breakfast and open up discussion with us all, family, friends and apprentices. So I have heard your arguments before and still think little of them! And when you speak of revolution, sir, you talk from the exalted view of a safe spectator. I have fought some private wars, sir, owing to my Quaker connections. England takes her religious quibblers seriously, and there were those who misliked the Scholes apprentices—whether they shared the Quaker faith or no. Had you been brutally waylaid, as I have, and fought until you were all blood and bruises—and then been beaten when you crawled home, for fighting!—you would not speak so freely of civil war. It is not battled on printing presses with paper and ink, sir!'

Charlotte sat white and still, her hands knotted in her lap. But Toby laughed and said he loved a good argument, and that they should open another bottle of wine. Then both men remembered the silent girl and her burden, and endeavoured to soften the conversation.

'Now, Will, I have a bone to pick with you,' said Toby gaily. 'I hinted broadly at your sister's new profession, and you did not so much as turn a hair. I had expected a better response from you.'

'I seldom respond as I am bidden,' said William, with dry pleasantry.

'There you are like your sister. For I thought her simply a pretty, gentle creature when first we met at Thornton House. Then I discovered the steel beneath the lace, the iron beneath the velvet. Did I not, my Lord Chief Justice?' Kissing her hands in turn. Which smoothed out Charlotte's forehead and made her smile again. 'Yes, our Lottie has the makings of a first-rate pamphleteer. I am already bringing her into the publishing side of the business. In fact, I have a capital notion for a new gazette and, given a year or two, Lottie shall edit it. There are quite a few lady writers hereabouts, are there not, Lottie? An odd but fascinating assortment! You shall meet some of them, Will. But Lottie has a cool head, a warm heart and a sharp pen, and that combination is as rare as diamonds in our business.'

William guessed that this show of pride and affection was for his benefit, but that it was also the truth. He forgave the one because of the other.

'We corresponded for a year together,' Toby continued, giving his wife's hands a playful little shake, 'and someday when I have money to spare, instead of always owing, we shall publish our letters as an example of love's growth from friendship. They are none of your mawkish rubbish. No miss's moonshine. But a titanic struggle, Will, and so I tell you!' And he turned to William with such charm and candour that the young man comprehended why his sister lived in a ruin with a ranter. 'Do not imagine that I took a mean advantage of Lottie's youth and innocence. I fought for my freedom like a lion, fought long and ardently. But she would have her way. You see before you an extremely happy fellow who was married in spite of himself!'

They were all very pleasant together after this speech, and as the evening was now getting late Lottie made fresh tea, and they supped off the remains of their dinner. Then retired at last, and William, who had enjoyed no more than a few hours' rest in three days, fell at once into a slumber so deep that it triumphed over the putrid odours of Lock-yard and the night-noise of a city. No scurrying rat could rouse him from this sleep, or even the most tenacious bed-bug bite him to consciousness.

The day after William's arrival Charlotte felt poorly and lay abed. Toby reported her to be somewhat low in spirits, and catching up a copper can with a hinged lid he suggested they take a walk to St James's Park, where they could buy milk fresh from the cows that grazed there.

'For myself I mind not,' he said carelessly, striding out into the turbulence of Fleet Street. 'I take milk but rarely—in coffee or tea. So what matter if it is somewhat sour, or mixed with water? But Lottie is a country lass, and bewails her lack.'

'But where could people keep a cow here?' William asked of the maze of tenements.

'Oh, they could not. But in many places near the city we have cowsheds, some of them underground, which are like to your mills, brother—dark, unclean factories employing their workers from youth onwards. The delights of fresh air and sweet grass are unknown there. The animals are milked until they can give no more, and then cast out to die. But the cow has one final use—she can be slaughtered for her meat and hide! So St James's Park is the answer, unless we take advantage of that she-ass there.'

The small grey donkey had caused a traffic stoppage along the Strand, though people, carts and wagons were beginning to move round her. She stood patiently while her owner squatted on his stool, squirting her milk into a pail, ignoring the trouble he had made.

'No, I think not,' said Toby. 'Her coat is something scabby. Oh, but look there, Will, at that fashionable she-ass!'

The lady in the sedan chair was regretting her toilette, which must have cost her maid and hairdresser hours of fabrication. Face, neck and bosom were painted white, lips and cheeks vividly rouged, a black star was placed cunningly upon one cheekbone, a black heart by her mouth. The lawn fichu swathing her shoulders was immense, and above all towered a vast white powdered wig raggedly cut so that the lady looked as though she had been severely shocked. Immobilised by the ass, she was the object of scornful eyes and mocking remarks, and William marvelled again at the frank rudeness of the London populace. They called, they mimicked, they caterwauled. The lady lifted a little fan to screen herself, but it was the hedgehog wig which entertained them and this reared over the pretty ivory sticks, unabashed.

'Will no one rebuke them?' William said indignantly.

'Why should they? Pox on the fool for looking so! Though I dare say she is poxed already,' Toby added cheerfully, 'for her paint is very thick. No, Will, be glad of our bad manners. The freeborn Englishman is free-spoken. It is a mark of his liberty. And at heart he is a republican who despises the rich. . . .'

But William knew exactly where this conversation would lead, and so remarked upon the bad breath of a fellow who had just elbowed him aside—and earned a diatribe on folk who would not be vaccinated.

At Charing Cross Toby stopped and bought *eau de cologne* for Charlotte, and left his change upon the counter, which William prudently picked up and restored to him. At the Haymarket he bought oranges from a barrow. While all the time he rattled on in the most diverting fashion.

'We must show you round, Will. Have you seen a circus? Or attended a play at the theatre?'

'As an apprentice to a Quaker master,' said William smiling, 'I was forbidden such wicked pleasures. Tho' I remember when I was in Birmingham that someone proposed a licensed theatre, but the church would have none of it.'

'We must see the wild beast show,' Toby continued. 'I shall find out what is on, Will, to divert you.'

The milk purchased, they adjourned to a coffee-house where Toby assuaged his thirst for debate, and both argued interminably. Then they began a roundabout stroll back home. William wondered whether this sort of excursion was in his honour, or whether Toby in fact spent more time away from his business than attending to it. But whatever the man saw he could use as grist for his political or social mill, and he nourished a decided passion for France.

'Our so-called pastimes are uncouth and vicious,' Toby said. 'The French, when they come over here, are aghast at our brutality. Cock-fighting! Bull-running! Bear-baiting! Football! (And what is that but an excuse for breaking coach-windows and knocking folk down?) Prize-fighting! Even our children will torment animals for their own pleasure. We take delight in cruelty. . . .'

'These are the free-born Englishmen you praised not long since,' William reminded him, 'and before the slavish French speak of cruelty may I remind you that Damiens was publicly tortured to death in Paris not thirty years ago? And the spectacle most lavishly advertised and attended, as though it were one of your entertainments at the pleasure gardens. . . .'

'But here the hangings are a public spectacle. . . .'

'An honest hanging does not compare with. . . .'

'And what of our nobility, so-named? A set of feckless gamblers who will stake house and land, aye, and wives and mistresses, upon the throw of dice or a hand of cards? Oh, we are corrupt!' Then suddenly changing the subject, as his attention was caught by a cookshop, he cried, 'I must buy some mutton pies. We shall go hungry, else. Here, Will, hold these like a good fellow!'

So that William fumed, even as he obeyed.

'But do not imagine,' Toby continued, coming out of the hot little shop with his savoury purchases, 'that I concern myself with our morals and our politics alone, Will. I have but recently wrote a pamphlet upon the Unprincipled Adulteration of Foodstuffs in the City of London. Ah, you who come from country stock, what shall you know of the rubbish with which we fill our bellies? You live off the fat of the land, while we are at the mercy of every poxy vendor who colours his butter and cheese to make them look fresh! There is sand in our sugar and dust in our tea, and soap-suds in our beer to give it a good head. And heaven only knows how much stinking horse-flesh we consume in the name of....'

Here they both looked suspiciously at the mutton pies, and walked on in an uncomfortable silence. Then Toby laughed.

'The devil of it is, Will,' he said frankly, 'that if governments were sane and people honest—how could I earn a living?'

Which made William laugh, and like him again.

THREE

A Lying-in

Charlotte had known, even as Toby swore he would fetch the milk back directly, that the two men would be gone for hours. At first she did not mind, for the strains and festivities of the previous evening had left her with a troubled heart and a queasy stomach. So she lay quietly until she felt able to rise, then manoeuvred herself out of bed and made her heavy way downstairs, pursued by the black kitten. The kitchen was dark and cold and empty. Where the servant was she did not know, and feared to ask or complain. And she thought how her mother would have dealt with such a situation, and made order out of chaos. She needed her mother then with an intensity that brought tears to her eyes. If only Dorcas could, by some miracle, walk briskly in, don the vast white apron worn for all family ailments, and put Charlotte back to bed and scold her, how preferable that would be to this solitary imprisonment. Since that was impossible she must brew tea for herself and sit close to the hearth for warmth and comfort.

The stitch in her side was nagging her, and she endeavoured to soothe it, but no matter how she shifted position and rubbed the place gently with her fingertips it would not go. The infant had been quiescent now for some days, lying low in the womb, and this morning the pressure was noticeable. She knew nothing of childbirth, too timid to ask her

35

new friends, too proud to ask Dorcas, so she entered each stage in fear and ignorance, hoping for the best.

'You allus take the hard road, Charlotte,' her father had said. 'I'm not saying that's wrong, lass, but many a time you punish yourself when you needn't.'

Well, this was her hardest road so far, and the most lonely. And now there was a stitch in her other side, and she felt as she used to before her monthly courses when the pain made her ill. The smell of hot tea which had been refreshing became offensive. She broke into a great sweat and knew she was going to vomit. Clumsily she pushed herself to her feet and hurried to the door, where she was violently sick. She leaned against the doorpost, trembling with shock and cold, knowing she had not the strength to move or clean up her own mess. Then as nausea ebbed, pain flowed: a seeking of pincers from the small of her back to her belly, a dull hot ache in the groins.

She heard the printing press clack steadily in the shop. Davy, an apprentice who taught himself while his master was absent, would be tending to business. She was too ashamed to call him, yet too weak to shiver in the November air without fear of catching cold. The pincers gripped her tenderly and retreated, then gripped again.

'Davy!' Charlotte called. 'Davy, will you come, if you please?'

He was out in moments, a good-natured round-faced lad of eighteen. The eldest of nine children, all conceived, born and bred in two rooms, he knew more about midwifery than his mistress, and grasped her plight in an instant. Carefully, supporting her weight, he walked her indoors, sat her down again, and brought a bowl lest she vomit a second time. Then he prepared to find the absent servant, the doctor, and Toby and William.

'Oh, do not leave me!' cried Charlotte, as the pincers seized her firmly.

'You'll be all right, Mrs Longe,' said Davy cheerfully, 'never fear. There's naught'll happen between now and tomorrow, with it being your first.'

'Tomorrow?' cried Charlotte, horrified.

'Aye, or the day after,' said Davy, more truthful than tactful. 'My mam was two days having me, and none so quick with the others!'

So he ran off, leaving her to her own sorry reflections and

to the claws which reminded her that life would crack her open.

It was four in the afternoon before Toby and William brought home the mutton pies, and were greeted by a self-important apprentice. Davy was a decent lad, but bad tidings are always more interesting than good, and he had run hither and thither to little avail for some hours. The doctor could not be traced, the servant had been found drunk and insensible in the larder, and Mrs Longe was now downright poorly and asking for her mother.

'Oh, my poor sister!' cried William, running up the stairs after Toby.

For once Charlotte took precedence over those weighty matters which so preoccupied her husband, and Toby being most grieved was most useless. First he ran into the room calling her name. Then he ran downstairs, calling for a doctor. Finally he put his head in his hands and reproached the God whose existence he denied. Though touched by this sincere affection William could not help doubting its efficacy, and himself (having spoken to his sister and bade her be of good cheer) ran for help in one direction, while Toby ran in the other.

London was a shade less intimidating to him now and, adopting the easy manners of its regular inhabitants, William dared ask advice of a kindly woman who recommended him to try Mrs Coates of Ludgate Hill.

'For she is both clean and sober, and will come if she can, sir.'

A message being left for Mrs Coates, which suggested that the Thames was afire, William hurried home again, threading and elbowing his way through the throng like a born Londoner, and found the household in a greater uproar. Numerous ladies had called, and were sitting round Charlotte's bed drinking tea and discussing their confinements, while his sister approached her ordeal with a brave face and a quailing heart.

'Oh, what shall I do?' cried Charlotte as Toby and William entered together. 'Oh, please to send them all away for they make my head ache. Oh, that I were home again. Oh, help me, God!'

'Out! Out!' Toby shouted, running into the press of callers like a madman, flailing his arms as though they were geese to be scattered.

Whereupon they departed with shrugs, smiles, frowns,

raised eyebrows and meaningful looks, leaving a litter of unwashed crockery behind them.

'Oh, help me!' cried Charlotte, holding out her thin young arms in supplication.

'God help us all,' Toby echoed, burying his head in her pillow.

The servant, now miserably sober, threw her dirty apron over her head and burst into loud sobs. While William, numb with apprehension, clasped his sister's fingers and felt the vibration of her pains through his own.

It was that hour of a winter's evening when fog descends and lamps are lit, and the house becomes enclosed in a private world. What Toby thought of no one knew, but brother and sister, handfast, had conjured up a childhood vision of Kit's Hill to shield them. There Ned forever stood guard, and Dorcas sat serenely in her parlour, and however wildly the wind called it could not harm them. As each contraction came Charlotte clutched her brother's hand and gasped, and as it ebbed she opened her eyes and smiled upon him. So that they did not hear the footsteps on the stairs, sounding hollowly, and stopping now and then as though their owner paused to take breath. And when the short sturdy woman pushed open the bedroom door and looked sharply about her, she too seemed to have risen from the past, with her high colour and small black eyes and her air of knowing best what was good for everyone.

Betty Ackroyd, their old housekeeper, would have stood thus: striped dress bunched over a plain petticoat, mob cap on her head. She would have taken off her woollen cloak in the same brisk manner, rolled up her sleeves in the same aggressive fashion. But when the midwife spoke it was the pert twang of a Londoner, not the broad Lancashire voice of Betty Ackroyd.

'I'm Mrs Coates, I am,' she said, announcing herself with a nod of importance. Then, seeing the disordered room, the distracted company, added, 'And come about time, too, I reckon!' She sized up the servant accurately. 'Now, Miss Sluts,' she said without ceremony, 'just you run downstairs and boil some water, and fetch up a bucket and scrubbing-brush. I like a clean room, I do, for the lying-in. And we'll have a fire lit—this place is cold as charity—which should have been done before, with the poor lady a-shivering of herself to death. So fetch plenty of coals. And I'll have a saucepan of hot posset, which if you can't brew—and that wouldn't surprise me!—I'll need milk and wine and spices. And be quick about it!'

She stared the girl into action and watched her disappear, then turned to the two men.

'Now which is Mr Longe? You, sir? Well, I should take your head out of that pillow if I was you, it don't do no good to nobody if you should suffocate. And this is a friend of yours, is it? Oh, your brother-in-law? Well, that's nice for you. Some gentlemen drink theirselves silly, and others work themselves tired, but to my mind a gentleman needs a friend to talk to in times like these. Now would you like to take yourselves off while I make the lady easier? And I'd be obliged, Mr Longe, if you wasn't to hang about outside the door, an-asking of questions every five minutes. For we shall be a while yet. And you might as well have this little feller, too, for we shan't be needing him neither!' Scooping up the kitten, who was swinging on a torn bed flounce.

William rose obediently and motioned Toby to come with him.

'For Lottie is in good hands,' he murmured, 'and we can sit the night out together if need be.'

Toby cried that he was the best of fellows, but still had to embrace Charlotte lovingly, asking her forgiveness, stammering his apologies. Until Mrs Coates had enough of his nonsense, as she told him roundly, and turned him out of the room by his shoulders and closed the door upon him.

'For it's no use a-saying he's sorry now,' she observed. 'He should have thought of it sooner, but they never do!'

The room scrubbed, the fire lit, the place in order, Charlotte began to feel better though her pains were stronger. Her courage returned with each word the midwife uttered: so safe they seemed within these walls, bent on woman's business, the meddlesome world of men excluded. And as the midwife worked she talked.

'Never a man but got in my way during a lying-in. Now, Mrs Longe, let's make you comfortable. There, lean on me, sweetheart. Ah, you're going to be one of those good ladies, I can tell, that don't make a fuss and pother. Brave as a martyred saint. Come, loveday, where is your clean shift? There's my lovely lady-girl. Aye, stop a bit when the pain comes, and breathe out, love. Never hold yourself. Let it go, for you won't stop it. Let go, sweetheart.'

Something good had entered the room with her, which Charlotte hazily recognised but to which she could put no name: something ancient, fundamental and well-tried. Living with Toby had been an unacknowledged war of attrition, resulting in her temporary defeat. She loved him and therefore could not be rescued, only encouraged to survive until she found herself. That he cared passionately for the many she did not doubt, that his ideas were far-sighted and humane she truly believed; but it seemed to her, in her simplicity, that it was best to begin at home before looking for problems abroad, to help a few loved people rather than rave over the wrongs of a multitude. Thus she proved herself to be merely a woman, caught up in personal concerns, rather than a man of wider views and greater intellect. So it was satisfying to engage in this venerable act of creation, and know that nothing was expected of her but to deliver a healthy infant, and be praised for doing so.

The birth was slow and hard, alleviated by drops of laudanum and constant attendance. She was aware of Mrs Coates's identity, though towards the end, as morning came, and pain and the hour were dark upon her, she confused both name and place. And thought she was at Kit's Hill, and called upon Betty Ackroyd—dead these six years—and Betty answered her, and gave her water, and told her not to fret, though Charlotte was terrified lest she burst open like ripe fruit and the sensation was unbearable.

'There's the head,' said Mrs Coates briskly. 'Hold back now, loveday! Don't go with it no more. Two or three more pains and we're through, sweetheart. Hold hard, now.'

Charlotte held as hard as she could, and then screamed aloud, and with the scream the child sprang forth, wailing at the loss of his warm lodging. And soon after, muddled with laudanum and exhaustion, his mother fell asleep.

It was bright day when she woke, to find the room at peace and the midwife sitting over the fire, dipping sippets of toast into her mulled ale and eating them with relish. The broad short back spelled strength, the round red arms comfort; and in the round red face now turning towards her, whose eyes were black cracks, whose smile gaped with lost teeth, past and present fused into one image. By her side, clucking and snuffling in his cradle, making good headway in a hard world, was Charlotte's son, whom the midwife now placed in her arms.

'You have been so good to me,' said Charlotte, smiling her thanks over the baby's cotton cap. 'I thought you were Betty, from home. She would have befriended me as you did, but she has been dead these many years. Oh, where is my husband, and my brother William, and how have they been?'

'Mr Longe's been a nuisance,' said Mrs Coates plainly, 'but then, they all are. A-rattling on the door knob, and a-calling on the landing, when a body has enough to do! But he's creeped in and see'd you and the baby. You've been sound off, sweetheart, with the laudanum. And now you've come to I'll go my way. Babies come in batches,' she remarked philosophically, 'so I lives betwixt and between, as you might say, never knowing when I'll get my washing done, but I'll be round tomorrow, all being well.'

'We were to have had Dr Southwell,' said Charlotte, uncertain of medical etiquette, 'but he was otherwise engaged. Should we not ask him to call in?'

'Leave him be,' said Mrs Coates, packing a great number of small articles into a large bag. 'He's best left. With gin at a penny a pint, why trouble him?'

'He was recommended by one of my husband's customers,' said Charlotte, and then drooped wearily, for all their arrangements seemed to be doomed.

'A respectable pig wouldn't recommend him to sleep in the sty,' said Mrs Coates sarcastically, 'for fear of breathing the fumes. You tell him to be off—if he does remember to come!—that is, if he can stand on his legs!'

'But you will come again, if you please, will you not?' Charlotte begged, afraid to lose this strange new ally.

'Ah, to be sure I shall. Now let me tuck Master Longe in his cradle—the which I found halfway down the bottom stairs to the kitching, and full of old books. And his blessed garments in a box under the dresser, and that kitting asleep on top of them!'

'I fear,' said Charlotte meekly, 'that the house is in some disarray.'

'Well, I know a servant as would suit, so long as you don't turn up your nose at the Afflicted. She might not be quick but she's clean, and having nothing else to think about she gets on with her work—which is more than you can say for Present Company Downstairs!'

'Since you recommend her, Mrs Coates, I should be glad to have her. Is her affliction. . . ?'

Her mind wandered through a forest of strawberry marks, rickets, rashes, and downright ugliness, unable to picture this marred treasure.

'Oh, she won't frighten the baby,' said the midwife briskly.

'Her trouble's elsewhere!' And she placed a finger on her forehead and turned it round, like an imaginary key in a lock.

'Mad?' Charlotte gasped.

'Back'ard,' said Mrs Coates, 'and all the better for it! Apart from breathing very hard while she polishes and scrubs, and not knowing when to stop—which you'll have to stop her, else she goes on 'til she drops—she hasn't a fault in the world. Only, she needs kindness and a bit of understanding, not to be made merry with and put upon. . . . I brought her into a Vale of Tears, Mrs Longe, thirteen years since. She was backwards way about then, and her mother took agin her in consequence. I'd like to see her settled, and you settled. And from what Mr Longe's been saying about Society he should be glad to do somebody a good turn! And, talking of Mr Longe, he's just the sort of gentleman as Polly Slack could take to—in a proper way—and she'd polish his boots until he could see his face in 'em!'

'Send her round as soon as may be, Mrs Coates,' cried Charlotte. 'She shall find a home with us.'

So had Dorcas said, many a time, and Betty always grumbled at the flock of red-nosed starvelings brought up from Garth village. But, fed and firmly trained, they had all married well according to their station in life, and left their good places for the doubtful delights of a small cottage and a large brood. And still Kit's Hill continued to absorb their little sisters and eldest daughters.

'That is settled,' said Charlotte, sounding exactly like her mother.

'Which goes to show,' Mrs Coates continued, 'how one good turn begets another. And now, Miss Sluts,' as the subdued servant entered with lukewarm tea and scraped toast, 'keep a-moving and do as your mistress tells you. And the next time a kitting does his business in the coal-scuttle, mind you clean it out, not leave it for folks to put on the fire and make a stink!'

'Yes m'm,' said the slattern, and those might have been her farewell words, for that afternoon Polly Slack joined the household and she left it, and they moved into a new phase.

Even in the three final days of his visit, William saw the beginning of a transformation which began in Charlotte's bedroom and crept down as far as the first floor. On the Thursday, he and Toby were requested to close the folding doors between parlour and dining-room. As they had been standing open for about twenty years, with Butler's *Analogy of Religion* and Berkeley's *Dialogues* acting as present doorsteps, this proved to be quite an undertaking. Toby was not even sure whether the books held the doors back or held them up, and the two men moved them gingerly (one at a time) to make sure, while William inspected and oiled the hinges as an extra precaution. Then Toby very kindly presented him with a fine copy of William Griffiths's *A Practical Treatise on Farriery* which had been published only the previous year, and begged him to stay on as long as he liked. But the purpose of the visit had been achieved, and William's mind was now bent on returning to his dying friend and master.

So early one dark morning he rose and dressed and knocked gently on Charlotte's door, to find her giving suck to the infant while Toby slept soundly.

'Our mother sent this,' said William quietly, delivering the final message in shape of a leather bag full of silver and gold coins. 'It was to be Betty Ackroyd's gift to you, upon your wedding day. It is Betty's savings.'

He wanted to say more and felt he could not, but Charlotte said it for him. One hand moved protectively over the little mound of earned money.

'It shall not be lightly spent,' she whispered. 'I shall keep it safe until I need it. Tell my mother I thank her and thank Betty.'

She lifted up her face to be kissed, and he marvelled at the change in her, weak though she still was from the delivery. Her eyes were calm, her face had lost its childish aspect, her mouth was firm and yet tender. She was no longer the victim of her impetuosity, or of the circumstances which had followed upon her choice. She was a survivor. The family might regret her difficulties, rail at them, be sorry for them, but they need not fear for her. Charlotte's weakness for self-sacrifice had been channelled by this dependant creature at her breast. Though her problems were manifold she would not yield to them lest her child suffer.

'Tell my mother,' she whispered, 'that we shall call him Ambrose, which was her father's name, and—though I have not been to church of late—he shall be christened.'

'She will be glad of that.'

'And tell her that all is pretty well with us, now.'

'I shall describe Mrs Coates and Polly Slack to her complete satisfaction.'

'And—though Toby cannot leave his business—in the summer, when London is unhealthy, I shall come home and bring the baby to see them all.'

'That will please her most.'

'And—oh, speak well of Toby for me.'

He kissed her cheek again in solemn promise, and she caught his hand, saying, 'And I am glad you came, Willie. And, Willie, was it not strange when Mrs Coates walked in to save us all? As though Betty had come back when she was needed!'

'I shall tell Mamma that, too. And now Lottie, dearest Lottie, I must go. For the Mail waits for no man!'

'Oh, I forgot to ask you, did you get your business done? The business that brought you here?'

Was there a teasing gleam in those velvet eyes? He could not be sure, and Charlotte was not stupid.

'The purpose of my visit is accomplished,' said William with dry humour, 'and Toby has promised to keep me informed of all future developments in the iron industry, both gossip and fact. He has already given me information about Mr Cort's puddling process.'

'I shall remember that, if he forgets!' Then her eyes filled with tears, her lips trembled, and she held out her infant, crying, 'Oh, kiss the baby, too, for he is your nephew—and, who knows, he may help you at the forge when he is older, as you helped Aaron Helm. And my father shall teach him to ride. And tell my mother he shall be as learned in Latin and Greek as any scholar. . . .'

'God bless and keep you, love,' said William, giving her a final resolute embrace, then turned to the door so that he should not be riven by her weeping.

Polly Slack made tea and toast for him, and he slipped a shilling into her unexpectant palm and bade her look after her new mistress, and left her staring astonished at the little coin.

He was troubled until he reached St Martin's-le-Grand, where an insolent fop wearing a sword called him 'Johnnie Bumpkin' and bade him step off the pavement to let his betters pass! William's gorge rose. Heedless of rank or sword or consequence, he set down his bags, dealt the fellow a blow like a sledge-hammer and left him lying in the mud with a little crowd about him.

'Pox on 'em all!' said William to himself, stepping victoriously aboard the Royal Mail.

He found a curious satisfaction in using this London oath against the Londoners, and settled back in his seat like a seasoned traveller.

FOUR

View from the Smithy

'I don't know as I'm man enough, let alone master enough, to fill your clogs!' William had said to Aaron Helm.

'Nay, lad,' the smith had replied, 'you might find as they slop about your feet at first, but time'll come when they're too rough and too tight for the likes of you. Then you'll be looking round for a pair of fine leather shoon wi' silver buckles!'

That fashionable era seemed far off. Aaron died shortly before Christmas, and William spent the festival at Kit's Hill with his family before opening up the forge officially at Flawnes Green. This was a poignant celebration for him: a harking-back to the past as the Howarths and their servants dined at one table; a vision of the future as his mother superintended his departure.

During Aaron's last illness Dorcas had employed a widow of good repute to cook and clean for him. Now that careful choice of hers would look after William. She had arranged the cramped living quarters behind his shop to the best advantage, and seen that the big farm wagon was packed with home produce. Ned and young Dick had driven it over, and the three men made a holiday of this removal: rolling the barrel of strong beer into the little larder, heaving in a sack of potatoes and another of Swedish turnips, hanging up a flitch of bacon, taking care that the salt pork was nowhere near the tallow candles, setting out butter and cheese and eggs upon the stone slab, stacking the wheat and barley loaves, fetching in a currant cake and a block of gingerbread.

To this bachelor bounty the ladies of Thornton House had contributed an exotic array of gifts. Besides the hundred gold guineas from Miss Wilde to mark the end of William's apprenticeship, there were a dozen bottles of fine old crusty port and his great-grandfather's silver-headed cane. Aunt Phoebe, not to be outdone, had bestowed upon him the last of her late father's claret and a little heap of pen-wipers, most beautifully stitched. And Agnes and Sally had presented him with red and white marmalades from their store-cupboard.

That late December evening, alone in his humble kingdom, William savoured the rare delight of independence and solitude. The kitchen beams, blackened by age and years of smoke, were low enough to brush the top of his head. In its deep recess, a fire glowed on the hearth. On the mantelshelf above stood a pair of iron candlesticks, a couple of blue and white china plates, and two pottery figurines such as farmers' wives buy from the packman when they have egg money to spare. Aaron's ingenuity was apparent in the wrought-iron chimney crane, by means of which pots and pans could be moved into different positions over the fire, and raised or lowered accordingly. There was a mechanical spit which turned by use of iron weights on a pulley, and even an iron fire-dog with a toasting-fork welded to his head. An iron kettle simmered on its hook. His chops were cooking in a hanging grill. Potatoes were baking in hot ashes. His table in one corner of the room was laid and waiting. William Wilde Howarth, blacksmith of Flawnes Green, was a happy man.

As well as the forge William had inherited Aaron Helm's last apprentice, Stephen Turner. He was a slight lad for this kind of craft, just fifteen years old, shy and withdrawn. William wondered why Aaron had accepted him, but did not wish to seem critical, though Aaron himself remarked that a shout, a clout, and a kick up the backside were all the boy was worth.

But in the three months of Aaron's dying William had contented himself with winning back old customers and setting the business on its feet again. So the shortcomings of Stephen were no more than a minor irritant, a brief disturbance in the routine, until the time when William was made responsible for the smithy and a human being he neither knew nor cared for. According to ancient law the apprentice must be provided for in the event of a master's death, so Stephen was duly transferred to William, with his first year's training already gone to waste. A study of his half of the indentures caused the new blacksmith further disgust. For the privilege of teaching Stephen the mystery of smith-ing Aaron had charged a mere ten sovereigns. Moreover, since the lad lived

46

out with his mother, she must be paid three shillings a week for his keep, rising by easy stages to six shillings and sixpence in the seventh and final year. Calculating his expenses, William found that he was training the lad at a financial loss, with nothing but the doubtful prospect of Stephen's usefulness to compensate him.

'We are given nothing without return,' Dorcas had said, when he complained to her. 'You have the smithy. Look upon Stephen as your payment for it.'

Winter was in its depths, heavy with the rains which had dogged the previous harvest. But on his first morning as master, William rose at half past five o'clock, washed in icy water, donned a coarse shirt and breeches, raked the fire together in the grate, and took a swallow of beer to start the day. Beyond the kitchen, in which warmth still lingered, the shop was closed and dark and cold.

From mid-September to mid-March, apprentices worked from daybreak to twilight: a short day compared to the other half of the year, when they laboured from five in the morning until eight at night. Yet Bartholomew Scholes had his apprentices up and about by six of a winter's morning, cleaning premises by candlelight. For as he said, 'This is not work, but making ready for work, my friends. When it grows light thou shalt learn what labour means!'

The silver watch proclaimed six o'clock precisely. William concealed it beneath one of the hollow figurines and marched into the shop. He unbarred the double doors with a flourish, letting in a bitter gust of rain, and took down the shutters. A metallic grey had taken the place of night's black. He tied his leather apron about him, put on his woollen skull-cap, and stood arms akimbo, waiting for Stephen. The rain beat in upon him with no more effect than it would have had upon a marble statue. He was master here. He would not fulfil the duties of his apprentice. So much had he learned of Quaker training.

'I do not punish honest ignorance, William Howarth,' Bartholomew had said, taking off his heavy leather belt. 'But neglect of duty and tardiness I cure with a whipping, my friend.' And so he had, upon William's bared backside, though merciful enough not to use the buckle-end as some masters did.

Now the sky became dull pearl, and a hurst of trees was visible on the hill beyond the river, opposite. He could glimpse the road running down to Millbridge, partly screened

47

by hawthorn. From the cottages tucked round the Green smoke lifted to heaven. A door opened, a voice called and was answered. Women were astir, blowing on the ashes, kindling the fires, cooking oatmeal porridge. A cock crowed guiltily. A robin trilled question. Flawnes Green was awake.

Still William stood, in the majesty of his calling, damping down his temper that it might flame more freely later on.

At half past six a little lad scurried round the corner of the smithy, holding a man's tricorne hat on his head to prevent its slipping into his eyes. His clothes, too, seemed to have belonged to a larger person. The breeches were held up with string and bellied over his knees. His clogs gaped. His shirt and coat overpowered him. William quelled a smile and remained grim and silent at the door of the forge, until the lad came to an uncertain halt and looked fearfully up at him.

'Morning, master!' said Stephen, whipping off the battered hat.

William waited an exquisite half minute before he replied.

'Morning?' he said sarcastically. 'I should have called it afternoon, Stephen. I have been waiting since morning.'

The boy rubbed his head and then his eyes, endeavouring to find words out of an inadequate vocabulary.

'Day's just breaking, master,' he said finally, pointing vaguely at a watery sun. 'Just broke.'

William caught him by one outstanding ear and pulled him inside the shop.

'Aye, and next time it will be your head that is broke!' he cried, in fair imitation of Bartholomew's manner. Severe but controlled. 'Now I will have you here as soon as the first light comes to the sky, not the last. Do you hear me? You rise in the dark, and breakfast in the dark, to get here in time. I'll have no gentlemanly dawdling, sir. This smithy is open and working at six o'clock.'

The lad nodded vigorously to prevent his teeth from chattering, and held his big hat to his chest. They stood by the cold forge together, one of them gloriously at war, the other ignominiously cringing. William folded his arms.

'Tell me your duties, Stephen,' he said.

The boy stared at him dumbly, afraid.

'Duties, duties!' cried William. 'What are your first duties here?'

A quiet voice from the doorway said, 'It's no use shouting at the lad like that, Mr Howarth. He don't know what you mean,' and Hannah Garside stepped in out of the rain.

William's housekeeper was no more than five and twenty, but sorrow and an air of authority made her seem older. Her figure was slight, and she wore her working clothes with grace. They were shabby but very clean, and she had bought a new black shawl in honour of her husband's funeral, which covered up the deficiencies of her wardrobe.

William stopped short, as though she had caught him out in an offence.

'Stephen's mother is a widow-woman, like me,' Hannah continued in her low pleasant voice, 'but she takes her grief harder. She's not a woman that can stand alone, like I can. Stephen tries to take his father's place, but he's o'er-young for that.'

She was unwinding her shawl, shaking the wet from it, touching her white cotton cap to make sure it was in place. Now she came beside the boy, and smoothed the hair out of his eyes, and rested her hand upon his shoulder.

'You won't know, perhaps, how a woman can grieve, Mr Howarth,' said Hannah, and there was no reproof in her tone, yet she intended that he should understand. 'Bess Turner cries in her sleep, and not wanting what the day will bring she don't like waking to it. The lad gets up first, and lights the fire for her and brews tea. He sits with her, listens to her, does what he can afore he leaves. Which is little enough, for what can anyone do? Farmer Boulton lets her keep the cottage, out of charity. She's got nothing but what she earns, cleaning, and the three shilling a week you give her.'

Then William saw that the lad was wearing his father's old clothes.

'And he's had no schooling like you and me, Mr Howarth,' said Hannah inexorably. 'He can't read nor write. His father died last year, and his master died last month, and his mother wants to die and all. So it's no good shouting at him, Mr Howarth. He's not backward, nor lazy, nor disobedient.' She smiled at William to show she did not blame him for his ignorance, but would enlighten him. And the smile was sweet and quick like a girl's, and lit her face and warmed her fine grey eyes. She put her hand on Stephen's cheek lightly. 'He's bewildered,' said Hannah.

She looked each of them fully in the face as if to say, 'Now make your peace!' and walked away into the kitchen.

The boy dared glance at William timidly; and William was ashamed, remembering how Aaron had always dealt kindly with him, and made a joke of his errors. So he cleared his throat and resolved to start afresh. It was his father who spoke out of him then, in rough and homely fashion.

'Hast had thy breakfast, Steve?'

The lad shook his head.

'Hannah!' cried William. 'Lay another place at the table, will you? I'm paying three shillings a week for nowt!'

Then he began to laugh and shake his head, and to wonder how Bartholomew Scholes would have dealt with this sorry starveling. But the Quaker master had no truck with the poor, except as outside charities. For each of his apprentices must bring a good boxful of clothes and under-linens, and a hundred pounds in gold, which restricted applicants to the ranks of the lesser gentry or the prosperous yeomanry. Nor was the smithy at Flawnes Green comparable to the network of blacksmiths' shops and small iron industries owned by the Scholeses of Birmingham. So William must learn to be master in his own way.

The boy moved nearer, hearing him laugh, and looked less fearful.

'We'll start again, shall us, lad?' said William. 'Now tell me what you know. What do you have to do here?'

Thus encouraged, Stephen found his tongue and consulted his memory.

'Sweep shop out and tidy up, master. Learn names of tools, and sizes of nails. Make the fire hot wi' bellows. There's a mort of names for the red and yellow of the fires, for different jobs, but I canna remember which is for what. And there's another lot of names for the welding fires, like *greasy* and *snowball*. And I have to draw the clinkers out, else they spoil the heat. And there's stock and dies, but I don't know them, neither. And dunnot face the horse when you're shoeing, but set your back to his backside—though I'm just as feared, any road! And tingle the anvil—only I weren't big enough to swing the sledge, and then Mr Helm was took badly. And'—his invention failing him—'sweep shop out and keep all tidy!' A pause, 'Master,' said Stephen.

'Aye,' said William, after another pause. 'Well, you've some way to go yet, haven't you, lad? We must teach thee to read and write. Where I was 'pprenticed, in a big town called Birmingham, we had to be able to read and write afore we started.'

Hannah was in the kitchen doorway.

'Food's on table,' she said, and added, 'I can learn him to

read and write in the evenings, Mr Howarth. Maybe I can get his mother to learn, and all. It'd take her mind off her grief.'

William sat in his big chair on one side of the table, and Stephen slithered into his place on the other.

'Where did you get your schooling then, Hannah?' asked William.

'The Methodists taught me, Mr Howarth. I'm a Methody.'

Stephen placed his salt pork between two thick slices of bread, and munched contentedly, swinging his feet.

'Are you not joining us, Hannah?' William asked.

For her food had been one of the arrangements made by Dorcas. A hungry woman does not work as well as a fed woman, and may even be tempted to steal.

'I can have mine when you've done, Mr Howarth.' Quiet and firm.

He looked at her curiously. She was poor enough to need this job, glad of a full belly and a few shillings, but she held herself proudly and met his eyes like an equal.

'How long have you been widowed then?' William asked, spearing another slice of salt pork with his knife.

'Five months, Mr Howarth.'

'Have you childer to care for?'

'No, I thank God. I shouldn't like to see them clemmed. This is a poor village, and a poor valley from all accounts. Except for Millbridge folk.'

'What about your family then, Hannah? Do you live with any of them?'

Something in her face and presence forbade him to intrude upon her any further. She answered him flatly, withdrawing from the conversation.

'I live in one of Farmer Boulton's cottages. My husband worked for him. I pay my way by doing a bit for Mrs Boulton here and there, and helping at harvest time. I'm a foreigner, you see, Mr Howarth. I come from Charndale, the other side of the valley.'

Then she busied herself with the fire, back turned on them both. So William addressed himself to Stephen, who had been blowing upon his tea like a man and supping it loudly.

'Hast done then, lad? Come into the shop and let's put some muscle on thee!' Then he cried over his shoulder, 'Thank you for a good meal, Hannah!' remembering how Bartholomew Scholes always paid this tribute to the woman of the house.

She inclined her head gravely, and began to clear the plates away. As he showed Stephen how to make a dull-red fire into a cherry-red one he pictured her sitting down at the table and taking breakfast. She would not eat hurriedly, apologetically, huddled over her food as poor women did, as though her want was a shameful thing, but with the detached and tidy manner of the more fortunate. So she was a Methodist? Flawnes Green was becoming quite a colony of Methodists. Aaron's preaching and principles had borne fruit here. William wondered whether Hannah ever preached. He imagined she would be rather good at that.

All morning she busied herself about the house, wearing stout clogs to protect her feet from the wet. She scrubbed out the privy which stood next door to the sty. She fed the brown sow and the four brown hens. She counted William's personal and household linen, observing how his mother had laid dried lavender between the sheets. She tidied his larder and scoured his cooking pots. From time to time he saw her walk by the front of the smithy, carrying two pails to fill at the village pump on the green. She spoke only once and that briefly, standing in the kitchen doorway, hands folded across her clean checked apron.

'I'll be off now, Mr Howarth. There's boiled beef and dumplings in the pot, and I've made you a morsel of oatcake, and a treacle pudding. I'll be back afore it's dark to get your supper.'

Then she let herself quietly out at the back door and walked across the fields to Boulton's farm. Stephen ran home for his dinner, and was back within the stated hour, looking anxiously at his master for praise. And William, having dined like a king, took out his own apprentice's masterpiece and prepared to show the lad what was expected of him. For his test-work William had made a set of horseshoes, so well fashioned that not a hammer mark could be seen.

'To show,' said William wryly, 'that I was sufficient in cunning and knowledge, as well as of good name and fame, Steve. Do you know what that means?'

'No, master.'

'It's a fancy way of saying that I knew my job and could behave myself, lad. Let's nail these above the smithy door, shall we? Then they'll see I know a horseshoe from a ploughshare!'

The lad smiled at the little joke.

'Do you know what being an apprentice means, Steve? My master told me, the first day in Birmingham. You're my servant, in a manner of speaking, and that's your duty to me.

52

But my duty to you is to care for your body and your soul, to treat you as though you were my son. Are you fond of the girls, lad?'

Stephen, after much throat-clearing and mind-searching, said no, he was afeared of them mostly.

'That's all to the good,' said William humorously, 'because you mustn't go courting until you're a journeyman. Do you play football? No? That's good, too, because you're not allowed to. Nor can you go dancing, nor mumming, nor watching plays at the fair—though I'll turn a blind eye to that, so long as you don't get drunk and disgrace the pair of us!'

Stephen said hesitantly, 'Can't I go pace-egging, master, at Eastertime?'

'I reckon we'll allow that, and all,' said William, 'seeing it's a religious festival. What part do you play then, lad?'

'Bold Slasher,' said Stephen, evidently aware that this hardly described his character or appearance.

'Try to be Saint George if you can,' said William, grinning, 'it'd look better, if we ever had to confess to it! And get your hair cut. Here, fetch us a pudding basin and I'll do it myself. And another thing, lad, you'd best take that silver lace off your hat and those ruffles off your shirt. They're not allowed. And give up fencing, wilta?'

The boy looked puzzled, then uncertain, scanning William's solemn face. He lifted his hat and looked at it. He pondered over his bony wrists. And at length a slow smile crept across his face.

'You're having me on, aren't you, master?' he said.

Then smiled even more broadly, and went for the pudding basin and scissors.

Stephen's hair was not the last pudding-poll cut by William. As village blacksmith he fulfilled many roles: tooth-drawing, toy-mending, pig-ringing at a penny-halfpenny a time, trimming the feet of cows and goats, soldering old pans, and even capping Sailor Pearson's wooden leg with a new ferrule. Seven years of Quaker commonsense had inclined William to look upon country folklore with a sceptical eye. He found it difficult to believe that bad luck, evil spirits and epidemics could be kept at bay by horseshoes, nails, or iron circles drawn upon the air, and was inclined to scoff at such superstitions. But he saw that simple people gained great comfort from them, whether they worked or not, so said nothing and allowed the pagan rituals of Flawnes Green to flow round him: accepting his central role in the mysteries with good humour. While the villagers, unaware that a heretic was in their midst, laid ailing children upon his anvil and asked him to bang his hammer on the other end to drive out sickness; dipped their rickety limbs, their wounds and their warts in his water-trough; begged bits of iron to lay in their infant's cradle, to prevent an elf-child being put in its place; and once brought a case of goitre to be cured by inhaling smoke from the hoof of a virgin ass which William was shoeing.

There was one old law which he liked to keep. He refused to use iron upon a Good Friday, in memory of the time when Christ's hands and feet were nailed to the Cross. Otherwise, William worked a six-day week from dawn to dark, and had been called out of church on a Sunday, more than once, to fulfil his duties as a farrier.

Goods and services were still exchanged here, though Bartholomew Scholes was grand enough to need a counting-house and rich enough to use a bank. But in Flawnes Green William shoed Farmer Boulton's oxen, and in return had his sow visited by the farmer's boar until she became fruitful. He was paid in produce (grown or poached), in manure, in a day's work at the smithy. The carpenter repaired for him. The baker allowed Hannah to put her weekly batch of bread, or her pies, in his oven; and on Sundays let her roast the meat with onions and potatoes under it.

Dorcas, who loved to be consulted and needed, presented Stephen with a sober suit of fustian, which fitted him, and called it her Christmas box: so bringing the lad into the family, instead of setting him a little apart from them. Life was smaller and closer, warmer than in the town. And now William laid down the rules which Aaron had laid down for him.

'Build yourself up with boxing and weight-lifting, Steve. A good smith needs good shoulders. Eat your victuals, crust and fat and all. Run and jump and pull and push with all thy might. And never use thy strength against the weak.'

Stephen looked at his master's great chest and mighty limbs, the hands that could bend a bar of iron, the fists that could smite a nail into a plank, and the handsome head that had sent every maiden in Flawnes Green to the wise woman for a love-potion; and he vowed silently that he would not rest until he could stand side by side with William. Now he began to answer quickly, look sharply, listen carefully. And

54

sometimes, sheepishly, he would bend over the village pond when no one was watching to see if the transformation was apparent.

F I V E

Fledged

1787

Having neither husband nor child to concern her, Hannah Garside was the good neighbour of Flawnes Green. Folk would not forget that she came from Charndale, and her passionate commitment to Methodism set her apart in another way, but she had gradually become indispensable to the community. When the midwife could not be present, Hannah brought forth the infant. When sickness came, Hannah nursed long and patiently. She sat with the dying, laid out the dead, and brought comfort to the bereaved. She looked after William and Stephen, taking pride in her work. From the kitchen window of her four-roomed cottage she could see straight across the barley field into the back yard of the forge, and unknown to William she kept an unobtrusive and caring watch upon his daily life. As he mounted his horse of a Sunday, handsome and tall in his best suit, bent on visiting his great-aunt in Millbridge or his parents on Garth Fells, she could commend herself on his appearance. It was Hannah who brushed his clothes and shone his top-boots, starched his linen and cooked for him, as well as any woman could. When he had gone she hastened over the field by the hedge path, to make sure that the house was immaculate for his return. She never entered the smithy on these occasions. That was a world apart from her. But she glanced everywhere else, seeking out small disorders and righting them. That done, she would throw the hens an extra handful of corn, give the pig a few dandelions or a couple of rotten apples, peep into the scrubbed privy, examine the donkey-stoned doorstep, and return home satisfied.

But once all the scouring and baking and helping were over, Hannah was alone. And at these times, when her vital

55

force was diminished or spent, it seemed that everyone asked of her and no one replenished her. She scorned to feel sorry for herself, but she knew empty hours and wakeful nights, when even prayers lay in her mouth like stones.

It was William's habit, in his first year as a fully-fledged blacksmith, to visit Kit's Hill once a month, where he attended morning service at St John the Divine in Garth, dined with his family, exchanged news, and rode back after supper. On this particular Sunday, early in 1787, there came across the Pennines a great gale of snow, and such a high wind that horse and rider must plod along, heads down, for miles. At Coldcote William halted, and hearing that conditions grew worse towards the Fells, relinquished the prospect of a hot dinner and a dry stable with regret, and turned again for Flawnes Green.

On these holidays the house was left to itself, no fire lit, no cooking done, since he was not expected home until bedtime, and food and fuel were too precious to waste. So he walked, as it were, into a domestic mausoleum, and reached for his tinder-box with hands red and stiff from cold. He was used to Hannah planning and catering for him, and endeavoured to light the fire while he wondered how to manage for his mid-day meal. And he reflected that he must be the only man in Flawnes Green who would not enjoy the tastiest food of the week. For even the poor families, their pig killed in December could fry up a black pudding; and the farmers ate like kings on Sunday.

The latch lifted and fell with a soft clack, and Hannah was standing in the kitchen with a basin held under her black shawl. They were more easy together these days, though she always held him at a distance. But the first sharpness of her husband's death had passed, she spoke more freely, smiled more often.

'I chanced to see you riding back, Mr Howarth,' said Hannah. 'I guessed it was the weather as brought you home. I've got a bit of dinner here for you. It's no sort of a day to go cold and hungry.'

He stood up, clumsily for William, and took the basin from her. He could find no adequate words of thanks. She had come when he needed her, and he realised for the first time how much he relied upon her, how much he took for granted.

'Nay, don't go back just yet, Hannah,' he said, as she

56

turned towards the door. 'Sit you down and warm you. The fire'll blaze up in a minute. I've put the kettle to boil.'

'Well,' she said, hesitating, 'just for a minute then.'

Still he stood, awkwardly holding the basin, staring down at her cap, pleated like a pie-crust in starched white cotton, and her brown hair shining in glimpses beneath it.

'You'd best put that to warm,' she said, glancing at him and glancing away, and she shook her shawl into the hearth to free it of snow.

'Have you had yours?' William asked, immobilised.

'Aye, I have. Here, eat it out of the basin. Have your dinner on your knees for once, like I do. I'll brew tea for you, Mr Howarth,' and she brought him his knife and two-pronged fork.

'I'll eat it if you'll stop for a bit, and have a cup of tea and talk,' said William, recovering his equilibrium.

She looked at him quickly, and smiled to herself. 'I'll stop,' she said, 'just you get that hot food inside you, it'll do you good.'

So he sat by the fire, greatly comforted, and ate while she watched him with absorbed grey eyes. He had needed her ministrations. She had ministered to him. Now she talked, easily, simply, as he forked the meat from his basin.

'Rabbit stew, that is, and never cost me a farthing. Farmer Boulton give me the rabbit, and his wife give me the potatoes. I dug an onion out of the field, and had a few dried herbs by me. Is it good? That's right! We had Sunday meeting at my house this morning. We were fair put to it to cram in, I can tell you. Two up and two down, and not enough room to swing a cat. Twelve of us, all told. Aaron Helm started up the Methodys in Flawnes Green, and got my husband Abel to join. That was before we were wed. He used to walk a lot of a Sunday, did Abel. He'd put a bit of bread and cheese in his pocket and think on the Holy Word, and walk. He was a jobbing carpenter, and Farmer Boulton let him have the cottage instead of payment. One Sunday he walked right over the top of Belbrook How and down the other side to Charndale. I was sitting outside our door, shelling peas, and he asked for a drink of water. Then he started coming every Sunday, to see me. My folk went mad when he said he wanted to wed me. A foreigner and a Methody! I'd never thought much of men before. Mother said I was a pisey cat, turning my nose up at this lad and that one, and my sisters married long since! But when I told her I would have Abel

57

she said worse than that. So I up and left Charndale and come here. I turned Methody, along with Abel. We never had no childer. and that broke my heart—until he died. Then I was glad. I've seen too many widow's childer go hungry. They say as the Parish'll look after you, but the Parish make starvation seem kinder than charity. I've done well enough on my own. I'm not feared of hard work. I give Mr Boulton a hand at harvest-time if he needs me, and they're good to me at the farm—like giving me the rabbit. Have you done, then? I'll pour us some tea.'

She had never spoken to him so naturally and so much before, and he had always been slightly in awe of her, so these simple confidences came like revelations upon him. He had identified her with her tasks: Hannah the whitster, pounding his linen in the dolly tub, heating her flat-irons on the hob: Hannah the cook, beating up a batter pudding, pressing out cakes of gingerbread: Hannah the housekeeper, keeping a stern eye on dirty feet and clean floors. Now he saw Hannah the woman, and she was a mystery and a delight.

It was her air of authority, her dignified reserve, that made her seem plain. When she spoke of her husband she was alive, shining like the girl she must have been when she upped and left her family in Charndale and became a foreigner in Flawnes Green. Her eyes were very clear and beautiful, meditating on the past. She sat as upright and gracefully as his mother did, nursing her cup in both hands. Her weekday dress had been changed for a black linsey-wolsey gown; her worsted hose and clogs for black stockings and shoes, her checkered apron for starched white, and a fine muslin kerchief (possibly handed down by Mrs Boulton, since it was quite elegant) completed her Sunday attire. And though her hands were not the hands of a lady, as Dorcas's were, Hannah had cared for them in between her tasks, and they were smooth and small and capable, not the usual red and roughened hands of a working woman.

'Who were your family, Hannah?' he asked curiously.

She pursed her lips in mockery of their grandeur.

'Oh, summat and nowt as folk say! My father was a weaver and earned good money, and my mother saw to our manners and wanted us to marry well. We were all girls, Mr Howarth. Six girls! The others, they did the right thing according to my mam. Susan married a baker. Prue a farmer. Tabby married an undertaker. You see what I mean? A jobbing carpenter don't compare to them!'

'Tell me,' said William, stirring his tea thoughtfully, 'did you grieve very much when he died? I mean, like Stephen's mother for her husband?'

He had wiped the joy from her face and she answered soberly.

'I never took it that way. I was never much for tears. But when Abel died there was a part of me went with him. I've heard women say, when they've lost a child, as they felt the loss of it in their bellies. But I didn't take Abel's death that way, neither. But for a long while I couldn't get warm. It was a lovely summer, the summer Abel died. And yet I just couldn't get warm. . . .'

She put down her cup and wound her arms about herself, remembering. Her sadness had penetrated to her clothes, and they lost their Sunday lustre, becoming mere widow's weeds.

'Aye, that's right. Aaron was always good to women, though he never had one of his own. It seemed proper, when he had nobody, to help out. And I was glad of the money. And it kept me busy.'

So she and her husband had lain together in love and warmth, the warmth Abel had taken with him, and yet their union had not been blessed. Her story was unfinished. She should have borne many children. He could imagine her in their midst, prodigal with giving.

'And do you know what hurts me most?' said Hannah, looking into the fire, holding out her hands to the blaze. 'I canna see Abel like I used to. Six year we were wed, and I knew every change in his face and every move of his body. And now I canna remember what he looked like. As if time was robbing me.'

He could not bear that she should change back into the sad withdrawn woman. He wanted her to smile again, to be young again. He wanted to be a part of her mystery, to share those thoughts she now told to no one else. He leaned forward and clasped her two cold hands, and looked into eyes the colour of sea on a winter's day.

'Nay, don't be sad, Hannah,' he said, coaxing her.

She answered very quietly, in that tone which held him at a distance.

'If I'd known you'd be home, Mr Howarth, I'd have made a pudding. But I never bother when I'm by myself.'

He let go of her as though she had struck him across the face, bent his head to ask her pardon, and walked over to the window not knowing what to say or do. She put on her shawl, picked up the basin, looked at his bowed shoulders.

'There's cold meat in the larder, Mr Howarth, as'll do for your supper. I shan't be coming back today. There's another meeting at my home this evening. I'll see you tomorrow. As usual.'

He said, beseeching her, not looking at her, 'Hannah, should I build thee an oven to bake bread? I could do. Then you needn't be always begging a bit of space from the baker.'

'That'd be handy,' she answered, cool and firm. 'You could have a pie whenever you fancied, then.'

He dared glance at her, to see if she had forgiven him.

'I could make thee a salamander to brown the pastry, Hannah.'

'That'd be grand, Mr Howarth.'

'And I'll get thee a box-iron, all the way from Birmingham, to smooth the clothes. Then you needn't be forever lifting heavy flat-irons, Hannah.'

'Nay, one treat's enough at a time,' she said, light and friendly. 'I don't have to be marred, Mr Howarth. I'm used to the baker, and my old irons.'

'But I should count it an honour,' said William, very low.

She flushed up quickly, for he had spoken to her as he would speak to a lady, and she was not prepared for that.

'Good-day, Mr Howarth,' she said, turning to the door.

The latch clacked into place. She was gone, hurrying across the field by the hedge, shawled head bent against the driving wind and snow.

William strode into the smithy and smashed his fist down hard upon the anvil, to drive out the devil in himself. And all afternoon and evening he was sorely puzzled, wondering how it was that he could live side by side with a woman for over a year and then discover that he never knew her, and now wanted to find her out. No room would contain his restlessness. The snow kept him indoors, the day forbade him to work. He revolved round that fateful half-hour or so they had sat and talked together, re-worded and re-made it. The night wrapped its shawl about him and still he had not found an answer.

Building Hannah's oven was one of the hardest and sweetest tasks he had ever undertaken. There had been a patent for an enclosed grate and oven as far back as the mid-seventeenth century, but in recent years a man called Thomas Robinson had invented a kitchen range suitable for the modern household. Bartholomew Scholes, with his network of connections and information, was among the first to install one, and William would have liked to present Hannah with such a complex iron monster as his. But the modest inglenook and kitchen could not sustain such a thing, and in the end he wrote and asked advice from his old master, and laid out a portion of his hundred guineas to buy a smaller novelty.

The metal was his metal, but the trade was not his trade. A village blacksmith does not possess a blast furnace. But he could assemble and fix it for her, build it in and make it trim, to please her. To please her. To make her smile and speak again as she had done.

The neighbours wondered what Hannah had done to deserve such a tribute. And though they came in one by one, to admire the basket grate and moulded hood with its fancy trim, and spy William's dinner cooking in the neat oven, there was much speculation. For William was a bachelor, and as such could not be expected to care how his food was cooked, provided some woman served it up hot and tasty at noon. Surely he could not be courting a widow on the wrong side of her twenties? Hints and rumours distressed Hannah, and she withdrew into a silence he could not break. Wretched, he neglected the ladies of Thornton House, and hardly went near Kit's Hill, so that Hannah might come to him on Sundays. While she, aware of all his stratagems, fearful that either Miss Wilde or Dorcas might hear something or make enquiries, cooked enough for both days on the Saturday, and steadfastly avoided every opportunity of being alone with him again.

So winter turned to spring, and spring to summer. William's homilies to Stephen ceased. He no longer took pleasure in his work, but found every task unwelcome. The ringing of his anvil became noise instead of music. A smiling customer meant mockery rather than friendship. Enquiries were veiled complaints. Sometimes his elbow went. At others the weight of the piece defeated him. He felt that he was losing his power, that Hannah had drawn all the virtue from him.

Others were enjoying life, or so it seemed to William. Either Toby or Charlotte wrote to him regularly of national and international events, stirring his quiet backwater into a river of discontent. Caleb Scholes the younger, fellow-apprentice of William's Birmingham years, scrawled entertaining tales concerning the trials and delights of working for his father the ironmaster. And occasionally Ruth Scholes of Birmingham, Bartholomew's wife, put pen to paper, for she had made a subtle favourite of him, and sent him news of her busy household and that ever-increasing network of iron men, bankers, and quiet wielders of power.

In his frustration William turned on Stephen. The silent little lad had become a youth of seventeen, grown four inches taller by the mark on the smithy wall. He could wield a sledge-hammer, or truss and throw an ox to be shod, nearly as well as his master. And he loved Hannah, who was more mother to him than his own mother. And he worshipped William, which made him vulnerable. So William chided where he should have encouraged, remained silent when he should have praised, and one summer Saturday was so unreasonable that Hannah came to the door and spoke her mind forcibly.

'You've done nowt but find fault all morning,' she cried, hands on hips, 'and the biggest fault of the lot is thee, William Howarth. Think shame on yourself! And remember this—he'll be as big and as clever as thee, someday, and if you get a clout round the head instead of a hand in friendship—don't say as I didn't warn you!'

He had never seen her angry before, and slight as she was her wrath defeated him. He let fall the hammer and followed her into the kitchen, where she clashed pans and slammed the precious oven door to with a ferocity that astonished him. He lapsed into his native tongue to deal with her.

'Never make a fool of me in front of that lad again!' he warned, but his tone lacked conviction.

She rounded on him, unafraid, though her cap did not reach his shoulder.

'Make a fool of thee? Tha makes a fool of thyself!' she answered, as broad in her dialect as he. 'Tha'rt nowt but a babby shriking for its sucking-rag! That lad'd go through fire for thee.'

He slammed the door between themselves and the smithy, to pay her back for her treatment of the oven. He loved her, and he could have killed her.

'I've done more than enough for thee,' said William in a fury, 'and let me tell thee summat. Tha'rt nowt! Frowning and hiding, when a man does his best for thee, and never a word of thanks. I paid out good money and worked and sweated all winter for thee, and by God I'm sorry as I did.

Now get off home and shut thy mouth. Dunnot fret about leaving me a bit of cold meat for my Sunday dinner. I'll manage for myself. Else go where I'm wanted.'

She tore off her apron, and then hesitated. There was a potato pie in the oven, and though she would not yield to him she had put her heart into the baking of that pie. She stood indecisively, holding her checkered apron to her breasts. He had turned the tables on her, and she was puzzled.

'Mind you take that pie out then,' she said, recovering a little.

He knew he had won this round at least. In turn, he placed his hands on his hips and played master in his own house.

'Bugger the pie!' said William deliberately. 'Get off home!'

He did not wait to see her go, but strode back into the smithy. Stephen was blowing the fire to welding heat, and did not look at him.

'All right, lad,' said William kindly. 'I'm sorry I spoke as I did. I'm in no humour wi' myself nor anybody else these days. We'll shut up shop for today. Get thee off home.'

'What about this here welding then, master?' Stephen asked.

'We'll do it Monday. First thing. It'll be a nice afternoon,' said William, looking at the fleecy sky. 'I don't fancy shutting us-selves up, welding, on a day like this.'

'Tha'rt the master,' said Stephen slowly.

'Come back Monday, lad. I'll be better-tempered then.'

He locked the smithy, feeling lighter of spirit. He remembered the pie, and his heart beat fast in case it was burned, but when he drew it out the pastry was crisp and golden. He put it in the larder to cool, and covered it with a piece of muslin like Hannah did, to keep off the flies. Then he stuffed a kerchief-full of bread and cheese in his pocket, slung his coat over one shoulder, and struck off down the dusty road, whistling. He had a mind to walk the four miles from Flawnes Green to Childwell, and climb Belbrook How to look over into the valley of Charndale, where she was born.

The wooden bridge which spanned the River Wynden between Childwell and Belbrook was a paltry thing. He scorned it, even as he used it. At this point, halfway down the valley, they should have an iron bridge: nothing grand like the one at Coalbrookdale but strong and plain. He looked up into the woods which clothed the hillside, and began the long ascent.

This place was now returned to its former wild beauty, but the soil had been deeply disturbed at some time, and the vegetation told its own tale. Yellow coltsfoot and spiky teasels indicated the presence of heavy clay. Guardians of wasteland, rosebay willow-herbs, stood sentinel. Dandelions and plantains, their rosettes of leaves clinging to the earth to survive the trampling of feet, marked old trackways. Birch trees sprang, silver and slender, the first wind-borne seeds to alight in clearings: now being shouldered aside by the oaks which had once taken shelter among them. On the uneven ground grew goat willow and elder. Thickets of bramble and hawthorn scratched his hands, snagged his homespun shirt and breeches. Nettles brushed and stung. Tussocks of tufted hair-grass made him stumble. Ground ivy caught at his shoes.

The busy stream, from which Belbrook took its name, lay in slow-moving pools here, silted up and choked by reedmace; then tumbled briskly again over the rocks to find a lower level. Under these clear noisy waters lay a motley multitude of pebbles, drawn inexorably forward along the bed of the brook. Shafts of sunlight illumined their subtle browns and greys, picked out a band of orange, a slab of black.

William stooped quickly, and fished one swart stone from among its fellows, turning it over in his hand. Incredulous, he found another, and another. He examined the banded stone with increasing excitement. Then followed the stream up to another pool, pushing his way past willow and alder, getting his shoes hopelessly sopped, tearing his clothes heedlessly. He stopped to take his bearings: not the bearings of the place, for he was lost there, but the bearings of an outrageous and wonderful plan in his mind. His heart was hammering so madly that the blood sang in his head. He took a great breath and closed his eyes, mastering himself. He needed all his wits now. Man had been here already, plundering the land. In return nature laid a hundred traps against invasion. Pits, ponds and caverns, seductively screened, could drown him, break his leg or his neck. He began cautiously, intuitively, to explore this area of Belbrook.

The furnace pool had been here: now all scum and bulrushes, and the remains of a wooden bridge turned to green bile. Down that steep bank should be the water-wheel, long motionless, and above it the crumbling launder.

He broke off a stout ash bough and attacked the tangled undergrowth. The wheel must have been thirty feet in diameter, hanging in its pit, and the huge wooden shaft was clad in rusting iron. William traced the shaft and found where the iron bellows had been. Kicking and pulling fallen bricks aside, he knelt down and brushed and scraped the earth away impatiently, revealing a sand pig bed. He stripped off his torn shirt, sweating and trembling with the joy and terror of discovery, and hung his coat on a thorn bush. He needed something sharper and heavier than his ash stick now, and poked among huge blocks of slag which stood like rocks to one side of the site, disguised with moss and lichen. His search uncovered a heavy iron pole, and this he wielded with both hands, flailing at the thicket beyond the sand pig bed, knowing this would be the greatest find of all.

The brickwork was surprisingly sound, and those vast oak beams, which had been young in the Wars of the Roses, would have held a mountain, let alone a roof. William caught up a switch of birch and brushed the back beam clear. The inscription was cut black and deep into the wood.

DEO GRATIAS 1515

He was standing, breathless, victorious, upon the fore-hearth of an old blast-furnace.

William Wilde Howarth, blacksmith, was at home here. He could have walked the site blindfold, had nature let him. As it was he must dwell lovingly upon those portions he had freed, and imagine the rest as it would be. Slowly he came back to the thorn bush, and wiped the sweat and grime from his face with his torn shirt. He sat upon a boulder of slag, and ate his bread and cheese, hands shaking with excitement and exhaustion. His silver watch insisted it was time to go, and the deepening shadows of the wood agreed. He endeavoured to think what must be done. The owner of the site found, and persuaded to lease it. Advice sought as to the cost of re-building and setting up the foundry. Help asked, coaxed, begged, to clear the place. But that it was his he never doubted, that he had been sent here to find it he truly believed, however long it took to work again.

He seized a handful of earth and stone and wrapped it carefully in his scarlet kerchief, as though it had been precious stuff instead of waste matter. Then the glory of discovery burst upon him, and he gave a great shout which sent small creatures scuttling for cover. But a jay answered him with its harsh screech, and seemed to have been personally insulted, for it scolded a long time afterwards as though the peace of its rural precincts had been wantonly destroyed.

Hannah saw him return home like a drunken man in the failing light, and ran across the field afraid. He was sitting at the table in the kitchen corner, head down upon his arms. She stared at his torn hands and wild hair, his soiled shirt and crumpled coat, and the self-imposed discipline of months left her in an instant. Softly she stepped to his side, touched his shoulder, spoke to him like the part of her he was.

'Eh, whatever's to do, my lad. Wherever have you been?'

He lifted up his head and smiled at her.

'I've found an old ironworks in Belbrook Woods, Hannah.'

She grasped the implications at once: interested, pleased, and afraid.

'Nay, you've never!' she cried.

She pulled the other chair out from under the table, and sat opposite him, hands folded in front of her.

'Well, tell us about it,' said Hannah, encouraging him.

His narrative tumbled from top to bottom of Belbrook. He told it back to front, and inside out, tripping up on facts, righting himself half a dozen times in his exultation. She could not have understood very much, but she listened attentively, marking his story with little movements of mouth and brow; watching him talk as she watched him eat, with quiet satisfaction. So that he saw the situation in a calmer light, and rubbed his head ruefully, and laughed at himself, even as he believed in its possibilities.

'There's not much I can do about it though, my lass. It'd take a year to clean the site. Then there's the mending and rebuilding and replacing. I don't know who owns it, or whether they'd lease me the land. And if it's worth summat then there's richer folk than me'll be after it. But I'd give my back teeth to have a try at it. I would, my lass, I would.'

She pursed her mouth and nodded her head, thinking. Then rose briskly.

'Take what's left of that shirt off your back,' she said. 'I'll brew us some tea and mend the fire. Then while I clean up those scrats and cuts I'll tell you summat as you didn't find out.'

In his weary and exalted state he was content to be cared for, and sat trustfully as she steeped the cloth in hot salty water and applied it to his minor wounds.

'You look as if you'd been pulled through a hedge backwards!' said Hannah sarcastically, nipping out thorns.

'Nay, I've been taking hedges apart, my lass,' he answered, loving her sharpness and gentleness.

'A good job you weren't wearing your Sunday suit then. You'd be daft enough to ruin that and all! Ironworks-mad, that's you, Will Howarth.'

He twisted round to see her face. She was smiling, but cried, 'Sit you still!' and clapped the scalding cloth on his shoulder, so that he shouted.

'They call one ironmaster Iron-mad Wilkinson, Hannah,' he said.

'That makes two of thee, then. I'll rub some Self-heal into the worst of these scrats. The rest'll do by themselves now.'

Utterly content, he let her scold and anoint him.

'I'll tell thee a tale,' said Hannah, and he settled like a child in his chair. 'Years ago, when Abel come courting me, he found that place. Sit you still! Nobody else is fretting for it, as far as I know. It takes somebody like Abel, or thee, to go ferreting after nowt!

'He was lettered, was Abel, and he liked finding things out. He liked to know where things came from, and how folk were, once upon a time. So I can tell thee who owns the land, just like Abel told me.

'Belbrook was a gentleman's manor, and belonged to a French family called de Quincey who came over with the Norman king, and they had it for two hundred year until the Black Friars came to Wyndendale. Then they gave part of Belbrook to them to build a priory, and it's still called Belbrook Grange by some round there. These monks were friendly-like. Not shutting themselves up and away from folk. They lived among them and did a power of good. And they cleared the forest and started iron-mining and iron-making. Then a king took against them, and he pulled the priory down and hanged the prior, and that part of Belbrook belonged to the Crown. And folks picked up the stones—like they do when a place is falling down—and used them to build their houses. Abel found stones in many a place that had come from the priory. And it all grew over, and nobody did anything with it.

'Then the Quinceys joined a Catholic plot against the queen that was on the throne, and they lost, and she took that part of Belbrook as well. But she let it go on as it had done. And then there was the wars, and the land belonged to the Protector, but he did nothing different. And then the other king came from over the water, and he was short of money and he sold Belbrook to six gentlemen, four in London and two here. One of them was Lord Kersall—as he was

67

then, like. The other was called Edmund Cotrell and he was betwixt a gentleman and a farmer. But he went down in the world and Lord Kersall went up, and the London gentlemen couldn't be bothered and they sold out.

'Farmer Cotrell owns that piece where the ironworks is. Abel found that out. And Lord Kersall owns all round it, and he's wanted to buy up Edmund Cotrell for donkey's years, but Cotrell won't sell. He'll see him—well, Abel said he'd see him damned first. So he might let you lease it, to do Lord Kersall in the eye, as you might say. But he'll never sell. And if ever you do get it going you canna run it on an island, my lad, you'll need Lord Kersall so as you're not boxed up. So think on, and don't say as I didn't warn you!'

William drew a great breath, and caught her hands as she rested them for a moment on his shoulders, and brought them to his lips and kissed them. She pulled away, but not quickly, or in offence.

'That's enough of that,' said Hannah. 'I'll fetch you a clean shirt. Are you starved?'

'I'm famished, my lass. Let's have some of that potato pie!' He twisted round again to see her, saying penitently, 'I took it out, like you said, and put a bit of muslin over it to keep the flies off. Have you supped yet, Hannah?'

'Nay. I'd only just got back from Boultons when I saw you come.'

'Aye, and I can tell what you've been doing since you left here,' said William, smiling, for they were so close he could detect the scents of food and field. 'You've been brewing beer, and baking bread, and giving Isaac Boulton a hand with the hay. Am I right?'

She laughed, and he watched her with delight.

'Kettle's boiling,' she said, not needing to answer him. 'I'll brew tea.'

'Shall you stop a bit, and have some pie wi' me then?'

'Aye, I might,' she said lightly.

For the first time they sat down and ate together. She delicately, as he had imagined she would. He ravenously, as became his appetite.

'You cook as well as our Betty did,' said William honestly. 'I know I ought to say you cook better, but I don't think anybody could.'

'Why should you tell me a lie?'

'Because I want to pay you a compliment.'

She said nothing, and began to clear their plates away, confused.

'Now I'll tell you something,' said William, musing. 'When you're vexed or worried you look like anybody else. But when I give you a bit of attention you look bonny, my lass.'

'That's enough!' said Hannah again, but without conviction.

'And I'm better-tempered when you're bonny.'

She looked about her distractedly, for something which was not there.

'I'll be off home now, Mr Howarth.'

'If you're looking for your shawl you never brought it with you,' said William composedly.

'No more I did!' She paused. 'Well, I'll be off.'

'It's a grand shawl,' said William. 'I think of that shawl as part of you. Did Mrs Boulton give it to you?'

She stood still, remembering sorrow but not ruled by it.

'I bought it for my Abel's funeral,' she said quietly. 'I had nowt else to show respect. And it covered the rest of my clothes. They wasn't up to much.'

They were silent, stripped of all artifice. He came over to her and put his arms round her.

'Oh, it's not right,' said Hannah.

'Aye, it is,' said William.

S I X

End of the Road

1792

Rarely did Hannah spend other than Saturday night with William in the small bedroom over the smithy, but he had been so despairing all the winter day that she hurried across the field after dark to offer consolation. They had lain together in a bed which filled two-thirds of the room, leaving space only for a wash-stand and wooden chair. She listened to his fears. They were only warming each other's body, and she comforting his heart and strengthening his spirit, for it was no time for love-making. Those halcyon days had passed long since in the fierce struggle for the ironworks. They lay in her mind ringed with fire, as became a mortal sin, but honeyed as was the lure of sin. Now, he needed her much as he needed food and sleep, and forgot her afterwards. From time to time he realised the value of her, and loved in repentance, but the physical demands alone of running a forge and clearing a site for four long years had exhausted him. The accumulated worries over Farmer Cotrell's health, Lord Kersall's cupidity, and his own unchanging state of finance dragged William's dreams down to earth, though in the beginning they had soared to heaven.

'I'll tell thee what I think, Will,' old Edmund Cotrell had said that fine summer Sunday in '87, garrulous over his late wife's dandelion wine, 'I think you was sent, in a manner of speaking. Me and the missis had a brood of childer like a flock of chickens, and only two of them come through. Well, the lad went off a-soldiering, a long while back. And the lass wed a foreigner. So the only time I'm like to hear from them is when they're short of a shilling. Neither of them gives a sow's squeal for this here farm, as has been in our family for I don't know how long. They're waiting for me to push up the daisies, Will, and then they'll sell up and divide up. And that's all the use I am to anybody these days. But mark my words! I say, mark my words! There's life in me for a good few years yet, and if I can do nowt else I can give owd Kersall a run for his money! Aye, you won't catch me Lord-ing him, Will. My great-grandsirs was as good as his, any day. They stood side by side, bidding for Belbrook, at one time. Bidding for Belbrook, and my grandsir's money was as good as owd Kersall's then. I'll not Lord him, no, no. Have another mugful, lad. It's a long while since anybody sat drinking wi' me. The land round here's not so easy to work. It needs a deal of clearing. Owd Kersall, he's waiting for me to die. He owns half the valley, tha knows, and leases it and works it.

'I'll tell thee what I'll do, lad. I'll rent that piece of land to you for five year, at the price my grandsir leased it. How's that for fair dealing? Nine pound, three shilling and five-pence. But I want summat for it. You can keep my oxen shod, and my horses, and do a bit of mending here and there, to help an old man. Aye, and call on me now and again, and give me the time o' day. Now if you make nowt of it in that time, the deal's off, and neither you nor me the worst of it. And if you make summat then I shall put the rent up. Aye,

aye, you won't catch me napping at mid-day, Will. I'm sharp enough for twenty Kersalls. Where's that there bottle gone? I seed it in front of me. just now. . . .'

It had been a hard bargain. Without his family, without Hannah, William could never have weathered those years. His spare time was either after dark, which was no use to him for outdoor work; or the Sabbath, on which he could not work; or public holidays which seemed either to fall in winter months or on rainy days. Stephen, growing daily stronger and more skilful, often minded the forge while William sweated at Belbrook. The men from Kit's Hill, led by his father Ned and younger brother Dick, would give a day's labour for nothing but goodwill. Dorcas graciously and very firmly called on Farmer Cotrell, to relieve her son of that penance, for he was a difficult old man. And in that relationship lay the only gleam of comedy, for Dorcas intended to improve Edmund Cotrell, and so dosed him and organised him into outward submission. But the farmer now had a living prey to torment, as well as a phantom enemy, and William paid dearly for every yard of land delivered from the undergrowth.

And what of Hannah? Between them lay an unspoken understanding that someday they would wed, and make this profane love a sacred commitment, but small things constantly disturbed their peace. Formerly, William had paid her wages into her hand and thought nothing of it. Now he felt awkward, and left them on the corner of the mantelshelf. He still visited his great-aunt and his parents once a month, and those times seemed to be exacted from Hannah. When any member of his family called in on their way to Millbridge, she was treated civilly and even warmly, but not as one of themselves. There was a great part of his life in which she could not figure, and yet she was his main support and encouragement. These matters grieved both of them, but how could they be helped? *One day*, they thought and sometimes said, *one day;* though that day was never delineated, only hoped for, and perhaps meant different things to each.

So on that wintry dawn, early in 1792, Hannah rose first from their bed. Clothes lay in little heaps where they had cast them down the night before. She folded his and donned her own, then slipped out by the backdoor, hurrying along the hedge path in the dark and cold. Though aware of her going, William pretended still to be asleep, and lay watching the dim wall long after the door had closed behind her. He had now

71

paid nearly half his capital in rent, and the five years was up on the first day of August.

'Forty-six pound, twelve shilling and one penny!' Edmund Cotrell had reminded him at Lammastide. 'That's what it's cost you, my lad, so far, and nowt but rusty iron and rough ground to show for it!'

As though he were William's adversary, instead of his landlord.

'We'st come to t'day of reckoning, lad!'

Oh, may he die in his damned bed! William prayed. And then prayed that Cotrell might live, for if he did not the farm and land and ironworks would go up for auction, and William could not buy them. Miss Wilde, now in her five-and-ninetieth year, had been approached to see if she would lend William money to bribe the farmer's goodwill and induce him to sell. But she pretended not to understand what was expected of her, and then had young Mr Hurst round and endeavoured to cut William out of her will, which the solicitor managed to avoid—afterwards privately warning Dorcas not to approach the old lady on financial matters, for she grew more capricious with advancing age, and he could not forbid such whims, though he would always endeavour to reason with her. (This interview was, of course, conducted with the utmost circumspection, and the information conveyed to Dorcas by way of a report on her aunt's health.) Nor would William allow his mother to break into her small annuity of twenty pounds per annum, and Ned was too busy setting good farming years against bad ones to give his elder son more than the strength of his arms and heart.

Knocking at the smithy door aroused William, and he saw that the watch had been keeping time while he fretted it away. Stephen, now twenty-one years old and recently out of his apprenticeship, was rousing his master.

'Not so good this morning, Mr Howarth?' said the young man, including William's mood and the weather in one remark.

'I'll be with you in a minute, lad. I'll make us some tea first. What's to do, then?'

'Mr Boulton wants his team shod again. The lady at Brigge House says what about that gate you promised her. They want a new sign at The Weavers Tavern. Jackie Slater's hoop needs mending, and so does the Cheetham's ploughshare. And Margery Higginbottom's youngest has the smallpox, and she says can she come and lay him on the anvil while you drive the sickness out with your sledgehammer.'

William's silence told him more than words. The kettle slammed down upon the hob.

'I'll get on wi' it,' said Stephen peaceably, 'dunnot mither thysen!'

They had changed places. Now Stephen was the youth full of joy and hope, and William grimly enduring. Life had lost its savour, and dreams their ineffable rapture. The day was as dark as his soul. They worked by candlelight and the tallow stank in their nostrils, along with the odours of burning hoof, hot iron and scorched leather. Hannah knew better than to cheer him on, and went about her tasks mutely. Only once, when they were alone for a few minutes after dinner, did she put all her trouble into a gentle comment.

'Eh, my dear lad, I wish I could do summat for thee!'

He was lad no longer. Lines carved their character beside his mouth which had been soft and full. He had lost his muscular leanness and developed muscular might. He spoke deliberately, moved more heavily. His plumage lacked its lustre.

'Nay, I must take life as it comes,' said William, without conviction. 'It was a gamble, my lass. I'd have done the same again.'

He had bought a great wheel to replace the crumbling monster in the newly dug wheel-pit, and rolled it three miles down the road from Garth to Belbrook. Ten men, a day's labour. He had bought an iron shaft from Birmingham, to replace the wooden one. Half his capital for rent, the other half for tools and a pitiful amount of materials.

'Shall you have owt left?' asked Hannah, hands in apron.

'Myself,' said William, and went off into the smithy.

Normally they would have shut shop at four, for they could not see properly, even with a little forest of candles; but William sent Stephen home and worked doggedly on. Hannah fried up cold beef and onions, and left them in the oven covered with sliced potatoes; and a milk pudding to tempt his appetite. He was glad to be alone, to be let alone, in his small cave full of fire and homely smells. Though the early evening was cold and dank his sweat poured from him. He listened to his anvil as a musician listens to his instrument. Just the two of them, and one inanimate, was all he wanted.

Hannah put on her old black shawl.

'I'll be going then, Mr Howarth!' she cried, for the benefit of any who might be close enough to hear.

He lifted his face to see her, and she came near to give and receive silent comfort.

'Eh, my lass,' he said softly, 'I'm about at the end of the road today.'

'Can I do owt? Shall I come back later on?'

He shook his head. Her mouth closed sadly, but she nodded, and he returned to his task. No one disturbed him. Flawnes Green drew in upon itself, closed its doors, huddled round its fires, stirred its suppers. Only a horseman riding by swelled the solitary concert of the anvil and smith.

'Ho, there! Mr Howarth?'

William came forward, wiping his hands down his sides, peering into the night. The gentleman dismounted and called him by name again.

'Aye, that's me,' said William, and then seeing the face said, 'Is it Mr Hurst?'

'It is. It is indeed. And with solemn news I fear. Can we go into the warm, Mr Howarth? Your great-aunt was found dead, my dear sir, not an hour since!'

They stood by the fire together, more astonished than sorry, for Miss Wilde was very old but had seemed to be immortal.

'Less than an hour since, Mr Hurst?'

'Aye, I had been with her. Every Friday evening, you know, upon the stroke of six. It was her last amusement. Thank you. Mr Howarth, I should be glad of a little something to keep out the damp—though you are well-furnished against it here!' Looking at the hot coals in the grate. 'Yes, Mr Howarth, we used to spend an hour going over the minor details of her will. An injury being punished here, a kindness rewarded there—nothing and something, you know, sir. Well, we enjoyed our usual pleasantries, I took my leave, and a short while later Sally came running round with the news. She is the only member of the household nowadays—Agnes so feeble, Miss Jarrett so easily distressed—who can be relied upon to deal with such a crisis. So I offered to bring the news to you, and hoped you would convey it to your mother yourself. One cannot pretend,' said Nicodemus Hurst honestly, 'that this will be a shock to her. One should rather be thankful for such a lengthy life, with many consolations and no material hardship. But I imagine Mrs Howarth would receive it better from you than from anyone else.'

William was ashamed of the hope that sprang in his breast. He opened a bottle of his great-grandfather's port, feeling this was somehow appropriate.

'Mr Hurst,' he said with equal honesty, 'there is no cause for grief, but my great-aunt was always good to me—and I am sorry for her death on that account. We liked each other very well.'

They sipped the port, remarked upon its excellence, and warmed themselves at the fire.

'Do you know, Mr Howarth,' said Mr Hurst, amazed, 'I shall find a hollow in my Friday evenings, without Miss Wilde. I have grown accustomed to her whims and fancies. I shall miss her.'

A dream-like quality had come over the evening. William saw his guest safely back on to the road, saddled Wildfire, and rode supperless towards Kit's Hill. The knowledge that he would benefit comfortably, if not considerably, by his great-aunt's will had wiped out his despair. A wind was clearing the clouds away, and the stars shone. The cold air braced him, the steady trot of the horse soothed him. Life was beginning all over again. His sense of destiny returned. He was god-like in his contentment.

Then remembrances stole upon him. He saw her, imperious, secretly delighted, at their first meeting when he was a lad of eight. Heard her voice cry harshly, proudly, 'You, sir? Why, you are a rascal and a scamp, and so I tell you!' She had called him to her, many a time, and smuggled a guinea into his hand, winking and whispering. She had shielded him as best she could from his parents' wrath when Mr Tucker expelled him from Millbridge Grammar School. When he went away to Birmingham she had risen at six o'clock in the morning to breakfast with him before he left, to give him his silver watch. He was her favourite, and he knew it. She paid his premium to Bartholomew Scholes, wrote him wavering letters full of sound but cynical advice. She disliked men, but had loved him.

He did not chide himself for the tears that now came to his eyes. They were her requiem.

SEVEN

New Company

Miss Wilde's death made William the richer by one thousand pounds, and transformed Dorcas into a lady of means. With his mother's backing and his own initiative the dream of Belbrook might become reality, but how to achieve that aim, or what to do best, he did not know. Then his long friendship with Caleb Scholes the younger decided him to seek help in that direction. He wrote, reminding Caleb of their boyish

May 1792

promise to form a partnership, setting down the problems and possibilities of the ironworks, leaving all questions open to advice from higher quarters. Of course, he hoped that the ironmaster would be interested, that wind of the venture would reach Bartholomew Scholes, and that the vast family network might throw up a few patrons eager to invest capital. For he would need upwards of twelve thousand pounds to start a company. He neither said nor hinted this, keeping his tone low and his story modest, but none of them were fools.

First, young Caleb replied in his usual dashing style, full of wild hope and pure delight. He was prepared, it seemed, to down tools in Warwickshire and catch the next coach for Lancashire, in the opening page of his letter. On the second page he mentioned that his own share of one thousand pounds would have to come from his patrimony, and he would need to consult his father. In the postscript, he scribbled, *'Wait and see, Will! Be patient!'*

In his own good time, Caleb the ironmaster, brother of Bartholomew Scholes of Birmingham, invited William to visit them all at Somer Court and discuss this new turn of events. His letter was brief, dry and courteous, but they read promise into it. Whereupon the best tailor in Millbridge was called in and, after much advice from Dorcas in person and Charlotte by return of post, created an ensemble fit to grace the occasion.

William twisted and turned and squinted sideways at his

76

reflection in the glass, but could find no fault in his grandeur. His green cloth coat was slimly fashioned, with cutaway tails, steel buttons and a high velvet collar. His fawn breeches were buttoned below the knee, in the French style. His waistcoat was striped in white and gold. His white stock was most splendidly frilled. His tall-crowned hat boasted a ribbon-and-buckle trim. His Hessian boots of hard black polished leather were gloriously tasselled.

'You should carry your great-grandfather's silver-headed cane!' cried Dorcas, entranced. 'And you should wear a wig. A Cadogan wig.'

'I shall not wear a wig, Mamma,' William replied firmly. 'You have but to look at my hands to see I am no gentleman. This is enough, and even so I fear I have made a popinjay of myself to please my mother and sister!'

He was confirmed in this by the men of Kit's Hill, when he displayed his finery there on the eve of travelling to Warwickshire.

'By Gow!' said Ned, laying down his pipe and grinning broadly. 'He'll think you've come to give him summat, instead of borrowing!'

'Dunnot let him into t'dairy, Nellie,' cried Tom the carter. 'He'd make cream turn!'

'You'll need to take care if you're playing cards wi' the Prince of Wales,' said young Dick impudently. 'He'll win that fancy waistcoat off thee!'

But Nellie and the kitchenmaids cried that it was a shame, and William looked proper handsome. And they reddened and frowned and bridled to such an extent that the men were reduced to nudging each other, and exchanging covert winks. While Dorcas sat very grand and silent, smiling proudly on.

William had first seen Somer Court a decade ago, and taken its beauty to his heart for life. Built in the reign of Elizabeth, the house had been designed for a country gentleman of ample means and large family. And from its walled kitchen garden to the fantailed pigeons on its roof, was an orderly delight. A long sloping lawn bordered with flowers, a wooded park, a driveway shaded by noble beeches framed this retreat. The ironmaster's inferno, down below, was another world, another place; even, it seemed, another time.

Then, as on his first visit, the warm afternoon had drawn Catherine Scholes and her children and their nursemaids out on to the terrace. She had changed very little, though her marriage was regularly blessed and her eldest daughter's first-born was the same age as Catherine's last-born. Today a mixture of children and grandchildren played together. Two boys rolled hoops across the shaven grass in keen competition. Two girls played battledore and shuttlecock, a toddler staggered half a dozen steps between one servant and another, and the youngest member sat on Catherine's lap and stared boldly about him like a miniature ironmaster.

Pray God my household be as this, years hence, thought William. He would have liked to stay on the edge of that tableau for a few minutes longer, but the elderly manservant was hastening over the lawn to inform his mistress of William's arrival, and then the children caught sight of their visitor and ran pell-mell towards him, crying welcome. While from the library, whose windows opened into the garden, came the ironmaster and his eldest son.

Caleb Scholes's height was not very great, and yet he held himself as if to say, 'These inches God gave me, and thou shalt see they suit me well enough!' so that William wondered whether John Wilkinson the Iron King could be half so imposing, and made his bow and shook hands with sincere reverence. But young Caleb and he greeted each other with boyish delight after their long absence from each other, crying, 'Seven years!' as though it had been a hundred: their friendship as fresh and green as in their Birmingham apprenticeship, now promising to blossom into partnership at last.

The girls hovered like gauzy butterflies, the boys jumped up and down, hoping for compliments. None but a strict Quaker could have quarrelled over the Scholes's taste in dress, but some quality set them apart from the sober members of their Society, marking them as being worldly. At the same time William realised that he had grossly overdone his own apparel, and was standing out in this subdued elegance like a parakeet. His shame lasted but a moment or two. His resolve to learn and change was constant in him.

They dined at the fashionable hour of five o'clock upon fried soles, boiled fowls, veal cutlets, roast duck and new potatoes and green peas; followed by gooseberry tart and cream, a rich custard, and strawberries in a green dish. Then Catherine took her place at the tea-table to dispense cups and small-talk, while Caleb the elder signalled to the young men that they should retire to the library.

'For the house will be full of folk by supper-time,' he observed, placing a hand upon William's shoulder, 'and besides,

I never know when I shall be needed down yonder,' nodding in the direction of the valley. He added slyly, 'But thou shalt bear that burden in thy day, my ironmaster, and oft find it a heavy one! Hast thou thy map and papers with thee? Let us see. Let us see.'

They sat very comfortably and privately, with the summer light coming in at the long windows, while Caleb Scholes spread out William's survey and bent over it, smiling to himself as though he had begun life again and would find it just as good the second time round.

Belbrook Priory had commanded a view of both the Wyndendale and Charndale valleys, screened by forest which reached down to the River Wynden far below. How much land had been theirs no one knew, but Edmund Cotrell had bought a broad strip down the centre, through which the stream ran like a silver serpent; later supplying a series of pools with water, one after the other, as the friars dammed them. The blast-furnace had been built into the side of the hill, and fuelled with charcoal from the surrounding trees. It was a sturdy but simple affair, capable of dealing with the modest seams of coal and ironstone located nearby. The bellows, too, had been a homely construction worked by hand. The results of their labours, probably domestic pots and pans, were in small enough quantity to transport by pack-horse and sell the length of both valleys. Supply and demand would be about equally matched.

The ironmaster smoothed his chin and nursed his elbow, musing. The map, marked with symbols for trees and buildings, was largely coloured green over and beyond the Belbrook area; an oblong in the middle blazed defiant red, as if to show it would not be underestimated; within this was a little shaded ironworks.

'The green is Kersall's land, the red belongs to Cotrell, I take it?' said Caleb, looking at William's resolute countenance. 'Thou art truly trapped, my friend. Thy site is not worth a farthing, without it can expand. A doll's industry in an age of giants!'

William grew sombre, but said nothing. Caleb the younger softly sighed.

'Will this Cotrell renew thy least next month?' asked the ironmaster.

'Aye, sir, at twice the price. But he is an old man, and his family will sell all if he dies.'

'Will they sell to thee, William?'

'They will sell to the highest bidder, sir, and that would be Lord Kersall himself. But he could squeeze me out, or use me.'

'Then thou must persuade the farmer to sell out now—site, farm, land and all. Make him a price a little above what he could fairly ask. Use thine adversary's weakness against him, William, and keep thine own hidden! That is good business parlance. Edmund Cotrell nourishes the weakness of hatred: hatred of his kin and of this Kersall. Put it to him that he stands to gain by selling now, to thee. Promise him that he shall live on his farm as long as his life shall last, and put that promise into writing. Promise what else will keep him sweet, provided that this site is thine. When that is done, we can speak again. Until it is done our words are mere speculation—pleasant stuff for an evening round the fireside, but not good business!'

And he folded up the map and papers and handed them to the astonished young man. Caleb the younger looked at his steel shoe-buckles. and lifted one eyebrow philosophically.

If I could have worn such a suit as his, thought William, staring at the ironmaster, I should not now feel like some foolish interloper. Oh, that a length of brown broadcloth and a plain stock should make such a difference to a man!

He saw the ironmaster's hands placed lightly upon the polished table, fingers splayed. He saw his own, clutching the precious documents: roughened, horny, dirty, in spite of patient scrubbing and anointing. He felt his anger rise, and welcomed its support.

'Sir,' said William, with a certain dignity, 'I have not come so far to be dismissed as an idle dreamer. Your son and I long planned a partnership. My mother is desirous to invest in this enterprise. I had hoped for advice that went beyond mere commonsense. I know that Farmer Cotrell must sell, and so he shall. I have not worked so hard and so long for nothing. But when he has sold, sir,' very firmly, 'what advice do you give me then?'

Caleb the younger pursed his lips and whistled silently, looking out of the long windows. Caleb the ironmaster did not show by so much as a twitch of lip or eyebrow what he felt, but answered in apparent surprise.

'Oh, it was but advice thee sought, William? I had thought thee looked for a major investor in this dream of thine!'

So he had, and for enthusiasm to meet his own, for encouragement to spur him to yet greater efforts, for an understanding. Bitterly disappointed, William spoke out.

'Why, sir, it was you that invited me here. I am not so foolish as to think you could concern *yourself* with such a little venture, but since your son and I proposed to throw in our fortunes together I had believed you wished us well, and would give us the benefit of your long experience.'

'My son Caleb is to invest one thousand pounds of his patrimony, if so I think fit. Was that thy whole proposition, William?' the ironmaster asked with gentle sarcasm. 'Thou'lt need far more money than that!'

'Deuce take the money!' William cried, jumping to his feet. 'Is this good fellowship? I crave pardon, sir, for wasting your time and mine!'

And he put away his map, incensed.

'Let not thy feelings ride thee, William,' said the ironmaster quietly. 'If thou would'st be a man of iron then stay cool, my son, and do not confuse business with friendship—unless thou art in trouble, when friendship in business is important. Think, William! If thou wert in my shoes would thee lend a young man a great sum of money for such a proposition? Think, now, and speak honestly.'

William sat down again, and considered the tassels on his Hessian boots.

Finally he said, 'It would be decided, sir, upon the matter of character. Certainly,' warming to the problem, as it became that of Caleb Scholes and not his own, 'certainly I should not lend one penny until the land was secured. But after that, judging the man in question, I should think it a fair though not a safe proposition. Yet, on the other hand, what should we call safe? Security is not in *our* hands. We may be carried off, in a night, by the cholera, by the smallpox, by a thousand diseases of the body and mind. So might William Howarth die without seeing the fruit of his labours. So might I, Caleb Scholes, die without reaping the benefit of my belief in him. Yet the Quakers say, *Think not of the fruits!*'

Father and son sat in silence, watching William expand. He had become his mother's mind: composed, detached, forcible, clear.

'I have more knowledge and more power, by far, than William Howarth,' William continued. He sat easily now, hands clasped between his knees, pondering. 'The question of my son's partnership is not important, except that I should not like to see him, too, fail. But what is a thousand pounds?

I have wagered more than that in half a dozen new enterprises which might also have failed. So I could let William Howarth find his way through the maze, slowly, for he will find it, if it take him a lifetime of endeavour. But if he die trying, then the reproach is not his, but mine, for I could have helped him. And if he succeed, with my help, then can I say, "This is my protégé, in whom I am well pleased." And if even with my help he fail, I sleep at nights, my conscience lies easy, I have done my best—and at little cost to myself. William Howarth—is a charity!'

He looked up, and laughed at his own eloquence, thus giving them permission to laugh at him and with him. But young Caleb leaned forward and shook both his hands, solemnly and proudly as became a close friend. And the ironmaster cried, 'Well said, William!' and added with wry humour, 'Spoken like a good Quaker!' And then they spread the map upon the table again, and all three bent over it to see how it might be transformed into a living, growing, financial proposition.

'First, the sale of the land,' said Caleb Scholes. 'Then, an approach to Kersall, with a letter from me, to suggest that he leases more land as it is required, and takes a share of the profits. Is the coalfield his? This area in Childwell and Swarth Moors? Good! Thou wilt have need of it. And the canal in Millbridge, is that his also? He is ambitious, that is his weakness! Offer him more power. Take care of him, William, and let him know that thy success is his. Find out his partners—those known and those unknown. Make sure that his interests are thine. Count me thy friend in this. I have many connections. Oh, I have asked my manager to call by and by, and fetch his chief foreman. They will give thee excellent counsel, and work out costs and materials for thee. One Tudor blast-furnace is not enough, lad! Thou shalt need three or four more! Aye, and they will counsel thee how to bargain, how to drive, and how to hold back, when to say nay or yea. Thee must start small, William and Caleb, and listen humbly now, my ironmasters—however mighty thou shalt become in the end!'

'So I may have my thousand pounds, father?' young Caleb asked quietly.

'Aye, lad, and others among us may put their money down!'

So this had not been a matter of confidence between father

and son, William reflected, and even Caleb had not known how the ironmaster would decide.

'It shall be deducted from thy share of my fortune when I am dead,' said Caleb the elder drily, 'and if that suit thee not, then say so, lad! And if all fail, which is in the Hands of Almight God—as William rightly said—then thou canst come home, Caleb. And William hath his forge at Flawnes Green!'

Nothing, thought William, could have been more calculated to make him succeed than the threat of remaining a country blacksmith.

'And now hear me,' as both young men started to speak at once, 'on the subject of thy partnership. I speak to each, and to both, and love thee both. Make sure that thy fortunes are not so entwined that thou hast no means to end a quarrel fairly. Thou art not the same men, though honourable men. Thou shalt marry different women, and set up different households. Aye, and sire different children. My cousin, John Scholes, and I began together, but we did not end together. Today, when thou art young and free and hearty, life seemeth light. Troubles come always tomorrow, together with age and sickness, and those many responsibilities which cannot be laid aside. Remember this. Differ only in small matters, and if thou differ in great ones—then part company in peace. There endeth my homily. God bless thee both. I embrace thee both.'

The two young men clasped his hands warmly and shook them. Tears had come to their eyes, and they laughed at themselves, and endeavoured to brush them away unnoticed. They clapped each other's shoulders in friendly mockery. Advice had been sought, without half the questions being known. They had received answers unbidden, and a gift of great price, and of greater value. While Caleb the ironmaster, as composed as ever, despite the affection he had shown, smiled to himself and stood a little apart, looking on at the emotion he had wrought and the hopes he had planted.

Unheard, in this happy commotion, came four polite knocks at the library door. A new face peeped in. A voice endeavoured to attract their attention.

'Father! Father! I am back for supper. My mother says that Mr Codlin and Mr Sharpe have come. And I have brought George Horsefield with me. Hast thou done talking?'

Then the ironmaster displayed another countenance, that of loving indulgence, and called the girl to him and kissed her fondly.

'Dost thou know who this is, William?' he asked.

And as he hesitated, utterly lost, they all laughed at his confusion.

'She was but a gawky gosling when last thou saw her, seven years or more ago,' said the ironmaster.

'And now has become a goose!' cried Caleb, grinning.

She was perhaps seventeen: a tall serene girl with dark-gold hair, dressed in a muslin gown, but its simplicity had been set at naught by the cashmere shawl which hung from her arms, scarlet and gold with a deep black fringe. And now the beauty of her face changed to impishness. She wrinkled her nose at William, and but for the years of her maturity would have put out her tongue.

'I beat thee at cribbage, William Howarth!' she cried.

He knew, and could not believe.

'Why, is it Zelah?' he asked foolishly, so that they all laughed again. 'Yes, it is Zelah. Of course, it is Zelah.'

She stood gracefully in the circle of her father's arm, and smiled at him, half-teasing and now half-shy, for she saw the changes of the years in him also. She perceived that his costume embarrassed him, that he had worked too hard for too long and was lost in this refined atmosphere, that he was brave and would not give up what mattered to him. She became grave, in contemplation of these insights.

'So thou art to be an ironmaster, William?' she said, building his esteem.

'If all go well,' he answered awkwardly.

The map upon the table caught her attention.

'Wilt thou show me?' she asked, smiling.

Aware of her presence, and of the watchful eyes of both Calebs, William endeavoured to convey his passion for the project without sounding a windbag. She listened carefully, glancing at his animated face, his workman's hands, cherishing his vulnerability.

'But it is not yet settled,' William finished, and his heart was heavy at the chasm between Flawnes Green and Somer Court.

She guessed that he spoke from the world of men, and answered from the world of women.

'I wish I could sit next to thee at supper, William,' she said prettily, regretfully, 'but George Horsefield has come home with me, so I must sit by him.'

She spoke the name without coquetry or embarrassment,

84

but William was very sorry in the next hour or so to observe that Mr Horsefield appeared to be a member of the family. Catherine smiled on him, and the ironmaster spoke to him as to an intimate. He was a quiet, dark young man of the Quaker persuasion, elegantly plain in his dress, with the self-assurance of one who has no earthly lack to trouble him, and is good enough even to hope for heavenly treasures also.

'Are they engaged to be married?' Willam whispered to Caleb, though he should have been attending to Mr Codlin.

'Whom? George and Zelah? Not precisely, but it an under-stood matter. They have known each other a long while,' Caleb replied, and turned to Mr Sharpe.

'I dare say it would be regarded as an excellent match,' William whispered, with some bitterness.

'Oh, in both senses,' Caleb replied, puzzled by this second interruption. 'The worldly as well as the spiritual,' he added, with a hint of mockery.

'What does he do for a living?'

'He is a banker, my good fellow. Now, pray, continue with Mr Codlin, for we must have this business at our fingertips ere thou return to Lancashire. More than *my* thousand pounds depends upon it! Reminding William how much more he had to lose. 'For if we fail we shall never dare show our faces in Warwickshire again. I may even be compelled to go to sea!'

So the company despatched a battery of cold meats, a side dish of goose pie, a pyramid of glowing fruit, and best of all a fanciful mould in the shape of a hedgehog whose bristling quills were almonds. A delicious sweet golden wine, such as William had never before tasted, loosened their tongues and made them eager for conversation. The talk was patted or tossed from one person to another like the children's shut-tlecock: a pleasing pastime rather than the earnest debates known to William in the Birmingham household of Bartholo-mew and Ruth.

The children being abed, Catherine brought out her sketches, and took William under her protection. Like her daughter, she sensed his unease and strove to allay it: speak-ing of his mother, encouraging him to talk of his smithy and of Belbrook. Then Caleb took out his flute, brother John pro-duced a cello, sister Mary a viola, and Zelah sat at the little scarlet harpsichord painted with gold flowers.

William was so charmed by this that he dared say to Catherine, 'Your daughter, madam, has matched her costume with her instrument!'

Zelah was removing her cashmere shawl, which George Horsefield received gallantly. Bright harpsichord, bright scarf, became symbols of gaiety in a muted Quaker world, and William took unwonted hope and cheer from this.

Observing his sudden lightness of spirit, Catherine said, 'I fear we are but half-Quakers in many ways, William. Yet though we do not walk by the same rule we mind the same thing.'

Zelah looked towards them, relieved to see William in a happier mood, and cried, 'What are you saying, Mamma? What are you saying?'

Playfully, seriously, Catherine repeated her remark. George Horsefield smiled civilly and inclined his head. But William, feeling more himself, smiled directly at Zelah.

'I call that fair compromise,' he said in his most engaging manner, 'for this household then enjoys both an Inner Light and an Outer Brilliance!'

Zelah clapped her hands and laughed, Catherine smiled, the company looked with great interest at this mighty young man who had seemed so dull, and the ironmaster gave a dignified bow.

But Catherine then placed her smooth hands on William's rough ones and besought him earnestly.

'But we *do* mind the same thing, William. So let not our frivolity hide our truth from thee!'

Had he been perceptive enough to scent a prophesy, he would have marked her words and the occasion. But, the musicians having tuned up, the entertainment began, and William was too absorbed in watching Zelah to concern himself with religious differences. She was at that loveliest stage of a girl's life, where she might play the child, or become the woman, from one moment to the next. Her inward growth had never been stunted by harshness or poverty. Her troubles had been slight and soon over. Being one member of a large family she was not spoiled. In another year or so she would be immersed in marriage, learning how to sustain others, how to discipline her own needs and desires: a second Catherine, handsome, capable, loving, selfless. The knowledge hurt him, for what he most wanted in the world was that slim white girl sitting at the scarlet harpsichord, crowned by a wealth of dark-gold hair, and turning—even this moment—to smile on him. Untouched, unhurt, unchanged.

The household rose at six o'clock, and while the youngest children learned their lessons, William was taken on a thorough tour of Caleb's kingdom. Three horses from the stables at the back had been saddled for them: a chestnut, a roan, and a black stallion for the ironmaster.

'Stand not too close, lads,' Caleb warned, 'for this fellow will have all the road to himself. And keep thy chestnut apart from the roan, William, else she will kick. But they are excellent good beasts,' he added, with an affection that touched William. Then he smiled wryly, and said, 'I find that good horses, like good women, must be considered and cared for if we would live in harmony!'

He clicked his tongue softly at the black stallion, and led them north of Somer Court. The morning was cool and fine, the horses trod neatly on the grassy ground. A sense of well-being came to them all. The conversation was friendly, easy, between equals.

'I dare say thou hast often heard from my sister-in-law Ruth how our family began, William? But I feel, in the light of thy one thousand pounds, that a little humility could be engendered!' Here he winked, to show that he meant no harm. 'My father, Zebediah Scholes, had a nail-shop which he worked with his brother until they could build their first blast-furnace. Sixteen years or so later their business was fetching in eleven thousand pounds a year, and they had workshops in four villages roundabouts. But he believed, and so do all his many children, that the only right a man has to expect is a good home and a good education. The rest he must do for himself. So as each son became a journeyman, my father set him up with a hundred sovereigns, and told him to find his fortune. Save for good counsel he then let us be.

'When I was one-and-twenty, William Howarth, I tramped miles round the countryside of Warwickshire, searching for a place to work and live. I found a village by the name of Longbarrow that was but a single poor street, and there I bought a cottage with a bit of garden, and rented the blacksmith's shop. For he had died and left the business to his daughter, and she had no use for it. I made anything to order, from a spade to a pair of gates. I ate little, and saved every penny I could. I studied my books by candlelight.

'My business prospered. Why should it not? I bought land cheap, and built my first foundry upon it. Cousin John Scholes came into business with me. I built my first house.'

87

At first William was inclined to be annoyed at this homily, for he could match it all the way along, and Caleb must know that. Then he saw that this was the ironmaster's way of cementing their friendship, of paying him tribute. So he sat his horse like a gentleman, reflecting that Caleb Scholes had once owned a pair of workman's hands and felt awkward in refined company.

They were now mounting a hill from which William could see the valley below. The ironmaster pointed to a doll-sized roof with his whip.

'Dost see, William? That house with the chimney at one end was where I took Catherine to wife. There our Caleb was born, our first son. Aye, and our second, John. I built cottages to house our chief workmen round the original site. And over there! Mark them, William. I bought ever more land, or leased it if they would not sell. I built more cottages, set up more blast-furnaces, more ironworks. I made not a penny-piece for twenty years that did not go back into the business, lad. And then, when it prospered exceedingly—and I thanked God, William, for all this while He had kept me safely in His Hand—why, then I saw Somer Court.'

They were riding higher and higher, and the horses went more slowly, picking their way over rough ground.

'Somer Court. The family and the money had all gone, and it was a poor fallen thing, William, a crumbling home of mice and beetles. But Catherine loved it.'

And you loved Catherine, William thought, which sometimes is the only thing I like about you, ironmaster, for you are a hard man!

'So I bought it,' said Caleb simply. 'I bought it, as folk say, for a shilling—but spent many a pound upon it. Zelah, our third daughter, was born there, the first summer. Seventeen years ago.'

Ah, that is so fitting, William thought. That Zelah should crown Somer Court.

He longed to say so, and knew intuitively that he must keep his compliments and emotions to himself. They had other plans for Zelah, and he was already wondering how to thwart them and yet hold their friendship.

'What dost think of that, William?' cried Caleb Scholes. 'Is it a good tale to be told round the fireside of a winter evening?'

He laughed aloud with pleasure, throwing back his head. There was pride in his tone and bearing, and though it was an honest pride and became him, still it was not a Quakerly virtue, and William smiled to himself. Find out thine adversary's weakness, he remembered, and keep thine own hidden.

'So you have been at Somer Court only seventeen years, sir?' William enquired. 'It seems as though you had all lived there for ever.'

'Nay, lad. We are but newcomers. Somer Court hath been there above two hundred years already, and shall be there two hundred years after we are gone. But now to business!' For they had climbed the hillside and reached a summit which overlooked the county. 'There is my blacksmith's shop, William Howarth!'

As far as the eye could see, on this cool clear summer morning, the works stretched the length of the valley. Chimneys marched in ranks, each bearing a straight black banner. Blast-furnaces erupted messages of flame. Row by row the swart brick cottages stepped up and down the valley sides, or clustered round larger buildings. In this pit of Acheron iron ruled. It clanged and resonated, scraped and ground. Water tasted of iron, air smelled of it, surfaces were chill and strange to the touch. Anything which could be cast into a mould was made of it. Fire transformed it. Men hammered and wrought it, lived by it, thanked it for their bread. It permeated the substance of the landscape, leaving no green and living thing untouched. Coal-dust lay in a fine gritty film over all, so that a child could not pluck a blade of grass without he left a mark on flesh or fabric. A parched and withered vegetation clung to the iron earth, rattled in the iron trees, straggled to the edge of the iron river. Scarred by waterways, wagon-ways, track-ways, heaped with slag, the land gave up her wealth of millennia to furnish the need of a day. And over the vale, in memory of its rural past, spread a sulphurous pall of smoke.

'There is Longbarrow, at the end,' said the ironmaster, pointing his whip-handle to the kingdom below. 'Then Bagbrooke, running into it, where the blast-furnace now flares. Pits End is beyond. Willowford, Mallowhall and Rossborne. Villages, did I call them? Nay, they are hamlets. Poverty-stricken places, with but a hundred souls apiece, scarce able to rack a living from the land. See now how they prosper! They are our children and we care for them!'

A memory stirred William's heart, of a grand May morning, twenty years before, when he and Charlotte were children. Driving in their mother's trap all the way to fine

Millbridge, through hamlets strung like jewels on the silver chain of the river. Poor places all, with but a hundred souls apiece, racking a living from the land and thanking God for it. Garth, Coldcote, Medlar, Childwell, Whinfold, Thornley, Brigge House, Flawnes Green.

And yet, the sombre grandeur of this new world. The power and sullen beauty of its workings. Buildings as high as Babel. Eerie lights and hellish tints. Sounds as awesome and compelling as the voices of old gods. Great cranes with iron arms. Coal-pits yawning open, their giant wheels driven by steam. Huge bellows pumping out blasts of air which echoed round the valley. Gloomy caverns dwarfing the men who laboured in them. The vastness of the enterprise consumed him. He sat his horse, black head bent, eyes very bright, musing on the benevolent despotism before him. So that the ironmaster, observing his rapt face, had no need to ask what he thought or what he felt. Caleb Scholes's investment, God willing, was assured.

Though William had been asked to stay as long as he pleased, he knew this was yet another of the Scholes's small courtesies, and having tested out his ground discovered that the ironmaster, at least, was done with him for the time being. Caleb, allowed a day's absence to greet his friend, was called to heel on Tuesday, and Catherine's second sister was expected on Thursday, with her youngest son who hoped for an apprenticeship. So it behoved William to depart, but he gave himself Wednesday to carry out the last and most unexpected part of his business.

Zelah and her elder sister Mary, being of marriageable age, took over a part of their mother's duties in the household to befit them for their future homes, and by dint of observation he discovered where he might find Zelah at any particular hour of the day. Before breakfast she gave Rebecca music lessons. After breakfast she read aloud turn by turn with Mary, for two hours, while Catherine taught Rebecca needlework and did her own. In the afternoon the two sisters walked, if it was fine, and visited those wives of their father's workmen who were sick or in childbed, taking various comforts and remedies with them. Then all drank tea, and rested in their own fashion until dinner-time. Between dinner and supper Zelah practised on the harpsichord and wrote her journal, while Mary sketched and painted. After supper the entire family mingled with friends and guests.

He seized an early opportunity of courting Rebecca, who was eight years old and inclined to find learning a wearisome affair, so that his unobtrusive attendance on her morning music lesson seemed but a part of his pleasant courtesy. And when he entered quietly, sitting well back in the shady part of the drawing-room, he took care to bring a newspaper with him and pretended to read it. But all the while was studying his lady's voice or face as she strove to train eight mutinous fingers and two awkward thumbs.

She, well aware that Rebecca was not the object of his attention, affected not to notice his presence, and sat with her back half-turned; though as she changed places, to show her young sister how the harpsichord should be played, she could not forbear glancing in his direction. And as the lesson progressed she lost her concentration, made little sounds of exasperation and despair which touched and enchanted him, and finally sent Rebecca off with an admonishment, ten minutes earlier than usual.

The child skipped off, delighted, while William lowered his newspaper and Zelah her head. For a few moments he sat watching her, and she gazed abstractly at her hands folded in her lap. Then she looked up, and he walked over. He had to dispense with the usual preliminaries. Catherine might look in, breakfast be served, a hundred small interferences come between him and his intention.

'Zelah,' said William, and the unbearable sweetness of those two syllables robbed him of self-command. 'Oh, Zelah,' William whispered, and took her hands in his and raised them to his lips.

She whispered back, desperately, 'I am spoken for, William,' and added, 'though not in words,' and so betrayed herself.

'George Horsefield?' said William grimly, softly.

'It is understood.'

He said, with a look she was to see intensified over the years, 'It must not be. I would marry thee, Zelah'—slipping into her Quaker way of speaking—'and I shall marry thee, I care not how long I wait, because thou art my wife. I knew thee when I saw thee, Zelah.'

She pulled her hands away, afraid of the trouble this would entail.

'But we are not of the same faith, William, and I know thee not.'

'I shall honour thy faith, Zelah. Thou shalt be Quaker as

much as it pleaseth thee. Aye, and our children. I shall build thee a meeting-house when I am ironmaster. Wilt thou wait for me? Zelah. Zelah.'

Then, practised as he was in pleasing Hannah, and not honouring by so much as a remembrance that instigator of love-making, he risked all by taking Zelah in his arms and kissing her upon the mouth.

She had never come into contact with a man before. Her father's gentle caresses, George Horsefield's proffered arm, were the limit of her experience. Now she was held by a man who knew how to hold a woman against him, and was not afraid to press his hand into the small of her back and feel her trembling through the muslin gown, and crush her lips. The physical shock immobilised her will. Terrified, ashamed, she let him kiss her again and again. She even put her arms around his neck, and was repelled by his warmth and scent and strength, and revelled in it. She was lost.

William recovered his wits first, though the possession of so much innocence and beauty almost unhinged him. He released her, and begged her pardon, then pursued the advantage he had gained over George Horsefield.

'If thou wilt wait for me,' he whispered. 'It may be four years, and small beginnings, Zelah, but I will marry thee. And I will build thee a house as beautiful as Somer Court and there thou shalt be queen. On Belbrook How, where the old priory stood, and we shall call it Belbrook Grange. This I promise thee. And with thee to wife I shall labour tenfold to achieve it. So I promise thee.'

She sank on to the stool in front of the harpsichord and buried her face in her hands.

'If thou wilt wait for me,' said William, 'then give me a sign this evening. I go tomorrow, at cock-crow. If thou wilt not, then do nothing, and I shall go my own way and never trouble thee again. Zelah.'

He took his exit quickly and quietly. Catherine, coming in a while later, found her daughter weeping over the harpsichord and saying she would never teach Rebecca again for the child did not practise and she was wore out!

They were a peaceable household, yet a small cloud hovered over Somer Court. But it lifted before dinner-time. Zelah wrote long in her journal, and earnestly, and secretly, endeavouring to counsel herself. She appeared at the table with her usual serenity, though a little pale, and was charming with everyone. By request, she played a spectacular piece upon the harpsichord: Mr Handel's third suite in D minor. Then embraced Rebecca warmly, kissed Catherine timidly and apologetically, and was remotely gracious with George Horsefield. She did not, however, give William the entire honours of the field. He received no sign that night, and lost his sleep and peace of mind in consequence. But as he was departing the next morning, so early that only one good-natured serving-maid was up to see him breakfasted, he felt an unknown softness in the pocket of his great-coat. He had the presence of mind to wait until he was aboard the coach for Manchester before he examined it, and then could have knelt in gratitude and relief.

She had crept down sometime while the household was asleep, and left the sign he wanted. Clinging to the folds of his cambric handkerchief lay a single pink moss rose.

EIGHT

An Understanding

August 1792

From her vantage point, high on the side of Garth Fells, Dorcas Howarth could see the valley lying beneath a morning haze, and however cruel the previous winter had been, this summer day promised to be glorious. She sat very trim and erect on the seat of the trap, holding her long whip, waiting for Ned to finish checking the wheels and harness—though this was needless, since Tom the carter sent out both horse and vehicle in immaculate condition. Nevertheless, her weekly drive into Millbridge, weather permitting, was subject to certain scrutinies and conditions on the part of her husband.

'All's well, Dorcas,' said Ned at last, coming up somewhat breathless and scarlet from bending, for he was no longer young except in spirit. 'Now take it easy down Garth Lane, and watch that sharp turn at the forge. Enjoy thyself, my lass, and dunnot fret about us. We'st have supper waiting. If owt keeps thee late I'll be riding out to meet thee. Give us a kiss, lass, and get thee gone!'

Thirty-one years of marriage had not thickened Dorcas's waist, or robbed Ned of the satisfaction of squeezing it. He kissed her heartily and liked doing so. He would now forget about her until six o'clock, and then begin to tap the time-piece in the parlour to make sure it was working, lift the lids off Nellie's cooking pots to smell the food, and walk his horse up and down the cobbled yard.

All this Dorcas understood and respected, while relishing the freedom of a day's outing, full of shops and gossip. Occasionally, though in the eight-and-fiftieth year of her age and old enough to know better, she had been guilty of lingering on the homeward road for the pleasure of seeing Ned riding towards her: white head purposeful, blunderbuss at the ready. This he may or may not have guessed, but accepted her occasional capriciousness as part of their long alliance, and cherished these small demands for his attention.

On this fine blue day her straw bonnet was tied beneath her chin with lilac ribbons which matched the sprigs in her muslin gown; and over all she wore a loose grey cloak and hood to protect her from both dust and showers. Her recent affluence was evident in such little vanities as a pair of silk knitted gloves, black kid slippers, and a new purple velvet reticule with a silver clasp: all of which lay in her basket at the back of the trap, ready to dazzle Millbridge on arrival at Thornton House. She looked exactly what she was: a handsome gentlewoman of some means, with a tendency to drive too fast.

The sun rose higher, the haze diminished, the air became diamond-clear. Beneath the wheels of her trap the way changed from country lane to broad road. Garth and Coldcote had been left behind now, and she could smell the dyeing-house at Medlar and hear the steam winding-engine at Childwell. Once this had been Childwell Way, but now they called it the 'Black Road'. She paused here, and shading her eyes she peered across the river at Belbrook but could see no one there, so drove on past the Swarth Moor mines and the big spinning mill at Thornley. She could scarcely tell the difference between one village and another these days, for as industries increased so did the workers and their ramshackle homes and sheds. Brigge House grew out of Thornley and spilled into Flawnes Green. And whereas William's forge had been seen clearly from the road, across the green itself, now it was hidden by a row of labourers' cottages and a new

Methodist Chapel, and Farmer Boulton had lost a field or two in the interest of progress.

Here she turned in, to be greeted by Stephen with a mixture of reverence and pride, for he still looked upon her as a benefactor of his boyhood.

'He's not here, Mrs Howarth,' said Stephen, coming out of his forge, arms akimbo. 'He's gone off with Mr Caleb to see Lord Kersall this morning.'

He delivered his information grandly, for these were great days full of great names, and Stephen was a part of them in however humble a capacity.

'I will come inside for a little while,' Dorcas decided. 'I have a message for him from his father and can write him a note.'

'Aye, come in and sit you down a bit, Mrs Howarth. I'll see to the horse and trap. Hannah's inside. She'll make you welcome.'

So Dorcas came from bright to dark, and stood in the kitchen doorway seeing the room in explosions of fiery green, and Hannah's figure flickering by the hearth. They greeted each other cordially, as usual. Dorcas accepted a glass of lemonade while she wrote her message, and Hannah finished black-leading the famous oven and put away her cleaning materials.

'It is about the ice-house,' Dorcas said, folding the paper in four and propping it where William could see it when he came in. 'My husband has drawn up a plan from the specifications, but I doubt you will have it erected here, Hannah. For it seems to be a vast beehive of a building that will take up over a hundred square yards of space and stand some twenty feet high!'

Hannah's face looked pinched and grey. She did not reply directly but stood before Dorcas, folding her hands into her apron.

'Mrs Howarth,' she said, 'could I have a word with you?'

Her voice held a beseeching quality which made Dorcas observe her more closely, and motion her to a chair.

'Thank you kindly, Mrs Howarth, but I'd sooner stand. I shan't take long over it.'

But she was so slow to begin that Dorcas said quickly and kindly, 'Come, Hannah, we have known each other seven years or more. If something is wrong then let us make haste to mend it.'

For she thought that perhaps William was expecting her to

do too much or paying her too little; which would be just like a man, who could think of building an ice-house but neglect his proper concerns.

'Mrs Howarth,' said Hannah, colourless but composed, 'this'll never be mended in a manner of speaking, but you're the only one as I can tell, and the only one as can help me. Only, I don't like fetching trouble to you, and I'm feared you'll think ill of me after.'

'I trust my judgement,' said Dorcas resolutely. 'I know you to be incapable of a mean or thoughtless act. Speak out. You will not offend me. Is it about my son? He can be heedless, I know.'

'It is about him,' said Hannah, speaking with difficulty, 'but I'm a poor hand at explaining, Mrs Howarth. So if I don't put the words quite right I hope as you won't hold it against me.'

'You should really sit down,' said Dorcas firmly, for the woman looked as though she might faint.

So Hannah sat with clenched hands, and fixed her eyes on the wall opposite so that she could not see the effect of her words.

'Mrs Howarth, I've been unwedded wife to your son for the last five years, and we've kept it hid from everybody.'

All the colour fled Dorcas's face.

'Mrs Howarth, I want you to know as I'm not blaming him for it, because it takes two to do what's wrong, but I swear to you as I never run after him. It weren't like that. I run from him, in a manner of speaking. I held out for five long months—and I were lonely, and I thought the world of him. But he'd made his mind up, and you know what he's like when he sets his mind on summat or somebody. I were weak. I don't deny that. Weak and sinful. But I loved him and I thought it might be made right in time.'

She said desolately, managing to meet Dorcas's troubled gaze, 'I felt there was an understanding between us, Mrs Howarth.'

A tremor of the straw bonnet served as a nod.

'Well, I were wrong,' said Hannah quietly, 'and if I'm to be truthful I've known that for long enough. But I dursen't face it. There was a long while, when he were pulling his heart out with that blessèd ironworks, and getting nowhere and nowt to show for it, when I were no more to him than a crust of bread or a sup of beer. But after Miss Wilde died, and he knew there was a chance for him, he seemed to wake

96

up to me a bit. It were only a month or two, Mrs Howarth, but we was right back to the beginnings again, and I'd been starved for want of a word or a touch from him. I thought it had all come right again, you see.'

She wiped her eyes on her apron and smoothed it out thoughtfully.

'Then he went down to Warwickshire to see that ironmaster. Mrs Howarth, if I'm speaking out of turn, or if I'm telling you summat as he doesn't want you to know just yet, I'd be grateful if you wouldn't let on that I told you. But he met a lady down in Warwickshire as he'd like to marry, better suited to him than I were or ever would be. I don't deny that, and I don't begrudge him, for he's younger than me, and grander. But it goes to explain why I say what I do, and why I come to you sooner than any other.'

At this fresh blow, Dorcas clasped her own hands on the table in front of her, and watched Hannah in mute sympathy.

'Mrs Howarth, he don't want me and he don't know how to tell me, so I shan't stop with him, but I've no means of getting away from Flawnes Green. You might well say to me,' Hannah continued bleakly, ' "Go and work for somebody else round here then!" But it isn't that easy. I must go a long way off, to where I'm not known. I'm four month gone with child, Mrs Howarth.'

Dorcas gave a short soft sigh. Her hands relaxed.

She said quietly, 'Does William know this?'

'No, Mrs Howarth, and I never want him to, if you please. Nor nobody else but yourself. I lay no claim on Will now, and never shall do. But I've got nobody to trust, and nowt but a few shillings as I've saved up against a rainy day. I lost my family when I come here to wed Abel Garside fourteen years since. And I've thought on, night after night, how to put it to you so that it sounded proper. But I can only tell the truth and hope you understand me. If you could help me out with a few pounds, to keep me while the child's born, and to get me far enough from here, I'll never ask nowt from nobody again.'

Stephen's hammer beat in their heads. The little room was stifling.

Dorcas said, 'I understand you very well, Hannah. I will help you all I can. Let us make a pot of tea and talk matters over together.'

Oh William, she thought, this is not the first time you have deceived us, and still we contrive to set matters right for you!

She remembered how he had kept them in ignorance while he worked at Flawnes Green forge with Aaron Helm all those years since: Miss Wilde thinking he was at school, the headmaster thinking he was at home, Aaron believing the boy had permission. Then his ordering of *The Gentleman's Magazine* on her account, and the way he contrived to get books for himself on her list, from old Mr Longe in London, Toby's father. And when Henry Tucker threatened to expel him, Miss Wilde pleaded for him, Ned came to some agreement with him, her own plans to reinstate him were turned upside down. So in the end William had books and magazine and his apprenticeship. Which was what he had wanted all along.

'Hannah,' she said, 'who is this lady in Warwickshire?'

'She's one of young Mr Caleb's sisters,' Hannah replied, empty even of sorrow. 'Will must have confided in Mr Caleb, because when he followed him up here in June he brought a letter with him. And they've been talking together, quiet-like, as they worked. I guessed some of it, and Stephen told me the rest—not meaning harm, just chatting-like, being interested. But the lady's very young, and her family don't know, and Will and Mr Caleb don't want them to find out, neither, because old Mr Scholes wants her to wed somebody else.'

'Dear God in heaven,' said Dorcas, horrified, exasperated.

For William had not been satisfied to ruin one woman, but was risking the ironmaster's patronage by courting his daughter.

'Do you know her name?' Dorcas asked cautiously.

'Aye, I do, Mrs Howarth. It's a strange name for a lass, though taken from the Holy Book. The name of the city where Saul and Jonathan were buried. Zelah.'

'And she is engaged to someone else?'

'They have an understanding,' said Hannah, without irony.

The knowledge that Dorcas would help her, and was sharing some of the responsibility, had released Hannah from the most cruel of her anxieties. She sounded tired, almost uninterested.

'Let us talk of you for a while,' said Dorcas gently. 'Where will you go, and how shall you live, when you leave here?'

The woman gathered strength, spoke with a rough eloquence which touched Dorcas closely.

'I've thought it all out, so's the child won't be shamed. I shall go far off. I don't know where I'll settle. But I'll put a few places between here and there, so's I can say truthfully as I was travelling round a bit. I'm a widow, and I'll pass for one again. Folk don't know what goes on from one valley to the next, and a big place like Manchester or Liverpool could be the end of the world for most. There's one thing more as you could do for me, Mrs Howarth. Would you give me a piece of paper as says I'm honest and hard-working?' Dorcas nodded, and clasped her hands a little more firmly. 'I could keep house for somebody, and have the child with me. And I don't want them gossiping at the Methodist Chapel, or round Flawnes Green, so I've been putting about that I heard my sister was in trouble with her health. A word here and there soon spreads. Mrs Boulton said to me the other day, "Hannah, you're not with us these days. If you feel you've got to go then your job's here when you get back!" But I shall write her a line or two, later on, saying as I shall stop there for good. And Will—well, perhaps you'd look around for somebody for him. I'd rather not tell him myself. I can leave him a line. You could say we'd talked together, so he wouldn't think I were leaving him in the lurch, like.'

'And you will write to me from time to time, will you not? said Dorcas. 'And send me your address so that I know where to contact you?'

'You'll excuse me, Mrs Howarth,' said Hannah, very low, 'but when I leave here I leave for good. You won't see nor hear from me no more, like I told you. You've got your lives, and we've got ours. I want to cover my tracks so's we all stand a fair chance. I don't want to be beholden to nobody.'

Dorcas bowed her head, and then said, 'But at least, if you are ever in difficulties, you can ask *me*, can you not? I could not rest if I thought you were so much alone.'

After a moment, Hannah said reluctantly, 'I'll send word if I must, Mrs Howarth. I know you mean it for the best.'

'I am ashamed,' said Dorcas, 'that you should suffer.'

Then she stood up, for there was no more to be said on that matter, only the practical side to be resolved.

'I shall bring you one hundred pounds in sovereigns from Millbridge, late this afternoon. Will my son be here?'

The sum stopped Hannah for a moment. She seemed about to protest, but Dorcas's upraised hand forbade argument.

On a lower note Hannah answered, 'Aye, he will, but I'll be in my cottage. You can see it across the field over there. If you wanted, you could say you were having a word with me, and walk over.'

'I shall do that. And I shall say nothing to him of your going. I can find somebody, if that is necessary. William and

Caleb are seldom here nowadays. A whitster to collect the washing . . . we are scarcely a mile from Millbridge . . . one of the Bowker girls. . . .'

'Aye, I know you'll manage summat for him,' said Hannah lifelessly. 'I'll give Mrs Boulton my notice.'

'The child,' Dorcas began, concerned for them both.

A subdued radiance was for the first time apparent in the weary woman before her.

'Eh, bless you,' said Hannah in her old warm way, 'dunnot fret about the child. I've allus wanted one. I wanted one so much that I can't see it as a judgement on me, nor think of it as a sin. I'm grateful, Mrs Howarth, for the child. And I thank you for helping us.'

The sun was at its height when Dorcas drove away from Flawnes Green, and the day which had begun so splendidly now became oppressive. Her new velvet riticule, her silk gloves, her fashionable slippers had lost their importance. The Millbridge shops had nothing to offer in the way of consolation. Thornton House was dull and languid, Phoebe Jarrett querulous, old Agnes forgetful, and Sally pre-occupied with jam-making.

During the afternoon the heat increased. Dorcas, fanning herself and making conversation, waited until six o'clock before venturing homewards. Then William and Caleb kept her talking longer than she wished, at the smithy, and her visit to Hannah was brief and unsatisfactory in consequence. And the weight of the secret dragged her down. Why should she be the one to know, to help, to cover up, to say nothing? Abruptly, she took her departure. The day had crawled along, getting nowhere. The hour was late. As the rim of the sun slipped down behind the Stoops she saw Ned in the distance, white head erect, brass blunderbuss at his side, and whipped up the horse in sorrow and relief.

'Why, whatever's to do?' he asked, as soon as he saw her tired face, her tired ribbons.

'Oh, such a day, but do not ask me! Let us talk of anything else, Ned. Oh, Phoebe is growing old, and Hannah Garside is leaving, and I shall be glad to get home. I wish there were someone else to hear all their troubles and make matters right. . . .'

'Well, I've told thee often enough,' said Ned kindly, 'as they'll allus drive a willing horse!'

'Calling me a horse!' cried Dorcas, lip trembling.

100

He dismounted, tied his stallion to the farm trap, got up beside her and took the reins.

'Come on now, my lass,' he said, 'let's get thee home. Nellie's cooked a pig's face for supper, and peas, and there's a boiled chicken if you don't fancy the other. You should never have gone visiting in this sort of weather. You know it tires you out. . . .'

So he pretended to grumble while she wiped her eyes and gradually felt a little better; and the evening came on cool and blue, and folk began to light their candles against the dark.

Hannah sat up until midnight, sewing one hundred gold sovereigns into her best black linsey-wolsey gown, and folded it to form the base of her luggage. She possessed very few belongings: some clothes, her Bible, a trinket or two which Abel had bought at a fair. Round them all she wrapped her black shawl. She had cleaned the cottage from top to bottom, and left her cooking pots and wash-tub behind her. A letter for Mrs Boulton lay on the scrubbed table. She walked across the field for the last time.

It was easy to avoid William, since he was avoiding her, and Stephen had gone over to Brigge House Farm to shoe a team of oxen, so she was spared explanations and farewells. The ritual cleaning done, and dinner in the oven, she picked up her bundle and stood at the side of the Black Road until a passing farmer gave her a lift into Millbridge. There she made enquiries, and found that an afternoon stage-coach called at The Royal George on its way to Liverpool. So it became quite a holiday for her. She ate a pie at the pie-shop and drank a mug of ale, and looked shyly round the town, and thought it all wonderfully fine. And at the appointed hour she obtained an outside place for the sum of ten shillings and sixpence.

Hannah Garside might have driven out of the world, that summer afternoon in 1792, sitting steadfastly on top of a coach for the first time in her life, with her bundle on her knees. For none of them ever saw her again.

NINE

Partnerships

The letter was waiting for him, propped up against the wash-basin in the bedroom which had been theirs for five years, carefully sealed with a blob of red wax.

My deer lad Im off and I shant cum bak for that is wot yu want. I onderstand so dunnot fret deer lad for I shall be orl rite. Yor deer mother nos I am leeving but I hav told evribody that my sista Suzan is ill and Im gon to luk after her. The rest is bitween thee and me and all-waze shal be and I thank yu for the hapines deer lad. Deer lad I wish yu luk wi the iernwerks and a happy lif wi yor ladiwife and childer to bless yu both. Tak cayr deer Will and may God kep yu safe. Yor luving Hannah. Amen.

William sat upon the bed, and between shame and sadness and relief could have wept aloud. He sat so long that Stephen mounted the wooden stairs to see if all was well, bringing with him an uncertain mood and tone: a compound of sorrow and accusation.

'It's a bit of a winder,' said William slowly, folding the note. 'Did Hannah say anything to you, Steve?'

'Summat and nowt. Mrs Boulton knows more nor anybody else. Oh, and your mother—Mrs Howarth, that is—left word that she's sending a woman in from the Green tomorrow.'

'So I am the last to know. Well, if Hannah felt she must go then she was in the right of it.' Heavily.

Stephen made a curious movement of the mouth as though he were about to spit, then checked himself and ruminated on his master.

'Aye,' he said finally, 'whatever Hannah did were right. If anybody tells me any different I'll punch the living daylights out of them. She were a good woman and there's not so many that we can afford to lose them!'

Then he turned and went clumsily down the narrow stair, leaving William to make what he would of that remark, and taking his own feelings out on the anvil. While the future ironmaster stayed deep in thought, until at length he put the letter away, being unable to destroy it.

From the first, William and Caleb's partnership in Belbrook Iron Foundry was very like that of husband and wife, for though their investment of money and work might be equal, their positions were not. William had originally laid claim to the wasteland, cleared it, envisioned it. He looked always outward into the world, always forward, seeing what could be and therefore must be, regardless of present circumstances. Whereas Caleb, accustomed to the subordinate role, toiled over domestic detail conscientiously and with a certain quiet enjoyment. Therefore it seemed that William was in charge, though he deferred to Caleb in routine business. Already folk were inclined to say, 'Th'ironworks? Oh, *Howarth's* tha means?' and to refer to William alone as 'Th'ironmaster'. The interviews with Lord Kersall were conducted by William, while young Caleb provided shrewd counsel from the background. But, the partnership being complementary, it looked to work well from the start.

Before the spring of 1793 all legal formalities had been concluded and the construction of the Foundry began. The little wooden hut which Ned and William had first built on the site, where they might eat and shelter, was now furnished with tables, chairs and shelves. Here, warmed by an iron stove whose pipe stuck rakishly through the roof, Caleb installed himself and his papers and the files labelled BELBROOK IRON FOUNDRY. Upon the door, under which blew a bitter draught, was nailed a plaque which read COMPANY OFFICE. The administration was complete.

Outside the hut William consulted with their foreman, Jim Cartwright, and the carpenter Harry Orrell. His tone was genial authoritative, so that they knew he was master and yet a fellow man.

'Now before we start,' said William briskly, 'I want the men to see what they're building. So I got Mr Ellis Field to draw up a simple plan, clearly marked, which they can understand,' and he smoothed out his map upon a flat stone to show them. 'Now then, Orrell, I want you to make me a frame to fit this plan, and make it strong and good. Set it here by the river, on stout posts, so that it catches the eye. And Jim, we shall want a sheet of glass over it, for it shall stop there until the Foundry is finished. And I'll be speaking to the men, so have it up there for Monday, will you?'

They nodded, touching their foreheads in respect, puzzled by this curious notion. For what did it matter, after all, that a labourer should comprehend his ultimate goal provided he reached it? But William was a great believer in inspiration.

The architect had allowed himself considerable scope, and flattered William, by being slightly fanciful in his vision of the future. Though his drawing was accurate in that it depicted the workings (from the upper furnace pool and dam, through the foundry buildings and lower furnace pool, to the upper and lower forge pools, and on to the wharf and warehouses) it flourished with trees as yet unplanted, workers' houses as yet unbuilt, and a general air of prosperity which could only be attributed to faith and optimism. Nevertheless, the picture was heartening to everyone concerned with this enterprise.

Caleb surveyed it with a wry smile, and produced a list of rules for William to read out when he exhorted the men to work. His vision was less popular, more practical, and quite as necessary.

'I shall give my speech first,' said William, and he was right. 'Then Cartwright can read all this out,' he added, and was right again.

So it came about on a cold March morning that William stood bare-headed before the little crowd of workmen, and spoke up loud and clearly.

'My name's Will Howarth, as most of you know. And this is my partner, Caleb Scholes, and a famous name in the world of iron. I wanted to say a few words to you all, so that you know who and what you're working for, and why! This is the Age of Iron, men. And, though England has been manufacturing iron goods for longer back than I can remember, she's never known such an age as this one shall be. This works you're engaged on building will be known as The Belbrook Foundry, and every inch of ground on which you build, and every yard on which you tread, has been cleared by me and a handful of others. You're not working for some fancy gentleman from Manchester or Liverpool, who wouldn't know a pick-axe or a spade if you put it in his hands, you're working for us. Caleb Scholes and I were apprenticed in Birmingham together as blacksmiths, and Mr

Scholes's father is one of the foremost ironmasters in the land. So we know what we're about, and we know what we want. We want Belbrook built as soon as possible. We want her working as soon as possible. And even then we haven't finished with you! Belbrook isn't the end, she's the beginning. Lancashire isn't rich in ironworks, like Yorkshire or Shropshire, but she's going to lead the world. This drawing may not seem much to you'—he knew that it had impressed them, that they were even now murmuring about it among themselves, seeing themselves as part of an idea instead of slaves to someone else's ideas—'but wait until you hear what we have in mind. You can be employed for ever!'

He had not intended to finish upon this note, but the hardship of the times was upon them, and they cheered wildly. So he cleverly forgot the rest of his speech, which was mostly statistics to impress them, and repeated his words with a great flourish of the arms as though he called for another cheer.

'Employed for ever!' cried William. 'For ever! For ever!'

They threw up their old felt hats and shouted, *'Hurrah! Hurrah!'*

'All right, Mr Cartwright,' said William calmly, 'you can carry on now.'

Caleb greeted his partner with a knowing smile as he stepped down from the improvised rostrum.

'I believe thee should have been a politician, William,' said Caleb.

'I may be, in the end,' William replied carelessly, 'but someone must inspire them. They must work as I did, not as though I were labouring but as though I drew breath. And I shall be among them at all times of the day and when they least expect me. There shall be nothing that the lowest and poorest of them are asked to do that I cannot do better. Thus shall Belbrook rise and flourish, Caleb. That I promise you!'

The quiet Quaker turned to watch the crowd, and smiled again.

'See how they greet my homily!' he observed, without disappointment or pique. 'So it always is with mankind. They can be exhorted to battle for glory, even at the cost of maiming or death, but the daily concern to live in harmony with themselves and their neighbours defeats them!'

'Well, it is difficult not to take a swig of spirits to keep out the cold,' said William reasonably, 'and the Irish will fight, whether they drink or no! As for profanity, my dear Caleb, they do not know it from the common tongue.'

'Yet our own workpeople must observe these rules when the Foundry is built,' Caleb replied. 'I am thinking already of their general welfare and health. When thou hast time, Will, wouldst thee like to discuss our Welfare Society? I had thought of a subscription scheme, with graded payments for illness, accident and death.'

William's attention was already wandering. The work-gangs were marching off: a dozen men to each gang, led by a ganger who would see that they laboured long and hard since his cut of the wages depended on it.

'My dear Caleb,' said William, in his most charming manner, 'what can I offer as advice or criticism? You know what you are about better than I do. And we have one aim in all this. I pray you, do as you think best!'

He walked rapidly after the men who were to dredge the upper furnace pool and strengthen the dam. There, they would be furthest from the office. But the safety of this dam was more important than anything else on this burgeoning site, William told himself, and he had promised to oversee everything personally. So he strode away.

Caleb stood looking after him for a few moments, then turned towards his hut, only to be greeted by the sight of Farmer Cotrell alternately hobbling and waving his stick. Courteously, the younger man assisted him into the warmth, thus compounding the destruction of his morning.

'I think nowt to this!' Cotrell began, looking round the cramped room.

'Ah well, we must begin at the beginning, my friend. Can I help thee?'

'It's about that Kersall. I should never have sold up. You're letting him have all his own road. Tha knows that the council is in his pocket, and the bank manager—that Pettifer. I've allus kept my money in a stocking and allus shall. . . .'

So he spun out his loneliness and wove misgivings wherever he could, and wondered why folk shunned him.

'You canna smelt an ounce of iron ore without Kersall dipping his hand into thy pocket,' droned the old man. 'There's not enough ore here to make a set of pans. You'll have to ship it up his canal, and buy his coal and pay his rent. If tha runs into debt he'll get Pettifer to foreclose on thee . . . art tha listening to me, young man?'

'We have many friends in business, Edmund Cotrell,' said Caleb firmly. 'Thee may be sure that we have not risked our enterprise upon the whims of one man. But I am not at liberty to give thee details. State thy business, and let me do mine, I pray thee.'

'I heard you was building a landing-stage at Belbrook Bottoms, and a railway to fetch up deliveries from t'river. And building a new blast-furnace, and buying them steam-engines from foreign parts. Tha'lt go bankrupt, I'm telling thee. I've seen folk come and I've seen folk go.'

Caleb said courteously, 'I have work to do, my friend. I pray thee excuse me!' And he held open the door.

'Oh, that's the way on it, is it? Buy the land from under an owd chap's feet and throw him out when he gives thee the time of day! Where's Will Howarth?'

Caleb compromised with the truth.

'He is not *here*, Edmund Cotrell.'

'Taking my name in vain! I know thy sort. Tha'rt a dissenter. They used to clap them in prison, and a good thing, too. It'll be some time afore I call on you again, you can take my word for it.'

Oh, how I wish that were true! Caleb thought.

'Good-day, friend,' he said aloud, peaceably.

The morning's letters had arrived. He opened the one from his father first. The Warwickshire ironmaster's yoke was comfortable, but both partners resented it a little. Still, his goodwill and advice and the twelve thousand pounds of capital he had helped them to borrow must be paid for in humility.

The letter began with Lord Kersall, who must surely be dogging their footsteps that day. Humphrey Kersall, the ironmaster wrote, was driven by greed and worldly pride and suffered from the sin of covetousness. In order to save him from temptation, with the morsel of Belbrook Foundry in his jaws, the elder Caleb now suggested that they do business with George Horsefield in the main part, giving the Millbridge bank manager enough money to please him but not enough to put themselves at his mercy. Furthermore, when cash was short and payments due, they should draw bills on either the London or the Bristol Quaker business houses. *'For if the fruit is ripe,'* Caleb had written, *'and Humphrey Kersall ever able to gather it, that will he do.'* He ended by saying that George Horsefield had spoken to him about marrying Zelah, and he had given him both permission and blessing to do so.

'Oh . . . Christmas!' said Caleb, which was the nearest he ever came to an oath.

The banker stood by Zelah's side in the conservatory at Somer Court, quietly pleased with an intimacy which had grown from childhood, which would flower into marriage. She seemed pale and ill at ease, unlike herself. He put this down to a natural modesty, for she must know what was afoot even by the way Caleb had brought him to see her, by the way Catherine had smilingly left the inner room and taken her younger daughters with her.

So he began by saying, 'This will not surprise thee, my dear Zelah—'

When she incontinently cut across his speech, crying, 'Pray thee, George, we have always been friends. Let us remain so.'

His speech was too firmly in his head and mouth, too rooted by years of belief and habit, to be stemmed in this fashion.

'Why, so we shall be, Zelah. For if a man is not his wife's best friend, and she his, then should they not be joined—'

'Exactly so, I pray thee. I pray thee, say no more. Be my friend, and say no more, dear George. Oh, heaven knows'—seeing his bewildered face—'I would sooner cut off this hand than hurt thee. So be my friend, and no more.'

He was both intelligent and kind. Perceiving that she was on the verge of weeping he pursued the matter no further. But touched the proffered hand to show they were friends indeed, and bowed and left her. Alone, she grieved openly for the life they could have led together had she not met William: then for William who, though always present in her mind, was absent in flesh: then for her parents who would be disappointed and troubled: and at last for herself who was torn between the life she knew and the unknown life at Belbrook, and the discipline of her Society which would surely expel her.

So Catherine found her, and endeavoured to mend the situation.

'For though thou knowest that marriage is a solemn contract, and that much is expected of all women (and no one gainsayeth that our way is difficult!) yet do not let thy heart fail thee at the prospect, Zelah. Though there be hardship there is great joy, and deeper than joy, in a good match. And thee knows that George is a fine man and we love him. Do not fear marriage, Zelah. It is to be approached with reverence and care, but not with fear, my daughter.'

'But I do not love George,' cried Zelah. 'I like him very much, Mamma, but I do not love him.'

Catherine assumed, as George Horsefield had done, that the thought of love-making was disturbing to her daughter. In truth, it was the lack of love-making, and not from George, which made Zelah weep.

'Thee will feel better by and by,' said Catherine. 'Perhaps he spoke too soon for thee. Shall we ask him to wait a twelvemonth, my love?'

The truth hovered on Zelah's lips, and was sealed by Catherine's next observation.

'Thy father hath persuaded George to be concerned in Belbrook,' she continued, endeavouring to bridge the conversation with more familiar matters. 'That will help Caleb and William mightily. I am amazed how much thy father hath done for them. But then, he sets great store by them both—though thee would not think it, hearing him chide them!'

'Hast thee heard from Caleb yet?' Zelah asked, drying her eyes and resolving to say nothing.

'Why, we heard only last week, child. Thou canst not expect them to write more often.'

'It seems much longer,' said Zelah pitifully, for they only wrote of business.

'Perhaps thee should visit one of my sisters for a month or two,' said Catherine, looking at her daughter's woeful face and drooping form.

The girl's mouth and eyes were swollen, vulnerable. She was suffering the inexplicable sorrow, the extreme sadness, of youth. Her long childhood was over. She stood at the edge of loss.

'Could I go to my Aunt Maria?' Zelah asked.

'I must ask thy father first, but I dare say he will not mind.'

For her sister Maria, closest of companions, had married a Church of England clergyman and gone over to the other side completely. They had never lost touch, but visits were not easy for either of them, and Zelah had not seen her aunt more than three times in her young life.

'I thought thee did not care for Sheffield,' Catherine commented.

'I care for Aunt Maria,' said Zelah, who would confide in her.

Catherine sat with her hands in her lap; as women sit at the end of a long day, wondering how they have got through. The defection of Maria had been a sad trouble in her family, and in twenty years the hurt had not healed.

'Well then,' said Catherine at last, 'if thee must, Zelah. Though why thee should have a concern for her above the others I do not know.'

The girl was silent. Her need could not be voiced.

'I will take counsel with thy father then.'

But how should he deny his wife or favourite daughter? For favourite she was, though the great Caleb frowned upon favouritism. Zelah was too like Catherine to be loved along with the rest. So husband and wife communed together: he spare and grey, she subdued but golden still.

'She is younger in heart and body than we thought,' said Caleb simply. 'Well, she shall not be forced. It took me more than a twelvemonth to gain thy consent, Catherine. And thou wast older than our Zelah.'

She mused upon that time. She had borne their last child. Their summer was over. They could only see how quietly splendid their match had been, how like to it that of George and Zelah could be.

'I shall speak with him again,' Caleb assured her. 'He will wait. His love is great and deep. Aye, let her go to Maria if she wishes. Though *of* us, they are apart from us, and that is what Zelah most desires. At the moment.'

My Dearest William, I am staying with my Aunt Maria at the Address above Until the Summer, and if Thee send me a Letter Pray ask Caleb to direct it so that my Aunt think it Comes from Him. Oh, how I do Detest this Secrecy, and feel I am Less than Myself in Our Love whereas I should be More. Aunt Maria hath Hearkened to my Story but will not say yea nor nay, and tho' she hath a Concern for me she Fears to Estrange herself Further with my Parents by Taking my Side. George Horsefield hath spoken for me, but I Refused him, poor George. Yet my Parents think Only that I need Time, and he will Ask again. How then shall I Answer without I Tell them of Thee and me? Oh, Dearest Life, tho' I would not Hurt thee in thy Dealings with George and my Father, shall thee not Confide in my Parents as to thine Intentions? Give me some Hope and some Direction, else shall I not know Where to Turn. I am so much Alone in this, and Separated even from mine own Sect in my Mind.

Tell Caleb that I am Poorer for my Brother, Friend and Messenger. It is nigh on a twelvemonth since thee told me that thee Loved me and would have me to Wife. Nigh on a Year since I have seen Thee. And those Few Letters, tho' so Dearly Cherished and Oft Read, are all I have of Thee. I know that thou art Embroiled in thine Undertakings, but All I have is Invested in Thee. Oh, Help me, William, and do not Cease to Love thy most Loving Zelah.

TEN

The Northern Correspondent

London 1792

Toby Longe's notion of finance could be compared with going to sea in a leaky boat. While the waters were calm he trimmed his craft pretty well, though without making headway. When a wind rose he was in trouble. A storm threatened to capsize all aboard. And he was sinking little by little. Charlotte early learned to waylay payments so that butcher and baker might be satisfied. Every article of value was pawned and redeemed in rotation, so that they never possessed all at one time, but so far had not lost any either. Meanwhile, Toby, affectionate and hapless, never enquired how his household stayed afloat. Care went to bed with Charlotte, rose with her each morning, and kept her company during the day. Her love for him never quite died. He was a great deal of trouble, but he truly admired and revered her. And occasionally life smiled on them, enabling a debt to be paid, a bill to be settled, and a little left over. Then, a family man, Toby would take wife and children and Polly Slack out for the evening and sail down the river to Vauxhall, to eat ice-cream and watch the firework displays; or hire a post-chaise and drive to the village of Islington for the day, and drink fresh milk and let the world go by.

For a long while he had been possessed by the idea of publishing a radical journal which would entertain and inform intelligent readers. His main difficulty was lack of money, so he was constantly on the look-out for a patron, and still had not found one early in 1788 when his daughter Cicely was born. Before the infant was three months old, Joseph Johnson, a far more successful publisher, launched the first literary and scientific journal of its kind, called *The Analytical Review*. It was a thick little magazine, closely printed and heavy with informed opinion, containing serious essays of great length and shorter notices, designed to appeal to the radical intelligentsia. It was so much what Toby had in mind for himself that for once he gave vent to loud ill-humour, railing against fortune to such an extent that Charlotte lost her milk, and little Cicely had to be handed over to a wet nurse.

But on the heels of this disappointment came a far more significant calamity. The bailiff put a stop to all Toby's activities by seizing the printing press, and threatening him with a debtors' prison if the bill was not paid forthwith. Longe & Son was saved only by Charlotte unearthing Betty Ackroyd's wedding gift of hard-earned shillings and sovereigns, to placate the creditor. She was understandably bitter about both these events, and on looking into the firm's accounts found them in a perilous state, which further roused both her anger and her courage. She resolved to work in her own right, instead of helping Toby out for nothing, and was about to defend this decision with considerable acerbity if he had questioned it. But he remained prudently silent on the issue, realising that another rocking of the boat might bring them all to penury and eviction. And among those publishers who would employ a jobbing writer was Joseph Johnson himself, who kindly put some reviewing her way. This suspicion of betrayal on Charlotte's part, and Toby's inability to condemn her action, brought a coolness to their relationship. The marriage became mere courtesy for twelve months, and they went their own ways, so Charlotte was never sure at what particular point Ralph Fairbarrow entered both their lives. But early in 1789 Toby went off to France, from whence came rumblings of change, and his expenses must have been defrayed, for Charlotte now kept guard over their ready money in a locked box: an arrangement with which Toby did not quarrel, since she paid domestic bills out of it. She did not ask questions about his assignment and he did not offer explanations, though he returned full of a suppressed excitement, and Fairbarrow's name cropped up in conversation, being referred to simply as 'an old friend'.

Stationed at her writing-table in the window of their living-room, Charlotte welcomed the distance between them.

She was busy from early each morning until early the next morning, overseeing the household and children, writing at all hours. Sometime during the day she would make her round of the publishers, delivering work, returning with further commissions, making introductions, following up connections. She was dealing with men on equal terms, meeting women like herself, earning a modest livelihood. She was no longer afraid of Toby's whims and moods, no longer courting his favour. She had little time for conversation with him, and none for leisure. Besides, she was afraid of love, of becoming pregnant. She sensed that she was safer in every way when no longer involved emotionally with a man. The barrier suited her very well.

But nothing remains the same. The summer of 1789 was extraordinarily fine and hot. A lighter mood prevailed, threats of bankruptcy retreated and an astonishing book had come into her hands, called *Le Rideau Levé, ou l'éducation de Laure*, published two or three years previously, which taught her a greater physical freedom. It was not, she learned, necessary to incur frequent pregnancies and live in fear of ill-health and possible death. If a sponge was inserted into the female passage, attached to a narrow ribbon, conception did not occur in the majority of cases. Afterwards, the sponge might safely be withdrawn. Sauntering homewards one bright blue day in high summer, Charlotte permitted herself for the first time in a year to think of Toby kindly. She had money in her pocket and in the cash-box, work to do, new people to know. She could afford to be his wife again.

As though in answer to this unspoken thought, Toby arrived back within hours of her return, bringing news that illumined and enjoined them. French peasants had stormed and taken the prison-fortress of the Bastille and slaughtered its governor. The revolution which Toby had long prophesied, and they and all their friends had hoped for, was made manifest. A new and better world was at hand.

That night, lying together after a mutual reunion, Toby dared say, 'Do you recall the idea I had for a radical journal, my love?'

And though Charlotte felt a customary pang of fear she answered, 'Yes, my love?'

Well, it has turned out differently, and far better, than I could have hoped. Ralph Fairbarrow is interested in publishing a news-sheet which will appeal to the artisans, the small masters, those who are literate and stand to gain by a com-

113

plete change of constitution. He feels that we could do this'—and here he kissed Charlotte's fingers, from which the day's ink-stains were not completely removed—'but what do you say, my love?'

Charlotte replied warily, 'Can we make it pay, Toby?'

He straightened at her tone, and though he continued to smile and shake her fingers gently from time to time, to remind her of their reunion, he now spoke more directly.

'He is willing to finance its beginnings, and to offer you a salary equal to what you now earn by working for others. Of course it must pay its way, but that it is almost bound to do. We plan to fetch it out once a week, charging twopence a copy—which these people can afford very well. Ralph already has a long list of possible subscribers and, once we begin, the readership will grow. I print it here in the shop. Ralph distributes it.'

'Here, in London? We shall not make it pay in this city!'

'No, no, in the north. Lancashire, Yorkshire, Durham, Northumberland. Up to the Scotch border. It will be a political weekly, giving informed opinion and reportage of events both nationally and internationally. I shall scurry round collecting the news, and you, my clever love, shall put it in your own inimitable way—so that it interests miners in Durham, cutlers in Sheffield, weavers in Manchester, and even sailors home from the sea!'

Charlotte was thinking so deeply that he rose from their bed and walked the room, humming uneasily to himself, glancing at her occasionally.

'Why only the northern counties, Toby?' she asked at length. 'Why not Scotland, and the Midlands? They are just as industrial there.'

'Well, Ralph has connections with this particular section of the industrial community. That is all.'

'And a weekly newspaper—for that is what it is! They cannot rely on us for the latest news, can they?'

'As I said,' cried Toby, striding up and down, 'we inform them. We distil, translate, give them the essence. Think of the influence we shall have! Think of the good we shall do! This is not like you, Lottie.'

'It is not like I was,' she replied composedly, 'but I wish to have some guarantee of earning a living before I give up the one I have established.'

'Oh, if that is all. Ralph shall speak to you. You will not mind dealing with him? He is a dry stick, but totally reliable!'

And in some pique he went downstairs to see if there was any wine left in the supper bottle. But he obviously needed her co-operation, for he was back again before long, his breath scented with claret, full of bonhomie.

'And how is our good friend Joseph Johnson?' Toby asked amiably, though the idea of *The Analytical Review* was still a bolus for him to swallow.

'I have grown to like him very well,' she said, smiling.

'We have each been so busy of late,' Toby continued casually, as though their year of non-communication had been an unavoidable weekend spent apart. 'I know so little of all your enterprises—though our very bread has come from them. And that I do not forget, Lottie, my love,' he added, with a sincerity which calmed and delighted her. 'Come then, tell me how you met with him. We have not gossiped for such a while!' and he settled himself down again, lying more comfortably upon the bed, by her side.

'Well, where should I begin?' she answered gaily. 'Our good friend Edmund Crowley sent me to him, and first I met Mr Johnson's assistant, Miss Wollstonecraft—who seemed in much the same case as myself. . . .'

Poor, talented, vulnerable, prickly, and too honest for her own good.

'The alarming red-haired mistress?'

'She is not his mistress, but his friend,' said Charlotte coldly. 'May not men and women be friends?'

He squeezed her hand in penitence, crying, 'Why should I not believe it, when you and I are such friends, my love?'

'Well, Mary is not his mistress—he set her up in the George Street house because he believed in her. But I digress. Mary heard my plea, looked at my work, and took me in to see Mr Johnson—who grasped my hand as though I had been a man, and said he dined at three! He says that to every poor and radical writer he employs, because most of them are hungry I expect! I know I was. . . .'

But had secreted food to take back to the children, just the same.

'So you dined at seventy-two St. Paul's Churchyard?' said Toby hastily. 'Whom did you meet? Some of our friends?'

'All friends in spirit, certainly. Yes, some I knew and some I did not.'

'You should not give up Johnson entirely,' said Toby, thinking of future introductions.

'I had no intention of doing so. We are not yet rich enough for that!'

'And you like Miss Wollstonecraft, I take it?'

'Better than any woman I have ever known—except my mother, but that is a particular relationship,' said Charlotte sadly, knowing how much it had diminished in the years of their separateness.

'Then I shall like her too. We must sup together, Lottie. Aye, and Johnson also. I am not such a poor creature that I can envy a man who seizes his opportunity as well as Johnson has done.'

He stole a glance at her downcast eyes.

'I used to discuss matters with my mother as I now discuss them with Mary,' said Charlotte quietly, 'but these days all Mamma and I have between us are our guarded letters. There is no freedom of thought or speech or written word any more. She was once my friend and mentor. Now? Oh, full of wit and anecdotes and wise remedies for small ills, but no more than another northern correspondent.'

'The very name!' cried Toby, thankful to divert her from this topic as well. 'You shall write the leading review of the day, Lottie, in letter-form, and we shall call our journal *The Northern Correspondent*, in honour of your mother.'

And he kissed away the tears which brightened her eyes.

The first issue, in December of the same year, carried a full account of Dr Price's discourse, preached the previous month at a meeting-house in Old Jewry, in praise of the glorious French Revolution. Charlotte reported the event with wholehearted fervour, and yet in such an easy and loquacious style that it seemed she was talking to her readers.

It was a fortuitous beginning for a swaggering, passionate, and honestly indignant courier such as *The Northern Correspondent*, and its subscribers grew steadily as the journal hammered away. Price's sermon drew forth a stinging attack upon the revolutionaries by Edmund Burke, in the House of Commons, three months later; to be followed by the publication of his thesis, *Reflections on the Revolution in France*. Both factions were up in arms. At Upper Marylebone Street, the reformer Tom Paine was busy composing his measured answer to Burke. But long before his *Rights of Man* could be published, Mary Wollstonecraft rushed in with *A Vindication of the Rights of Men*, which Joseph Johnson printed sheet by sheet as she wrote it. Hers was the first refutation, and captured the public fancy. A second edition, early in 1791, carried her name upon it.

Charlotte, wearing paper cuffs to protect her sleeves from ink, was writing a note to her that first bitter winter of the '90s, and waiting for Toby to come back from France—whither Ralph Fairbarrow had sent him, as foreign correspondent.

So y^r Name is now Illustrious, and I Rejoice for you, but Pray do not Forget me Utterly. Tho' I Look Up to you I sh^d Destest y^r Looking Down at me! *The Northern Correspondent* does Well in my Home County of Lancaster, and in Yorkshire also, among those who have both Wealth and Insight into the Evil of our present Society, and those Strugglers after Truth—less Fortunate in the Worldly Sense, but with the Wit and Courage to think for themselves, and the Desire that their Children may Live in a country where Liberty, Equality and the Brotherhood of Man may Prevail. . . .

A small rough hand put down a cup of tea on her writing-table. Charlotte acknowledged the attention with an abstract glance, which Polly Slack received as thanks.

I shall send this Letter by Personal Messenger, since they tell me that Government Agents are Watching the Mail. Folk are linking y^r Name with that of Tom Paine, but I am Sad that Mr Jordan published his book instead of our Friend, Mr Johnson. Take Care of y^{r}self. If They can bring such Pressures to Bear upon J.J. then They will not Hesitate to Muffle Others, and tho' I Like You very well—you was never Discreet! It is close on Midnight and I have not yet Done. Farewell, Amazon: y^r Friend, Lottie.

She reached out for the cup, and sipped while she read through the proofs Davy had just delivered from downstairs. The candles were flickering in their sconces as she drank tea and made her corrections. She initialled the leading article Y.L.C. and snuffed their flames with a pinch of the fingers.

Jack Ackroyd, son of a Millbridge weaver, adopted son of Henry Tucker the late headmaster of Millbridge Grammar School, graduate of Cambridge University, and present headmaster of the same Millbridge academy picked up his copy of *The Northern Correspondent* in March 1792 and began to read Charlotte's monthly letter.

. . . and after a Supper of bread, cheese and porter, these nine Honest Men lit their pipes and Discussd the subject of Parliamentary Reform. History will Remember this winter night at The Bell Tavern in Exeter Street, for the Occasion was the First Meeting of the London Corresponding Society, whose Purpose is to Communicate with Groups of people such as themselves Throughout the Realm, and thus Little by Little to Build a Mass of Opinion which shall Topple the present System. The Founder and Secretary, Mr Thomas Hardy, is a shoemaker, who dresses Plainly and speaks Frankly. The Shoemakers are Prominent in Revolutions! But the Society Welcomes all those who seek Reform. Whether Artisans or Labourers, Professional Men or Small Masters, Dissenting Clergy or Soldiers and Sailors, they Belong to the Brotherhood of Man and claim the Rights of Man. The weekly Subscription is One Penny—a Humble sum to make a New World. The First Intention is that Every Adult Person, unless He is Mad or a Perpetrator of Crimes, should be able to Vote for a Member of Parliament. And the Membership of the Society is—UNLIMITED:——Y.L.C.

> School House,
> The Grammar School,
> Millbridge,
> Lancashire
> 7 March 1792

Dear Madam,
I have long been an Admirer of y^r Journal, both for its Aims and its Achievements, and to my Astonishment I now discover that Y.L.C.—Y^r London Correspondent?—is None Other than the former Miss Charlotte Howarth, whom I Knew as a Learned young lady Teacher at the Misses Whitehead's so-called Academy. You Graced that Ridiculous Establishment in a Manner w^h both Amused and Moved me, and I sh^d have liked to know you Better, but I was never a Parlour Gentleman and so Millbridge ladies Seldom received me. But I do not mean to Run on merely in a Social Vein. I mean

118

to Pick a Bone with you. In y^r latest issue you Cry up this London Corresponding Society as tho' it were the First of its Kind, whereas Sheffield, Derby and (not Least) Manchester have already formed such Radical Organisations. Pray remember y^r Loyalties, Y.L.C., for you come from the County of Lancaster y^rself and are writing to Lancastrians—and Those across the Border! London is very Fine, but it is not the Only School of Ideas. Furthermore, I Wager that Radical London is something like its River, a Fluid Mass, while here the Radicals form round Centres of Industry, thus making a Heart of Belief rather than a Head of Opinion! Yet do not think I Decry you or the Society, for I wish Both of you Very well. Y^r Humble Servant, Madam. Jack Ackroyd.

> Longe & Son,
> Printers, Publishers & Booksellers,
> No. 3 Lock-yard,
> off Fleet Street,
> London

14 March 1792

Sir,

I Remember you as an Alarming Person, tho' I do not Doubt I sh^d now find you Less so, for my life has led me into a Very Different Sphere from that w^h I knew Formerly. In one Respect you have not Changed, sir, for you Still declare War upon the Slightest Pretext! Tho' I Cried Up the London Corresponding Society with Fervour, in not One instance did I *say* it was the First of its Kind, nor ever Hinted at such an Untruth. The Reason my Husband, Mr Tobias Longe, Directed *The Northern Correspondent* at Lancashire and Yorkshire in particular was Because these places were foremost in Radical Thought and Action.

Having said my Piece, sir, may I condole with you upon the Death of y^r Benefactor, Mr Henry Tucker, last year? He w^h have been greatly Heartened by the Choice of his Successor, and the Grammar School is Fortunate in you.

There is great acclaim for the Second part of *Rights of Man* by Mr Thomas Paine, w^h we think even Finer than the first part. Sh^d you Require a copy we shall be

Pleased to send one. I also Suggest that you study its Female Counterpart by my Friend, Miss Mary Wollstonecraft. When she had done Writing her *Vindication of the Rights of Men* I asked her, 'What shall you do next?' She has Answered me with *A Vindication of the Rights of Women* and we can Supply you with a Copy of this too, if you Wish.

We grow Wiser, I believe, as we grow Older, but oft our Wisdom is Ingrained in us. Tho' Ignorant of my Mission at the time, I did Endeavour to Amend the puerile Education of young girls at the Misses Whitehead's Academy! Y^{rs}, Charlotte Longe.

ELEVEN

Bitter Winter

London, January—March 1793
That morning Charlotte had to break the ice in her water-jug before she could wash, and sat over her work breathing on her fingers to uncramp them. A little fire struggled to make an impression on the chilly room. Last night, with Toby still away in France, she had brought both children into the high bed, and the cat joined them all. Now Ambrose and Cicely were downstairs with Polly Slack, sitting upon tall stools like islands in a sea of soap-suds, while Polly scrubbed the flagstoned floor. In the printing shop Davy carried on their shrinking trade, and waited for Charlotte's editorial. *The Northern Correspondent* was in troubled waters, politically speaking, and the Longes had once again fallen on hard times.

What a year 1792 had been, with only the alleviation of Miss Wilde's legacy to Charlotte: tied up so that the capital could not be realised. This was a double blessing, for had the gift been a lump sum it would have become another of Toby's lost causes. Whereas Mr Hurst invested it wisely and sent the interest direct to Charlotte on the first day of every month. This, and her salary as editor, kept their domestic side running, while Toby's business was supposed to pay for extras and overhead costs. He became evasive whenever she enquired about his financial affairs, so until recently she had been forced to comfort herself by remembering that she could earn a living. But the ominous tidings from France, and the increasing fear of an English revolution, had driven King George III to condemn all radical meetings and writings as treason, and *The Northern Correspondent* was in danger of extinction.

Since May of last year they had printed and distributed it under cover, and for the main part it was read under cover too. Many a Lancashire free-thinking gentleman concealed his copy beneath the papers on his desk, as the artisans hid theirs inside their jackets. But what precautions the Longes could take were flimsy in the extreme, considering how many government agents were infiltrating societies and watching suspected Radicals. Possibly the journal was less important than they themselves believed, but it could only be a matter of time before it was harvested. So Charlotte lived from day to day, from hand to mouth, and Toby had been absent for three weeks now, without so much as a letter to plead for him.

She was half expecting Ralph Fairbarrow that afternoon, for in these days of severe political crisis he had become almost a regular visitor, though she would not have called him a close friend. He did not appear to have wife, child or home. When he was in London he stayed at an inn. His northern addresses changed constantly. He was care of anybody with whom he was engaged at the time. And though he often supped with them at Lock-yard, and Toby's hospitality was open-handed, he was never drunk or talkative over his wine. He remained curiously anonymous, so that if Charlotte had been asked to describe him she would have chosen subdued adjectives. His image retreated even as she strove to imprison it in words. Only his aims and beliefs brought him to life, and then he was possessed of a cool violence far more frightening, and more credible, than Toby's wildest flights of rhetoric. In this she was afraid of him, but on the whole they understood each other pretty well. She was adept at dealing with difficult and clever men. She had learned patience and perseverance in a hard school. And they both took great pride in *The Northern Correspondent* and thought it the finest radical newspaper in existence.

This bitter winter's day she struggled with her editorial in vain, her spirit chilled by the weather and the latest news from France. Just now, as the dull light waned, she had written to her mother to ask if Mr Hurst could forward her allowance a little earlier than usual. As she read the letter through again Polly Slack came in with the candles.

'And Mr Furbelow's downstairs, ma'am,' she said, with a lowly servant's usual disregard for names, 'a-talking to the children, and would like a word with you. If convenient.'

He knew that her convenience was of no account, but preserved a punctilious regard for the proprieties he was endeavouring to overthrow. His brief conversation with the children, too, was another mark of convention. They had nothing to say to each other, but he persevered in a wooden manner, convinced that this was the correct thing to do: aware also that he was addressing the future citizens of a radical age, whose minds needed improving.

'Pray tell Mr Fairbarrow that I shall be glad to see him,' Charlotte replied, 'and fetch us some tea presently, will you, Polly?'

'There's only potatoes for supper, ma'am,' Polly observed, more in interest than dismay, for though she toiled willingly she relied upon Charlotte to give orders and take responsibility.

Obedient to the hidden request, her mistress searched pockets and drawers and finally looked into the empty cash-box in hope that something had filled it.

'Then potatoes we have, Polly,' she said finally.

'Yes, ma'am. I can bake them, and put a bit of salt in them.'

'You are very good, Polly. I should be lost without you.'

The girl was now twenty but seemed far younger, though her backwardness had become forwardness in this benignly careless household. She had been Charlotte's mainstay for seven long years; and the children loved her, for she was a child with them, and yet an adult who could tell stories and cook simple meals.

'I'll fetch the tea, ma'am,' said Polly, 'and put the potatoes in the ashes. We ain't got no more coals, neither,' looking at the sad grate.

'I shall attend to that tomorrow,' said Charlotte, with more confidence than she felt. 'Please to show Mr Fairbarrow up, Polly.'

He was dressed in the same snuff-coloured suit, wore the same dingy linen, as always. His long sallow face was pierced by a pair of slate-blue eyes. He bowed, and his hair slunk forward with the movement, and retreated as he straightened. He carried a black felt tricorne hat which he brushed with the cuff of his coat as he waited for her to speak.

'Why, Mr Fairbarrow,' cried Charlotte, hoping he might advance her something, 'you are the very person I need, for I have laboured all day over my newsletter, and a sorry spectacle it is, both in mood and content, since I heard that King Louis was guillotined Monday last.'

'Aye,' said Ralph Fairbarrow, parting his shabby coat-tails as though contact with a chair would damage them, 'our Citizen Capet has lost his head for the last time!'

'You cannot be glad of this?' cried Charlotte, though even the September massacres had left him unmoved, and they quarrelled over the policy of the journal in consequence.

'No, not glad,' said Fairbarrow deliberately. 'Sorry that the French have done their cause and the radical movement such a disservice.'

'We should denounce these actions in the name of humanity. We should have done so in the autumn, when priests and prisoners were murdered in Paris.'

'Oh, Burke will do that for us. And the puling King and government. Your friend, Miss Wollstonecraft, left us quite cheerfully for France, last month. And Toby preferred to find out for himself, rather than listen to hearsay.'

'Mary was too wretched to stay in London,' said Charlotte, on a lower note.

'Aye, you women must always muddle love and politics, and nourish high-flown notions about both. I care not tuppence for Citizen Capet or his wife. They are on the losing side, that is all, and too dangerous to keep alive. . . .'

'But their degradation, their humiliation. . . .'

'Mrs Longe,' said Fairbarrow, hard and cold, 'you must learn the rules of this game if you would play well. We are speaking of power, not good manners. We may see similar acts of violence over here before many months have passed. The north of England is like a tinder-keg that needs but a spark set to it. The Secretary for War did not send a Deputy Adjutant-General to Sheffield for nothing, last summer. The King did not issue a royal proclamation against seditious meetings and writings for nothing. The government has not banished Tom Paine and taken proceedings against his publisher for nothing. Mobs are not being incited to burn his effigy in the streets for nothing. And you, Mrs Longe'—fixing his eyes upon her—'are not encouraging a workers' revolution for nothing!'

'I am not a child,' cried Charlotte, 'that thinks its rights are toys. I know as well as you that there must be turmoil and adversity for us all before we establish a better system in our country. And I know, too, that in our own case we risk imprisonment by continuing to publish *The Northern Correspondent* secretly, and to distribute it secretly. And if Toby and I are gone, and the press seized,' she added, faltering at the notion, 'what shall become of our poor children?' Then she straightened and spoke resolutely. 'But if I thought that our movement would, in its turn, refuse justice and mercy in the name of liberty and equality, and set up a scaffold in Leicester Fields to butcher their brothers in the name of fraternity, then, Mr Fairbarrow, I should know that we had worked in vain.'

'Why, Mrs Longe,' he said, holding up one hand to ward off her anger, 'you are far warmer than this room! I do not commend the guillotine as a salve for all our ills. But we must not switch sides in a moment because a section of the revolutionaries are—perhaps—misusing their authority.'

She said, not knowing what to think, 'I shall not change sides, sir. I am no weathercock.'

'In any case,' he said peaceably, 'I did not come to cross swords with my friends, Mrs Longe. Tell me, have you no news of Toby?'

She was confounded, realising that subconsciously she had hoped Fairbarrow brought tidings of him.

'Then where the devil is he?' said Fairbarrow, half to himself, uneasy.

'I know not. I have heard nothing since he went. Sir,' said Charlotte, desperate, 'is it not possible to have an advance upon my salary? The newsletter shall be ready tomorrow, and the rest of the material is here for you to read before it goes to press.'

'Have you no money at all, Mrs Longe?' he asked abruptly.

'Not one penny in the house, sir. No food but potatoes, and no more coals. I have borrowed all I can, and pawned what I can. I have wrote to my mother only this afternoon, to ask for an advance upon my allowance. And Toby is not here to think of some other way. And I am at my wits' end with worry and hunger and cold!'

And here she put her head into her two stained hands and sobbed aloud.

Awkward in such a situation as this, Ralph Fairbarrow first rang the bell, and then, finding it did not work, shouted down the stairs for Polly.

'Here, Mrs Longe,' he said, placating her, laying down a guinea upon the little table by her elbow, 'cheer up, devil take it. You are not alone in the world. You have good friends yet, ma'am.'

His dry embarrassment brough her round, where sympathy would have prostrated her. She dried her eyes and cheeks, dried her fingers, begged his pardon, sitting very upright in her chair to show she was in full command of herself again.

'Set that tea down, Polly!' said Ralph Fairbarrow, as the maid came in with the tray. 'Now, Mrs Longe, should Polly not run out and buy something from the pastrycook's, and some coals? I'll sup a dish of tea and leave presently, when you are better.'

Charlotte nodded, red-eyed, and Polly whisked the guinea into her pocket, unconcerned.

'That's a good girl,' said Fairbarrow to the servant. 'Be off with you, and take care of your mistress!'

Charlotte said, turning the conversation to less personal matters. 'They say that two hundred thousand copies of Tom Paine's sixpenny pamphlet have been sold so far, and there is not a cutler in Sheffield without his *Rights of Man*.'

'Should I pour tea?' asked Fairbarrow, very kindly for him. 'Rest yourself a while, Mrs Longe. By God, this room is cold! Here, ma'am, drink this and warm yourself.'

'I believe,' said Charlotte, keeping her mind upon safer topics than Toby and his absence, 'that our country will have a different revolution from the one in France. The French are a choleric nation.'

'They think us a brutal one!'

'Perhaps,' Charlotte continued hopefully, 'what the Fall of the Bastille was to the French, Tom Paine's pamphlet will be to us. I know I seek to change the cast of thought rather than to cut off the head of the thinker.'

He was careful not to arouse her sensibilities again, and perceptive enough to see that she needed to keep her mind occupied. So they roamed peacefully over the growth of corresponding societies and their vastly increasing membership, the demonstrations in the North and the variety of craftsmen, tradesmen and labourers involved, and the sterling qualities of *The Northern Correspondent*. When Polly returned, Ralph Fairbarrow stood up and took his leave.

'I shall be in London a while,' he said, 'and, with your permission, will look in from time to time. As soon as one of us has news of Toby let him or her contact the other. I shall be staying at The Bell Savage in Ludgate Hill.'

'Thank you,' Charlotte said, holding out her hand. 'Thank you, sir.'

He gave the hand an abrupt little shake, and followed the maid down the stairs. She was grateful to him, and glad he had gone. Soon Polly would stoke up the fire and bring her something hot to eat. Then, warmed and fed, she could return to her writing with confidence, and might, sometime in the early hours of the morning, find herself so caught up in the future of mankind that she could forget her own future, which seemed bleak.

A week later, France declared war upon Great Britain, and Toby was still missing.

They came late one night, Ralph Fairbarrow and the stranger, when Polly and the children were long abed. Charlotte knew, even as she held the flickering candle high to see their faces, that the news was bad, but lighted them up the stairs with a still composure reminiscent of her mother. Either they were in a hurry to be done, or found the room colder than they could wish, but they stood uncomfortably in their great-coats, holding their hats, and looking anywhere but at her. Then Fairbarrow fetched a bottle of brandy from his baggy pocket and asked where she kept the glasses.

Very pale, Charlotte motioned them to sit, then she mended the small fire and rubbed her hands to warm them: a tall, fine-boned woman, hair garnered carelessly into an ashen knot, wrapped in an old brown velvet pelisse trimmed with grey fur.

'You'd better have this,' said Ralph Fairbarrow, putting a glass beside her. He said abruptly, 'It was an accident, Mrs Longe. Toby died by accident. In the streets of Paris.'

The young man now lifted his head and glanced at her. There was a guilty air about him, as though he felt the message should have been given by him, and not so baldly. She sat, face averted, and sipped the brandy.

'How did Toby . . . ?' she began, and could not finish.

'You tell her,' said Ralph Fairbarrow. 'You were there, damn it. I was not.'

The unknown was a man of some gentility, most probably a convert like herself, immersed in his own traditions and fighting nobly to overthrow them.

'Forgive me for bringing such news as this, Mrs Longe,' he said courteously, 'I wish to God I could have fetched him back again.'

'Get on with it, man. We are not concerned with your fine feelings!' cried Fairbarrow.

'It wasn't safe, you know, the streets weren't safe, those last days. Toby and I met, by arrangement'—here he glanced at Ralph Fairbarrow—'and we liked each other, madam.'

She looked at his bright young face and white linen, saw that his enthusiasm would break through, his ideas beckon him ever forward, despite the onslaught of life.

'Yes,' said Charlotte quietly, 'I imagine you did, sir. Pray go on.'

'We saw Capet executed. He died with dignity. Aye, poor stupid fellow, with more dignity than he had lived. And, oh God, the people there. As if the streets were running with rats. Such faces and such voices. The sense of evil, the feeling of being watched. Nay, not a feeling but a fact. Everyone watches, and is watched. Fear your enemies, for they can denounce you, have you tried and guillotined, within the week, within the day, as fast as they can fill and empty the tumbrils. I took care not to seem conspicuous. The cleanly are not well regarded over there, just now, nor are the English. But Toby took not a ha-porth of notice. He stood out among that filth and they misliked it. Everywhere we went there would be eyes, peering from under a dirty mat of hair. Sometimes they threw things at him, sometimes called "Aristo!" for all that he wore the cockade, talked and believed in the revolution.

'Then—oh, all shouting and running feet, I know not what, some fellow escaping capture or being captured. I pulled Toby into a doorway. Saw his face change. Before God, Mrs Longe, it was so quick he could not have felt the bullet. Sagged against me. And I held him. Stared at him. Cursed them, Mrs Longe. Cursed the damned lot of them. And then the questions, and the difficulty over papers, the lack of money. The English community over there paid up and saw him decently buried. I've written down the name of the cemetery. Brought his few things. Poor Toby. God damn them all, he was a fine gentleman. A brave gentleman. We are all the less because Toby's gone. Forgive me for bringing news such as this, madam.'

'Drink up,' said Fairbarrow roughly, and took a gulp of spirit to encourage them both.

With the stilted kindness of that other day, recently, he then asked if he could rouse Polly Slack to attend her. Charlotte shook her head, stunned.

'When you're feeling more yourself,' said Fairbarrow, 'we must think what is to be done about you. I shall help you as best I can, of course.'

'If you would give me a day,' said Charlotte stiffly, 'just a day, Mr Fairbarrow. And then I should be grateful for any suggestion you could make that was practical. For what we shall do I cannot think.'

He laid another guinea, as unobtrusively as he could, on the table by her glass, and coughed to indicate his departure. But the young man, whose name she never knew, lifted her cold hand and kissed it and bowed low.

'Put that down there,' said Fairbarrow softly, and a packet was set next to the guinea. 'We are going now, Mrs Longe.'

'But will she be. . .?' she heard the young man say anxiously.

'Yes, sir,' Charlotte answered him, 'I shall be well enough, I thank you. I should prefer to be alone. A day's grace, if you please, Mr Fairbarrow.'

The clock ticked quietly in the corner. She sat silently, gazing into the fire. After a time she stirred a little, and picked up what was left of Toby's worldly goods. His watch, which she would keep for Ambrose. A purse, containing a few French coins of no great value, which she would give to Cicely. His papers in a leather folding-case: passport, notebook, and a letter of some age, much-read and fragile. She opened it, wondering, and recognised her own young hand and mind in the words.

'*. . . I do not charge you with being Mean and Paltry, sir, but you were not Compassionate enough to Shield me from Misfortune. . . .*'

Then Charlotte bowed her head and covered her face, and wept for her husband.

Even grief, it seemed, was a luxury. Within forty-eight hours Toby's death brought his creditors about her ears. She wrung payments from a few debtors, and sat up at nights calculating how she could maintain the business. Ralph Fairbarrow did what he could, but his help finally amounted to finding a purchaser for Longe & Son. Two gentlemen drove a bargain which left Charlotte and her children with the clothes they possessed, and no home. So she took the only course left to her, and wrote to Kit's Hill, asking if Dorcas and Ned would care for Ambrose and Cicely while she found work and lodgings, until such time as she could support all three of them.

Post-haste came the finest and tenderest of letters from her mother, enclosing a banknote to pay the coach fares to Millbridge and provide immediate necessities, urging Charlotte to keep her small family together.

> . . . for they who have lost a Father sh^d not lose their Mother also. I Comprehend and Admire y^r determination to Support y^rselves, but this you c^d do in Millbridge. Thornton House is but a Hospital these days, with Sally caring for Agnes—who is Ailing—and y^r Aunt Phoebe—who is Rapidly Ageing. They are Provided for, why sh^d not You be also? You have y^r own Allowance, and can Earn a Little by means of y^r Pen—perhaps y^r Friends in London will put Work in y^r Way! You was always Fond of Millbridge, and Thornton House will Come Alive again when the Children are there, and you have many Friends here. Think, too, that you will not be Over-strained and the Little Ones will Benefit from this. A Tranquil Mother makes a Tranquil Family. But sh^d you Decide to stay in London then y^r Father and I will Care for Ambrose and Cicely as we once cared for You and William. Take y^r Time, my Dearest Child, to make up y^r Mind. We Grieve with and For You in what can be the Greatest Loss of all— that of a Dear Husband and Friend. Indeed, I Weep as I Write. God Bless you All from our Hearts. Y^r Loving Mamma.

The decision cost Charlotte another night's sleep. Time was short. The next day she wrote back, assenting.

There had been many callers at Lock-yard, and Charlotte was moved and amazed that they came with love and admiration for her, as well as compassion. She had assumed that everyone adored or deplored Toby, but took her for granted. Now a personal regard was made manifest which both humbled and strengthened her. On this last evening, when Ambrose and Cicely were abed, came Ralph Fairbarrow at his own request to discuss the final arrangements for *The Northern Correspondent.*

He arrived punctiliously upon the stroke of ten, bringing a

bottle of claret with him and some sweetmeats for the children. As always, he was lost where human relationships were concerned, and his thoughtfulness embarrassed rather than touched Charlotte, though she thanked him kindly. He had, in his way, been good to her. Now he sat with his feet upon the fender, and watched her mull the claret with a sort of dreary gaiety, as if they were celebrating a friendship rather than mourning a friend. She was very quiet, keeping her despair to herself.

'Now, Mrs Longe,' he began, as they sipped the claret in a ghastly essay at companionship, 'we grieve over Toby, certainly, but life must go on, and I believe you will find that matters have turned out very well in the end.'

She deplored his choice of words, and his ineptness, but knew him too well by this time to feel offended.

'I have not been entirely frank with you,' said Ralph Fairbarrow, musing over the flames. For, as this was the last night, Charlotte was burning coals as she had never done in Lock-yard.

'Indeed, sir?' she asked, since some comment was expected.

'Yes, ma'am, but I am about to confide in you, and I must ask you not to reveal this confidence whatever your choice might be.'

Now he was his true self: that curiously cold yet passionate being, who could see what was best for mankind, and yet be unable to communicate with a single member of it.

'You may be assured, sir, that I shall not speak to anyone, now or in the future, of this matter.'

He inclined his head, in thanks, in acceptance. Then took a swig of claret, and looked so lonely and disagreeable in his dingy linen that she wished he was anywhere but with her. There was about him an untouchable quality. He was unlovable. She was sorry for him on that account.

'Mrs Longe, I represent far more than myself. What that may be it is better you should not know, lest at any time you are questioned, but you may be assured that it is more than a vehement radical with some money to indulge his convictions. Your husband worked for me, and so have you worked for me, and I should like that work to go on. Am I understood, ma'am?' In her turn, she inclined her head. 'The revolution in this country may not take the extreme form of that in France, but it has begun, and it has begun in the North. Until its objects are realised, Mrs Longe, I shall foster that revolution by every means within my power. I should like you to

130

be with me in this endeavour, but the personal cost will be high, so you must know what you are undertaking. Allow me to outline the situation as I see it.

'We are now at war with France, and many a Radical will turn his coat in consequence, and many another for safety. The success of Tom Paine's pamphlets, and the fear of insurrection, will make the government redouble its efforts to crush a radical movement over here. English Jacobins will have a lean and dangerous time of it, and as they grow more powerful they will be treated more roughly. Our societies must go underground, our literature must be written anonymously and distributed privately. Because the punishment for discovery will be imprisonment, transportation or death. Do you follow me, Mrs Longe?'

'I understand very well, sir,' said Charlotte.

'Very good, ma'am. Now whether poor Toby had died or no, *The Northern Correspondent* must have finished. We dare not continue from this shop, even if we could. But his death—tragic though it was—has opened up a new prospect for you, and possibly for us. Toby took responsibility for the paper though you were its chief scribe and I its financier. Therefore, to all outward purposes, the *Correspondent* was Toby's venture, and he was long known to be a fanatical radical. So, Toby dies, and the newspaper dies with him. His wife is left penniless and disappears up north to live with her relatives. Therefore the journal, and its publisher, and its editor, are rendered null and void. Harmless. Exploded fireworks. You follow me, Mrs Longe?'

'I begin to perceive your intention, sir.'

'But, ma'am, what have we now in our revolutionary hand of cards? An experienced editor, a gifted pamphleteer, a convinced Radical with excellent connections, in the form of Mrs Charlotte Longe! And where is she by chance to be placed, but in the very centre of our activities?'

'You are asking me to spy for you, sir?' Incredulously.

'No, ma'am. I am asking you to act as an organiser of the growing movement in Wyndendale Valley and around, to work in conjunction with one of our central agents there, and to preserve an unimpeachable facade.'

Charlotte thrust the poker into the heart of the fire, and mulled some more claret. She had forgotten everything that troubled her in contemplation of this new proposal.

'Think now,' said Ralph Fairbarrow, accepting another

glass, 'of all that entails. If you are caught you will be hanged, no doubt of it! What of your children then?'

Charlotte said, through cold lips, 'My mother would have them.'

'Point one,' said Fairbarrow, marking if off on his fingers. 'Point two. You will lead a life of deception, and you have a very nice mind, Mrs Longe. You must become two people: one of them the loving mother and daughter and niece and so forth, the other. . . .'

'*The Northern Correspondent*,' said Charlotte, not without a certain doleful humour.

'Aye, very good, very good. But this will be the harder part for you, so consider it well, this point two. Then, point three, although you must lead a social life you must not become entangled emotionally—do you understand me? It is of no use coming to me in a year or so, with a blushing confession that you have fallen in love with the Mayor of Millbridge—or some such *réactionnaire*—and would like to tender your resignation. You will hold too many lives in your head and hand for that sort of indulgence, Mrs Longe.'

'Of that you need have no fear, sir,' said Charlotte bleakly. 'I shall not marry again. I have no mind for marriage.'

'Well, you speak now out of grief, and so forth. But you are young yet, and a woman. Women can never distinguish between head and heart.'

'This woman can,' said Charlotte quietly, 'though you must take her word for it. I promise you that this is the easiest condition you have asked of me so far. Are there others?'

'You must not confide your position or your beliefs to anyone outside this agent, or his fellows. Moreover, Mrs Longe, you must seem to suffer a conversion. This will be the more credible because of your sex, which is notably fickle in its opinions. You come to Millbridge shocked and chastened. In any event, you are not pleased with the state of affairs in France, so that should not be too hard for you? Then, gradually, your views become less extreme. I should think it unwise, in a woman of your intelligence, to revert to Toryism, but a moderate stance will appear to suit your new condition in life.'

'So I cannot teach my children what I believe to be good?'

'They above all must remain innocent, ma'am, for out of their mouths can you be proved guilty!'

She wrapped the shabby brown pelisse more closely round her, imagining that betrayal.

'Mind, I do not expect you to decide in a moment,' he said, emptying his glass and standing up. 'You may let me know in a month or two, when you have settled in. For once you put a foot upon this road there is no turning back, Mrs Longe, and no one can promise you what lies at the end of it.'

'Oh, come,' she answered drily, 'no one can promise anything. That lies in a higher province than our own, Mr Fairbarrow!'

'Ah! I am an atheist. I would not know about that, Mrs Longe!'

She followed him down the stairs. The house sounded hollow, cleaned and swept out, ready for the new occupants. In the hallway stood a very little luggage. Outside, the rusting sign of Longe & Son, Printers, Publishers & Booksellers had been removed. Another name swung in its place upon oiled hinges. And now Ralph Fairbarrow shook hands in silence. They had said all that was needful. Charlotte lingered on the threshold, listening to the sound of his boots on the cobbles until they died away.

The city was not yet ready to sleep. Time and again it had kept her company at this hour of the night. She could hear a fragment of song, the shout of a reveller, the cry of a watchman, hooves and wheels. In one corner of the narrow court a whore plied her trade, regardless of the bitter weather. A window was flung up into the night, a name called into the darkness. No answer.

'Toby,' said Charlotte to herself.

He had left her, as though he had never been. And all that was once his had gone with him. Shop and house and friends, even London itself, were no longer any part of her. At daybreak she would leave almost as she came here, with a few personal possessions. Almost as she came, since two young lives now travelled with her, depended upon her and in the background Ralph Fairbarrow waited for his answer.

It had been such a winter as this when Toby Longe first met her, and she sought a greater freedom than Millbridge could afford. The belief pierced her, as she stood shivering upon the doorstep, that she would never be free, that every flight was followed by retribution. Her eyes, glazing with tears, saw Polly's forgotten broom against the wall as the symbol of a dark tale.

'Why, they have swept our lives away!' she thought. In her pain.

Part Two

Man of Iron
1793—1800

TWELVE

Thunderstorm

Summer 1793

William had a knack of seeing the quality in a person and choosing him in a highly flattering manner, so that the man belonged to him, as it were. Jim Cartwright, the foreman, was such a one, and a handful of skilled workers could be reckoned in with him. But William would have more than that. Ideally he wanted his labourers, too, to be first-rate: like navvies, who were accounted the strongest and bravest workers in the country, and had even dazzled folk abroad with their achievements. Mind you, a navvy must eat and drink well and prodigiously to keep up his strength, and therefore be paid higher wages. Nevertheless, William hired a gang of them for excavation and hoped they would set an example to the rest.

Millbridge had a long memory, and old tales of the navvies who dug the branch canal back in '74 still percolated through the valley. So no one would lodge them, and William had to build a large hut on the Belbrook site, where they slept and cooked and ate in rough comfort six days of the week. But on Saturday night and Sunday they would dress up and roam Wyndendale in search of amusement: their white felt hats stuck jauntily on one side of their heads, their plush waistcoats gleaming like rubies, bright kerchiefs tied round their bull necks. The lower taverns put up with their roistering for the sake of their custom, but among the people they were greatly feared, and with some reason, for their reputation was violent. There were incidents whispered, concerning women of low morals, who thought to earn easy money and had nearly been put out of business in consequence, since the navvies would pass one woman between them all night. Drunkenness, fighting and swearing were commonplace. But every Monday morning they would be back at work: sober, silent and industrious.

Caleb deplored them from the beginning, but William

thought them a wonderful acquisition. They had a style of their own, and he liked that.

Their ganger was a man called Ignatius Riordan. William's shoulders grazed the doorposts of the men's living quarters, and he had to duck his head to get inside the hut. But Riordan's shoulders would have fetched the doorposts with them, and he could have beheaded himself entirely had he stood upright and walked straight through.

On what bog had he been bred, this mighty child of nature? By what mountain was he fathered? Unlettered, inarticulate, he did not know his age let alone the day of his birth. His hair was the colour of his temper, his blue eyes unfathomable. He had a charisma of sorts. He could lift greater weights, drink more heavily, swear more obscenely, and whore longer than any of his gang, and they worshipped him.

Now the need to make money being pressing, William and Caleb had decided to open the Foundry as soon as the upper furnace could be used, and to carry on building the lower furnace and fill out the rest of the architect's plan at the same time. This would be hectic and require considerable organisation, but both partners felt it could be done. And William used his imagination, making each completed building, each machine installation, an occasion for mild celebrating. Thus it was free ale all round when the steam-engines arrived from Boulton and Watt: free ale when the first load of coal was hauled up the inclined plane: and promise of a roasted ox when the furnace was lighted.

'Thee should not bribe them, William,' said Caleb reproachfully.

'This is not bribery but encouragement, my friend.'

'Aye, but thy gifts and promises make them reckless. Accidents are too frequent for my liking.'

'See to the payments then, Caleb, according to our welfare scheme. So much for maiming. So much for death. That is only fair.'

'My dear Will,' said the Quaker, with a hint of reproach, 'this morning a workman fell from the scaffold, and hath left a wife and six young children to face the world without him. Money cannot recompense them.'

'The men are not forced to take risks.'

Caleb shrugged his shoulders, unhappy, unconvinced. But the work went on. They toiled like the beasts they used. Their efforts were herculean, but the results of their labours dwarfed them, threw the men into shadow.

No longer part of a rural landscape, Belbrook now bore the ponderous burden and sombre housing of a foundry. Its workers hazarded their lives and limbs daily, hourly. Cumbrous wagons tilted tons of spoil into new hills. Iron barrows teetered heavy loads up narrow planks. Iron cranes swung massive weights. They could be crushed like beetles, toppled to oblivion. Flesh and bones were fragile things in such a place. This monster they created could overwhelm them in an instant, in the weakest of its workings and the least of its parts. It towered above them, fell away beneath them, yawned to receive them, threatened them on the earth, in the air, with water. Soon they would add the final element of fire, and only the dominion of mind could hold all this in check and make it serve them.

William stood outside the completed furnace with Caleb. His navvies and labourers, in a vast half-circle, joined them in contemplation. This house of sacrificial fire had been enlarged to produce an appropriate quantity of pig iron, and was perhaps fifty feet high: flanked by gigantic bellows. The area around it was walled against the pressure of water from behind. Sheds housed the bellows and the sand pig bed, and to one side the great waterwheel was poised in its pit.

All was prepared. Boys ready to wheel barrows of coke from the coke heaps on the right of the dam, to carry baskets of fuel and lime and iron-ore and pour them into the circular mouth. The sluice-gate waited to be opened. The ox roasted.

Caleb nodded in silent satisfaction, smiled on the assembly and stood back. But William stepped across the forehearth and into the belly of the empty furnace, and lifted his face to the little hole of sky far above, and looked and looked as though he would imprint every brick upon his mind. And to his side, without the least embarrassment, came Ignatius Riordan, saying nothing, simply looking as William did at this colossal artefact.

After a minute or so master and man turned to regard one another, again without need of explanation or apology. And William said, 'This is good.' And Ignatius said nothing. But in the depths of his eyes he answered William, and the meaning was the same.

Then the spell lifted. Ignatius ducked his head under the arch and came out to join his gang. William gave the order to begin work, and Caleb walked back to the office to deal with the day's requirements.

As evening approached, William's family converged upon Belbrook to see the furnace fired, and a number of well-wishers and time-servers also joined the crowd. Word had spread throughout the valley that Wyndendale's first ironworks was about to go into production. The smell of roast beef was perhaps an even greater attraction.

'Now it will make a vast noise, Mamma,' said William, taking Dorcas's arm, 'so be prepared for it. There is nothing to be afraid of. It is all sound and fury, merely signifying—in the long run—pig iron!'

She laughed and clasped his hand, so proud of him in this first moment of glory, wearing her new bonnet.

Dick Howarth, a raw young man of eighteen, spoke little and smiled shyly: not quite at his ease in this iron realm, being used to green fields. While Charlotte talked animatedly to Caleb, and her children looked solemn and held fast to her skirt.

'Is everybody ready?' William cried.

'By Gow,' said Ned Howarth, staring up and around him. 'Tha's getten a right hell's kitchen here, our Will!'

Now the firer came forward with stately tread, bearing his beacon, and approached the waiting altar. Now the audience was hushed, and also waiting. The working shift hovered: ready to begin their twelve-hour vigil before they were relieved the following day.

'Of course,' said William to Dorcas, in defence, 'this is but an ordinary type of furnace. The ones we are building lower down will be three in number, and powered by a pair of steam-engines. But it does well enough. For a start.'

She could not have been more impressed.

'It is a question of chain reaction,' William murmured. 'Water runs, wheel turns, bellows blow, fire brightens. . . .'

The torch was thrust into the kindling.

. . . and so the Works was opened and I took out my Watch to observe both Minute and Hour of Belbrook Foundry's birth. Then to the Ox, w^h Caleb and I carved so Poorly that my Father took over in our Stead. And all the while a steady Roaring in our Ears, as tho' we were under Cannon Fire, and Blasts of air w^h Sounded like the Compound Shriek of Poor Souls in Purgatory. But, sweetest Zelah, my Heart beat every Moment in thought of Thee, for now I have Asked thy Father if we can be Engaged. And I shall marry Thee as soon as Possible, and Pray that it be Tomorrow, dearest Love. . . .

Old Caleb walked out of the library with William's letter in his hand, and Zelah let fall her own into her lap at the sight of his face.

Th ironmaster had suffered a double blow, being deceived by two persons close to him, and Quaker though he was he could not be called a forgiving man. Like one of the ancient prophets he stood now, and his daughter rose trembling before him with her love-letter tumbled to the carpet, while his wife did not know whom to comfort or for what.

'Zelah, thou hast betrayed me, and all thy family, and a man who did not deserve aught but honour and fair dealing from thee. As for William Howarth, who hath crept like a serpent among us, and now expects to be rewarded for his treachery, let his head be bruised by my heel as the Scripture sayeth. . . .'

'Caleb,' said Catherine, understanding everything. 'My love. Caleb.'

And she came to him at once, warding off his wrath, beseeching Zelah to be silent. Caleb Scholes held his tongue with difficulty, mastered himself, turned on the heel which was to bruise William's head, and left the room. Catherine followed him. Alone, Zelah picked up her letter, but could not read the words. So sat there, waiting for her mother's return, and all the sun had gone from that summer day.

It was characteristic of Catherine Scholes that she dealt with what was uppermost, and did not trouble herself with details of what was past. This and this must be done, therefore she did it. Why and wherefore would be revealed in time, but that was not her province. So she returned in half an hour, not smiling, and certainly concerned, but calm.

'There will be no engagement, child, nor thought of one,' she said, kissing Zelah's cold cheek. 'But thy father sees now that young folk will be young, aye, and loving even when they should not. So do not speak to him again of this matter. He will write to William. And if he seem strange and silent with thee in the next few days—bear with him, for he loves thee. And if thou must weep, daughter, then save thy tears for me.'

The year's frail castle had crumbled in moments. Disbelieving, Zelah held out William's letter that her mother might understand, but Catherine motioned it gently away.

'Thou hast no love for George Horsefield, so that is over,' she continued, 'but the other may not be. Though I have a concern and care for William he hath done wrong in courting thee, and double wrong in courting thee behind our backs and swearing thee to silence. Thy father will have none of him. Do not hope, for hope can only make thy heart sore.'

Then Zelah comprehended the enormity of her offence and of her father's retribution, and began to shake. She could not stop herself. Her teeth chattered as though she were cast out into a winter landscape. Catherine held her close and spoke soothingly, smoothed her hair and kissed her cheeks, rubbed her hands. Still the girl shook, and could not form the words she needed to say, and she drew air in gasps, staring ahead of her with wide and frightened eyes. So they put her to bed with a copper warming-pan for company, and burned feathers under her nose, and poured drops of brandy down her throat, in an effort to revive her. Caleb sat in his library like the God of Wrath, and would not spare his child's suffering because it made him, too, suffer.

William turned over the coin which he carried as a talisman. On one side sailed a small brigantine, possibly commemorating the launching of Wilkinson's first iron ship in 1787, though it bore no resemblance to that vessel. On the other side a homely middle-aged gentleman in a curled and flowing wig presented his profile. Round this bust ran the legend JOHN WILKINSON IRON MASTER.

'We must mint our own coins,' said William, thinking aloud.

It was a secret regret within him that they could not inscribe them with WILLIAM HOWARTH IRON MASTER around a portrait of himself, but must use the name and picture of the Foundry, and something in the nature of clasped hands as a symbol of partnership.

'Let us earn the value of the coins first, my friend,' said Caleb, and though he smiled he intended to rein in the wilder of William's fancies.

'Oh, I was but remarking,' said William, halted by the smile, 'that since industrial wages are well in excess of national coinage we should do as others do, and make our own tokens.'

'Aye, and drive a four-in-hand as Ironmaster Crayshaw doth, and have folk running out from here to London to watch us pass!'

'Nay, none of that!' cried William, laughing, but he flushed up just the same, for he had dreamed all of that and more besides.

'We should have been born earlier,' Caleb went on, determined to root out this worldly pride, 'and then King Louis of France could have invited us both to Paris, as he did Boulton and Watt. And perhaps, hearing of our fame, Queen Catherine of Russia might visit England and stay with us in our country retreat. Though I imagine she would find the smithy at Flawnes Green somewhat crowded!'

But here he put his arm about William's shoulders, for he saw he had wounded him; and began to lead him towards the office, where their dinners awaited them in pudding basins.

'You mock me, Caleb, but I believe in us and in Belbrook. I do not picture myself cutting a fine figure at Court, but I confess to more practical day-dreams, it is true.'

'Then tell me thy practical fantasies, Will, for I would indeed hear those!'

They walked on, close as brothers.

'Well,' said William, laughing at himself again, 'I think how Josiah Wedgwood walks through his workshops every day, and breaks every imperfect pot he sees. And how he writes in chalk, upon the benches of careless workmen, *This won't do for Josiah Wedgwood!* For I love that in the man. He lives like a gentleman and toils like a slave. And I would do likewise.'

He looked for approval, but Caleb grinned and made one observation.

'Thee would have some difficulty in breaking an iron bar!'

Then they laughed, and pretended to spar, and cuffed each other's head, and raced each other to their wooden office: boys rather than ironmasters.

Caleb's letter was waiting for them, addressed to them both, written to them both, and he thrashed them both in spirit. He wielded words as if they had been swords, cutting his offenders down with accusations of treachery, hypocrisy and dishonesty. He referred only once to the triumph of the firing ceremony, and that at the end of the letter in a postscript.

'*So thou hast begun work at the Foundry? Then get thee about thy Business, for there is Much to be Done*'.

They could not eat their dinners that day, but worked on in silence.

143

Even the weather was oppressive. From being very wet it had turned very hot, and the Foundry was not the best of places to work in such conditions. The men glistened with sweat as they laboured in their various crafts and trades. Tempers were short and appetites poor. The greatest need was for water, and at dinner-time many of them preferred to plunge into the dirty river rather than sit at its bank and eat their hunk of bread and bacon. Ignatius Riordan and his navvies toiled on, unmoved by such frivolities. Naked to the waist, every giant worked smoothly and silently, raising his ten tons of soil a day, filling his seven wagons. And the men in the casting house laughed at the lot of them, for the stoves in there were heating to the boiling point of mercury, and they said that they only came out into the molten sun for a breath of fresh cool air.

Heavy of heart and spirit, William and Caleb mingled with their labour force at every level. The silence from Somer Court was complete. No word, even from Catherine, who usually acted as mediator in these times. At Kit's Hill there had been some sympathy, but William felt it was for the unknown Zelah rather than their son. And though Ned Howarth had not the temperament of old Caleb, he managed to compress a marked disapproval of the whole affair into one comment.

'Why the hell not come out wi' it at the first? Instead of taking his money and courting his daughter on the sly!'

Charlotte and Dorcas were concerned lest Belbrook suffer, but Caleb Scholes was too fair-minded to vent his rage upon their business as well as themselves.

And Charlotte said curiously, 'How did you come to act as messenger, Caleb? You must have known what trouble that would cause?'

Whereat young Caleb said unhappily, 'Well, I love Zelah and I love William, and they love each other. And who else could they have asked to go between them?'

'We pray your sister do not break her heart,' said Dorcas at last.

Therefore they worked in leaden duty. The sun poured down, the cupola fires blazed up, the cranes carried their ladles of incandescent iron, the liquid metal ran in tongues of fire into the sand pig bed. From the bellows house came the eternal roar, the god-like drawing of breath, the hissing cry. Into the mouth of this underworld the boys emptied their baskets of fuel, seeming like insects on the top of the furnace.

And above the works hung great dark clouds of choking vapour, for there was no wind to drive them away.

The tension increased, as though the atmosphere were a balloon blown to capacity, its skin about to burst. With aching heads and smarting eyes men found fault with one another, were abusive, savage. Then Ignatius Riordan thrust up his shaggy head to the heavens and shouted, 'Rain, will you? You. . . ,' followed by such a stream of profanity that they feared to see God look out upon them, and damn their souls to all eternity.

The sky grew livid, startling. The light was thick and bright and dense, as though filtered through a metal screen. Then a pair of cosmic scissors ripped across the tight silk, followed immediately by a thunderclap so loud that it drowned the noise of the ironworks.

'You roused Him, Riordan!' one man cried, and there was an uneasy ripple of laughter.

The sky drew in upon itself in a great scowl and then exploded again.

'It is directly overhead,' said Caleb.

The massed black clouds were illuminated suddenly, beautifully, fearfully. God's drums rolled from end to end of the valley.

'They've a bigger works up there!' said William, grinning.

He had always enjoyed thunderstorms. They seemed to him to come from some pagan forge. He thought of the Grecian gods, and of lame Vulcan. He and Ned had viewed such holocausts from the heights of Garth Fells when he was a boy. But Dorcas and Charlotte used to sit on the stairs with the house cat, afraid.

Now the rain came in fat warm drops, and they could hear the spitting of the coal-hearths, where forty-ton fires transformed coal into coke. The rain ran, it poured, it roared like a river. And overhead the sky cracked and lit and cracked again. Ignatius considered the result of his oaths for a few more minutes, and then, seeing that further work would be hopeless, he threw his spade into a heap of earth and strode towards the big hut. The other labourers followed his example.

William and Caleb had been about to ride back to Flawnes Green for supper, but they stayed now, feeling a need to watch over the ironworks, though there was nothing anyone could or should do. The evening shift of men tramped up the road, sodden with rain, and changed places with the tired shift which had marched in that morning. The storm raged and abated, raged again.

'There's nowt we can do, Mr Howarth,' said Jim Cartwright, 'and it's all running right and running to time. A storm's a storm, sir. We canna stop it, nor mend it. I should go home if I was you.'

So when it was ebbing to a growl they mounted their horses and trotted back. But not to rest or to sleep. All night they lay awake, listening to the rain beating on the roof of the smithy. And when they rose next morning the valley drooped beneath a weight of water, and the river ran high up the bank and lipped the wharf, heavy and swollen, bearing upon its swift current small wreckages which spoke of other places along its course.

Caleb Scholes, the ironmaster, stood by Zelah's bed and looked upon the work of his will. She had lain there a week, at first unspeaking and then feverish. It was as though all her strength had gone into the waiting. Now there was nothing to wait for she left the world: went somewhere else, to a place no one could follow her. Catherine had stayed with her night and day, relieved by maids only that she might rest herself for an hour or two. Finally, she had gone into her husband's room and brought him back with her to the bedside.

'It is his fault,' cried Caleb. 'It is William Howarth's fault.'

Zelah stared past and through him. They had remarked that she was quiet when anyone other than Catherine was there.

'Well, then,' said Catherine, 'it is his fault. But what shall thee do about it?'

He looked at his wife and scowled. He walked away. Catherine sat by the bed and wrung out a cloth in clean water, and smoothed it on her daughter's forehead. Presently, sensing that they were by themselves, Zelah began to ramble on again. And Catherine cried silently, and watched by her.

On the second night of the rain William pushed his supper to one side and reached for his coat.

'I shall go back to Belbrook,' he announced.

'What concerns thee so much?' asked Caleb, concerned himself.

'The dam,' said William.

'It could not be safer,' said Caleb, endeavouring to calm

146

him. 'Thee knows that better than I. Thou wast there when they rebuilt it. What, then?'

'A feeling,' said William. 'A feeling that something is wrong.'

'Then I shall come with thee, when I have ate my supper. So thee must eat with me, William. If thee need thy strength thee must eat.'

So, sensibly, he prevailed upon his partner, and they finished supper together in a quieter state of mind. Then set forth in the dank green twilight.

The new excavations were awash with water. Water was swilling soil down to the wharf, leaching the earth from under the rails on the inclined plane. Steam rose in clouds as dense as smoke where heat met moisture. But against the downpour Belbrook thrust up its mighty towers, and lit the sky with its own eerie fires, and thundered back at heaven with its incessant roar. And in its midst, stripped to the waist, its slaves ministered to it, and fed its fires and received the molten iron and transformed it into humble utensils.

'So much for so little,' said William to himself. 'We should be casting cannon. The mountain brings forth a mouse else.'

For he had been studying drawings of Wilkinson's boring-drills, and felt himself more in sympathy with ordnance than pots and pans. But the Quakers had financed him, and he was but a cog in his own machine as yet.

'Besides, I have done them harm enough,' he murmured, thinking of Zelah.

They mounted the side of the hill, threading their way through this fiery town until they reached its upper slopes. There they stood, as they had done not long since, before the old furnace.

'Everything all right, Lem?' William asked the night foreman.

'Everything's grand—except t'weather, Mr Howarth.'

'No more explosions in the moulding rooms?'

'Nay. There were but one or two, and nobody was hurt. Just covered wi' dust. Th'air hadn't enough discharge, and didna take fire until t'mould were filled. It's common enough, Mr Howarth, at first. We've getten it sorted, now.'

'Come,' said William to Caleb, still uneasy, and they mounted to the top of the furnace which was filled, as usual, with its toiling human ants.

The vast black stretch of water in the upper furnace pool seemed tranquil, in spite of the rain that pitted its velvet sur-

147

face. Yet William could not rest. He sensed a mindless evil somewhere, and descended in no better spirits than he had come up. And to him, out of the gathering dark, came Ignatius Riordan, hands in pockets.

He was dressed shabbily as usual, in his working clothes, but his bearing seemed resplendent in the pelting night.

'What now, Riordan?' William asked, 'What do you do here, man?'

The heavy face could have been hewn from granite.

'Somethin', sor,' said Riordan. 'Somethin' wrong.'

They understood each other.

'Yes,' said William. 'I'm worried about the dam,'

Riordan walked past him then, up to the dam wall, and inspected it minutely and at length. Shook his dirty felt hat from side to side, and returned to his master.

'I'm going to tell the men to get out while this downpour lasts,' said William, on an impulse.

'But what about the iron?' Caleb asked.

'I want them out,' William repeated. 'Go back, Caleb. Go to the hut and wait for me.'

'My men,' said Riordan slowly.

He meant that their hut was in the line of water, should the dam go.

'I'll send everyone out,' said Caleb, suddenly convinced, but of what he could not say, and he ran off, shouting orders.

'You, Riordan,' William said peremptorily, 'go with him.'

But the Irishman shook his head. He had helped to build Belbrook. It was his responsibility too, or that is how he saw it. They stared at each other: master and man both adamant, both leaders.

The workers were moving, quickly but in an orderly fashion, out of their shops and down to the road, headed by Caleb and the foreman. One of them alerted the navvies, and they joined the throng to the iron gates.

'We shall look pretty foolish,' said William grimly, 'if it's for nothing.'

But Riordan said, 'No, sor.'

In the immediate flare of cupola fire he was illuminated, and in the light of that same flare he looked and shouted and pointed to the dark trickle in the dam wall.

'Dear God,' cried William, cold in spite of the heat. 'Run, man. Run!'

And he set off pell-mell down the hillside. While the

workforce, hearing him shout and seeing him run, themselves began running and shouting.

The trickle was stronger, making a little bulge in the wall as though a tongue were stuck into the side of a cheek. The bricks were swivelling outwards as though on pivots. The wall bulged like a lower lip, like a giant pout.

William could not forbear looking over his shoulder as he ran, and then saw that the Irishman had not followed him.

He had taken charge of that wall and it was letting him down, making a fool of Ignatius Riordan. And beyond the wall was a blind force in the dark which had always been against him: something he had fought, dumbly, obstinately, uncomprehendingly, all his days. He had known he could not win, but he would not be beaten either. It could overcome him, but he would not yield. It must take him on his own terms. So, for a few moments, he attempted to stop up the trickle with his great body, and hold the wall. And as he exerted the might of his muscle he swore defiant oaths out of the night of his soul, and against the weight of black water.

Now it was Belbrook's turn to give a cosmic firework show. From the far side of the river William and Caleb and their cohorts had a ringside seat, as the pool dam flooded the furnace, and the furnace blew up. Situated as it was, almost in the centre of the valley, that explosion blasted the ears and widened the eyes of all Wyndendale. Old ladies in bed woke with a start and screamed for the constable. Card-players dropped good and bad hands alike, and forgot them after. Horses panicked in stalls. Women near their time went into premature labour. Men ran and shouted and swore. Even work in the cotton mills stopped until they had ascertained what was afoot. And yet only one was killed.

No woman would come near the navvies' living quarters, so they washed him and laid him out themselves; and someone sponged his best clothes and dried them and brushed them, until they were as good as new; and dressed him in them, top hat and all.

William paid for his funeral, and commissioned Joe Burscough of Garth to make him an oak coffin, and Joe said it was the biggest coffin he had ever fashioned. Then they asked a priest to bury him, supposing that he had been born into the Catholic faith, but as he had never been near the church or proved his faith in any way, none would do it. Nor did any holy place want Ignatius Riordan lowered into its sacred soil. So in the end they buried him in a corner of Belbrook,

149

near the river, and William and Caleb said a few words over him. And navvies came from all over the valley, and formed into an orderly procession without being warned or told, and marched behind his coffin, linking hands. As a mark of respect they had tied black handkerchiefs about their bull necks, and wore their Sunday clothes.

'. . . receive thy child, O Lord,' Caleb prayed, 'and be merciful to him. The light that thou kindled in him was small, and he could not make it bright.'

He spoke with supreme compassion, and Riordan's mates gave him credit for his feelings, but it was William who reached their hearts.

'O Lord,' William prayed, 'Thou knowest this man better than we, for thee fashioned such a one in Samson: strong and fearless and yet blinded by lust. Yet in his captivity was his freedom found, and in his blindness his greatest strength, and his last moments were his mightiest. Therefore, Lord, redeem his spirit. For if it serve Thee as his body hath served us, then hast Thou a great and goodly steward in Thy heavenly mansions.'

And they cried 'Amen! to that.

Caleb the ironmaster had not been established in The Royal George for above half an hour when he called for a horse, and made his way down to Belbrook despite a night and a day travelling. The two young men were working with their labourers on the site, clearing debris, and there was no fear left in them when they greeted him. They had reached a limit of suffering. He could inflict no more, whatever he did. But he had not come, upon the heels of their letter, to add to their tribulations. His handshake was warm and firm. His smile kindly. His unshaven cheeks bore witness to his concern.

'The Lord hath laid His Hand somewhat heavily upon thee both,' said old Caleb. 'Take me round, and let me see, my sons.'

His eyes approved what had been, saw that what was could be fast mended. The dam had only been breached at one point. Shattered windows were the worst affliction in the workshops. The furnace itself had taken the full force of the explosion and must be rebuilt.

'A month or two, my masters,' said Caleb, much relieved. 'I bring thee greetings from thy shareholders, much sympathy, and the promise of money where and when thee need it most. This is but a step backwards. We shall stride forth again, and all the stronger for it. Where dost thee live?' Abruptly. 'William, I know thee well enough to say that thou hast not spared thyself, therefore will my son spare thee for an hour. I will see Flawnes Green on my way back. Wilt thou accompany me there?'

His manner had not altered in the slightest, but neither of them knew whether William was to be praised or chastised. So old and young ironmaster set forth on the Black Road, and Caleb talked pleasantly of his journey and the speed of the Royal Mail. In the same fashion he looked round the smithy, shook hands with an awed Stephen, and gave the two apprentices some sound advice. Then made his way through the living quarters, tickled the sow's back with his riding whip, was interested in Hannah's oven and grate, and finally turned face to face, and spoke sternly.

'My daughter cannot live here, William," he said, as though that had been in question. 'Thee must find her a suitable house. Not like to Somer Court. We do not expect so much at first. Catherine and I began small and ended great. Until then thee may consider thyself affianced to Zelah.'

He set his hat more firmly upon his head, strode through the smithy and mounted his horse. Dazed, incredulous at the swings of fortune, William followed him, but could find nothing to say. The ironmaster looked benevolently down at his future son-in-law.

'When thou hast re-fired the furnace,' he said, 'we expect thee at Somer Court. Ah, and thee must bring Caleb tonight to dine at the inn. Tomorrow I go home again.'

'Tomorrow, sir?' said William, roused to speech.

'Aye, tomorrow, William,' the ironmaster replied testily. 'There is work to be done, my son!'

And rode away as though there were not a moment to spare.

Father and daughter sat together under the tree on the lawn that September. Summer, in dying, had given forth one of those lovely days when light and warmth and freshness mingle, reminders of past glory. They were content in this and in each other. Zelah's thinness, the care with which Caleb adjusted her shawl, her cropped hair under the muslin cap, were signs of convalescence. But William was expected hourly, and her animation threatened to outdo her strength.

'Thou hast had thy way,' said Caleb, without rancour, 'but

before thee embark upon marriage thee should see William for what he is. Mark me, child!' He pointed his forefinger. 'I shall show him to thee, and then thee may answer for him.'

'I do not fear it,' said Zelah, though she gathered her shawl closer.

'He is of the earth,' said the ironmaster. 'His faith is in himself, not in his Maker. He is honourable, but only so far as it shall serve him. He loves, but with fire and passion. We do not know how constant, nor how continent he may be. Yet brother Bartholomew thought highly of his parents, and that is a goodly thing in William. For our parents—though thee may not think it, Zelah!—watch over us alway, and oft guide us even after their deaths. So, thy future husband is brave, fearless, ambitious, industrious, and will rise high in the world's view. Is this enough for thee, daughter?'

Her face was troubled. She looked inwardly upon her love.

'Well then, doth he not need me?' she asked. 'For my faith is rooted in Almighty God, my love is given once and shall be honoured by me until death, and is this not my part?'

'He gives thee crude ore, and thee transforms it into gold?' Caleb said ironically.

'Nay, father,' she cried, with her old humour, 'I am no al-chemist. Let the iron be transformed into a cooking pot, and I shall do well enough!'

'I shall go and find thy mother,' said Caleb, rising. 'For I fear that she too, like all good women, was given a lump of ore for a husband. And, in the manner of good women, hath made me more than I was, and thinks me more than I am. Thou hast chastened me, daughter!'

She laughed then, and lay back in her long chair, at peace with herself and life, and dozed a little in the late afternoon. So William found her, and sat at her feet tracing the marks of their trial upon her unconscious face. She had a way of holding her lips, a sharpness of bonework, a hollowing of eyes, that had not been there before. Above all, the cropping of her, dark-gold hair hurt him most. He put out his fingers tenderly, to touch the tendrils which escaped her muslin cap, and the movement woke her.

Zelah and William, at the beginning. Zelah and William.

THIRTEEN

Chiming Clocks and
Silent Rooms

Autumn 1794

Charlotte had now been twenty months at Thornton House, arriving as a bereaved young widow with two dependants, followed by Polly Slack and the cat on a slower stage-coach: servant and animal both surviving a prolonged journey in a hard winter. At first there were difficulties with Sally, the buxom young housekeeper. In her two-and-twentieth year, the girl was becoming an amiable despot with her two elderly charges, and did not welcome even Charlotte as a new mistress. She suspected Polly of attempting to usurp her position, said that the cat got underfoot, and that the children made a deal of work and cooking. There were a number of small scenes, much tossing of the head, and finally an interview with Dorcas; during which that cool and experienced lady suggested that Sally came as assistant housekeeper at Kit's Hill, and lived in her parents' cottage at Garth.

On the following morning Sally personally made Charlotte's chocolate and lingered at the bedroom door, remarking on the likeness between young Ambrose and his father, remembering what a pleasant gentleman Mr Toby was, and recalling high moments of that Christmas in 1783 when he first illuminated their lives. From then it was only a matter of minutes before she and Charlotte picked up the threads of their girlhood; discussed the goodness and simplicity of Polly Slack, her lack of ambition and her capacity for hard work; set Thornton House in order, with every member in her right place; and forgot their differences.

This first disruption over, the house returned to its former tranquillity and Charlotte became young again. She woke early in the morning, rising with her servants and working in her room until the children needed her for their lessons. She went last to bed at night, loving the hours when she could recharge herself, as it were: walking the silent rooms, hands clasped before her and head slightly bent in contemplation: sitting at her writing-table in the front window, looking out at the quiet High Street or the lights on the fells. As before, the clocks marked the passing of each day: time for dinner, for the afternoon calls or the afternoon walk, for tea-drinking and conversation, a musical evening, supper and bed. Her angularity of body and spirit melted under these gentle, steady auspices. She smiled more frequently, laughed on occasion, lost the cough she had acquired in smoke-laden London, took an interest in her dress, received gentlemanly callers, and for a while became the family centre in Millbridge.

On Sundays she attended St Mark's Church and listened to the Reverend Robert Graham, whose views were diametrically opposed to those of her late husband. His congregation, well-dressed and prosperous, flocked to hear him denounce the enemies of the King, the French Revolution and General Unrest. His sermons upon 'That place to which it hath pleased God to Call us', and 'The Poor are always with Us' were considered particularly fine, and came out regularly in different guises. He was exceedingly popular, and though he might lack the elegance of his predecessor, Walter Jarrett, he was innocent of that ironic humour which had often disturbed Millbridge in Jarrett's heyday. Though poor Phoebe Jarrett, withered virgin, always whispered in church to Charlotte, 'He has not Papa's eloquence, I fear!' and wiped her eyes in fond remembrance, forgetting how often she had been a victim of her father's wit.

Then there was a delight in taking up pianoforte playing once again, and of teaching little Cicely, who early showed a surprising talent for music. The pleasure of receiving Mr Hurst, who delivered her allowance in person once a month, and came round every Friday evening to drink tea and ask how she did, with occasional talk of her investments. The piquancy of knowing that Dr Standish's partner and nephew, Dr Hamish Standish, did not call so frequently just to enquire as to the state of her lungs and her children's health; but sat hemming and hawing while he sought a way to captivate her attention. The slightly disquieting knowledge that William's partner, Caleb Scholes, was far fonder of Charlotte than she of him, and must not be hurt. So that Ned, who called on market days, chaffed her about being the most sought-after widow in Millbridge. Dorcas was inclined to favour Caleb above the other suitors; but had a fondness for Mr Hurst because he had looked after all their interests so well with the late Miss Wilde; and a partiality for Hamish Standish on account of Dr Standish who had, in his dry way, been good to them.

In the third month of her stay at Thornton House Charlotte wrote circumspectly to Ralph Fairbarrow, and said she believed she would not be able to accept his offer of work. She proffered many excuses: the constant attendance of Aunt Phoebe, which allowed her no privacy, the demands of her family, the needs of her children. The truth was that she did not want to be absorbed again into that difficult, exciting, dangerous world she had once inhabited with Toby. Fairbarrow replied simply that if she changed her mind she should contact him again. Then all communication between them ceased.

There existed a tacit agreement among family and friends to say nothing of Charlotte's past. Her former outrageous beliefs, her suspected part in a weekly journal which even the rector described as 'that damned radical rag!' belonged to yesterday. They were too relieved to have her safely back again to stir up old differences, and too polite to mention them. They felt that she had in some way lost herself in London, influenced by her husband's opinions, but was now restored to her senses and her proper place in life. She had been misled, and saw the error of her ways.

Tuesday had been Callers' Day at Thornton House for longer than anyone could remember, certainly back into the reign of Queen Anne when great-aunt Wilde was a girl. It had remained the best day for Dorcas to call, since her reconciliation of 1772, because she could meet most of her old friends there. And Charlotte continued the practice, or perhaps the practice continued and Charlotte countenanced it. At any rate, the faithful knocked upon the front door between the hours of three and five o'clock, to find Charlotte sitting in readiness, Phoebe Jarrett twittering, and the children summoned to hand round cakes and biscuits.

This day in the November of 1794 was cold, with a rough wind. From the parlour window Charlotte watched her visitors battle their way up the High Street, holding on to their hats, holding down their skirts, and almost taking to the air as great gusts swept by them. Phoebe sat close to the fire in Miss Wilde's old chair. At the age of sixty-four, devoid of her life's tyrants, she was ageing rapidly. One would have thought that a peaceable existence without care or personal responsibility might suit this gentle spinster, but her father's selfish charm and Miss Wilde's unfairness had provided an interest, demanded a response of some sort. No one now asked or needed anything of her, and she had for so long done what other people wanted that she did not know what she needed for herself, and was too submissive to find out. So she harboured grievances.

Ambrose, just nine years old, sat at his mother's escritoire in one corner of the room, scribbling and drawing industriously. His curly brown head was held to one side, observing effects, his legs twined ecstatically round each other, his tongue protruded between his teeth. He was living each moment to the full, in the sheer delight of creation.

On her stool at Phoebe's feet, six-year-old Cicely was embroidering quite an intricate sampler. She had inherited her mother's deceptively sweet expression, and her ash-coloured hair.

Now Dorcas, having refreshed herself with a nap, called the family news into the old housekeeper's deaf ears, made sure that Sally was content and Polly not put upon and the new scullery-maid showing promise, joined the circle. She saw that none of the parlour inmates needed her, and so hooked her spectacles into the thickest part of her grey hair and reached for *The Wyndendale Post,* making but one observation.

'That child,' she said of Cicely, 'besides having my mother's name is the very image of her! And she is adroit with people. Yes, she is very adroit.'

She was adroit with Phoebe certainly; while Ambrose was only polite, and endured the old lady's fulsome compliments and easy tears with some embarrassment. But Cicely understood the child in Phoebe, and would call her up to play companion. Thus, Cicely's talk of sewing had brought forth a faded sampler stitched for the Reverend Walter Jarrett when Phoebe was nine years old; and Phoebe had taught the little girl both simple and complicated stitches, and was making a fine needle-woman of her: a skill which Charlotte conspicuously lacked, Dorcas rarely used, and Polly had never attained.

'Yes, Cicely has leaped three generations,' Charlotte agreed, 'but that young man persists in being exactly like his father! He says he is writing his own newspaper, for ours is such a dull one!'

'Dear Ambrose!' said Phoebe, plucking out her handkerchief. 'Poor Toby!'

Dorcas looked expressively at Charlotte, who shrugged and sighed. Ambrose, observing the exchange, smiled to himself. Then, meeting his mother's gaze, wiped the smile off his face with one hand—which made her lips twitch in spite of herself.

Cicely said, lifting her eyes from her sampler, 'I hear someone at the front door, Aunt Phoebe. Perhaps it is your friend Mrs Graham.'

Of all the callers, the rector's wife was most likely to dry Phoebe's tears and stiffen her resolution, because she had taken Phoebe's place at St Mark's Church, and though she was not to blame for that Phoebe would never forgive her.

'Mrs Graham indeed!' said Phoebe, and became very dignified.

'Do you see what I mean, Charlotte?' said Dorcas, nodding at her grand-daughter, putting away the dull newspaper.

It was not Mrs Graham but the elder Miss Whitehead, who had left her sister in charge of the Young Ladies' Academy that Tuesday, and next Tuesday would stay at home while Miss Frances paid her call. Ambrose had early nicknamed her, 'Miss Oh-Whatter', and been strictly chided by his womenfolk, though Dorcas and Charlotte could not help but be amused every time Miss Mary spoke.

'Oh, what a day, my dears. I am blown to pieces! Oh, what a wind. Mrs Howarth, however did you manage to drive all the way from Garth? Oh, what a week we have had. Two of the young ladies threatening to have putrid throats! How are you keeping, Miss Jarrett? Oh, what a lovely fire. . . .'

She carried apologies from old Dr Standish's newly acquired wife: a rich widow who had won his cold hand by offering to endow a hospital of his creation. Then in walked the self-conscious Mrs and Miss Harbottle, wife and daughter of a cotton-mill manufacturer recently come to the valley, who were courting Millbridge's social circles with timid obstinacy; accompanied by Mrs Pettifer the banker's wife, who was introducing them by reason of Mr Harbottle's bank account. Finally these ladies were followed by Mrs Graham, upon whose entrance Phoebe came to life with a remark about the shabbiness of the old altar-cloth.

The weather, the new cotton-mills, rising prices and the altar-cloth being given due consideration, the visitors came to the nub of that afternoon's call. For Farmer Cotrell,

William's benefactor and *bête noire,* had been found dead in his bed the previous week, and they were all anxious to know how this would affect William's long engagement to Zelah Scholes. Since none of them knew, or would have cared to know, Edmund Cotrell, they endowed him with amiable qualities to fit him as an object of conversation.

'A lonely death, I fear,' sighed Mrs Graham, 'but then he lived a lonely life these many years. A stoical old fellow, and genteely connected in the past I understand. And what a friend he was to William, to be sure. Now, do tell us, Mrs Howarth, shall William leave Flawnes Green and reside at the house in Belbrook in the near future?'

She was so anxious to avoid the words 'smithy' and 'farm' that Dorcas supplied them in her answer, though civilly, so that Mrs Graham's smile lost its sugar but did not leave her face.

'Oh, William certainly intends to live at the farm, and of course his journeyman will now take over the smithy entirely.'

Mrs Pettifer leaned forward with a conspiratorial air, for like all the ladies she had become her husband's shadow, and since her bedfellow was a banker it was naturally presumed that she dealt with the financial side of any discussion.

'But does this not mean that William now has a house suitable to offer his future wife? Refurbished, of course, but then with a patron such as Lord Kersall, and the ironworks already doing well, the house could be made most elegant. Oh yes'—nodding sagely round the little circle—'very elegant indeed!'

As though she had glanced over William's accounts before she came.

'I believe William hopes that his patron the *ironmaster*'—with slight emphasis on this august personage, as opposed to Lord Kersall who was merely an investor—'will consent to the marriage in view of their having a home on the site. I understand that William is shortly visiting Mr Scholes at Somer Court to discuss the matter.'

Charlotte's lips again gave that slight twitch of amusement. So far she had not minded Dorcas presiding over her Tuesday afternoons. It was a relief to find herself part of a respectable *milieu* again. Though she had been somewhat piqued that the headmaster of Millbridge Grammar School had not sought her acquaintance, but kept himself formally polite and at a distance. And yet these sleek cats measuring each other's striking-power were hardly any thinking person's choice of company. Sometimes she wanted to clap her hands smartly together and cry, 'Shoo, puss!' Irony was her only weapon.

Phoebe suddenly said, smoothing her handkerchief upon her knees with trembling fingers, Zelah was very ill. No one considered her feelings. She was like to die last summer, and all because of her father and her lover quarrelling. Oh, William is the handsomest and cleverest man you could wish to meet, but he is absorbed in his work. And Mr Scholes, I dare say, is a good man in his way—though Papa could never abide a Dissenter!—but he has his work for solace. And she, dear Zelah, had no love but William, and nothing to do but think of him, and so was took dangerously ill and they cut off her beautiful hair. . . .'

'Phoebe dear,' said Dorcas quietly, 'we were all very sorry for Zelah, but she is quite well now. And let us not forget that her illness made her father relent and allow the engagement. Much good came out of that.'

'But it is always the woman that suffers,' cried Phoebe, mouth working, 'and until we are about to die they do not consider us.'

The ladies were aghast at this unexpected ugliness, and sought to cover it over.

'There is so much suffering in the world,' said Mrs Graham, in her capacity as surrogate rector, 'it does not bear thinking of. We must be very strong, and have faith.'

'It is a woman's part to love and a man's to work,' Mrs Pettifer suggested. 'We have so much heart.'

'Let us hope that we have heads too, and can use them,' said Dorcas briskly. 'I do not divide the sexes quite so sharply.

Cicely put her sampler into Phoebe's shaking hands saying, 'I fear I have forgot how to do rose-knots, Aunt Phoebe. Could you show me again, if you please?'

Charlotte rang the bell for tea. Ambrose pursed his mouth and applied himself again to his newspaper.

Miss Mary Whitehead said, 'Oh, what a gusty day it is!'

Watching the boughs of trees clash and saw in the wind.

Mrs and Miss Harbottle said nothing, which showed that they knew their place.

'William has asked Charlotte and me to look over the farm-house at Belbrook,' Dorcas said in a lighter tone, 'which has been much neglected all these years. And, in any event, whether or not Mr Scholes allows the marriage to take place earlier than he stated, William and Caleb will be living there. It has been so inconvenient for them to be divided between their work and their lodging these last two years.'

'Ambrose. Cicely. Pass the cakes, if you please,' said Charlotte, as the tea-trays came in, followed closely by a large black tom cat.

He was now grown enormous, unrecognisable as that brave kitten who had fallen into William's top-boot nine years before. His life at Lock-yard and his protracted journey to Millbridge had made him resourceful, and he regularly besieged the parlour when food was part of the entertainment.

'Oh, there is that dear puss,' said Miss Whitehead, who detested animals. 'What is her name?' Though she did not care in the least.

'He has two names,' said Ambrose, proffering a plate. 'We call him Wibs for short, but his real name is William Wilberforce, ma'am.'

'Take the cat out, Polly, if you please,' said Charlotte, scenting trouble, for the Misses Whitehead had once employed a little Negro servant.

'Oh, what a strange name. Why do you call him that? Why do you not call him Blackie or Nigger?'

'He was named by my father, after Mr William Wilberforce, ma'am, who wishes to abolish slavery.' Then some hereditary demon made him add, 'I dare say we *could* have called him Nigger, but would that not suggest that our sympathies were on the wrong side, ma'am?' And before she could answer, 'Pray have a macaroon, ma'am!'

'Ambrose,' said Charlotte, 'take the cat out to the kitchen, and stay with him!'

The cotton manufacturer's wife leaned forward and spoke to Dorcas, while the other ladies exchanged meaningful looks.

'How many rooms are in your son's house at Belbrook, ma'am?' she asked.

'Let me see,' said Dorcas, grateful for the question. 'There must be eight. It is a very pleasing place, symmetrical in its design, and two rooms deep on either side of a passage. The lower floors are flagstoned. The windows are well proportioned. Cleaned and painted and papered it should be charming. . . .'

Polly said to Ambrose in the hall, 'Putting yer blooming foot in it again, Mr Ambrose! Sometimes I think you do it a-purpose.'

'Sometimes,' said Ambrose, with bland brown eyes, 'I do,

Polly. Come on, Wilberforce, back to the kitchen, you old slaver!'

In the front parlour Dorcas was skirting the perilous topic of mixed religions with Mrs Graham.

'Of course, Zelah will join the Church of England when she marries William. The Society of Friends is very strict, and will unhappily—I am thinking of Zelah's background and beliefs when I use the word "unhappily", of course—will expel her from the sect. She is, I understand, deeply religious and has been very torn by this prospect, but now quite come to terms with it.'

'Well, that is a good thing, at least,' said Mrs Graham very stiffly, feeling that the Church of England deserved better than a fallen Quaker.

Emboldened by Dorcas's difficulties, Mrs Pettifer slipped into the fray.

'Why, Miss Scholes must be quite besotted with your son, Mrs Howarth. She will give up her home, religion, her friends, her former betrothed, and her father's goodwill for him. It is very brave! I fear I took the easy way and married Mr Pettifer because we had so much in common!'

Miss Whitehead, guessing this was an oblique reference to Dorcas's own marriage cried, 'Oh, but love is worth the sacrifice!' For she had never been asked to make it.

'Certainly,' said Mrs Graham, 'love is a woman's duty!'

'I did my duty by my dear Papa,' said Phoebe, sipping and thinking. 'They said that the flowers in church was never arranged so well as in my day!'

Mrs Graham, unable to reply to Phoebe, turned upon Charlotte.

'Of course, you were just as brave as Miss Scholes, were you not, my love? For you left all behind you as she will do!'

'What heroines they are!' cried Mrs Pettifer in affected admiration.

'Oh, it is not heroic,' said Charlotte, so quietly that at first they missed the sting. 'We do not marry out of heroism but out of ignorance. The heroism comes after, whether we love or not.'

'Dear Charlotte,' said Miss Whitehead, mercifully bewildered. 'Always so clever.'

The silence was broken by the sound of Dorcas setting her cup upon the saucer with a little click.

'Do you know,' she said, looking out of the window, 'I believe the light begins to fail already. I must go, Charlotte dear, if you will excuse me. No, do not let me break up the party. I live at the end of the valley, not close at hand!'

She began her meticulous round of farewells. The banker's wife studied her watch, the Harbottle ladies stirred obediently, Miss Whitehead murmured something about her sister being afraid of the dark, and Mrs Graham picked up her reticule.

'Goodbye, dearest child,' said Dorcas, kissing Charlotte lightly on her cold cheek, for she saw that her daughter had been wounded and would have liked to soothe her, but did not know how to, and she was angry with everybody except little Cicely and the Harbottles. 'I shall be here next Tuesday, weather permitting, of course.'

'Weather and father permitting!' Charlotte replied, with a ghost of a smile.

'Ah well, if we court these tyrants we must expect tyranny, must we not, Mrs Pettifer?' cried Dorcas smiling, which was unkind, since the banker's temper was unstable and Ned Howarth's known to be particularly mild. 'If they are not charitable with us we must turn the other cheek!' This to Mrs Graham, because the Reverend Robert's charity stopped short at the pulpit and he was known to be mean with money. 'Pray remember me to Miss Frances, Miss Whitehead. Take care, Phoebe dear!' As that sad lady crossed the hall with Cicely in tow, 'Bless you, Charlotte, for putting up with us all!'

'I shall go to my room until it is time for supper,' said Phoebe to herself, but quite distinctly. 'I have done my duty even when it was most onerous. But I could be like to die before they considered me. It was always so.'

Charlotte closed the door behind her visitors and put her forehead against its smooth cold surface for a few moments. From the kitchen came sounds of china being stacked and washed, and the voice of Ambrose entertaining Sally and Polly. They were all right without her for a while. Just for a while she could wonder how far she had retreated from herself in the search for peace, and whether the price of a haven was not too high. She went into the parlour and drew out her footstool. The long clock stood at a twenty minutes to five. Then the brass lion on the front door was knocked peremptorily, twice, thrice. She listened for Polly's steps, but the kitchen must have been in an uproar with Ambrose for no one came. Savagely she pulled the bell, damning all callers.

Polly came running, and shortly appeared before her mistress, saying in utter amazement, 'Mr Awkright, ma'am!'

'Ackroyd, girl. Ackroyd!' said the owner of the name, and walked into the parlour holding out his hand with brusque courtesy.

'Pray come in, Mr Ackroyd,' said Charlotte, not altogether pleased.

'Have I got the day wrong?' he asked, looking at the used cups, crumpled tea-napkins and crumbs. 'I thought you were at home on Tuesdays, Mrs Longe.'

'Oh, I was. I am. We rarely expect gentlemen. Apart from husbands that is. And they are not often at liberty.'

'Ah! But I did not come to trifle, Mrs Longe. I thought it an opportune time to speak of your son's future education. Did I make a mistake as to the hour?'

She concealed a smile, for his presence this particular afternoon would have been more than usually disastrous.

'No, no. You are perfectly correct, Mr Ackroyd. My callers left a little early today, that is all. Pray do sit down, and Polly will fetch fresh tea for us.'

For he was roaming the room, glancing accusingly at the pictures.

'I never grasp these social niceties,' he said loudly, abstractly, standing with his back to her, holding his hat behind him.

Mistress and servant grimaced privately at each other.

'He wouldn't give me his hat, ma'am,' Polly whispered.

'Never mind, Polly. Take these trays away, and see if there are any cakes left.'

A burst of laughter from the kitchen caused Jack Ackroyd to turn his head enquiringly.

'My son Ambrose,' said Charlotte, smiling, 'is a born jester, but this afternoon his wit was out of place, so he stays in the kitchen until supper-time.'

She had decided to treat the visit with polite irony.

'He seems to have found the proper theatre for his talents,' said Jack Ackroyd drily, 'and an appreciative audience. Is that your notion of punishment, Mrs Longe?'

'No, sir. Of restraint,' she replied, daring him to criticise.

She glided past him, motioning to a chair.

'Yet, Mr Ackroyd,' she continued lightly, 'I could have wished you to call earlier, for I believe we touched upon every topic but that of education!'

He looked her fully in the face and said with an irony that

matched her own, 'I am astonished you should say that, since I believe Miss Whitehead was of the party!'

Charlotte accorded him silent respect, but asked, 'And how should you know that, sir? I had not thought you and Miss Whitehead were on calling terms with regard to education!'

He dropped his hat upon her little escritoire, saying, 'Do you work at this pretty toy, Mrs Longe?'

'No sir, it is used for social purposes only. Letter-writing and household accounts. Nothing of importance.'

'For social purposes,' he mused. 'Is there then another writing-table where you can fulfil your anti-social purposes, Mrs Longe?'

Her remembrance of him called forth the image of a wild young man with a menacing gaze, and a habit of saying the right thing at the wrong time and to the wrong people. She was relieved to see that he had mellowed somewhat. His forty years sat kindly upon him, clothing his scarecrow figure with a little more flesh, touching his rough dark hair to distinction, softening his tone and gestures. He now wore a fairly fashionable grey suit which needed brushing, and a clean cravat which was not properly tied. She guessed that he had conformed sufficiently to make himself acceptable for the post of headmaster, but would conduct his work according to his principles. Thus he examined her. An outrageous pedagogue. An unconscious heckler. And she let him advance that she might shoot him down more closely.

'Oh, my professional work is done at my great-grandfather's desk, upstairs in my room,' she answered calmly, 'but these days it could be read by any of my afternoon callers.'

'If they had a mind to read anything serious, which I doubt!' he said, and sat down abruptly.

It annoyed her that she had thought exactly the same thing. But she merely smiled sociably, for now Polly had brought in the tea things, and they were silent until she had gone.

'If I were one of your parlour gentlemen,' said Jack Ackroyd, 'I should say that I was guilty of a mild deception. Since I am not I can tell you plainly that I waited until your visitors had gone before I ventured across the road. But I so far bowed to convention—a deplorable commodity!—as to seem surprised they were not here. That was for the benefit of your servant. And now the proprieties have been observed—deuce take them!—we can talk freely!' Without giving her a chance to comment upon his singular behaviour he said, 'Tell me, are you not very bored in Millbridge, Mrs Longe?'

She took her time, pouring his tea, and asked if it was to his taste.

'I dare say,' he replied, stirring it absently.

He did not repel her as Ralph Fairbarrow had done, but she felt instinctively that he had some power over people and would use it where necessary. So she was wary with him.

'I am glad to lay down my former burdens,' said Charlotte simply, 'not the least of which was a fear of ending my days in prison, either for debt or on account of our politics. You spoke of Ambrose, sir, did you wish to see him? I had not thought of sending him to school as yet.'

'I take it that you would wish to send him to Millbridge Grammar School, madam?'

'I had hoped so, sir.'

'You are very wise. There is no other school as good for sixty miles. So that is settled.'

He seemed to her to have pared away all the inessentials of life in order to concentrate his being upon life itself. His lean body, on which the respectable suit hung like a disregarded costume, was full of vitality. His eyes were intent upon some inner vision. He stirred his tea too long, forgetting what he was doing. The amount of sugar was not important to him. He did not care whether he had cream or lemon. He drank it.

'So they released Thomas Hardy after all,' he said thoughtfully. 'We are not an entirely brutal nation, Mrs Longe. A charge of high treason carries a penalty of death by hanging, disembowelling and quartering. One does not condemn an honest shoemaker to such an end for starting the London Corresponding Society! But what a victory for true justice! After lying about five months in prison, and withstanding the fears and fatigues of a nine-day trial, to be drawn in triumph through the streets of London to the acclaim of the crowd! Why, it was almost worth his sufferings to see such a public affront to the Church and King mob.'

She knew he was trying out her sympathies, and resolved not to yield to his persuasion.

'Was it worth his *wife's* suffering, I wonder?' Charlotte said coolly. 'To see her home ransacked by officers. To lie in bed, helpless and pregnant, while they burst open the bureau and hunted through her linen for evidence of treason? To watch her husband being arrested, to hear the charge and imagine

165

his death over and over again? And then to die in childbirth? Was that also a triumph, Mr Ackroyd, in your opinion?'

He looked up, surprised by her words.

'That is bitterly spoken, Mrs Longe.'

'It is bitterly felt,' Charlotte answered, cold with recollecion.

'At least it was honest,' he remarked, equally coldly. 'I dare say it was the most honest comment you have made since you came here!'

She made up her mind to confront him.

'What do you want with me, Mr Ackroyd? For I am not such a willing debater as will use the late Mrs Hardy for a topic!'

He was not a man who laughed out of enjoyment. Life had been too difficult, and in many ways too puzzling and contradictory. So he laughed short and sharp, admiring the economy of her behaviour.

'I had not thought you could be so direct, Mrs Longe.'

'Then you misjudged me, sir.'

'I shall not do so again,' he replied gravely, and ate his little cake in two bites, and wiped his fingers on his breeches, forgetting the tea-napkin she had laid beside him. 'Mrs Longe, you will recollect Ralph Fairbarrow?' A compression of her lips, a darkening of her eyes, answered him. 'I saw him recently and he asked me to give you a message. I quote his words exactly, lest you think I am being impertinent on my own account. He said, "Tell our northern correspondent she has played long enough with her tea-parties. There is work to be done!"'

So that was what he was after?

Charlotte said coldly, 'I gave Mr Fairbarrow my answer eighteen months ago, and it was final, sir.'

'He seems to have thought you would change your mind, madam.'

'Sir, I shall be very frank with you. All I have suffered since I came to Millbridge are fools, and I grant you they are hard to bear. But I sleep of nights without fear of the bailiff or of government agents. We can eat without wondering where the next meal will come from. Our clothes are warm. We can put coals on the fire, knowing the scuttle may be filled again. These are not small mercies to people who have lived as we did once. Perhaps you would repeat my words to Mr Fairbarrow, sir, as exactly as you can?'

He bowed his head, considering, then spoke in contempt.

'I did indeed misjudge you, Mrs Longe. I had thought you asked more of life than its creature comforts. Man does not live by bread alone, though I know he must eat. But the woman's world is a very small one!'

'You seem to overlook my children, Mr Ackroyd, who must be cared for.'

'Madam, your children cannot take up too much of your time or you would have none for gossiping!' Here he looked scornfully round the pretty parlour.

He had gone far enough. Charlotte spoke with chilling rebuke.

'You have been very free, sir, with your opinions—and those of Mr Fairbarrow—though I did not ask for them. Allow me to expound my own philosophy, which is drawn from close observation and owes more to practice than verbal brilliance. When I first met my husband I adored him, for I had never before heard such eloquence, seen such energy, known such visions. It seemed to me that he was exalted above all other men. Nothing was too trivial for his humane concern. He would argue half the night, travel half the country, write and publish tracts often at his own expense. What money he had was generously bestowed. He was entirely sincere, and without malice even to his enemies. Who could find fault with him?

'But, sir, though he was constantly in attendance upon his ideas he neglected his human responsibilities. His family, who should have come first, came last and least. It was I who saw that they were clothed and fed, that the landlord was paid and the most pressing debtors satisfied. And this is something I have noticed in many men who call upon God or themselves to reform the world. They are so busy with Utopia that they do not mind their proper business. I know very well where mine lies. and I shall concern myself with it despite your opinion. Pray tell your friend to find some meddling *fellow* instead of me!'

She rose and rang the bell with such violence that Polly fairly ran to answer it.

'Mr Ackroyd is going, Polly. Good-day to you, sir. Your hat is on my writing-desk!'

He bowed curtly, without reply. What reply could he have made? He took his leave of her. She watched him striding furiously across the High Street, one loose tail of his cravat whipping behind him in the wind, his hat crammed down upon his head. But the discourse ran on in her mind, and she gripped the curtain thinking of it.

'A woman's world may *seem* a small one, its horizon limited, its details petty, its pace immeasurably slow. But from these little daily tasks comes forth the whole of mankind. Were governments to run their nations half so well as a good woman runs her household we should have no war, no debt, no famine. So do not dismiss our lives out of hand. We know very well what we are about. And if you are intent upon righting the wrongs of the world, sir, then look closer to home and begin there!'

'Told 'im off, 'ave you?' said Polly knowingly, collecting the china. 'Just like old times, Mrs Longe! It does you good to light off now and again, ma'am. You've been a-bottling up ever since we left London.'

She did not expect either a snub or an answer. She had acted too long as friend and spectator to give offence.

'You can have your supper in peace and quiet tonight,' Polly went on. 'The children is having theirs with us, and Miss Jorrocks is properly put out and taking hers in her room!'

'Why, what has put Miss Jarrett out?' cried Charlotte.

'She says as the rector's lady looks down on her, ma'am.'

'Oh, fiddle!' said Charlotte crisply.

She did not mind a bit. She wanted to sit by herself and think over all she and Jack Ackroyd had said to each other, and to discover what had incensed her so much. He had acted, unwittingly, as a touch-paper to the anger pent up inside her. She had been wanting to quarrel with somebody all afternoon, and he had served her purpose very well.

It was true that she found Millbridge empty of excitement or purpose. For now she was thoroughly restored in strength she often recalled old friends and old times in Lock-yard; sometimes dreamed she was back there, but with her present safety and prosperity to soften its harsher outlines. And though she believed every word she had flung at Jack Ackroyd, still she had not told the full truth.

She had delighted in doing battle in a man's world. She enjoyed the company of men, their toughness and simplicity, their direct approach to life. She missed Toby's passionate commitment, his flow of ideas, his ability to make magic out of an evening with two friends over a pie from the cookshop. Even his faults had been fascinating, and he always admired her complementary virtues and had sworn to do better in future. She was sad to think she had used him only in the context of an argument. He was worth more than that. In her heart she asked his pardon, and received it.

Charlotte sat alone and late, lifted the velvet curtain and pondered on the quiet street, walked the silent rooms: listening to the long clock chiming her life away.

FOURTEEN

A Family Wedding

3rd day, 1st month, 20th, 1795

My dear Friend Dorcas Howarth,
For Friend thou hast been to me over these Difficult years, while Our Children strove for their Happiness even against Us who most wished them Joy. I am at last able to take upon me the Sad and Loving Task of writing to thee Concerning their Marriage. The Discipline of our Society being necessarily Strict, my dear Husband cannot Consent to this Union, but he can give his Assent—thus saying that he Loves his Child and w^d let her have her Way, but yet does not Approve it. It is with a Sore heart that I tell thee we cannot Give our Daughter her Wedding, nor sh^d we Attend it, and so I must Beseech you to take our Place in this Matter. Can I ask thee to be such a Mother to our Zelah as you w^d be to y^r own Sweet Child at such a Moment in her life? I fear thou wilt Misunderstand or Mislike us hereafter, but I Pray you do not. I remain thy Sincere Friend. Catherine Scholes.

26 January 1795

My dear Catherine Scholes,
I believe we know each other Well enough, tho' but Good Friends on Paper, not to Mislike aught but the Circumstances in w^h we find ourselves. Nor are we such

169

Bigots as to believe that God may not be Worshipped in Many Ways, and still Bless and Keep us, out of His Mercy. It is with a Full Heart that I accept the Joyful Task of giving Zelah's Wedding, and even to Ponder upon the Mysterious Goodness of God in allowing me a Second Daughter whose Marriage will take place within the Family. For my Charlotte, as you may Recall, was married Secretly, w^h caused Great Grief, tho' now she is Safely Home again. But surely you can Visit y^r Child once she is Settled? For we sh^d all Wish to Meet you and Love you as we Love y^r son Caleb. Please tell Zelah that I shall write again to her Shortly, but the Weather had been so bad that the Apples were Froze in the loft! And Charlotte and I have not been Able to Continue with our Work at Belbrook. Last Week we met there with Two Maids, but the Well was a mask of ice. Perhaps Zelah w^d let me know if she Wishes me to Engage her Servants from Garth? I desire to be of Service to her, but not to Intrude too much upon her Future Life. Y^r Sincere Friend. Dorcas Howarth.

3 February 1795

My dear Zelah,

Tho' we know each other not as yet we shall be Sisters hereafter, and therefore I write to Welcome you into our Family and to tender the Hospitality of Thornton House for the time before y^r Wedding. I am to act as Chaperone when William Calls but you shall not find me an Oppressive one! We thought it good that you and William sh^d have Belbrook Farm to y^rselves for a Week after y^r Marriage, so Caleb has Invited himself back to Flawnes Green and will Work from there. We wondered whether you sh^d be Married at St Mark's Church in Millbridge, and have the Wedding Dinner at Thornton House, but William thought—and we believe him to be Right—that the Simple and Homely Ceremony at St John's in Garth w^d Suit you better. My Mother is Agog with the prospect of a Vast Reception at Kit's Hill, w^h she Swears shall be a Deal more Elegant than her Boisterous Feast of Four-and-Thirty Year ago! Of that, and of Much else, you shall Hear from our own lips. God bless and Keep you, dearest Zelah. Y^r Sister Charlotte.

My dear Dorcas,

We have a Black Frost this morning, with a Cruel Easterly Wind! The poor Birds lie Dead in the park, tho' Zelah hath them Feeding almost from her Hand and Strives to keep all Alive in this Wicked Winter. Dear Friend, I cannot let my Child be Joined with her Husband and we not there to see it. My own dear Husband thinks that if we do not Attend the Ceremony but come to the Wedding Dinner this will be accounted sufficient by the Society of Friends. Let us Pray so, else shall I break my Heart! We sh^d be a Great Party, for I do not Doubt that Mary and her Husband will Join us, and the three Younger Children are Coming, then there will be the Elder Grandchildren. Dear Friend, I shall not Weary thee with a List of them, but if thou wilt Engage the Largest and most Respectable Inn in Millbridge we Promise to Fill it for the Wedding! We shall be Travelling in our own Carriages, and of course we shall be very Circumspect—not thinking to Play the Host or otherwise Disagree in any way with thine own Arrangements. Only, dear Dorcas, may we Visit with thee, then? Thy Friend Catherine.

'Ned!' cried Dorcas triumphantly from the parlour. 'Please to call in at The Royal George and enquire as to the number of rooms. The ironmaster will attend the wedding!'

It was one of the sweetest moments in her life. But now they must consider the date. Usually a marriage took place within the month, but the winter was such a terrible one that even the Prince of Wales's bride was forced to wait on the other side of the Channel, the navy being unable to put to sea on her account. The Scholes family inclined to a summer wedding, considering this a pleasanter season to travel the country.

. . . but, dearest Friend, [Dorcas wrote] we cannot consider it at the Farm, for in June we have the hay harvest—if Harvest there be, after so much Cold and Wet!—and the Sheep-shearing, and the Feeding on both Occasions. In July and August we are greatly Concerned with Crops and Stock, and the Grain harvest and Mell Supper and Lammastide. Indeed, Autumn would be

171

the Best Time but William Chafes so at the delay that I Dare not suggest it! Then, tho' I do not bow to Superstition, there w^d be an Outcry if the wedding was to fall in the month of May, and a Similar Chorus if it were to Take Place during Lent. Betwixt Christian and Pagan Niceties, we are come upon the last week in April when we shall Offend Nobody! But what of the Day? Monday will be Fair Day in Millbridge, and Saturday is Market Day, and both of them in an Uproar. Moreover, you will Wish to be within Reach of a Meeting-house for y^r Sunday Worship, and the nearest I know of is at Rawtenstall, w^h is above Twenty Mile from here. Dear Friend, shall Our Children ever Wed? ...

Lawyers drew up the marriage settlement. Seamstresses sat in hillocks of linen and lawn and cambric, of silk and satin and fine cotton, stitching the trunkfuls of fine clothes which the bride would take with her: a dozen of everything to clad her from morning to night, and the handkerchiefs embroidered with her new initials, and six pair of silk stockings. At Belbrook the farm was re-named Quincey Place, after the original Norman owner. In spite of the cold weather, Dorcas and Charlotte drove themselves on, and their workmen even hoped to finish the outside painting before Easter.

Nellie, housekeeper of Kit's Hill, and her niece Sally in Millbridge were given the bill of fare for the banquet. With wheat at an exorbitant price because of the war, parsley at two shillings the ounce, and everything hard to come by, they worked out amounts and costs for the campaign ahead, called up a troop of minor assistants, and allotted tasks from master to the youngest lad who scared crows. Snares were set for rabbits and hares, geese and ducks and chickens had their necks wrung, hams were cured, an ox set up for roasting, sheep slaughtered. In the dairy, cheeses ripened, butter was stacked. Syllabub would be made fresh in the milking-pails, jellies were set in fanciful moulds, cheesecakes and fruit tarts and custards piled in tiers on the larder shelves. The new icehouse, which stood behind the farm like a giant beehive, was filled from floor to ceiling, and they thanked God for it.

The ironmaster graciously sent up two cases of fine foreign wines. From Kit's Hill cellar came casks of home-brewed beer, strong and mellow. From Thornton House came bottles of home-made wine: damson, elderflower, cowslip and blackberry. But with the wedding list now reaching enormous proportions, and the Scholes's party overflowing The Royal George, Ned arranged for The Woolpack in Garth to remain open from morning to evening of the day at his own expense, so that this giant thirst might be truly slaked.

For four days both households baked bread and stored it. For the whole of one day Sally Sidebottom hand-raised, baked and glazed a tableful of meat pies: each one a work of country art, crowned by a brown shining wreath of pastry fruit and leaves, and wine-jelly poured into the centre-hole by means of a narrow-spouted jug, and left to set.

Garth, always pinched by poverty, now ground by starvation, looked to Kit's Hill for invitations to fill their bellies with food and their mouths with loud rejoicing. Lord Kersall, condescending to wealth and industry, invited himself to a supper-party with the ironmaster at The Royal George the evening before the wedding, and brought with him a most handsome set of silver cutlery, but declined an invitation to the feast. While the ladies of Millbridge, who had been so difficult to please during William's long and curious engagement, were now wholly devoid of criticism in their anxiety to attend the most interesting union Wyndendale had beheld in years.

On the last Wednesday in April 1795 both households were astir by five o'clock in the morning, though the bride stayed abed until seven. Tom the carter took his breakfast of ale and bread and cheese with him, drove the big wagon into Millbridge to collect the last of Sally's contributions, and helped to unload. A host of voluntary servants was busy about the house and barn at Kit's Hill, setting up tables and laying them. Cutlery and china had been borrowed from every farm on the fells. Linen cupboards stood empty. Garlands of flowers hung from ceilings and graced trestles. Wicker baskets stood at intervals by the walls, filled with bread and bottles of wine.

Here was Ned in his best blue suit, looking uncomfortably splendid; and Dorcas in gold brocade with blond lace on her silk hat; and Dick a young edition of his father and twice as uncomfortable, but the handsomest bachelor in Garth; and all the servants in new clothes. Caleb and William had not arrived back until early hours, and were sleeping off the effects of a lavish drinking session. There had been some difficulty over the duty of giving away the bride, since the ironmaster was forbidden to do any such thing, and young,

Caleb was acting as groom's man. But Dorcas suggested Ned, who offered no objection, so that was settled. Indeed, Dorcas thought, looking at their preparations with considerable satisfaction, anything could be settled if one used common sense. Though she had found that sense to be rarer than its name supposed.

'Well, it's no good standing round doing nowt,' said Ned, tapping the long clock in the parlour. 'Let's broach one of them casks of beer and see how it's kept!'

At Thornton House they were all in tears. Catherine had come over to dress her daughter for the wedding, which accounted for her state of emotion. Then William had sent a child's basket of primroses to Zelah, with a lover's note tucked in their heart, which set the bride weeping. Charlotte felt the contrast between this family festival and her own hurried and meagre nuptials, and Phoebe cried because she had never been married at all.

They were saved by the appearance of Ironmaster Scholes, gold time-piece in hand, to announce that the hour was well advanced and they would be late if they did not dry their eyes at once. So the stately progress from Millbridge began, with folks standing on the pavements and peeping from windows, waving handkerchiefs and calling good wishes, as the line of carriages rolled down the High Street promptly on the stroke of nine. First came the great Caleb Scholes, with Catherine and their three youngest children, and the giant bride-cake baked at Somer Court having a seat to itself. Then their married children and elder grand-children, an aunt or two of liberal mind and persuasion, and a sprinkling of close cousins: all soberly but elegantly dressed, plain and expensive as became their state in life.

At Belbrook William and Caleb's chief workmen climbed into Tom's big wagon, while their lesser fellows marched two or three abreast down the road to Garth, to watch the ceremony and hang upon the outskirts of the feast, until plenty itself bade them join in.

Garth was garlanded from steeple to cow-shed, and as the first guests drove into the village they were cheered by a contingent of hopeful children. Gravely bowed the ironmaster, courteous to all, rich or poor. And Joe Eccles the blacksmith, who was to fire the anvil when bride and groom left the church, was so overcome by the grandeur of the occasion

that he let fall his hammer too soon, and the discharge of
gunpowder made the horses start. The Scholeses had been advised to leave their carriages below, since Garth Lane was
never meant for fine transport. Fortunately the weather was
holding, so the entire party mounted by foot to Kit's Hill in
the most splendid crowd imaginable, and all smiling and talking—as Jacob Burscough remarked—'Just like other folk do!'

A little flurry rose in Dorcas's heart as they met, but in
Catherine she recognised the friend of her long correspon-
dence, and both ladies succumbed to the second weep of the
day. While Ned, who treated everyone alike, whether king or
commoner, offered the ironmaster a mug of beer, which was
accepted.

An hour behind everyone else, so that the company might
arrive at church together, came the bride's carriage bringing
Zelah, Charlotte, Phoebe and the two children. Agnes was too
feeble to leave her bed, but Sally rode on the crupper of her
father's horse, and he set the gelding to a canter and overtook
the bride's party in no time. As Zelah approached Coldcote
she heard the first peal of bells ring out from St John's
Church, and now the sun shone upon her as though Dorcas
had ordered his presence at that precise moment. She lifted
her face to the warmth and light, smiling.

Then down the lane came the Howarths and the Scholeses
and all their people, wearing white ribboned favours, to be
greeted fervently by the small populace they would shortly
feed. William was clad in chocolate brown with a gold-and-
white striped waistcoat: Caleb in gunmetal grey. Both looked
pale and serious, as well they might, for Ned had finally to
arouse them with two buckets of cold water, and Dorcas had
brewed coffee according to Charlotte's method to settle their
stomachs. At the lych-gate they all paused, and turned expec-
tantly towards the sound of hooves and wheels. The bride's
carriage was just visible, and now half a dozen children
stepped forward to strew the ground with primroses, butter-
cups, bluebells and daisies. One small boy cast down an arm-
ful of rushes, and a small girl stood sentinel with a single
stalk of wheat saved from the last harvest. Zelah would enter
married life on a path of beauty, fertility and plenty, and so
continue all her days.

The carriage halted. Out jumped Ambrose and helped
down Cicely who was acting as bride-maid. Caleb took Charlotte's hand, and looked hopeful while she looked away. Ned

helped Phoebe down and offered her his handkerchief. And William came last to greet his lady.

Divested of her cloak, Zelah shimmered in the cool sunlight: the vision of a bride rather than the substance. A white and silver ghost, entering uncertainly upon the occasion.

Their courtship had been so long, so fraught with difficulties, and the outcome so sudden, that William and Zelah looked at each other in this moment almost with disbelief. He was handsomer, harder, more powerful than the youth who had first courted her. But she seemed even younger and more vulnerable. Then she set her white shoe tremulously on the carpet of flowers. He took her arm and steadied her. They smiled on one another in mutual triumph.

A singular decorum was observed during the ceremony. Perhaps the grandeur of the occasion subdued rough spirits, or a boisterous age was passing, for though the church was packed with villagers they were quiet and well-behaved. At the altar stood one symbol of the century to come: William, self-made man. By his side the proper helpmeet for such a future: Zelah, daughter of such another man, bringing both money and connections to the union. Yet she was far more than this, as the Howarths had found even upon a fortnight's acquaintance.

They had allotted her an honourable even a generous place in their family, and she had already discovered ways of expressing her gratitude without obvious thanks, her affection without utterance. She sensed that she might clasp Ned's arm as tightly as she would have clasped her father's, and feel an answering pressure of reassurance. She could rely upon Dorcas, as on her mother, to set her skirt aright before entering the lychgate. She knew that Cicely would be ready to hold her bridal posy at the correct moment, and be watchful at each stage of the service. Provided she usurped no one, the Howarths were for her.

So she concentrated on the ceremony and endeavoured to be pleased by it, in spite of a regret that she and William could not formulate and express their own vows; and that afterwards she could carry no document home, signed by a hundred Quaker witnesses, only leave behind her the image of a parish register, and the parson pocketing his fee.

Still, here they were, man and wife: William's heavy gold ring upon her finger, his name superimposed upon hers, his future setting the pattern of her own. She had seen so little of him in these three years, and discovered less, for even that

little was pure courtship, that she felt afraid to set forth on
life with such a stranger. But the choice had cost her so much
that she must go through with it, and find her way to him
without guidance. For how could Catherine advise her on a
marriage so different from that of her own?

Then one of those insights illuminated her as they passed
the grey army of Howarth's tombstones. Zelah pressed
William's arm that they might pause in their progress, and
stooped and laid her flowers on Betty Ackroyd's grave. It was
the thought and work of a moment: spontaneous, loving, inspired.

Ah, that is the heart of Zelah, Dorcas thought. And
resolved to watch over her, since such a heart is easily
bruised.

No rice was thrown. With wheat at fifty shillings and barley at seventeen and sixpence, all grain was precious. But
some children had shredded wild flowers patiently, and a
shower of their petals caught in the bride's shining dress and
gemmed her hair with blossom.

No lad shouted for her garter, since Zelah's shyness made
them shy. The usual uproar of approval had dwindled to a
murmur of pleasure. Folk hung back, fearful of offending
this slender girl, and William saw that his apprehensions had
been in vain. The wedding threatened to become a friendly
funeral. So when Tom stepped forward with the big bay stallion, which was there to rescue bride and groom from a mob
of well-wishers, William quickened the tempo. With a whoop
he leaped into the saddle, caught his wife round the waist,
and pulled her up in front of him shrieking and laughing.
They were suddenly at one with their audience, and a chorus
of shouts and hoots rose to keep them company. This was
something like a wedding! And as William drove his heels
into Wildfire and clattered off up the lane, the village came
close behind him on pony, horse and foot, yelling and firing
blunderbusses, ready for the fun.

They had been divided into house guests and barn guests,
with stronger tables and beer and heavier fare in the latter
place, but as the afternoon progressed and spirits rose and
bellies were filled the two parties mingled. So the ironmaster
was to be found biting into a slice of suet pudding and
treacle, while Charlie Grundy, saddler of Coldcote, hopped a
spoonful of ice-cream round the inside of his mouth until it
astonished him my melting. And he informed the ironmaster
that he earned above twenty shillings a week in his family

business. Whereat Caleb Scholes expressed polite surprise, though he earned above ten thousand a year in his enterprise. So they conversed with mutual esteem, and from this short acquaintance came the order of a new saddle for the ironmaster's horse. After which, Grundy's Saddlers shop-sign bore the sincerely meant if misleading inscription: *Suppliers to Royalty.* Furthermore, having asked permission of his host, Caleb the elder was pleased to bestow sixpence a head upon the poor of Garth, in memory of the occasion, and so to descend in the village annals as a public benefactor.

The old custom of bride-bedding, wanton revelry and public gaping was dying out. It was fashionable among the rich and aristocratic to take a bridal tour, but even lesser folk endeavoured to begin their married lives with a little privacy. As the light waned and festivities began to flag, William and Zelah drove off to Quincey Place for a week's holiday. And though all twenty of her family had been invited for dinner the following day; and all the Howarths the day after; and, Saturday being market day, Ned called in again and brought a brace of roasting fowls; and Sunday they dined at Kit's Hill; and Monday Caleb brought news of the ironworks and talked to William all evening; and Tuesday saw Dorcas, on her way to Millbridge; still they had the nights to themselves, and breakfasted in each other's company, with shy delight.

FIFTEEN

Love and Power

1795–1796

In the small front garden of Quincey Place a sapling shivered in the morning wind. Caleb the ironmaster had planted it with his own hands, the day before the wedding. For his mother was of Dutch extract and had brought this ancient European custom with her. He had done the same for Kate and Mary, would do it for Sarah and Rebecca in their turn. The symbol satisfied something very deep and secret within him: a reverence which had nothing to do with his religion: a belief far older than Christianity. And though the slim silver birch bent and swayed in every current of air, and seemed as though the first gale would uproot it entirely, there was a toughness in its pliability which promised very well.

William spent those first brief days together in courting Zelah afresh, partly out of consideration and partly in awe, for her innocence made him pause even on the threshold of fulfilment. Ned's advice, though well-meant, had been unnecessary.

'Now don't go at it like a bull at a gate! Think on!'

'I am no novice, father!'

'I wasn't saying you was'—drily—'I said, think on. There's plenty of men want a bucket of water thrown on them *after* the wedding, never mind afore it. And don't go dragging her down wi' childer every twelvemonth. Some men wear a wife out as if she was a suit of clothes. Nay, a suit'd last them longer, for they'd take better care of it!'

William swallowed his irritation, and thanked him kindly. Still, he did not know whether he would be confronted by ignorance or duty, and set about explaining his task with some delicacy when they woke on their first morning. But she surprised him by saying that her mother had told her what to expect, and though the act sounded unseemly it became a loving part of life together, for wife as well as husband, and that she should be very patient if it was not to her liking in the beginning.

She looked so solemn and child-like, sitting up in the vast four-poster bed, proffering her bit of knowledge, that William could not forbear smiling outright and finally laughing aloud, even as he begged her pardon. It is an advantage to be brought up in a large and rational family, and Zelah had learned very early in life to subdue excessive sensibility, so after a puzzled moment or two she joined his amusement, which effectively robbed William of his manhood for a time. But they employed the interval to good advantage, and took their first hurdle in high spirits: lying afterwards for a long while in mutual warmth, with the added delight of knowing that a cold spring day lay outside their little world among the bedclothes.

'And was that unseemly, Zelah? And will you be patient?' William asked, as she drowsed with her head on his chest.

'It was most odd,' she said honestly, 'but I did not entirely mislike it.'

'We shall do better by and by,' said William, with great

179

confidence, and they wound their arms about each other and laughed again.

Yet his conscience dealt him a blow, for he remembered his first bedding with Hannah, when the positions were reversed and she was teacher, he pupil. She had been generous and good to him: a raw, inexperienced youth, full of his own desires, his own importance. When he wanted her she gave herself to him. When he wanted freedom she set him free. And in this final gift, from a woman who had bestowed so much, lay a cold truth from which he would never escape.

So even in his present joy, Hannah's quiet ghost rose in his heart, looked on him briefly, smiled and vanished. As she had done. Presently he got up and dressed to drive the memory away.

If anyone had asked William what he most lacked he would have said, 'Time!' though the need for ready money came hard after it. There was never enough of either for his purposes, and he could never wait for anything unless he was forced to do so. Even while the paint was drying on the walls of Quincey Place, William was searching out the site on which his great house would be built. And from what he could gather, among the business minds of Millbridge, the war was not going to end in five minutes, and if a man were not supplying the troops with material for uniforms he should be supplying them with weapons. That was where the big money would be made in the next few years.

His marriage provided him with the means, his father-in-law with the idea, and both together gave him the opportunity to change course.

Standing in their dusty little office, the day before the wedding, old Caleb Scholes had pored over a map of the Wyndendale Valley and delivered his judgement.

'Thou art not the only new business hereabouts,' he observed, 'and this monster'—tapping the small square which indicated Thornley spinning-mill—'is but the first of many. So land will become expensive. Even the scrubbiest and most unpromising patch can house a factory. Therefore, as soon as thou art able, lease or buy what land thee can, even though it be idle for a space.'

William's eyes lighted on the area between Coldcote and Garth, where folk hung on to life by their finger-ends and would be glad of work.

'Thee had not thought to follow Abraham Darby at all, in

the gun trade, had thee, Caleb Scholes?' William asked innocently, in good Quaker fashion.

The Warwickshire ironmaster was plainly displeased.

'Why, that was many years ago, and for but a short while, when Ford and Goldney were managing the company. Abraham the second was in his youth then. Quakers do not take part in war, William Howarth.'

'Well, then, I beg thy pardon,' said William frankly. 'It had puzzled me, I confess. Perhaps I should have asked thee outright, which was what I meant to do. Quakers do not make guns?'

'They do not,' growled old Caleb.

'I thank thee. I did but wish to make the point clear in my mind,' said William reasonably.

He had given them their chance, Zelah's dowry, though tied up in one or two respects, belonged to her husband and was all of ten thousand pounds. Some he could use, against some he could borrow.

'Pray,' William cried, 'bear me no ill-will. I have ever been open with thee about my own beliefs. I have no wish to offend thee in such matters.'

The cloud dispersed. No more was said. William had reached a conclusion which involved him alone. Within a month of the wedding he had negotiated a private and separate deal for a vast tract of land called The Snape, at the other end of the valley. To ease his conscience he also searched out more land, and leased and bought at his own expense little islands of property between Belbrook and Snape, which could be used when the original foundry expanded.

Dorcas and Ned were pleasantly surprised to see more of their newly wedded son, as he came and went about this business, than they had expected. He was vague about his reason for calling in on them, and after a week or two he disappeared again, as was his wont, and they forgot about it.

On the fourth of June, having a contingent of horse and foot soldiers in the area, not long back from the Continent, Millbridge decided to celebrate King George's birthday in style and show themselves to be loyal to the Crown. For though the town burghers and their servants were eating regularly, the rest of Wyndendale was not. Discontent among the poor in the valley echoed discontent throughout the country, and the weather was so cruelly disposed towards them that new-born lambs had frozen to death in the fields that spring. Beset from all sides, their protests grew loud, and there had been incidents of an alarming nature: a boatload of flour and cheese held up on the Grand Trunk Canal, a miller robbed, an ugly scene in the Corn Market, food thefts. There was trouble enough abroad without civil unrest, and the spectre of the French Revolution stalked the dreams of all but the hungry. So Lord Kersall threw open the lower grounds of Kersall Park for the day, and the Council subscribed £50 to refresh the troops, and recouped it from renting out space for market stalls which would refresh the spectators.

Since the King's birthday fell upon a Tuesday, and Dorcas could be expected to come, Charlotte sent a note to Zelah suggesting they made up a family party for the occasion: quite forgetting that a military display on behalf of a monarch might be an inappropriate event. But as Zelah hesitated over the invitation, William declared that he and Caleb would accompany their womenfolk. Caleb's own hesitation was overcome by a promise to squire Charlotte and her children, and the assurance that he and William would work at the foundry all Saturday to make up for lost time. And so it was arranged.

At twelve noon precisely, the —th Lancashire Foot drew up in Millbridge Market Square and drilled for the benefit of the populace. Any doubts as to the wisdom of war, and its dire results upon the country's economy, were quickly dispelled by the sight of these splendid and immaculate puppets. The lines of weathered faces, red coats, white breeches and black gaiters stood to attention, shouldered and presented arms, fired salvoes into the air to the accompaniment of charming little screams from the ladies, and came to attention as though they were one soldier. Then, band playing, brass shining, they wheeled in unison and quick-marched off for their dinner of beef and beer. The cavalry were due to perform later that afternoon in the Park, and were said to be even more gallant and fearsome a spectacle.

Many hearts were fluttered by these displays of military strength and beauty, and Charlotte's children declared the sentiments of the majority.

'Mamma, how old must I be before I enlist? Ambrose asked, yearning for glory and white plumes.

'Mamma, I should like to marry that tall soldier on the black horse!' Cicely cried, tugging at her mother's skirt.

'You would do the country more good with an honest

newspaper, my son,' said Charlotte, her conscience pricking her as Toby's offspring joined the enemies of the people. 'And you would not really like to be a soldier's wife, my pet. They have no proper home, but follow the army from place to place.'

'Thee must not kill, Ambrose,' Zelah added softly, 'nor consort with those who do, Cicely.'

The children were doubtful of this point of view.

'What nonsense you are talking, my loves,' said Dorcas briskly. 'You have many years of education yet before you. Let us look round the fair. If Mrs Bottomley has a sweetmeat stall here I shall buy you some treacle taffy. She boils it herself, and it is very wholesome.'

'Caleb,' said William in a low voice, 'shall you take care of the ladies? I have that unfinished business with Lord Kersall over Ayside, which I may as well do while I am here. Do not wait supper for me. I may be some little time.'

The Kersalls' prosperity had begun in the fifteenth century with Sir Ralph Kersall, a country gentleman who rose in the world by choosing the right side at Bosworth Field. Marching a small band of twenty-five Lancashire bowmen down to Staffordshire in 1485 he had bent his knee reverently to Henry Tudor, and cast in his fortunes with that other unknown adventurer. The future king did not forget this loyal knight, and Ralph was made a baron and married to the heiress of a nearby estate at Thornley. Once given a chance, the family never looked back.

Over the next three centuries the Kersalls indulged in bursts of building activity. Their medieval courtyard house now boasted the addition of an Elizabethan hall, a Jacobean staircase, and an early-Georgian façade. Capability Brown had landscaped their park. They had given St Mark's Church its octagonal font, its lady chapel, and a set of stained-glass windows. They sent their sons to Eton and Oxford, supplying the church and the army with younger members, seeing that one of them kept a seat in Parliament. They married their daughters into good families, offering money to nobler husbands, breeding to richer husbands, and ensuring a strong sound bond of kinship with influential people.

Humphrey Kersall combined the best of all their abilities. He was a man of his time, with a flair for quick decisions. Coal found on his own estates made him even richer. The advent of the Leeds-Liverpool Canal gave him the idea of cutting a branch canal, down which he shipped his coal and limestone. The first spinning-mill in the valley was built on his land at Thornley, and when rioters burned it down he built a second and larger mill, and would follow it with others. He headed committees, held shares in all the important valley enterprises, drew profits as well as rents, and controlled the policy of *The Wyndendale Post*. Now close on sixty years of age he indulged in no vices, unless power could be called a vice, which he thought not. He preferred to gamble upon greater issues than a hand of cards. He ate and drank abstemiously, thus avoiding gout and heart disease. He hunted for exercise rather than excitement. He had married sensibly, lived with his wife agreeably, regretted her death suitably.

Until recently, William's only connection with the Kersalls had been a tenuous one: young Ralph Kersall's hunter had been foaled by the same dam who foaled Wildfire. And this eldest son of Humphrey Kersall, much the same age as William, once called him out of Flawnes Green forge because the hunter had cast a shoe on the Black Road. The heir's manners were negligent, but he did comment upon the likeness between their two horses: receiving information of their kinship with some astonishment, and looking twice at the blacksmith before he tipped him handsomely. This meeting had pricked William's pride, and as he watched Ralph Kersall trot away he said to himself, 'By God, sir, we shall sit at the same table yet, or my name is not William Howarth!'

Ten years after that episode William Howarth was closeted in the library at Kersall Park, discussing business.

'You come alone, I see, Mr Howarth?' said Humphrey Kersall pleasantly.

Cool-headed, cool-blooded, with a quiet taste for autocracy, he had much in common with Caleb Scholes the ironmaster. Between these two ageing lions stepped William, determined to tame the pair of them with his title-holding to Snape.

'It is good of you to spare me time, my lord,' said William, bringing forth his plans, 'and though this is a dark horse which may not even run,' he added lightly, 'I thought to show you its paces!'

And he laid out the thick sheets of paper upon the library table, as he had done at Somer Court three years ago.

The Snape, so-named for its pasture, spread much like Belbrook from hillbrow to river bank, as though some long-dead planner had decreed each owner an equal share of rock and marsh. William had cross-hatched the faults in red and marked them clearly: needs draining, needs levelling, to be cleared of scrub, and so on. On the second sheet, headed SNAPE IRON FOUNDRY, he had drawn up the finished works. On the third were his estimates of time and costs in detail. It was a highly efficient scheme for the production of cannons.

'An expensive animal, sir,' said Kersall negligently, using William's metaphor, 'and if it do run will carry a great deal of money upon its back!'

'But cannot fail to win its present race, my lord. Iron is the sinews of war, and the war seems like to be a long one.'

'And you come to me first, Mr Howarth, to do your horse-dealing? That is most amiable of you. May I ask why?'

'Because you were good enough to take an interest in our present enterprise, which I believe you will agree does very well.'

Kersall gave him a dry look.

'And perhaps because your Quaker friends would not feel kindly about making a profit from war, Mr Howarth?'

'Abraham Darby's ironworks made cannon, my lord,' William pointed out.

'Ah, but Abraham Darby was only a titular holder at the time,' Kersall replied, surprising him. 'A man who has but three-sixteenths of the shares calls a small tune. Your peaceable partner might see matters very differently.'

William's expression did not change. He had inherited his father's mouth and jaw: features expressive in Ned of tenderness and strength, in his son of an uncommon tenacity. His mother's bright quick intelligence had become in William a steady flame of intent. Every movement, every mannerism, had been schooled to the purpose in hand. He would no more have wasted a sign of approval or apprehension upon Humphrey Kersall than that cool and noble gentleman would have wasted one on him. So they pondered over this latest plan: the older man grey, spare and elegant; the younger man powerful, dark and dignified.

'Well, my lord, principles are a private matter. It is of business that I speak. You would stand to gain a large profit very quickly. Indeed, to risk least and gain most. Therefore I had thought you might be interested.'

'Your proposition, Mr Howarth?' Kersall asked, head held enquiringly to one side.

'That you, my lord, or you and others of your choice,

185

should lend me the sum of twenty thousand pounds, to be re-paid at one per cent above the highest rate of interest, in five years' time.'

'You judge very finely, Mr Howarth, as to both time and interest. I would suggest two per cent above the present rate, and give you seven years to repay.'

But this was mere bargaining, both knowing they would settle for something in between. Kersall laid a thin finger on his lips, meditating.

'Your collateral being, Mr Howarth?'

'My share of the Belbrook Iron Foundry and the title-deeds to Snape.'

'Mr Howarth, I would not give you a tenth of the sum for either!'

'My lord, you are gambling on my ability to continue to double the Belbrook output every year, to have Snape open-ing in twelve months' time and begin work on orders which shall make Belbrook seem a tinker's business. Snape is not an end but a beginning. I am no pot-vendor, to fret over a few hundred pounds' worth of trade. I am thinking in terms of ten thousand gun-barrels a month! If I cannot make this work in the time given me, then you will take over and repay yourself at a longer interval. But you cannot lose, my lord. Perhaps I could! Like yourself, my lord, I am prepared to look somewhat ahead of the present, and gamble accordingly. The whole world is changing, and it is industry which will lead the rest. I am willing to wager my life upon that!'

Kersall said, with mild irony, 'Unlike myself, you have a trade to fall back upon if all else fails! Though failure is, to my mind, an excuse of the weak.'

'My father says that failure is the inability to get up off the ground,' said William, smiling.

'It amounts to the same thing. Well, Mr Howarth, you must give me a week to cast about me. I have not such a sum lying around!'

William bowed his head, collected his papers, and waited. Lord Kersall tapped his lips contemplatively.

'Let us keep this horse of yours secret and well-stabled while I consider him as a proposition, Mr Howarth, shall we?' he asked, and smiled most charmingly.

'As your lordship pleases,' William said, smiling in his turn.

In the hall he met Ralph Kersall, and they exchanged bows: cold towards each other, as became two men with high opinions of themselves and a vast difference in station. But

William heard the opening words between father and son as the library door closed.

'May I crave the humblest of audiences, sir?' Ralph Kersall asked with mock humility.

'Deuce take it, Ralph, not money again?' Suddenly vulnerable.

So that is his other weakness? William thought. I shall do well to remember it.

He knew that a primary weakness had been played upon in the last hour. Humphrey Kersall could not resist the opportunity to own a very much larger share of the Belbrook Foundry in the event of William's failure; and the further bonus of a second ironworks, in which none of the Scholeses had any part at all, had probably clinched the matter. In the event of success, and Kersall was not a man to back failure though he might gain by it, a decent profit would be made and a promising business partnership consolidated for future purposes.

He sees me in terms of a useful and talented puppet, William thought, who will help him own the whole valley. And I see him as a staircase which I shall mount on my way to greater things. We shall find out who is right.

The late afternoon was cold and clear. Kersall Park stretched before him from terrace to lake, and put him in mind of his future residence.

I must look about me for a different site, he thought. I cannot be too close to Belbrook after all this.

It occurred to him that the ironmaster could see some treachery in using Zelah's dowry to buy the site of a cannon foundry, in which he would not be asked to take part whether he wished it or not. Then his wife and partner, Zelah and Caleb, would be both morally and personally distressed, and the whole family troubled by divided loyalties.

'But I am not hurting them,' he said aloud, striding through the wrought-iron gates without so much as a glance at their fine craftsmanship. 'Snape is at the other end of the valley. They need never visit it. And we must have more money. There is no way of standing still in this world. We go either forward or back. And I am damned if I am going back!'

The wedding at Kit's Hill had been a single prodigal gesture in a sorry year. The poor summer brought forth a poor harvest, and the price of grain soared. Only the rich and genteel could afford to eat wheaten bread. Most made do with dark barley loaves, and working folk were encouraged to grow potatoes instead. Young men enlisted, preferring unknown dangers to semi-starvation. And the grave-diggers kept busy, burying the old and weak who died of want.

To that penurious end of the valley, at the end of 1795, came William with money to spend and the need to build his new foundry as fast as possible. He could not have chosen a more propitious time. Men were desperate for work, and when word went round that labourers were needed at Snape they tramped in from miles around. Among them came the Irish, despised for their poverty, disliked for their foreignness, hated because they would accept less money for the same job.

William had learned a great deal from the building of Belbrook, and he knew how to find good managers to whom he could delegate work. He conceived the organisation minutely, and as a whole. Then he portioned it out to others. Thus he left himself free to pursue future objectives, and yet had a hand upon the reins and could twitch those reins when and how he pleased.

So he stood upon a hastily erected platform, looking exceedingly well-fed and prosperous in the midst of these hungry faces, and harrangued the crowd. He was not yet a thorough-going *capitaliste*—as Toby would have dubbed him—being still influenced by Ned, who was fatherly towards his labourers. And though he could not hope to know and care for this mass of unskilled men, who would toil for a few shillings and be laid off when the job was done, still he endeavoured to give them a sense of purpose and participation.

'My name is Will Howarth,' he cried, and his deep voice reached the furthest worker. 'I'm offering you hard labour and fair pay!' This raised a ghost of a laugh and a cheer. 'You deal well with me and I'll deal well with you. You're not just building Snape Iron Foundry, you're bringing more work to the valley for yourselves and others. And though the first blast-furnace will be fired within the year, God willing, your job won't stop there. I've got plenty of building for you!' The cheer came more strongly this time, and some of the younger men looked hopeful but the others reserved their judgement. 'It's healthy work here. Work with a bit of heart and interest to it. You won't be cooped up in a mill, watching the bobbins go round. You'll be making bricks and mortar grow! Give me all you've got and I'll stand by you. There's my hand upon it!'

His foreman, standing by his side, now threw his cap into the air and shouted, 'Three good cheers for Mr Howarth!'

They whipped off their own battered hats and gave William something of an ovation. For he looked a splendid fellow, towering above them on the temporary platform, in the full flower of his strength and vitality. And he had come out and shown himself and spoken directly to them: none of your high-nosed, low-born manufacturers, keeping at a distance and letting others do the dirty work.

'I thank you! I thank you!' said William, lifting his hands for silence. 'Now we'll put matters straight before we start, and then we all know where we are. The wages are a fixed price, whether you're English or Irish or anything else!' A murmur of doubtful acceptance. 'And we don't employ childer. The only young folk here will be craftsmen's apprentices with proper articles of agreement!' Another confused murmur. They were not sure how these rules would affect them in practice, though the theory seemed to be benevolent. 'I'll be here to set the first spade in the earth tomorrow morning at six o'clock!' William cried. 'And I'll work alongside you. If any man thinks he can dig harder—let him try!' They loved that, and something like comradeship glimmered in their gaunt faces. 'And here's my foreman, Mr Cartwright, to have a word with you about your pay!'

The terms were reasonable but not generous: a shilling a day to fill, wheel and empty heavy barrows of rock and soil from dawn to dark; nine shillings a week as bricklayers' labourers and spadesmen. But then they were unskilled and paid the penalty for their lack of status. A carpenter would take home a pound or more on a Saturday night, and engineers were paid between twenty-five and thirty shillings a week.

Now William stepped down from his eminence and moved freely among them. A few he recognised as belonging to the villages of his childhood, and to these he spoke personally, remembering their Christian names and enquiring about their families. Most were strangers, and many rough enough to strike fear into any respectable heart: such scarecrows as had crowded about the French guillotine to watch their masters die. But William was accustomed to command. If they did not respond to his broad smile they respected his broad shoulders, and his bright black gaze could harden until the other man looked away. Besides, he represented work. They cherished him for that.

If summer had been bleak, autumn was savage. Heavy thunderstorms, high winds and driving rain, plagued the labourers and slowed the building projects. In London, King George was mobbed on his way to open Parliament, with cries of 'No King! No war! Give us peace and bread!'

Relations at Quincey Place were difficult. William could have dealt with tears, reproaches or open anger, feeling his decision to be a rational one, but Zelah and Caleb had withdrawn into a stunned silence. The nature and scope of his enterprise bewildered them, who asked no more than honest trade and fair profit, but his secrecy appalled them most.

Caleb had only said, 'We are partners, William. I had not expected thee to go behind my back.'

In vain William used their religious dislike of war as an excuse for his reticence on the subject, and pointed out that Snape was four miles away and a completely separate business. They knew very well that if Snape had been on their doorstep he would have pursued the same course. He had made up his mind and they must adjust to the consequences. Brother and sister drew closer together, not casting him out but grieving for the loss of trust. He felt, when he was home at all, that they had to struggle to seem as they once were. Something had been broken. He endeavoured to mend it with affection, with gifts. He was truly sorry for the rift, but unrepentant about Snape. Meanwhile he was working as he had never worked before.

The middle of the parlour at Quincey Place was delightfully warm, owing to an abundance of coal upon the fire, which a little maidservant replenished as soon as it grew red and coagulent. But Zelah preferred, on this winter afternoon, to take herself and her sewing into the cooler perimeter, and sit at the window to enjoy the last of the sunshine.

With her dark-gold hair drawn into a Grecian knot, and her simple gown, she was in the very height of fashion, and secretly grateful for the comfort of her cashmere shawl. Ned had delivered judgement on both daughters as to the unsuitability of such clothing in a northern climate. But, though Dorcas might still wear her little corset and swathe herself in wool and linen underwear, Charlotte and Zelah preferred to shiver in one thin petticoat, a chemise, and a pair of cotton drawers. Frills and tight-lacing were out: the French revolution had influenced more than English politics.

At this time of the year gentlefolk kept indoors as much as

possible, and distance conquered sociability. So Zelah had been alone all day, with only the view from her parlour window for company. Formerly part of a large family, she found her enforced solitude a grave problem, though she strove in every way to lighten it. When she had given her orders, and written home, and said her silent prayers time hung heavily upon her. From breakfast to dark she saw nothing of husband or brother, who ate their dinners at their foundries in a couple of basins. And when at last all three gathered to sup together, Caleb would bring his accounts and William his building plans, and apart from a civil enquiry as to her well-being, the evening revolved round iron. The only sure way was to divert them with congenial company, but they could not entertain visitors six nights of the week. And nowadays, when she played her harpsichord, however raptly William seemed to listen, immediately afterwards he would say something like, 'Ah! I have hit upon a solution to that trouble in the moulding shop, Caleb!' As though even music were but a means to his iron ends.

So Zelah gazed through the window at the frosty garden, with nothing to cheer her but the thought of her mother coming to Belbrook in the spring, when their first child was expected; and the little garment in her lap received a baptism of tears.

Her labour started just before breakfast on the tenth day of April, and Caleb was despatched at once to Millbridge to inform old Dr Standish and Charlotte, while William rode to Kit's Hill to alert the Howarths. Catherine Scholes had journeyed northwards for the event, and such was her influence that no one apart from the family knew anything untoward was happening at Quincey Place. There was no running to and fro, no muffling of knockers or laying of straw on the threshold or rousing of near neighbours. Zelah sat for a few hours by the parlour fire, sewing with her mother, and assuring them that she felt very well indeed. Dr Matthew Standish pronounced himself satisfied as to her progress, and said he would call back at tea-time. While William, viewing his wife afresh, sat humbly by her. Occasionally he would touch her cheek or her hand, and then she would pause for a moment to smile at him, and sometimes clasp his fingers as the mild contractions came and went. It was the quietest and pleasantest Sabbath they had spent together for a long while, and William's conscience smote him when he reflected that it was his driving ambition and impatience which threatened the domestic peace. He endeavoured to learn a lesson from Zelah, and so refrained from pacing the room, drumming his knuckles on the table, and behaving in his usual restless manner. Dorcas and Ned drove up in the trap towards dinnertime, but Zelah could eat nothing and at two o'clock was forced to retire, when the contest began in earnest.

They had prepared a small bedroom at the back of the house, especially for the birth: a new procedure of which Matthew Standish deeply approved.

'For you would not operate upon a man in a four-poster bed,' he said belligerently, 'nor swaddle him in bedclothes and suffocate him with feather pillows and mattresses while you were about it! Birth is as much an operation as any other. The organism is just as profoundly shocked, the danger as great, the rate of mortality still higher than one could wish. So let the mother lie upon a firm and narrow bed in a well-warmed room, with a sheet and blanket over her, and so make matters easier for both doctor and patient.'

Thus he provided Millbridge tea-parties with fresh cause for disapproval, and ladies continued to prefer midwives and four-poster beds.

The child came forth into a cold and barren spring, borne by its young mother with gasping prayers for fortitude, while Catherine spoke loving encouragement, and Dorcas held high the candlestick so that Dr Standish might see what he was about. Downstairs, the men sat together: William now quite overcome by the length and severity of the ordeal, Caleb bereft of his usual humour, and Ned quietly smoking his pipe. Supper was a scrappy meal, and every time a door opened or shut, an order was given, or footsteps sounded up and down the stairs, they looked at each other in hope and fear.

At ten o'clock Charlotte joined them, saying that a neighbour had come that way and set her down at the gate. William was too distracted to care, but Ned guessed that she did not mention any name for fear of upsetting Caleb. So it would be a gentleman, he conjectured, looking shrewdly at his daughter. Possibly Nicodemus Hurst. She was looking flushed and well, decidedly handsome, and younger than her nine-and-twenty years.

'Come and sit by me, my lass,' said Ned, loving her.

There was something both ashamed and defiant in the way she glanced at him, as though she would be sorry to hurt him but had no choice. Which he also noted. Then she smiled, and sat in the circle of his arm, and became his child again.

"You don't wear enough clothes!' he grumbled, content to have her near him.

A woman's wail from the back of the house silenced them. Like a soul parting from its body and mourning for the passing, it came into the parlour and lingered on the air. At this despairing cry William jumped from his chair and would have run upstairs, but for his father's kindly admonition.

'Sit you down, my lad. That's good news, or I'm a Dutchman!'

They all watched and waited and did not speak. The silence was profound. All sounds of the struggle above had ceased. Then they heard Catherine's foot upon the stairs, Catherine's voice at the door. She came in smiling, and embraced her son-in-law.

'Now God be thanked, William. Thee has a daughter, and thy wife is spared. Nay, do not go just yet. Thou shalt see them in a little while, my son. Thee has cause to rejoice!'

But he buried his face in his hands, and wept.

One by one they came in, making as small a noise as possible, and kissed Zelah's cheek or patted her hand, and peered into the cradle by her bed. None of them was disappointed that the child was a girl. There would be time enough for sons to come.

'So, Mr Howarth,' said Dr Standish, as Ned helped him into his greatcoat, 'I begin to bring forth your second generation!'

They had nourished reservations for so many years that friendship itself could not be closer.

'I don't know so much about that,' Ned replied. 'Our Will were born before you got there!'

And the doctor had taken his guinea just the same.

'Well, well, sir,' said Matthew Standish, 'let us not be so particular. We are neither of us growing any younger, and need not argue over a shade of opinion.'

'Speak for thyself!' said Ned, grinning.

The doctor gave his thin smile.

'At least I may offer to take this lady home,' he said of Charlotte. 'And in this case I cannot be accused of evading my medical duties, for I certainly delivered *her*!'

Raising a laugh on his own account.

Rheumatism prevented him from horse-riding these days,

and he now travelled to and from his patients in a gig. So Charlotte was wrapped up in her cloak by Ned, and helped into her seat by Caleb.

'I am an aunt at last!' she cried, to excuse the radiance she could neither subdue nor explain. 'Oh, what a dragon I shall be!'

They laughed again, for Charlotte was notoriously indulgent with all children.

'Come on, my lass, let's get thee home,' said Ned, fussing over Dorcas's cloak and shoes. 'There's a sharp frost in the air! Give us a light, wilta, Caleb, for the horse-lanterns?'

'Another bad summer, said Dorcas, 'will find us sorely troubled to make do!' And was momentarily downcast at the thought.

'Nay, our Will'll take Dick and me on as labourers at Snape!' Ned replied, a-gleam with good humour.

So they all departed. Only once on the way home did Ned voice a note of disquiet.

'Our Lottie looks like a cat wi' a saucer of cream! What's she up to now, I wonder?'

For they could never be quite sure of Charlotte.

William rose at daybreak with a lightness of heart he could not at first name. Then he remembered that he was lying on the mattress which yesterday had been Zelah's bed of pain, and that she was safely delivered. He lifted himself on one elbow and listened. An infant wailed. A door opened and shut. Someone was about. Catherine, most probably, whom he loved next to Dorcas and his sister. She had been understanding of his courtship, forbearing towards Snape, kind to him, hopeful of him, always. No sharp word or quick frown had marred their friendhip, even when he had erred. She seemed to preserve her affection for people in spite of their misdemeanours: loving them for what they were, rather than what she would have them be. He put on a wool morning-gown and slippers, and walked quietly along the passage to the main bedroom. The thin high cry of hunger was now hushed. He knocked gently on the door, and Catherine opened it.

'Thy daughter is feeding, William. Shall thee come and sit with them while I order tea?'

Like Dorcas, she clung to the old fashion. Her hair was plainly brushed beneath its linen cap, her fichu immaculate, her waist neatly corseted. He kissed her hands in gratitude, feeling new-born himself, and sat by the bed with profound humility.

The baby was very small and perfect: her round head covered in silver down, like a dandelion clock. Her little hands clasped and unclasped in ecstasy as she nuzzled at Zelah's breast. Momentarily done, lolling against her mother's shoulder, she contemplated William with unseeing dark-blue eyes.

He put a finger into the pink bell of her palm, and she clutched it with surprising strength. The first rays of sun were lighting the room, illuminating both mother and child, and William felt himself to be caught up with them both in a memory so old that he could recall nothing but its beauty and familiarity. In that moment he was utterly content, and at one with himself and the world.

SIXTEEN

Old Debts

Charlotte had ceased trying to please people, which accounted for the apologetic but defiant look she gave her father before sitting at his side. And the reason for her subdued radiance had been growing for half a year.

One Tuesday afternoon back in the autumn of 1795, Simeon Judd, being destitute but persevering, had the temerity to cross the boundary of his parish in search of work. Though Millbridge was rich in its own poor, the town's obvious prosperity still deluded the hopeful, and Simeon was willing to turn his hand to anything. He was not a lucky man. Life had set an obstacle course before him which he set out in his youth to overcome; but youth being over, and his strength waning, he was at last brought face to face with want. Now, unknown to himself, he carried within him the ripe fruit of death, long disguised by privation. For if he felt faint, or staggered in his walk, or suffered pains in his belly, was that not due to hunger? If, having partaken of a handful of rough oats or a sour crust of bread, he sweated and vomited and purged himself, was that not the result of coarse food upon an empty stomach? So he entered Millbridge at four o'clock in the afternoon, to keep an appointment he had not made, and to disturb the peace.

As he had eaten no food since yesterday, and that not much, he was also guilty of stealing a turnip from a field and gnawing it surreptitiously as he walked. He had begun to feel its ill-effects as he trod the cobbles of the High Street, and sometimes stopped outright and held his aching guts, and sometimes stumbled. Had he been well-dressed, the shoppers would have looked compassionately into his face and diagnosed him as being sick; but his rags told them all they wished to know, and they sent for the constable because they were sure the man was drunk. Meanwhile a couple of young red-coats, with nothing better to do, fixed their bayonets in fun and advanced upon Simeon Judd, telling him to be off and not frighten the ladies. Brought to bay, he supported himself by means of Charlotte's horse-post and confronted his tormentors.

'I'm doing nowt wrong,' he said, in sorry dignity.

'He is the worse for liquor!' said one lady decidedly.

'I've nowt to buy liquor with,' Simeon persisted, and attempted to turn out his pockets as proof of that statement.

Constable Letherhead, being informed that there was only one desperate ruffian, and that two infantrymen were guarding him, now pushed his way to the front of the gathering crowd.

'What's your name and business?' asked the constable, very short and sharp as became his position.

'Simeon Judd, sir. Looking for work, sir.'

'Looking for trouble more like!'

'Nay, I were my own master once,' cried Simeon, 'and worked on my own land, and built my own cottage.'

'Master nowt, more like! Where do you come from?'

'Charndale way,' said Simeon wearily, for he knew now that there was no hope for him.

'Well, get back there,' said Letherhead, 'and let them find you summat!' The onlookers murmured their approval. 'We've got enough of our own to look after, without foreigners disturbing the King's Peace!'

The red-coats still held him at bayonet-length, though by now they felt a little foolish.

'Nay,' said Simeon Judd, 'I'm the one as is disturbed, mister.'

'Off with you!' the constable commanded.

Simeon was incapable of walking another step, and

doubted whether he could hold on to the post much longer. So he made a statement which would stand in his stead.

'Here I stop, and here I drop, until thee gives me work!'

Then he vomited up the turnip, looked piteously at his indignant audience, and fell to the ground.

At the window of Thornton House half a dozen shocked ladies stood holding china tea-cups. The comments of five of them echoed those of the scandalised people outside. The sixth hurriedly left her parlour and opened her front door, crying, 'Bring him in here, constable. He looks faint and ill.'

'He's only shamming, Mrs Longe,' said the constable sagely. 'You know what they're like, ma'am.'

But she ran down the steps and bent over the bundle of rags.

'Fetch a doctor, if you please,' she said impulsively, 'I believe this man is dying.'

'Dying?' said the constable. 'He mustn't do that, Mrs Longe. Not here. He's out of his parish. Hey there, Charlie! Joe!' to two gardeners who had come to watch the fun. 'Fetch a wheelbarrow, wilta?'

'Is there a doctor among you?' cried Charlotte, holding Simeon's dirty hand. 'Please to fetch a doctor!'

'My dear Charlotte,' said Mrs Graham, coming to her side but keeping her skirts out of the way, 'you are all heart, dear, but do leave the poor creature alone. He may be suffering from gaol-fever or all manner of things. Let Constable Letherhead deal with him. The constable knows best.'

Thus she paid tribute to mercy, but relied on justice.

'Here's a wheelbarrow, constable,' said Charlie Hargreaves.

'Right we are. Would you mind moving, Mrs Longe? Just while we lift him into it.'

Charlotte put her arms round Judd's soiled body.

'Leave him be!' she said, so fiercely that they moved away, touching their hats.

The crowd made a curious sound of disfavour.

'There is a poor man here in desperate need of help,' said Charlotte. 'If someone will go for Dr Standish I will pay the fee. Charlie! Joe! Carry him into my house, if you please!'

They looked irresolutely at the constable, but he waved them to stay where they were.

'Mrs Longe, ma'am,' he announced, in his loudest and most official voice, 'this here vagrant is not a man. He is a beggar. And there is a law against them. Furthermore, he is not a member of this here parish. If he dies, this here parish has the expense of burying him!'

This statement brought them all to attention. But Charlotte became very still, and listened as though she could not believe what she was hearing.

'Now then,' said the constable, satisfied that he had everyone's understanding, 'put him into the wheelbarrow, and wheel him along to the far side of the turnpike road, and lay him on the grass, comfortable-like.'

'You would leave him to die at the roadside?' Charlotte asked.

'Eh, don't you worry yourself, ma'am,' said the constable. '*He* don't mind where he dies, bless you!'

And heard the crowd's assent, and one or two laughs.

'My dear Charlotte, you are making an exhibition of yourself, behaving in this fashion,' said Mrs Graham in a low, hurried voice.

The other ladies nodded agreement, mouths pursed.

Charlotte asked, with ominous calmness, 'Do you believe the constable to be right, Mrs Graham?'

'Of course he is right!' cried the rector's wife, relieved to see her hostess coming to her senses. 'Pray do get up, and come inside with us. Do not distress yourself further. We thought'—in a louder voice, for the benefit of the spectators—'that you were looking pale today!

'I have never felt better in myself than I do now!' Charlotte replied, with supreme bitterness. 'Stand aside, ma'am, if you will not help me. I see you have learned nothing from your husband's sermon. Or would he, too, have passed by on the other side?'

'Hypocrite!' cried Phoebe, seeing her enemy retreat. 'Whited sepulchre!'

Then she fainted into Sally's arms.

'Come, ladies,' said Mrs Graham, mortally wounded. 'This is no place for us!'

'Mrs Longe,' said the constable, sorely troubled, 'he can't die in this parish, ma'am, even if he is in your house!'

'I shall also pay for his funeral, if need be,' Charlotte answered.

She relinquished her hold of Simeon Judd and spoke to the crowd.

'If any among you will help me, let them come forward. Would the rest please go about their business?'

Assistance was coming from two directions at once, unasked. Ambrose was already at his mother's side, closely followed by Polly Slack. From the back of the crowd Jack Ackroyd pushed his way, crying, 'Let me through, damn you. Let me through!'

'Now, ladies and gentlemen,' said Constable Letherhead, soothing them, 'Mrs Longe has agreed to pay all expenses. The parish will be quite satisfied as to that. We're all yuman beings, I hope.'

'You nincompoop!' roared Jack Ackroyd, reaching him. 'There is a law against what you are doing!'

'A law, sir? What law, sir?' asked Letherhead, aghast.

'It has not long been passed, you jackass, but this Act takes away from the parish its powers of preventive expulsion. In brief, constable, you have no right to move a dying man out of the parish!'

'Ah, the new law!' said Constable Letherhead, who had never heard of it. 'It's been passed, has it, sir? That's good news, that is, sir.'

'If I were you, my brave fellow,' said Jack Ackroyd, looking hard at the constable to frighten him still more, 'I should send these people away as soon as possible, lest Higher Authorities hear of your criminal stupidity.'

'Yes, sir. At once, sir.'

'Or you might all be arrested and tried for taking part in judicial murder!' shouted Jack to the silent crowd.

As fast as they had hurried to watch they hurried off, while the headmaster stooped to lift Simeon Judd, who was not at all heavy.

'Bring his bundle, Ambrose!' he ordered. 'Lead the way, Mrs Longe. You, girl, what's-a-name, fetch one of the doctors. You, other what's-a-name, put that lady on the hall floor and get a pair of blankets.'

'Yes, Mr Awkright,' said Polly, and ran up the High Street.

'Yes, sir,' said Sally, preparing to lay down her burden.

But Phoebe suddenly recovered, said 'Pho!' of the dying man, and shut herself in the parlour; where Cicely joined her, afraid.

'I would advise you to leave him in the hall, Mrs Longe,' Jack Ackroyd continued, 'until you know what is the matter with him. If it is cholera or typhus or smallpox we are at risk in any event, but we need not spread it all over the house.'

'I wish my mother were here,' said Charlotte. 'She would know what to do.'

'You have done well enough,' said Jack, which was high praise from him.

He lifted Judd's eyelid and felt his pulse, turned over his hands and looked compassionately at them.

'He has worked hard all his life,' he said quietly, 'and they grudge him a death.'

'Why, what have we here?' said the dry voice of Matthew Standish. 'They tell me you are fetching vagabonds from the hedgerows, Mrs Longe! Well, you will find plenty of employment. Let me see him, if you please.'

He examined the man carefully, nostrils distended, for Judd stank. Then called for a basin of warm water and a towel.

'He has been dying these many months,' said Dr Standish, washing his hands thoughtfully, 'and will not be long over it. You need fear nothing for yourselves, apart from his body and head vermin. His sickness is his own.'

'His sickness is a social one!' said Jack Ackroyd savagely of the emaciated creature.

'That too,' said Matthew Standish coolly, 'and he is not the only one to suffer it!'

'Is there anything we can do for him?' Charlotte asked.

'You could clean him, Mrs Longe, and keep him warm. Give him tea and slops if he asks for nourishment. No more. But I warn you that if this story is bruited about you shall have every beggar in Christendom knocking on your door! Let me take him to the hospital. There we can make his last hours comfortable, and his corpse will serve medical purposes, thus saving you innumerable complications.'

'No, I thank you, sir,' said Charlotte slowly. 'I should feel I had in some manner betrayed him.'

'Pure sentimentality,' said Standish, 'but I shall not dispute the matter with you. No, no, ma'am,' waving away his fee. 'If you must be so foolish I shall not charge you for it—unless it becomes a habit!'

Simeon Judd opened his eyes, though they saw nothing. Took three quiet breaths. Was gone from them.

His onlookers formed a tableau for a few moments: Polly holding the basin, Sally with her apron to her mouth, Charlotte clasping her hands and Ambrose standing protectively by her, Jack Ackroyd about to speak, the doctor in the act of putting on his hat. Then they all bent over Simeon Judd.

'His sorrows are done,' said Matthew Standish, and closed the empty eyes.

'Mrs Longe,' said Jack Ackroyd, too loudly in the quiet hall, 'I shall look to the arrangements for you, and with your permission will pay for the funeral myself.'

'Another sentimentalist!' the doctor remarked, covering the empty face.

'Someone should settle the debt,' said Jack, taking it upon himself.

'I commend your good heart,' said Matthew Standish cheerfully, 'and hope it does not lead you into too much expense! Mrs Longe, you would oblige me by lying down until suppertime. You have sustained an emotional shock, and I do not wish to be fetched back here in half an hour for a fit of hysterics. Polly, will you see to your mistress?'

'Yes, Dr Sandwich,' Polly replied, curtseying.

'Then good-day to you all!'

And the doctor departed, as lean and trim as any youngster, only his rheumatism conceding his sixty years.

It was the first time Jack Ackroyd had been in Thornton House since that disastrous visit twelve months previously, and he was anxious not to commit the same errors.

'You will, please, rest as the doctor recommends, Mrs Longe,' he said awkwardly. 'I shall have this poor fellow removed at once. Perhaps Ambrose would take a message for me—if you would allow him to do so.'

'You are more than kind, sir,' said Charlotte, striving to put him at his ease. 'Ambrose, you will be pleased to help Mr Ackroyd, will you not? Sally, will you see that Miss Jarrett and Cicely are kept in the parlour until Mr Ackroyd has seen to the arrangements.'

She paused at the foot of the stairs, looked down at the pitiful body, looked up into Jack Ackroyd's face. The same compassion was in his countenance, the same anger in his voice, the same resolution in his bearing, as in her own. She had found him and herself as she knelt on the muddy cobbles beside Simeon Judd. Someone should settle the debt, he had said, and he was right. Today, she had thanked those strangers who picked up Toby's body from the fatal doorway, carried it to a strange house, paid for and attended his funeral in a strange grave in a Paris cemetery. But she could not say all this, though she needed to explain.

So she only said, 'Once, he belonged to somebody.'

The scandal was mouthed down the valley as far as Kit's Hill. Dorcas penned approval, though Charlotte felt that her

201

mother would somehow have managed the matter without recourse to the drama. But Ned had written at the end of the elegant script, in his round, self-taught hand, *'Well done, lass!'* Caleb extolled her action. Zelah accepted it as right and merciful. William, with that mixture of admiration and mockery brothers reserve for well-loved sisters, dubbed her 'the family heroine'. And Millbridge turned its corseted back on her.

The following Tuesday afternoon Charlotte made ready for social battle and was disappointed of it. For two hours she sat in her parlour while Ambrose composed his weekly newspaper, Cicely sewed her sampler, and Phoebe quarrelled with the absent Mrs Graham in whispers. None of them commented upon the lack of callers, but all of them knew the reason why. When Polly entered with the usual tea-tray Phoebe rose in dignity.

'I refuse to stay in the same room with Beelzebub's mistress!' she announced, and swept out, head high.

'Stay where you are, Cissie,' said Charlotte, as the little girl stood up, sewing in hand, 'You can see Aunt Phoebe after tea.'

Polly jerked her head towards the door, and winked.

'Miss Jorrocks ain't right up here, if you ask me,' she said, pointing to her forehead. 'You oughter get Dr Sandwich to have a look at her, ma'am.'

'Miss Jorricks,' said Ambrose, with Toby's glint of humour, 'is barmy. She thinks there is a man hiding under her bed. Tell Dr Sandwich that, if you please!'

'Ambrose!' Charlotte warned terribly.

'My dear Mamma,' he replied, 'I always take my tea in the kitchen of a Tuesday. Can I not have it here with you for once?'

'She does, Mamma,' said Cicely, 'for she always asks me to look under the bed when I am in her room.'

'She comes to my room in the middle of the night sometimes,' said Ambrose, very matter-of-fact, 'and says she has escaped him, and will I call the constable—though what old Letherbrains would do I cannot imagine!'

Charlotte set down the silver teapot, feeling chilled.

'Oh my dear children,' she said, 'why did you not tell me before?'

'It was but Aunt Phoebe's fancy,' Cicely replied. 'If I had seen a man I should have told you, Mamma.'

'But in the night, Ambrose, when you are asleep? What do you do?'

'I take her back to her room,' said Ambrose, smiling, 'and peep behind the curtains, and shout—very softly, so's not to wake anyone!—"Be off with you, you villain!" And then Aunt Phoebe climbs into bed and goes to sleep again.'

'I do not know whether to laugh or cry,' said Charlotte, on the verge of both.

'You fetch Dr Sandwich to her, ma'am,' Polly advised, and added in exactly the same tone, 'and try them Bakewill tarts. Sally had the recipe off Miss Whitebread's cook.'

Then the front-door knocker astonished them all. Polly ran. They conjectured which of the faithful had been faithful. They listened.

'It is our good friend Mr Awkright,' said Ambrose, grinning. 'I can hear them arguing about the disposition of his hat. Well, he will be the only friend we have if Mamma persists in her scandalous behaviour!'

'You will take your tea in the kitchen, Ambrose!' Charlotte was crying as Jack Ackroyd walked in, carrying his hat.

'Mrs Longe,' he said, without preamble, 'your son is too old for petticoat government. You should enter him at the Grammar School. Aye, and upon a weekly basis, so that you do not amend our discipline daily!'

'Is that what you have called to say, sir?' cried Charlotte, thoroughly out of temper.

'Do let me have your hat, Mr Awkright,' said Polly, placating. 'And you come along of me, Master Ambrose. I told you how it would be if you didn't hold your blessèd tongue!'

Cicely sat timidly upon her stool, not knowing what she should do among these clashing people.

Then, visibly, Jack Ackroyd began to correct their first impression of him.

'Wait a moment,' he said, and put his hand to his forehead as though he had forgotten something. 'Here, Polly. Here is my hat. I forget these trifles. Mrs Longe, I should like the pleasure of some conversation with you on a private matter—but after tea, if you please. And could the children stay awhile, for part of the matter concerns Ambrose? Pray sit down, miss, and do your needlework. I don't bite, you know!' And as she looked even more alarmed he asked gently, 'What is your name, little miss? Cicely?' Catching the whisper. 'Well, sit you down, Cicely. I know so few small girls that you must teach me how to behave towards them. Is this your needlework?' Holding it up the wrong way. 'Well, it looks very neat indeed—though I am no judge of such matters. But I am sure you will not frighten me, and turn me out of the house, as your mother does, will you, Cicely?'

At this notion, which had a grain of truth in it, both children laughed aloud, and glanced slyly at Charlotte to see how she would take such splendid humour.

'Polly, fetch more cakes, if you please,' said Charlotte, smiling. 'Mr Ackroyd will take tea with us.'

'I shall sit by you, Cicely,' said Jack Ackroyd, genuinely relieved. 'You will not scold me!'

She saw at once that he was another child, a damaged child, and no longer felt afraid of him.

'Pray sit on Aunt Phoebe's chair, sir,' said Cicely kindly, 'and I shall fetch you the nicest cakes. You must not be frightened by Mamma. If you behave well she is very nice indeed.'

Ambrose said seriously, 'I should like to go to grammar school, sir. Here is my weekly newspaper. My grandmama says I am cleverer even than Uncle William was—though she is partial, of course! Pray keep my *Gazette*, sir, if you wish. I have a number of copies. I find *The Wyndendale Post* somewhat stuffy, and of a high Tory persuasion!'

'And how do you like your tea, Mr Ackroyd?' Charlotte asked ironically. '*Very* sweet?'

He met her eyes, under the children's protection.

'Aye, madam. For I need sweetening. I am aware of my defects.'

Before such humility she was robbed of her weapons.

Softened by tea and conversation, he no longer looked formidable. His thin face was defenceless without its frown, his grey eyes gentle. He was turning over her ideas in his mind, giving them full consideration. The short silences between them did not clamour to be broken. They sat quietly together before the fire, as they had done these two hours past.

Then he said, 'I have never spoke with a radical woman, Mrs Longe. For that is what I take to be the trend of your argument. Indeed, I have never before heard any woman speak to such effect—but then, I was an admirer of your prose long ere this. I fear my opinion of women has been much akin to that of Ralph Fairbarrow—how did you put it? "He thinks we are puppets, fools and breeders?" Well, you are scarcely representative of your sex, Mrs Longe, for most of them match that description! Grant us that excuse, at least!'

'I grant *you* that excuse, sir,' said Charlotte, animated, her cheeks flushed by fire and argument, 'but I would never grant it to Mr Fairbarrow. For though he was never part of our London circle—nor of any circle that I knew of!—he moved freely among us, and met with women who would put me to shame for intellect, achievement and discussion. But he does not like us at all. He is afraid of us, dreams us into tyrants who must be put down. When we show skill or courage or integrity in his own field he is lost, for his narrow creed does not allow of our virtues. He dismissed my friend Mary Wollstonecraft as being an idiot in love and a vixen in temper. Well, I grant you she has not been wise in her loves—if wise we can be!—but her affections are deep and true. And if she grow angry in debate, sir, have we women not cause for anger, and is she not our representative? When the fox mauls, shall not the vixen scratch? But no, he will not consider that. Like a picker in a rag-bag he cries, "Oh, this piece will not match, and that piece is an ugly colour!" and so casts all away. No, sir, it is easier for men to keep us for their private purposes, and give the better part of themselves to their friends and the world. And, sir'—holding up her hand as he seemed about to speak—'men are not our only, nor yet our worst enemies! Women themselves clutch the chains that bind them, nay even forge the links. Such mouthers of cant and convention as form the bulk of my tea-parties are enemies of women—and why I entertain them,' she said suddenly, aware of her words, 'I cannot imagine!'

Jack Ackroyd burst out laughing and slapped his knees, delighted.

Polly, knocking on the door as she pushed it open (for she had never learned to knock and wait a moment before entering) was amazed to hear him. In fact, seeing that they sat together like old friends, she resolved to mend her ways in the future lest she might sometime embarrass them.

'Hem! Mrs Longe, ma'am,' said Polly loudly, as though they were both deaf. 'Sally wants to know if Mr Awkright is staying for his supper. Because if he is she'd beg to let you know as she warn't told early enough. And there's only hashed mutton from the Sunday joint, and cold bread-and-butter pudding from yesterday, else the cakes left at tea-time. But if you'd wait a bit she'll think of summat else, and shall she do that instead, ma'am?'

'Mr Ackroyd,' said Charlotte, lit by laughter, 'you are being introduced to the less formal end of our housekeeping, I fear, but if you care to join us you are very welcome. Polly can fetch a bottle of claret from the cellar, to enhance the mutton!'

'Nay, stand on no ceremony with me, madam. I cannot abide your genteel supper-parties. Hashed mutton and bread pudding will do very well for me, I thank you. As to the wine—well, if you would drink with me, there is nothing I like better than an occasional glass of claret.'

SEVENTEEN

Conspirators

January 1798

They had tiptoed about the house all day while Charlotte sat in solitary grief. It was that wretched time of year, when Christmas is over and spring is nowhere near arriving, and this as much as death in the house had depressed its mistress. For Polly voiced their opinions very well.

'It warn't the wet beds, and the running up and down stairs, with Miss Jorrocks, but the downright badness of her at the end. For she'd soil her nightgown a-purpose, just when I'd put it clean on. And I've seen her throw a dish to the floor, just on account of it being the pudding she hadn't called for. As for the language—well, my old father were a blessed saint in heaven compared to her. Where she learned it from I'll never know!'

Yes, Phoebe had gone out in great style, reduced to the naughty child she had never until then been able to indulge. Dorcas, saddened by the change in her old friend, had even braved Ned's admonitions to attend to her; while Charlotte went through agonies of embarrassment as Dr Standish listened to the ravings of a foolish virgin.

'I feel,' said Charlotte, after one session, 'that I do her an injury by calling you in. I had not realised she feared men so much. You understand, of course, that I speak not of you but of any man, Dr Standish?'

'My dear Mrs Longe,' he replied, with his thin smile, 'your feelings are most praiseworthy, most delicate. But your diagnosis of the case—which is senile dementia—appears to be at fault. These are not the hallucinations of morbid terror, madam, but of raging desire! She does not fear my sex. She has been most cruelly deprived of it!'

'Indeed,' said Charlotte faintly, and kept that information to herself.

At last the ravisher under the bed, and behind the curtains, came forth in the shape of death and claimed his victim. All this they concealed, and her burial was demure and proper. They laid her with her father and mother, *And Phoebe, devoted and beloved daughter of the Above,* and prayed that the Almighty would overlook this last antic revel, in view of the patient years before. Left her to heaven, as it were, and came home relieved and ashamed.

Then, within the week, Agnes had followed her, and in such a different manner that the entire household was red-eyed and subdued. Though feeble and bedridden, the aged housekeeper had contrived to play a part in the household almost to the last. Propped up on the pillows, she would darn and mend the linen finely, with the aid of her spectacles and a good wax candle to enable her to see clearly. Cicely had been invaluable to both patients, and there was something extraordinary in the way the child comprehended derangement and death. A voice raised in anger, a door slammed, would make her jump. But the harrowing sights and sounds of terminal illness left her unmoved, except for the sympathy with which she would anticipate a need or want.

Whereas Phoebe had rushed towards death in sublime ignorance, garrulous to the last, Agnes approached oblivion in an orderly manner. On her final day she had asked to see Sally, and apparently interrogated her clearly and minutely as to the condition of cupboards and drawers: ending with a brief but practical homily on the virtues of spring-cleaning early. Then, perfectly composed, she had asked if Charlotte could spare her a few moments. She wished to hand over to her god-daughter the contents of a woollen stocking, in which she had collected her life's savings; and to leave a message for Dorcas. She thanked Dorcas for inviting her to become Charlotte's godmother: an honour of which she had always been proud. Then, perhaps a little blurred by this time, though quite coherent, she put Charlotte through her religious catechism—a feat which that lady afterwards recalled with

207

some misgivings—and so partook of a glass of mulled wine and a slice of toast, and said she would sleep.

An hour later, peeping round the door to ask if she fancied anything else, Polly found her fallen against the pillows, looking steadfastly into the heavenly mansion prepared for her.

Charlotte had borne up until the second funeral was over, and then cast aside all pretence of heading her household, and mourned its losses in the abandon which follows a period of intense strain. So the kitchen staff heard the door knocker, that Saturday afternoon, with a hint of temper.

'Set of old pussy-cats!' said Sally. 'They come spying round when a body's dead that they wouldn't give the time of day to alive!'

'I'd forget to hear it,' said Polly, 'except that Mrs Longe'd be vexed with me!'

'I believe it is Mr Awkright,' said Ambrose, recognising the peremptory sound.

'Well, he can turn tail. She won't see nobody, today!' said Sally.

'I should let him in,' Ambrose advised. 'He may annoy her thoroughly, and then she will not cry so hard.'

'You're too sharp for your own good!' said Polly, and ran down the hall before Jack Ackroyd could assault their ears again.

'And you know what happened to Sharp, don't you, Master Ambrose?' said Sally, warning him.

'He cut himself!' the two children chorused, and smiled covertly at one another.

They heard the parlour door close behind their visitor.

'How is Mr Awkright behaving himself, Polly?' Ambrose asked, as she returned.

'He ain't put his foot in it so far. But give him five minutes!'

He stood uncertainly, arms held stiffly by his sides, the pockets of his good dark suit stuffed with papers, his clean cravat awry.

'I beg your pardon for this intrusion, Mrs Longe. Polly explained that you were low in spirits. I would not have come in, but she thought I might cheer you, ma'am.'

He took two or three steps towards the bowed figure, and paused.

'Though I am the poorest person imaginable on such occasions,' he added, 'I have never seemed to master the art of conveying what I feel.'

Charlotte said with difficulty, 'Polly had no right to place such a burden upon you, sir. Will you not sit down?'

'I thank you. She said she would bring us some tea, and make a toast.'

He sat upon the edge of Grandfather Wilde's chair and spread his hands towards the glowing fire, glancing sideways at her. Charlotte dried her eyes and smoothed her hair, drew herself upright and avoided his gaze.

'I had not realised that your good servant's funeral took place yesterday,' he explained. 'I tend to overlook domestic matters. Mrs Longe, I have been endeavouring to compose a handbill, and your opinion and advice would be most acceptable. If you could bring yourself to glance at it for a moment.'

He attempted to withdraw a paper from his pocket, whereat the rest fell all about the carpet.

'God damn my carelessness!' he muttered in self-disgust, stooping to pick them up.

A slight smile hovered involuntarily on Charlotte's mouth. Then her eyes welled tears again, and she whipped her handkerchief from her sleeve.

'Mind you, Mrs Longe,' said Jack, in kindly admonition, 'the best medicine for grief is hard work!' He peered about him for stray documents, and drew a moral from this statement. 'I have suffered a deal of trouble in my life, but was never one to sit feeling sorry for myself when there was work to be done. I might say that by thinking of others I have forgotten myself, madam.'

Charlotte stopped on a sob, and stared at him in disbelief.

'Your want of tact is quite prodigious, sir!' she cried, and wiped her eyes as though to dry them for good.

He stood holding his papers, nonplussed by her reaction.

'You misunderstand my meaning, madam,' he protested.

'Then you should speak plainer, sir!'

Polly, entering, heard the intonation and registered her mistress's annoyance, but set down her tray as though she were deaf.

'You may leave the bread, Polly,' said Charlotte. 'I shall toast it myself. I might ask you to do so, Mr Ackroyd'—as the door closed—'but that you would be sure to burn it!'

'Upon my soul, you are too provoking, madam!'

'You should consider, sir, that I have been provoked in my turn!'

But she was feeling a little better, and began composedly to toast the bread while the tea brewed. While he, who was no sort of fool, pondered on the possible shrewdness behind Polly's simple façade. The woman who had crouched in her misery before him was now sitting upright, thinking of other matters. He had, after all, cheered her, however unwittingly.

'I hesitate to suggest any comfort, Mrs Longe,' he said, somewhat forlornly, 'but the two friends you have recently buried were both aged. They led lives which might have been richer, perhaps, but were at any rate useful and comfortable. And, forgive me if my view seems too forthright for your present mood, they were dependents who sapped your time and energy. Mourn them by all means, for the affection you bore them, for the kindnesses they did you, for what they were to you—but do not mourn for yourself, madam. You have been given a freedom you did not possess before. Think, rather, what you shall do with it.'

Then he sat watching her, with the firelight on her face. Even in two and a quarter years of a friendship which had scarcely stirred the gossips in Millbridge—for they all thought him a poor catch, and paid far more attention to the visits of Hamish Standish, Nicodemus Hurst and the Quaker Caleb Scholes—even in this long time he had not learned to gauge her moods. He saw, with relief, that she was rational once more. He rubbed his hands softly, thoughtfully, and extended them to the friendly heat.

'Mr. Ackroyd,' said Charlotte kindly, 'if you would be so good as to attend to the toast I will look at your handbill!'

And smiled on him.

He buttered three slices of bread, stuck them together on the fork, and held them before the red coals.

'I assure you, Mrs Longe, that I shall be no King Alfred, but mind my business,' he said in earnest, and applied himself to the toasting.

But she was back in Lock-yard again, studying the information before her, judging how best to present it, dealing with fearful facts in cool objectivity.

'This is something greater in scope than you have attempted before!' she observed, in passing. 'No sporadic risings, but a concerted effort, and yet in a peaceable fashion. You seek, in short, to organise the whole of the valley?' He inclined his head. 'Then, Mr Ackroyd, you are no longer speaking to the artisans, who have some education, but to the mass of men who will be illiterate. This handbill will, of necessity, be read out to them. So they want a simple explanation and a few facts, which they can grasp on the instant. Remember the truth and simplicity of the parables! You need, therefore, to make your matter colourful, to draw pictures rather than morals—for the moral should be drawn from the tale. No need, no use for rhetoric. Speak to them, address them, directly, forcibly. Tell them what is to be done now—do not wax poetical on future worlds. The man who is hungry would rather have a crust of bread than the finest sentiment! Tell them what you want of them. Let today act, and tomorrow shall take care of itself. And Latin quotations, sir, are *persona non grata*'—here her lips twitched, and she added—'except between us, of course, Mr Ackroyd!'

'I am obliged to you, madam,' he said generously. 'Forgive me if I do not look at you as I speak, but I must watch the toast lest it burn. So I have far to go before I become a pamphleteer worthy of *The Northern Correspondent*?'

'Oh, sir,' said Charlotte, 'you speak to my condition, as the Quakers would say. Forgive me, I beg. I do but seek to couch your words more surely. But I believe I know what you wish to do, and therefore I speak as I have done.'

At this juncture she poured the tea, and he proffered the toast in homage. He took the other documents from his pockets, brooding on them.

'Oh, Mrs Longe,' he said fervently, 'I need your help. I should be loath to put you to any risk, both for your children's sake and your own. But though London may have twenty political pamphleteers to the square mile for aught I know, there is but one in this entire valley and her talents are lying unused!'

As he spoke he gained confidence, ceased to fumble with his sheaf of papers, shook them neatly together and laid them upon a table by her. His whole body was bent upon the discourse. He leaned forward, hands planted on his knees, eyes eloquent, and held her with fire and conviction.

'Madam, I confess myself to be a follower of William Godwin rather than Tom Paine. For ever since I read Godwin's excellent book *Political Justice* I knew that evil could not be patched up but must be eradicated. The French were right, madam! Oh, I am not advocating their methods, nor condoning their bestial excesses. It would avail no one if we were to hang Pitt, shoot the King, take over St James's

211

Palace and rob the Royal Mint! These are the dreams of ignorance and malice. But our present system must go, madam, for as long as a handful of rich men own the country we shall continue to subjugate and sweat a majority of poor wretches.

'Now Paine would use our present social system, while giving every man his opportunity to work and eat according to his talent. On this I disagree in principle, but it may well be that we must make haste slowly. Paine first, and Godwin after. I am willing to go along with Tom Paine for a while! Tax the rich and give to the poor. Make each mill or shop or mine supply medical care for its employees, and a pension for the aged who can no longer toil. Let the workhouses provide work of a proper and dignified sort. And, since the human race depends upon propagation, dispense allowances: a sovereign when a poor couple marries, another sovereign to the mother when each child is born, and a payment to the parents for every child under the age of say, fourteen years who is still at school. Subsidise education, so that everyone can at least read and write. Build schools everywhere, fill them with teachers of a proper sort—and may your Misses Whiteheads' Academies and the old dames' schools go hang! Fill their bellies, clothe their bodies, put a plain roof over their heads, teach them to think.

'Madam, I confess that I have been at the back of most revolts in this valley. Since I was a young man I have helped and encouraged any little group who were oppressed. I led the weavers to burn down the first spinning-mill ever erected at Thornley, seventeen years ago. But I have never been able to organise the mass of workers. I labour for the day when I can see this valley as one great union, and hold their services in abeyance until they are paid fair wages. I look to the time when every man has a vote, and will elect a Parliament of Radicals. Then, madam, we shall see Reform!'

Like most women, Charlotte had learned the trick of dividing her attention. So even as she turned over these ideas in her mind, she rang the bell for more hot water, sliced bread, and coals. While Jack Ackroyd strode the parlour impatiently, stopping to say *Pshaw!* at any ornament he especially despised. But she took her time, and supplied him with further refreshment before she spoke on the matter.

'Sir, what you say reaches my heart and echoes my principles. In theory I am with you. It is the practice that falls down! Your organisation, sir, would be riddled with government spies in five minutes. And, upon all being discovered, no government would enquire into the purity of our motives, but despatch us both on the scaffold!'

'Not both, madam. Me, certainly. Your name shall never be mentioned, nor your presence known. If you would be our pamphleteer even Ralph Fairbarrow shall know nothing of it!'

She smiled in spite of herself at his ingenuousness.

'My dear Mr Ackroyd, Mr Fairbarrow and many others—unless they have forgot me quite!—would recognise my style. And if I agree to work with you then I agree to the penalty for working. That would be only honest in me.'

He struggled with a notion that was still new to him: the value of herself as an individual over the value of the cause itself.

'Then,' he said with infinite regret, 'I withdraw my offer, Mrs Longe. I know a little more of you and of your children since we made up our quarrel of that other year, and I cannot allow you so to risk your safety. It does not matter about me. I belong to no one. None shall miss me.'

In her astonishment Charlotte let the toast burn.

'There, sir!' she cried. 'Look what I have done!'

'It is not my fault, surely, madam?' he protested, brought down from his heights.

'No, sir, but I must scold someone for it!' Smiling at her wilfulness and his amazement. Then, threading fresh slices on to the fork, 'Mr Ackroyd, you have spoke of talents lying unused. What of your talent for teaching? Certainly, Millbridge regards you as an odd fish, sir. But they do not think you dangerous, and they are prepared to overlook a few eccentricities because of your ability as their headmaster. In the field of young minds you will plant a greater and more fertile crop of radical attitudes than by rousing an illiterate mob. For I must risk your displeasure, sir, by warning you that what you begin in this valley you will not end! Whereas in your grammar school the whole object is encompassed peaceably. Your pupils need you, sir, and they would miss you.'

He was restored at once to his theme.

'First, madam!' Holding up his forefinger in reproof. 'I know that he who sows the wind will reap the whirlwind. I dislodge a clod of earth, and start a landslide. I know, I know. You speak of ideas. Ideas are very well, but they are not enough. It is by our actions we are judged, madam. I do not seek merely to educate some hundreds of benevolent

213

young men. I wish to awaken the dormant spirit of thousands of oppressed human beings, to make them aware of their rights and their powers. Millbridge would find another headmaster but I doubt that such another weapon as myself has yet been forged in this valley. My predecessor and benefactor, Henry Tucker, used me as an educational experiment, madam. Oh, he was never unkind. He treated me fairly. I was not ill-used. But I was proof of the assumption that if you take an intelligent boy from a poor family, and instruct him well, he will prove as good or better than your educated gentleman.'

'So you were not unhappy with your family, sir?'

A wound had been opened which he had long chosen to ignore. He left his fresh toast untouched. He became cold and awkward.

'No, madam, they were kind to me, but kindness does not extend the intellect, and love can hamper it! I left them far behind me. With wisdom which, as a child, I did not realise, Mr Tucker cut me off from my family. I was allowed no dealings with them. They, being equally wise, though so much humbler, agreed to the stipulation. A boy of six or seven, madam, finds such a situation harrowing. A man over forty sees its inevitability.'

The line of his mouth was stoical. He coughed, folded his arms, crossed his legs, and stared fiercely at the fire-irons.

'Such a weapon as yourself?' Charlotte prompted, picking out the expression he had used so bitterly.

He looked directly at her: dark and hard and isolated.

'Madam, Mr Tucker did not consider human nature in his pursuit of education. My feelings were for my family, my intellect was for him, and socially I belonged and now belong to nobody. When I entered this room today I believe I remarked on my inability to express emotion. It arises from the division in me. I am not a loving, trusting, believing person, madam. I am of no use to myself. Therefore, my affections are directed to the mass of people—since they do not demand of me an attention which I could not give. I belong to everyone, madam, and therefore to no one. So no one will miss me.'

'Oh, Mr Ackroyd,' said Charlotte compassionately, 'I begin to understand you better. Pray eat your toast, sir'—briskly, endeavouring to put him at his ease again—'I should have thought we had gone to sufficient trouble not to leave it!'

She had been making up her mind for a longer time than

he would have thought possible: for well over three years, since his first visit. She spoke simply, frankly.

'Sir, I know myself to be an excellent pamphleteer. And I do not say this out of vanity, for my husband taught me, and what I am I owe to him and the need to earn my bread. And my principles are yours, sir. I shall be pleased to help you.'

Now he was beset by so many emotions, rational and otherwise, that he could not deal with her or himself. He jumped up at once, spilling his toast, knocking the table in his flight, stuffing the papers pell-mell into his pockets.

'I am no weathercock, madam,' he cried, 'to change direction with the wind. I had not thought about such matters as your style betraying you. I had thought I would take all upon myself, and so protect you from possible consequences. I see it cannot be. I beg your pardon if I have in any way offended you. And good-day to you, madam!'

Whereupon he departed, forgetting his hat, cravat tails flying, banging the front door after him.

'And how did Mr Awkright offend Mamma this time?' Ambrose asked.

'Now bless me if she ain't forgot to tell me all her private business!' Polly replied with tremendous sarcasm.

'But has Mamma stopped crying, please, Polly?' Cicely asked.

'Oh, she ain't grieving no more, love. Just a-setting by the parlour fire, a bit on the thoughtful side. Leave her be until bed-time. She'll be right as rain tomorrow.'

Charlotte had picked up the toast and righted the table by the time Polly came in to see what all the noise was about.

'Mr Ackroyd has forgotten his hat,' she said. 'If he comes back for it, do not trouble him to enter—unless he wishes to, of course—just give it to him. He has some problem on his mind.'

The handbill had been forgotten. She sat with her feet on the fender, shoulders hunched forward, reading it. From time to time she smiled impishly, involuntarily, at some scholarly turn of phrase, some solemn passage, some flight of rhetoric which would have adorned an essay better than a tract. Then she brought writing materials to the table by the fire, and began to draft a new broadsheet. The children came to say good-night and she kissed them fondly, promising they should spend the whole of tomorrow with her. Polly fetched her supper on a tray. Jack Ackroyd did not return. Their separate windows shone long into the winter night: mute witnesses to separate thoughts. But whereas Charlotte mused philosophically, Jack Ackroyd struggled in rage and misery.

Love is never a kind business, but by dint of meeting it early in life and possibly repeating the process a few times, a man learns how to parry its keenest thrusts and keep up a reasonable show of defence. The headmaster had no such experience. At the moment of bringing himself to confess that he was incapable of love he found himself impaled upon it. The irrelevance of the emotion damaged his self-esteem. Had he not ignored lovely faces, graceful figures and pretty speeches for twenty years or more on his solitary road? Only to be brought down by time and toast and firelight, perception and compassion, which he had interpreted under the very different name of friendship. The enormity of the enterprise appalled him. The more he considered the relationship between himself and Charlotte the less he felt able to cope with it.

'I shall not see her again!' he said aloud, resolutely.

Then the thought insinuated itself that she did not care for him anyway. Reviewing her many moods, he found aggression, apology, amusement, contemplation, dedication, comfortable companionship. None of these represented a woman in the throes of tender passion, according to popular lights. But did he want passion and tenderness from her?

'Certainly not!' cried the puritan within him, shrinking back.

But suppose one of those other boobies possessed her instead? That finicking solicitor, Hurst. That silent Quaker, Scholes. That stupid young Standish? What then?

'How soon can I see her?' he wondered, panicking. 'But then, what can I say to her?'

Charlotte, feet on the fender, head in hands, pondered on the infinite mystery of the human heart. It had been fifteen years since she fell in love with Toby Longe, but she remembered the girl in her, suffering, as though she had been a younger sister: the sudden knowledge of love, the struggle to interest and hold him, the need to possess him and lose herself in him. What folly, what immeasurable ecstacy! The cost of that expensive escapade had rendered her all but immune to a second encounter.

This time love had besieged her subtly, undermined her

slowly, disguised itself as anger, irritation, diversion, respect and liking. She accepted it, but in trepidation. What place was there for it in her present life? She shrank from involving her children, her family, in an affection they might dislike or despise. She had run that gauntlet once. And then there was this work between them, which must be done. Well, she supposed everything would take its course. She hoped they could survive the outcome.

In the meantime she could guess the extent of his bewilderment, his wretchedness, and was moved to compassion at the thought of that respectable scarecrow alone in his barren field, and yet could not help smiling at the picture.

'Oh, my poor Jack!' she cried, between tears and laughter. 'Oh, my dear Jack!'

From the time that he fled her presence, to the time he returned by means of her excuse, was only a matter of days. But days can be deserts, and Jack Ackroyd's deserts were stony places. Perceiving his dilemma, Charlotte wrote a friendly letter, saying she appreciated his concern for her family's well-being but had quite made up her mind about the matter they had discussed, and did he find the enclosed handbill to his liking? She then sent Polly across the High Street to deliver this bombshell personally.

'. . . and your hat, sir, as you forgot,' said Polly, clapping it down on his desk. 'Should I wait or shall you be coming round, sir?'

He did not answer. She observed the tremor of his hands as he unsealed the letter. Watched him glance at the enclosure and put it aside, scan Charlotte's message rapidly, and turn from white to red and back again. Then he read through once more, paying great attention to each line.

'Should I wait, Mr Awkright, or shall you call?' Polly asked.

He lifted his head and she was sorry for him. Such puzzlement and painful indecision.

'Pray tell Mrs Longe,' he said with difficulty, 'that I thank her. And shall reply presently.'

'Very good, sir,' said Polly, reading him with far more ease than he had read Charlotte's careful note. 'Mr Hurst generally comes by for his glass of wine at six o'clock. But she'll be on her own for supper tonight. Tomorrow being a Sat'day she gets caught up with one thing and another all day. And Sunday she spends with the children.'

'I thank you, Polly. That will be all,' he replied sternly, to show that he knew what he was about.

Which he did not.

She dropped her curtsey and departed, to report to Charlotte.

'He hasn't said nothink definite, ma'am, but I reckon as he'll be here for his supper, meself. Shall I tell Sally to cook somethink special?'

'No, I think not, Polly. That would seem contrived. Just tell Sally to cook a little extra, if you please.'

Jack Ackroyd wrote several letters that day, and tore them all up. He could not eat, but drank many glasses of wine. He remembered the handbill and read it over and over again, without comprehending it, so finally locked it safey away with his other papers. By eight o'clock that night he was light of head, heavy of heart, and totally disorientated. He crossed the High Street stiffly, arms rigid at his sides, mouth dry. He nerved himself to knock once, but softly so they might not hear it. Polly, waiting behind the door, wrenched his hat from his clenched hands and drove him into the parlour, where he stood for a moment: a most pitiable spectacle, if anyone had noticed.

But there was Charlotte sitting on the carpet in a perfect nest of papers, reflecting none of his terrors or concerns, intent upon some document. In the moments that she was so preoccupied he breathed more easily. Then she looked up and smiled, brandishing her spectacles at him as she did when excited about something.

'Ah, Mr Ackroyd,' she cried, 'I had hoped you might spare me half an hour. I have been so busy, picking up old threads and weaving them together. Pray sit down, sir, while I bombard you with questions!'

He settled himself stealthily in Grandfather Wilde's armchair, seeing her once more absorbed in her task. The fire crackled companionably, and he extended his hands to the warmth. He heard her reading to him, as he had looked at her handbill, without comprehension. Then gradually her words impinged upon his understanding. He relaxed and listened.

'. . . I have paid greater attention to political events than possibly you realised, sir. And from time to time our mutual friend, Mr Fairbarrow, has given me a jog, or fed me information to whet my appetite for more. So I know that the London Corresponding Society has adopted a new constitution, and gone underground. That there is also a secret committee, meeting in Furnival's Inn cellar, and from this centre comes the organisation known as the United Englishman. That there are several branches all over England, that they work with the United Irishmen, and are very strong in Liverpool and Manchester. There are also other societies with similar aims and principles, but in other guises, such as the Friends of Freedom in Rochdale and Royton, who are linked to a Manchester centre—which has such an essay of a name as I professionally deplore! Dear God in heaven, who shall remember the Institute for the Promulgation of Knowledge amongst the Working People of Manchester and its Vicinity? However, I digress! The Radical cause is healthy and growing stronger. No doubt the naval mutinies last year were due largely to poor pay and poorer food, but it is believed on all sides that the rebellion was instigated by our people, for there were members of the Corresponding Society among the sailors. We are sympathising with the Irish Rebellion, but are divided as to the action we should take if the French invade our shores. Am I well learned in my lessons, sir?'

'Admirably, madam!'

'What name had you thought of for your own organisation, sir?'

'I?' Startled. 'I had not thought of any, madam. The idea is yet in its infancy, and I was too deep in its aims and possible achievements to think of names. It would be a good thing if we could become affiliated to the United Englishmen, or to the Manchester centre. But the name is not important, is it, Mrs Longe?'

'The name is of the utmost importance,' she replied gravely. 'It evokes an immediate response in both friend and enemy, and we must take care what inference is drawn from it. You are seeking to establish a general trades union in the valley, so beware of such a title as Friends of Liberty which suggests we support the French Revolution—unless you plan to make England part of the French Continent!'

'No, no,' he said hastily. 'I do not dabble in foreign politics. Our own are quite enough. But if we are United Englishmen, a title already in fairly wide use, this would help bring about a national organisation.'

'Mr Ackroyd,' said Charlotte earnestly, 'that is the sort of dream which, pray God, another generation than ours shall realise. But to indulge in it at the present time is folly. I speak not as Mr Fairbarrow would have me—for he is an-

219

other dreamer as my husband was—but from the information he has given me. We have a number of dedicated and clever men initiating these movements—and, I dare say, more than that number of dedicated and clever government agents spying on them! But what I find in the mass is a great many separate and loose-knit groups, working sporadically for our cause, meeting regularly in inns, and singing seditious songs! It is of no use advertising our allegiance to those who cannot help us. We are best to keep in touch with national events, but to work for and by ourselves in the valley. We are not Sons of Freedom, we are Wyndendale reformers!'

She was sitting back on her heels, hands linked in her lap, wholly animated. There was some endearing fault in Charlotte which denied her elegance. Though she had brushed and curled her hair assiduously, strands were escaping over neck and bosom. Though her muslin gown was delightful, the skirt had been crushed as she sat. Her slipper was about to leave her foot. Momentarily, she gave the impression of a graceful, vivid, but untidy girl. The charm lay in her unselfconsciousness.

The sound sense of her proposal registered with him, but so strongly did love move him that this good sense seemed but one more delicious attribute. He was as rapt as a youth with his first sweetheart. His fears had vanished. His feelings came uppermost.

'Oh, Mrs Longe, I love you,' said Jack.

And sat appalled at his temerity.

Though she had intended mostly to put him at his ease by speaking of their common interests, she had become involved in her own argument. His statement toppled her composure. She opened her mouth to speak, and no words came.

The light went from him in an instant. He sat woodenly, twisting his hands.

'But I expect nothing of you,' he said too loudly.

He stared at the ring of papers, picked one out at random, clumsily, to give himself time.

'You have applied yourself with commendable zeal,' he said, endeavouring to speak naturally. 'We must discuss this matter at length.'

Then his heart failed him.

'Another evening, perhaps,' said Jack. 'At the moment I have a late appointment to keep. And must leave you.'

'Oh, why do you always make me laugh and cry at the

same time?' cried Charlotte, treading over the fruits of her labours to reassure him.

She took his head between her hands and kissed him long and tenderly, while he clutched her to him, loving, unbelieving. So that Polly, bouncing open the door, had hastily to close it again and call, 'Supper's ready, Mrs Longe!' very loudly, until they heard her.

They sat with plates upon their knees, eating and speaking very little, looking at each other in wonder from time to time, smiling from the joy of revelation. Then Jack's face clouded again. He had indulged the dream for a while, and now reality was upon him.

'Oh, Charlotte, it will not do,' he said. 'I blame myself for weakening. I should have let you be. Let us preserve our friendship and our common interests, not throw all away for the sake of a delight which could destroy the pair of us. We have no future together, Charlotte.'

She was thoughtful, feet on the fender, cheek propped on one hand.

'It is not even a question of the two of us,' he said awkwardly. 'There are your children to consider. There is your family, who would not welcome me as your husband. And Millbridge, I fear, would doubly detest us—we offend them separately as it is. I can say, "Go hang yourselves!" as far as I am concerned, but I cannot say it for the three of you whom I must cherish. And if we had children of our own, Charlotte, what hostages we should be offering to fortune. No, marriage is out of the question.'

Her old spectres rose before her: the grief and disruption caused by her love-affair with Toby, the terror of imprisonment for debt or treasonable acts, the pinpricks of social snubs and cold shoulders, the ultimate fear that Ambrose and Cicely would suffer through her and their young lives be stunted.

'Yes, I agree. The acceptable answer to our situation is unacceptable,' she answered as lightly as she could. Then, like Jack, she turned to the papers lying on her parlour floor, and sought solace from them. 'Jack,' she said, 'I had such an idea for your society!'

'Then tell me of it,' he said kindly, and endeavoured to help her turn the conversation on to matters which would once have been of prime importance.

'For some little while,' Charlotte began, her voice growing

stronger as she became engrossed in her project, 'I have felt I should use what teaching ability I possess, since Ambrose's education is now in your care and there is only Cicely. And that great mouthful of a title for the Manchester centre made me think to further the education of working people. I had thought, though folk will say it is very odd, of using the back parlour as a schoolroom one or two evenings a week. I can take a dozen people in a class, and teach them to read and write. I know,' she said hastily, 'that I am but scratching the surface, for there are hundreds in the valley who would like to learn and cannot be taught, but it is a beginning.'

The schoolmaster in him saw infinite possibilities.

'Mrs Longe,' he cried, forgetting their new intimacy, 'I think it a splendid notion. You have given a lead which the grammar school can follow. I have two young masters there (of my own political persuasion) who would also take an evening class, every week, and our facilities are greater than your own. We must form a committee. We must have a name for this new social venture!'

And he walked the room in his excitement, and threw up his arms in a gesture both clumsy and touching, as though his body would not contain him. Charlotte smiled, and then laughed, crying, 'That is not all!'

'My—dear—Mrs—Longe,' he said, sinking slowly back into his armchair. 'My dear Charlotte! What an astonishing woman you are!'

'Mr Ackroyd, "The Society for the Furtherance of Literacy among the Working People" if I may so call it, though sufficient in itself, will serve another purpose besides. (Yes, my dear sir, we *need* that monumental title to convince folk that our morals are pure and our aims charitable.) Jack, there may be held meetings within these meetings, a committee within this committee, a society within this society. Do you not see? Outwardly, both of us are behaving much as they expect. We have radical sympathies, but they come out in this harmless fashion. We may thus rouse Millbridge's amusement or annoyance but not their suspicion and hatred.'

He sat, faintly smiling, seeming to look right through her.

'You have a devious mind, Mrs Longe,' he observed, ironic, affectionate.

Charlotte gave a little shrug, and smiled directly back at him.

'Well, sir,' she said ruefully, 'I want to do what I feel is right. And I should not like to be hanged for it!'

He was very bright, very quick, drawn in on himself, thinking. His eyes were clear and cool, his whole demeanour changed.

'I fear,' he said slowly, 'that however careful, even cunning, we are, we both risk that in the end, Lottie.'

They enjoyed a silence of complete accord. Even the risk, shared, was nothing compared to the possible achievement.

'Should you like me to act as secretary?' she asked hesitantly. 'To either?'

'Would you, Mrs Longe? To both!'

'Yes, sir, with the greatest pleasure in life.'

'You see, we could enlarge this society, both in itself and in its radical heart,' he cried, running on ahead of her. 'I would—I think it best it should seem to come from me—begin with the evening classes at the grammar school, and you could take others here as a sort of branch meeting. Do you see, Charlotte? Then we enrol members of our persuasion throughout the valley. It does not matter how long it takes us, if we are growing steadily. Branch upon branch of the teaching society, and within each branch—as you said—a nucleus of committed Radicals, who can use the society as cover. Dear God, it is bigger and better than I dreamed of!'

She sat smiling, her hands in her lap, her papers all about her.

'We must be careful, and we must evolve,' Jack continued, pacing the parlour, throwing up his arms from time to time in that strange, moving gesture. 'No impatience. No slogans. No violence. Simply an organisation that runs like clockwork. Quiet, efficient and effective. Mrs Longe, I salute you!'

'Now, sir, I have chose—with your permission—the name of our teaching society. What shall you call your inner centre?'

'Well, let us be both simple and colourful, Mrs Longe!' he cried. Then, snapping his fingers, 'As Yorkshire lights up "The Black Lamp", should we not grow "The Red Rose"?'

They put their arms about one another, laughing, triumphant. The laughter gradually became a peaceful smiling silence, the triumph a delicious langour. He stroked her hair as though it were something very fine and precious, and she was emboldened to take up the subject they had let drop.

'Jack! When I lived in London, the last three years at least, I learned how to avoid . . . well, Toby and I had no more children. It is nothing new,' she hurried on, for she felt him withdrawing from her, 'the practice has been known among middle-class families in France for thirty years. Jeremy Bentham mentioned it recently. At least,' she persisted, 'we could have something of a life together. . . .'

'What? Creeping furtively across the High Street?' he cried, more wrathfully than he felt, but he had never been able to deal with emotions.

'How else are you proposing to conduct your secret society?' she answered, genuinely angry and deeply hurt. 'Why should a political organisation be so moral, and a personal union be dubbed furtive? Oh, you are detestable!'

And she fairly pushed him away from her. She could have wept with mortification.

His colour rose. His face changed. He stood before her, bowed in remorse, helpless to mend this error of judgement. He decided to be truthful, since he had failed to be diplomatic.

'You have chosen the most maladroit fool in Millbridge, Charlotte,' he said gravely. 'Pray forgive me.'

'Well,' she said, attempting lightness again, 'we have had a deal to do this evening, without fetching ourselves into the midst of it. Let it be, Jack. Good-night, and though you do not believe in God—God bless you.'

'It is like dragging oneself naked across sharp stones,' he said bitterly. 'I should have stayed where I was with you.'

'Believe me,' said Charlotte, with difficulty, 'you have not so much choice in the matter as you seem to imagine. Go now, Jack.'

At two in the morning, having tried in vain to sleep, the headmaster wrapped himself in an old and shabby mantle that he might not be recognised, and stole across the High Street to look at his lady's window. It gleamed out upon the night, and he cursed himself for a stumbling fool to have upset her so. Why had he not said that he knew of the French practice, and that it was not faultless? That he feared to hazard her life and reputation and destroy her peace of mind? That it put yet more responsibility upon her who had more than enough already? But, he must burst out with some sarcastic remark calculated to keep her at a distance from him. Only, she had come closer than any, just the same. She was a part of him whether he liked it or not.

Ashamed of himself, then and now, he picked up a pebble

and threw it as accurately as any of his schoolboys could against the window-pane.

Charlotte looked up, looked out. Then, shading the candle-stick with her hand, she crept down the stairs of the sleeping house, and let him in.

EIGHTEEN

Rise and Fall

Spring 1798

As the century drew to its turbulent close, William's reputation still exceeded his capital while his profits continued to span the gulf. Gradually the bond between him and his partner had loosened: on William's part with deliberation, on Caleb's with regret. William retained his share of Belbrook, and his interest in the first foundry, while Caleb directed it and was backed by Quaker shareholders. The change had been peaceable, business went on as usual, the Scholes's network absorbed this traitor within their midst, but William had been registered as unreliable and could therefore expect no special favours.

At the far end of the valley the Snape ironworks devoured ore and coal, poured forth its liquid metal, belched smoke and flame, and roared by night and day for more fuel, while the sky was lit for miles around and the ears assaulted by noise. And as Snape expanded it grew nearer to Belbrook, for William continued to buy up or lease land and build upon it: houses for officials, cottages for his workmen, another blast-furnace, another rolling-mill. He was mortgaged beyond reason, and yet, given money to clear one debt, would extend his business further and so contract another. He had survived the bank crisis of the previous year by sheer impudence, and an implicit belief in himself and his destiny. So far, neither had failed him.

Recently he had chosen and bought a new site for his house. Higher Cunshurst, midway between Belbrook and Snape, commanded a view of both foundries and the valleys on either side. Typically he said nothing of this until he could bring the architect and his plans to supper. Quincey House had palled on him long since, and his apologies were impatient as he cleared a space on the parlour table.

'For we are all a-top of one another here!' he cried. 'And my good brother-in-law will be glad to see the back of us! Mollie! Lettie! Take these things away!'

'Here, let me help thee, William,' said Caleb, even-tempered. 'Do not put the maids in a fluster. Zelah will be down again shortly, and Mr Field will not mind waiting over another glass of claret, I dare say.'

The architect was only a young man. He coloured up as though he had been at fault, and stammered an apology for nothing, clutching the plans to his best waistcoat.

'The new baby demands a great deal of my wife's attention,' said William unnecessarily.

'A very p-p-pleasant family,' said Mr Field nervously, for he had met two-year-old Tabitha on her way to bed. 'Did you say the new b-b-baby was a b-b-boy?'

'A second daughter, sir. Mollie, you can leave the fruit. We need something to hold down the corners. Now, sir, spread out your plans and pin them with oranges!'

And his face smoothed as the latest vision unfolded.

'There, what do you think of that, old friend?' William cried, and put his arm round Caleb's shoulders and drew him to the table.

'Shall we not wait for Zelah?' Caleb asked.

'Oh, I do not mind going over the plans twice. She will be a while yet. Pray continue, Mr Field.'

Ellis Field was one of the many gifted young men whom William collected about him, and who rose with him: the new ironmaster being an excellent judge of character. This latest protégé looked more unlikely than most. His movements were jerky, his slight frame angular, his eyes protruberant, his speech halting. But as he expatiated over their joint dream his stammer disappeared and he used the plural 'we' in a confident manner. Caleb could not decide whether the architect meant himself and William, or whether he reverted to royal status when his work transcended the man.

'At first,' Ellis Field began, 'we thought to crown the site with an Italianate mansion. See how commanding, how magnificent, would be this place upon the hill! Then, as we worked, the site imposed itself upon the house, and we saw that it must grow from the land, be a part of the place. We considered local stone, rejecting sandstone because of its coarse texture, its poor weathering quality and above all else its attraction to soot! For industry, my dear sirs, means smoke and grime. You would not thank us if she needed cleaning every few years! So we came to limestone, and one of them in particular which comes from the Ulverston neighbourhood, and when polished resembles marble—a superb stone. The roof to be made of Rossendale flags for harmony and strength. They do not care enough about appearances in this part of the country. Provided a building will keep out the rain they do not mind using ugly materials. How posterity will throw up its hands, my dear sirs! These harsh red bricks, these sombre slates and dreary stones . . . I digress. Ah, Mrs Howarth, you have missed my sermon and thus come at the right moment.'

He was so overjoyed at his project that he could even joke about it.

'Zelah, see what we have to show you,' said William eagerly, pulling her close to him and kissing her cheek.

He forgot that her baby had disturbed their meal and conversation, and made him irritable in consequence. And she, responding to his changed mood, became her honeyed self again, and forgave him for springing both guest and surprise upon her when she had but lately risen from childbed.

'So, dear madam,' Ellis Field continued, 'we have our house of five bays and two and a half storeys. The porch with Ionic columns—unfluted, naturally. A pavilion at either side. You see how she commands the hill? Let us go indoors! We are ahead of our time in domestic appointments. There is a water-closet on each floor, fitted with the new trap so that one is not troubled by unpleasant odours. A room designed solely for bathing purposes. . . .'

'Good heaven!' said William, amazed, delighted.

'. . . The cess-pool is set well away from the house, so that again one is not troubled, *etcetera*. The kitchen is fitted with the latest and largest range—courtesy of Belbrook ironworks, my dear sirs—and we have running water throughout the house, heated by means of a boiler in the cellar—again by courtesy, *etcetera*. Very modern. But!' Here he held up his hand. 'I pay tribute to both beauty and practicality, lady and gentlemen. Observe the beauty now. The golden mean is used throughout—the length just one and a half times the breadth. The height of the ceilings gives a sense of space and serenity. Matchless proportions! (Pardon me, if I put this sheet to the other end of the table. Ah, thank you, Mr Howarth.) Now we come to detail. Simple, elegant decoration. The baroque is quite charming. We do not quarrel with it. But it is a little too much. Observe our ceilings, our doorways, our fireplaces. Consummate grace! And here, Mrs Howarth, a touch, a hint, a mere nothing, but rather nice—the door at this end is curved to round the corner, which would otherwise be abrupt. You shall study these at your leisure, of course. I do but give a cursory survey.

'And now the final suggestion. There she stands. An austere elegance without, a gracious elegance within. The marriage of strength and beauty. I cannot think that "The Grange" should be her name, though Mr Howarth mentioned this in passing. A grange is a country house or farming establishment. No, let her take her name from the place, as she has taken her form. Cunshurst means "The King's Wood". Shall we say—Kingswood Hall?'

They stood astonished at his eloquence, for he had found even the weather a laborious topic at supper. They stood silent before the vision.

Imagining the worst, the architect tumbled down to earth again, and cracked his knuckles one by one to comfort himself.

'Of c-c-course,' he said feebly, 'this is but the f-f-first draft. . . .'

'It is the final draft!' cried William, elated. 'Marvellously conceived, Mr Field. And finer than I dreamed, sir!'

Even Caleb and Zelah, inclined to a Quakerish reticence, were warm with praise.

'But how much will thee pay for such a mansion, William?' Caleb asked, smoothing his long chin as his father did when confronted by a proposition.

'Oh, what matter? If the war. . . .' He had been about to say *if the war goes on I can pay for anything*, but altered this out of consideration for their feelings. 'If the war do not prevent me, I can start building at once. The site is already cleared.'

Zelah and Caleb exchanged glances. Neither of them had heard of the site before this evening.

'The cost,' murmured Mr Field, passing a scribbled note to William, 'is, of course, subject to any price rise due to the war, but you hinted that I should not cheese-pare, Mr Howarth.'

'It is not cheap,' William agreed, looking sideways at a

small fortune, 'but only the best is good enough. Now, Zelah, are you satisfied?'

'If thee can afford it, William,' said Zelah cautiously, 'but remember that after building it we must appoint it, and live in it.'

'Aye, and think of heating this great place, William!' said Caleb.

'Servants both indoors and out,' Zelah continued. 'I see that the garden is left blank. . . .'

'We plan to design that later,' said William.

'And unless these fine stables are for show. . . .'

Ellis Field had shrunk into himself, but William seemed to grow taller and more imposing. He spoke tenderly to Zelah now as though only the two of them were in the parlour.

'Love, dost thee want the house?' And as she hesitated, 'I hurry thee on and give thee no time to think. Say what thee wants, Zelah. Thee shall have what thee wants, love. Mr Field can come again, another evening.'

'Oh, c-c-certainly, M-m-m. . . .'

Zelah smiled on her husband, who had not courted her for a long time.

'Mr Field,' she asked gracefully, 'would thee take me through the house and make me see it?'

Then the place grew round her, and she walked from room to room.

'Oh, it is full of light,' she cried suddenly, and laughed. 'Here is my private parlour. And a room by the kitchen where I can do the flowers. And your dressing-room, William. And nursery and schoolroom and childrens' bedrooms all in one wing. Willie, we shall need twenty servants!' She clasped his arm with both her hands, and give her hurried little laugh again. 'Willie, we cannot live here! We shall never afford it!'

'But wouldst thee *like* to live in it, love?' he insisted.

'Oh, yes, Willie. I should like it more than anything.'

'Then it is thine, Zelah, even as I promised thee,' he said fondly, grandly. And in a different tone, incisively, 'Mr Field, we begin building as soon as possible. I do not want the new century to be far advanced before we move into Kingswood Hall. Indeed, I should like to celebrate its turn with all my family about me, in that very place!'

'But the t-t-time factor, my d-d-dear sir!' stammered the architect, aghast.

'My dear Mr Field,' said William. 'Money can buy time. Did you not know that?'

'A bad harvest gone, and another hard winter to come, from what I can see,' said Ned Howarth, standing at his parlour window. He thrust his hands deep into his breeches pockets. 'Look at them rowan berries. Dorcas—aye, and look quick afore the birds nip them all off! We'st be snowed in again by Christmas, my lass. You'd best get old *Robinson Crusoe* out. You'll be reading him to us when the nights draw in.'

Dorcas was casting up the farm accounts, which showed no great profit, and did not answer him directly.

Eventually she said, 'We seem to stay much in the same place, Ned, financially. Some crops do well one year, and badly the next. A good season sets us up. A bad one pulls us down again. I had thought by this time we should have progressed.'

'Nay, farming's not like ironmastering,' he answered. 'Our work lasts one year at a time, and then starts all over again. But Kit's Hill is better off by far than it were when we first wed, Dorcas. Thanks to thee for much of it. And we've never gone cold nor hungry, and we've got a roof over us head.'

'Well, it is easier to think of ideas in a warm parlour than to carry them out in a cold field,' she said fairly. 'You do that harder part, Ned. And that reminds me. I wish you would leave the heavy work to Dick and the men. At four-and-seventy you should take life more comfortably than you do.'

'Dorcas! If I've towd thee once I've towd thee a hundred times. Let me be, my lass. I know what I'm doing.'

'But you should rest more,' she persisted.

'Rest?' he cried scornfully. 'How can I rest, my lass? I'm not like thee, able to pick up a book and while away the time. I'm all hands and no head, lass. I were brought up to work from morning to night, and that's the way I'll work 'til I drop. So say nowt!'

She did say nothing more, but the line of her mouth showed disapproval, and she was obstinate enough to return to the argument another time. They were as intent upon each other now, in old age, as they had been in their youth and prime. Each strove to shield the other. She left her accounts and came over to the window, to slip her arm through his and watch the rooks tumbling in the wind above their ragged nests.

'I have been thinking of next year's harvest, Ned,' she began.

'Oh aye! Give us thy orders then, Dorcas!' Sarcastically.

'You know very well,' she answered, smiling, 'that these are but thoughts to be shared.'

'I learned summat a long while since,' said Ned. 'The thoughts go one way—from thee to me. Say thy piece, lass.'

'It occurred to me that we could extend the arable land, Ned, without really robbing the sheep, and so grow more and better food for ourselves. There are still a few acres, west of the Nick, that are limestone, love. It seems a pity to waste them upon sheep-grazing. Of course, I know they are rough and would be difficult to till—but with William's special plough, and the plough-horses he bought specially for you. . . .'

'I'll bet you set him up to do that for me!' said Ned, seeing matters in quite a different light.

'Indeed I did not! I am not so cunning as you wish to think!' she cried indignantly, and would have pulled her arm away from his, but that he chuckled and held it fast. 'And the plough is a great improvement, is it not?' she asked. 'And cuts more cleanly and deeply than your old one?'

'I've nowt to say against it so far, my lass. We've nobbut tried it out on regular-tilled land, and on the level, so I'm none so sure of it on grass slopes. Billy tells me it handles on the heavy side.'

'Well, it is but in its infancy,' said Dorcas, settling the matter to her satisfaction, 'and William was speculating on the future possibility of a plough worked by steam—though that is a wild notion!'

But she believed he could do anything, and was proud of him.

'He's steam-mad is our William,' said Ned roundly. 'If he thinks as I'm ever having one of them engines smoking and splothering in my fields, instead of a good team of beasts, he's got another think coming.'

'It is but an idea in his head!' Then, fondly, 'But it is a clever head!'

'Any road, your notions and his seem to match up,' he said, looking at her directly. 'Two shire-horses and a fancy new plough have to be used on summat special. I can see further than the nose on my face, Dorcas. So you want Breakneck and Sluther turned up, do you? You've had your eye on them for over thirty year! I knew we'd get to it in the end!'

'Breakneck and Sluther, indeed!' she cried, pink with mortification. 'Why, what a pair of excuses those names make! I will lay you a sovereign to a shilling, Ned, that when they yield up their harvest next year you will christen them more kindly!'

'When they're harvested, eh?' he said, nodding his head wisely. 'We may as well hitch up them horses and start ploughing!'

Penitently she kissed his cheek and cuddled his arm.

'Aye, you're sweet as sugar-cane when you've got your own road,' he said, knowing her. 'Right you are, Dorcas. I'll get the two lads to clear the stones, and we'll try Sluther first. It's none so steep as Breakneck, and we can get the feel of it with our Will's plough. But it'll be new-broke ground, and that means three or four furrowings. Then again, it's been natural grass for as long as I've known it, so you won't be able to use it for owt fancy—like wheat!' he added, watching her closely. 'You can make your mind up to 'taters, else turnips, to clean it up. And go easy on it for a year or two while it settles.'

'Such good rich soil,' said Dorcas, passing over the mention of wheat, for she could argue that point later. 'And so sheltered. Yet the sun comes upon it early and stays late. I have often noticed.'

'Aye, I'll bet you have, my lass. I'm none so daft as I look!'

The following Sunday William brought his family over, to dine early on roast sirloin of beef and baked rice pudding; while Caleb dined late with Charlotte on fried soles, a brace of partridges, and damson pie.

These visits were an especial joy to Dorcas, for William always brought the latest news and fresh ideas, Zelah confided small domestic problems and asked her advice, and the little girls delighted the entire household.

'How's my two pennorth o' copper then?' cried Ned, as Tabitha ran to him, and Catherine staggered four paces and suddenly foundered. 'Come on up!' Lifting them both tenderly. 'They musn't have any more babies at your house, I've nobbut got two arms to hold them! What shall us see first? Chickens or horses? Shall us see the new shire-horses? Punch and Judy, your Aunt Lottie calls them. She's allus got a fancy name for everything has your Aunt Charlotte! Aye, we'll take Punch and Judy a carrot apiece, and a morsel of sugar from the loaf. Oh, by the way, Will, I'm trying out that new-fangled plough-share of yourn on untilled ground, one day next week. Your mother's having them limestone fields off me, for cropping!'

'We knew she would, in the end,' William commented, unsurprised. 'Let me know how it handles, Father, and in particular how the edge wears. We are trying out a new process at Belbrook, chilling the bottom face of the share in a metal mould so that it sets harder and lasts longer.'

'I'll tell thee what I think to it, lad. And to the shire-horses, and all. Billy's had them so far.'

'Now there you have the finest draught-horses in the country, Father. Take my word for it.'

'I've got nowt against your word,' Ned replied, grinning, 'but I'd sooner give you mine. I've allus ploughed with oxen. They're easier to train and cheaper to feed, and they can shift heavier loads. But your mother says as I'm not to stand in the way of progress. So I'll give them shires a try. They're good horses, I'll say that for them.'

'Will thee not look at the plans for the garden, Father?' Zelah asked, as William began to unroll the sheets which nowadays accompanied him almost everywhere. 'Mr Field hath found us a fine landscape gardener.'

'Show them to Dorcas,' he said, hoisting the little girls to his shoulders, 'while I keep these two out of mischief. Dorcas knows better than me. She'll tell me all about it when you've gone.' For he was not really interested. 'Now then, Tibby and Kitty, hold tight like I showed thee and we'll have a gallop to t'stables. That's capital! Now say "Hup! Dobbin!" and off we go. And if I'm galloping too fast for you, you say "Whoa!" Right? Hup, Dobbin! Off we go!'

And off they went, little hands clutching his neck, silver heads bobbing to his motion, silent and smiling in delight.

'Oh, how elegant!' cried Dorcas, putting on her steel-rimmed spectacles.

She became a girl again in her enthusiasm. William watched her, smiling. For she echoed his moods more clearly than Zelah did, and many were the small harmless plots they hatched together.

'All the trees are to be felled from here to here,' he explained, 'just leaving a screen of them to shelter us against the prevailing winds, and to offset the house. We have had many difficulties, owing to the slope of the land. Some can be levelled, but if one builds a house upon a hill—then a hill one has to contend with! In this instance Mr Stirling has shown great ingenuity, setting aside the conventional plan

233

and creating something far less formal, and yet in keeping with the house and precincts. . . .'

She noticed, as he pointed out detail, that his hands and nails were now well-kept. They no longer marked the craftsman, they were a part of the administrator. She was at once pleased and saddened by this discovery. He was moving so quickly out of their knowledge of him.

'. . . lawns, paths and shrubs—thus contrasting with the rougher, nobler aspect of the woods behind. . . .'

'But what is this delightful nonsense in the corner? And why these empty circles?'

'That nonsense, Mamma, is an ornamental summer-house. Those circles will house statuary, but we have not yet decided what. I am for iron, but Zelah wants stone.'

'It will be even grander than Somer Court,' said Zelah, laughing, and was half-afraid of such splendour.

Dorcas whipped off her spectacles in her excitement, and scanned the garden closer by holding them like a magnifying glass over the paper. Then she smiled up at her handsome son.

'Oh, I could not be happier for you—for you both!' she cried. 'It is exactly what I should have wished. Only I could not have imagined anything half so fine. Oh, how I wish poor Phoebe could have lived to see it. Her godson building such a house! And poor Agnes, always so proud of you. . . .'

'And my great-aunt Wilde, and Aaron Helm, and Mr Jarrett!' said William, teasing her away from melancholy.

Dorcas laughed, and wiped her eyes, and called herself a fool.

'And what does dear Zelah think to all this?' she asked, mindful of her quiet daughter-in-law.

'Why, what should dear Zelah think?' William answered, embracing his wife, speaking for her as usual. 'She will come home again in Kingswood Hall, though something grander as she says. She was born at sunrise, and the sun shone on her face and hair, so I am told. The sun shines upon Zelah, and for her, and always will.'

'You look a little pale, nevertheless, my dear child,' said Dorcas, observing a pensiveness in her countenance.

'We cannot be certain,' said Zelah, smiling, 'but we hope to be five in the spring. God willing.'

'Oh, you always bring such splendid news to us!' cried Dorcas, ringing the bell. 'You must rest upon the sofa until dinner, Zelah. Susan, a glass of cordial for Mrs Howarth, if you please. William, fetch a cushion for Zelah. And Susan, how long shall we be until dinner?'

'Now do not fuss, Mrs Dorcas!' said Zelah, laughing, mocking.

'Oh, let her fuss,' said William lovingly, 'since she enjoys it so much.'

Master, mistress, guests and servants, all stood round the long table in the front parlour, and bowed their heads as Ned spoke his own form of Grace.

'Lord, we thank thee for this good meat and drink. Help us to remember them as has none. Bless our food this day, and us in thy service. For Jesus Christ's sake. Amen.'

'Amen,' they cried reverently.

Then there was a great scraping of chairs and stools as they sat down. Ned sharpened the carving-knife until it became a formidable weapon. A vast sirloin of beef was put before him. Two small maids, fresh from Garth village, and overcome by their new gowns and aprons, stood by to hand the vegetables.

'About that plough of yourn, Will,' Ned began, slicing with the expertise born of long practice. 'Billy tells me it handles on the heavy side. I've a mind to thong a leather strap to t'handles and run it over one shoulder, to give it a bit of leverage. What do you think to that?'

'But Billy will plough Sluther, surely, Ned,' Dorcas interposed.

'Dorcas! Let me be, my lass.'

'The plough is larger and heavier than the one you have been used to, certainly,' said William, considering the matter, 'and should be kept stable on such an incline as Sluther. But a strap over one shoulder may tend to unbalance it upon the turns, I should have thought.'

'Well, round my back, then,' said Ned, somewhat testily. 'To take the weight a bit.'

'A third horse?' William enquired, smiling.

'But why not let Billy do it, my dear?' asked Dorcas earnestly.

He was exasperated with the pair of them.

'Because I want to do it myself, my lass. And I'm better by a long road wi' horses—even three of them!' Glaring at his son. 'Billy's used to ploughing wi' oxen. I don't fancy him using them shire-horses on Sluther. They'll take a bit of coaxing and handling—and so will that plough!'

235

'Well, Father,' said Dick, who spoke as little as Ned and always to the purpose, 'you tell me I'm as good wi' horses as you are. And I can plough as well. And I'm younger than thee. Let me have a go at Sluther.'

Ned said, 'No!' and struck the table with the handle of the carving-knife.

Dorcas and William and Dick looked meaningfully at one another. Something underlay Ned's determination: a refusal to admit encroaching age, curiosity about this new ploughing system, a quixotic gesture to please his wife with a gift of his own making, perhaps even the need to stress that the land was his and he must be the first to cultivate it.

'Any road,' said Ned obstinately, '*I'm* ploughing Sluther!'

'So am I!' cried three-year-old Tibby, and banged her spoon in sympathy.

'So my!' Kitty echoed.

And in an effort to outshine the others she turned her dinnerplate upside down upon her head.

The argument was lost in laughter.

On that November early morning, Garth was a dream floating through the valley below, its chimney-tops barely clearing the mist. But up on the fells the air sparkled in the rising sun, and rills of water ran cold and sweet between red banks of bracken. Underfoot, the harsh grass was crisp. A man might lose all earthly cares in that space between moor and sky: hearing nothing but the call of a peewit, the bark of a dog on a lone farm, or the wind worrying the hollows. A man might lift his eyes unto the hills and be thankful for such a day as this: to the autumnal hills, sitting in judgement like old gods.

Such a man was moving slowly against the landscape behind his heavy plough, acting out an ancient rite, becoming part of this time and this place. Ahead of him the big brown horses, seventeen hands high, plodded a deliberate course, led by a little lad whose father and grandfather had trodden the same patient path. In their wake the earth had been turned by the chilled blade into a sea of furrows.

The man had removed his battered hat, stained by age and weather, to allow a slight breeze to ruffle his white hair. He was working out of habit, out of love. This was his land they tilled, and would be offered up to his wife to be made fruitful. The labour was hard. To take the weight of the iron machine he had wound a strong strap about his wrists and shoulders, thus harnessing himself to the wooden shafts. Man, boy and beasts toiled from side to side of the steep field, and on each turn the man lifted the dark metal coulter from the earth, suspending it at the curve until it drove into the land again, to draw another clean deep fold. From the farm below, the ribboned field could be seen emerging: order brought from green anarchy.

He had left his woman abed, as he always did at that hour, seeing in the first light her hair upon the pillow, her linen corset on the chair. For nearly forty years it had been so. He could not remember the years before her, except in the context of a long reverie. His humility, and his capacity for love, had brought him this richness in marriage. He reaped what he had sown. Another man could have used her virtues without regarding them, or made much of her faults. Because, to him, her faults were peculiar virtues, and her virtues faultless, he had possessed her wholly. And since, each day, love must be earned, on this November morning he ploughed Sluther for her.

'We'll take another turn,' he shouted to the little lad, 'and then stop for a sup of ale.'

'Right you are, Mr Howarth,' said young Amos Bowker, and confided in the towering horses.

'A good pull and a long 'un,' he said, 'and you can rest you for a bit.'

Slowly they wheeled in a half-arc, fetching the plough with them. And the man took the weight, eyes like cracks in his weathered face, lips clamped, heart straining at the load. The massive coulter swung clear, the ponderous plough hung suspended on the curve, the mighty horses pulled, and an imbalance threatened both man and machine. Unknowing, the boy urged the beasts on. The finest draught-horses in the country, William had said, and he was right. Against both plough and ploughman they set their great shoulders, their powerful haunches and monumental limbs.

'Steady!' Ned shouted urgently, harnessed as he was, a puppet in the midst of this impedimenta.

But in the moment that his set teeth chopped at the word he knew that he was lost. That the freed word would float unheeded. That the boy would drive mindlessly on, that the driven steeds would respond, the machine heel over, the strap bind tighter, the whole mass tumble and roll down the steep fell flank.

On me! he knew. But his sense of urgency was done. For

237

after all he must die. The surprise was immense. The event, small and familiar, seen from a great distance, permitted him both to observe and take part. Perhaps he had been through it before.

'You daft buggers!' he shouted, into oblivion, spinning.

The earth in his stopped mouth, the crushed amazement, neck snapped like a twig. No pain. Too quick for pain, or so much pain that the mind rejected it. Falling, slowly, gracefully. Falling away. Fallen. Over. Done. With his cheek at last cold against the cold soil. On this fine November morning, in the year of our Lord 1799.

The lad stood silent, hands over his mouth, tears trickling down his cheeks: aware that though the horses could be fetched round and calmed, the plough righted, the man brought out, he was alone in the landscape. Alone, he crept back to look. Alone, he brushed the dirt from that astonished face, felt for the still heart, cried the name into deaf ears. Then ran, shrilly calling, down the hillside.

The great shire-horses ceased to snort and plunge. Their size soothed them. They stood quietly, heads bent. Then, dragging plough and ploughman stealthily behind them, they found a patch of untilled earth, and grazed thoughtfully, waiting for someone to come to them.

NINETEEN

Taking Leave

Susan had lit the parlour fire and helped her mistress to dress. Nellie had made her breakfast, and closed the parlour door firmly upon her. The death was an hour old.

Dorcas knew that they wanted her to stay here while they made arrangements; and though she could not swallow she poured the tea, and sat obediently before the toast. She had been rendered powerless, but so long and so well had she ordered her household that it could move on without her for a time. The day was clouding over, the mist rose from the valley and covered the hill slopes, she could scarcely see the wall of the kitchen garden from her grey window.

Sounds were translated into sights which would have distressed her to watch, but provided needful information. A clattering of hooves out of the cobbled yard meant that the stable-lad was off to Garth, Snape, Belbrook and Millbridge with his dark news. The hammering and sawing of hurried carpentry told her they were nailing a rough stretcher together, to carry the body down from Sluther. The front door, not opened since William's wedding four years since, was being tried stealthily and its hinges oiled with goose-grease. The wedding recalled Zelah to mind, and Dorcas started up hurriedly to ring the bell.

'Nellie! They must break the news carefully to my daughter-in-law. She is with child, you know.'

'Don't you fret, ma'am. Mr William'll see to everything. Sit you down and drink your tea, ma'am, do.'

The door closed. She sat before the tray again. The tea had gone cold.

The stable-lad reined in at the wheelwright's shop in Garth, and leaned from his saddle.

'Mr Burscough!' he called into the dim shop. 'Mr Burscough, they'll be wanting you up at Kit's Hill. It's Mr Howarth. He's dead.'

Joe Burscough paused in the act of planing wood, blew the soft feathers from his tool, and set it on end.

'Nay, never,' he said in disbelief. 'Ned Howarth? However did that happen?'

'He broke his neck, Mr Burscough. Ploughing Sluther. Broke his neck.'

The lad's mouth trembled. He dug his heels into the bay mare.

'I've got to go, Mr Burscough. There's a mort of messages to take.'

And he was off to the vicarage.

'Did you hear that, Jem?' said Joe Burscough. 'Ned Howarth's dead. Would you believe it? Here, take over, wilta? I'll walk up. Oh, and look out that seasoned oak at the back of the shop, wilta? They'll want the best for him.'

Margery Cheetham, who dealt with the beginning and the end of life in the village, wrapped herself in her old shawl and knocked at her neighbour's door.

'Hast heard t'news? Ned Howarth's dead! Aye, I'm off to lay him out. If anybody wants me tell them I'll be back after dinner.'

239

The sexton, Zachary Sidebottom, spat on his hands and grasped the bell-rope. The traditional nine tellers, for the death of a man, were followed by four-and-seventy solemn tolls for the years of his age. 'It's a good age!' thought Zachary. The parson donned a clean collar, that he might comfort the widow in a seemly fashion. The grave-digger shouldered his spade. Garth was abuzz with the news that would travel from end to end of the valley: interrupting such homely actions as the lifting of a pint-pot, the milking of a cow, the baking of bread.

'Have you heard about Ned Howarth, up at Kit's Hill? Dead!'

'Nay, never!'

And a humble procession wound its way slowly down from Scarth Nick: two men carrying a third upon a home-made stretcher, and a little lad leading a pair of shire-horses. From time to time he thrust the knuckles of one hand into his eyes, but the great beasts moved ponderously forward, unknowing. On the dark field behind them all lay an iron plough, and the long leather strap which had been used as a harness.

The oak coffin stood on trestles in the front parlour at Kit's Hill. They had laid a dish of salt upon the farmer's still chest, and pennies on the blinds of his eyes. They left the bolts unbarred, the doors ajar, the window of that cold room a little open, so that the soul could stream freely out into the fog. The mirrors were shrouded. The clocks were stopped. At nightfall they lit candles and watched by him.

His widow sat at the head of the coffin because it was all she could now do for him. Her children repeated that she must rest, must eat, must drink. She was content to let them rule her, but obedience was not at the moment within her province. So finally they let her be, and she spoke to him when they were alone together, in a confused medley of old memories, present perplexities, and future speculation.

In the kitchen the ovens had been stoked all day, baking currant bread and buns. Nellie brought out last summer's stock of elderberry wine and spiced it. The new maids hurried round the village, offering sprigs of rosemary and biddings to the funeral. Then the women servants put on their black Sunday gowns and starched white aprons, and prepared to receive the mourners.

It seemed they would never get everybody in. But they all

collected together at last. The men removed their hats, the women bent their heads, the children were silent. There was a smell of camphor among the yeomen farmers' families, who had best clothes for the occasion; a creaking of freshly blacked boots, subdued conversation, pale faces. The many poor, who had eaten hungrily of the bread and made their heads spin with unaccustomed wine, stood in their sombre daily dress.

Dorcas held herself very upright. Her small gloved hand put a glass of wine to her lips now and then, for form's sake. Someone closed the kitchen door so that she should not hear them nailing the coffin down in the front of the house.

'I think they are ready now, Mamma,' said Charlotte in her ear, and took the glass from her.

Grey, white and black. No colour anywhere, except perhaps in the coffin which gleamed tenderly. His two sons, mouths set, eyes bleak, took the lead. His old servants, Tom Cartwright and Billy Sidebottom, followed. Between them they raised the box shoulder-high. It was heavy, broad, sturdily-built. They had some difficulty easing it through the front doorway. Outside stood Gowd and Siller, Pearl and Di'mond, Ned's team of oxen: harnessed to the wagon, ready to draw him down to the churchyard, according to the custom of his forefathers.

The way seemed long and hard, even with a son on either side of her. Dorcas was glad of the privacy afforded by her veil. The loss was a continual quiet grief within her which would make her weep dumbly, unexpectedly, without immediate cause. She could not comprehend why, after so many years together, he should die alone. She had never parted from him for so much as half a day without asking his leave, nor he hers. It seemed monstrous that he should set out on this last of all journeys, and she not there to comfort him. She had not known God could be so unkind.

May 1800

By unanimous consent, William and Charlotte and Dick held their council at Thornton House one Saturday afternoon in the spring, while Dorcas visited Zelah and the little girls at Quincey Place.

As head of the family William took Grandfather Wilde's armchair. Charlotte presided over the teapot, and Dick supplied material for the meeting. He had just come from the market, and looked the picture of a prosperous yeoman farmer. Into Charlotte's bees-waxed and flower-scented room he brought the homely odours of saddle-soap, new milk and hay. His gentlemanly brother, his educated sister, were fond of him, benevolently disposed towards him, but the bond was one of a family kind. Less and less did they have in common. So, though he needed their advice, he had excused himself from Charlotte's invitation to dinner, and consumed mutton pies and strong beer at The Red Lion, in company with his fellows. Now, though he still worried about the dried mud on his gaiters, and wished his teacup was larger and thicker, he placed his trust in their superior judgement.

'It's about our mother,' he began, for he loved Dorcas deeply but could not deal with her. 'And it's about me, too,' he added honestly. There was a long pause while the red reached his neck. 'And—and Alice Wharmby.'

William and Charlotte exchanged smiles over his bent head.

'Which of the Wharmby girls is Alice, Dick?' William asked kindly.

For the Wharmbys were rich in daughters.

'Ah, she will be the nut-brown maiden who steps out like a queen,' cried Charlotte, remembering the girl at the funeral looking at Dick.

'Aye, that's right. That's Alice!' Dick said, pleased and relieved.

How could he have described her, driven to doing so? He wished he could say what he felt as well as Lottie did. *The nut-brown maiden who steps out like a queen.* He must memorise that. Say it to Alice.

'Well, Dickie dear,' Charlotte coaxed, as he remained rapt and silent in contemplation of his love, 'could you explain a little more to us? Does Mamma not approve of Alice?'

Which would not be surprising, her eyebrows signalled to William. Knowing Mamma!

'Eh, I don't know. I haven't said owt to her!' he cried, alarmed.

'How long have you been courting Alice?' William asked, tackling the situation from another direction.

'Nigh on twelvemonth. But quiet-like. I mentioned it to Father, and he promised as he'd tell Mother—at the right time, he said. But it didn't come about. Father were talking about doing up old Luke's cottage for us. He said that when I were five-and-twenty I should have the running of the farm, and he'd stand behind me. Then, when t'family started coming, he and Mother would go to Luke's, and Alice and me could have Kit's Hill.'

Once he started to speak he seemed unable to stop, and they listened to the pent-up chronicle which must have run unheeded in his mind as he strove to assuage his mother's grief, and to hold Alice without holding her off. The last six months had been hard on him, as well as on the two women he loved.

'But he died, you see, afore we could set the notion in her head or speak wi' the Wharmbys. And though I'm five-and-twenty in another week or two I canna see Mother making way for Alice. And I canna see Alice sitting round doing nowt. And whereas my father might've got Mother to live in old Luke's cottage, I dursen't ask her to go there by herself. It's too near and too far, if you get my meaning. Besides, *I* canna stand up agin Mother, never mind Alice trying! She's got a hundred ways of getting her own road, afore you know what's going on in her head. I allus knew that Father could handle her, but I never give him credit enough. Nay, I never did!'

And here he rid himself of the troublesome teacup, and wiped his forehead with a large yellow handkerchief.

They could not help themselves, but burst out laughing. After a moment or two of bewilderment he joined in, sheepishly at first and then with relief.

'It is unfair to laugh,' said Charlotte penitently, 'and of course you and Alice must have Kit's Hill to yourselves. Dear Dick, you have had the burden of Mamma's grief, and said nothing until now!'

For he was still her baby brother, and she soothing and protecting him, though he could have picked her up with one hand and sat her on top of her own pianoforte.

'But it is only right,' said William, 'that Mrs Dorcas should have more in life than a shepherd's cottage on the fells. She farmed Kit's Hill, side by side with my father, for nearly forty years.'

'Well, we Longes are living in the house that is hers,' said Charlotte. 'But what should *we* do if she took us all over?'

'Caleb will rattle round Quincey Place like a solitary pea in a pod when we are gone to Kingswood Hall,' said William, looking at his sister, half-teasing and half-serious. 'I suppose you would not simplify matters by marrying him, would you, Lottie? You always cared for Quincey Place!'

Dick took upon himself the embarrassment Charlotte might have felt. He blushed, but she laughed.

'My dear Willie, I shall need a better reason to take another husband than the house he lives in!'

'Then that is that!' Philosophically. 'Zelah is devoted to my mother, but the devotion could be strained at close quarters. They are both matriarchs!'

'Sweet Zelah a matriarch?' cried Charlotte. 'Why, she is the most tractable of us all!'

'A matriarch, my dear Lottie, in fact, in spirit, and even by sheer inheritance. You articulate Wilde ladies are milk-cheese compared to the steel of which the Scholes women are fashioned!'

'We shall surprise you yet!' Charlotte retorted. 'When do you move to Kingswood Hall?'

'As soon as Zelah has recovered from the birth of our latest infant. Summer, I suppose.'

'She would need to be made of steel,' said Charlotte drily. 'And when you speak of close quarters, have you no lodges, stables, pavilions or orangeries at Kingswood Hall? Is there no corner for Mamma in all that vast mansion, where she could put her parlourful of Grandmother Wilde's furniture?'

'Mrs Dorcas's considerable talents must be housed separately,' said William, quite firm on this point.

Dick looked trustfully from one to the other as they talked. He was his father's son. He knew what was right for him. They were his mother's children. They knew what must be done.

'We are perhaps forgetting,' said Charlotte thoughtfully, 'that though Mamma is withdrawn and unlike herself, she must be well aware of this problem. She would not intrude upon any of us. Perhaps she would be glad to leave, but cannot think where to go, and has not the will nor the energy at present to apply herself to the problem.'

William's zest for fresh challenges was as sharp as ever.

'I have the answer!' he cried. 'Mrs Dorcas needs not only a new home but a new interest in life. Caleb and I have purchased a large area of land at Upperton, between Belbrook and Snape, in which we plan to build a model village. On this site is a farm I was going to pull down. Old, small, and lacking any convenience. Instead, I shall persuade her to re-make it to suit herself. She shall mark out her ground, borrow my workmen, use my materials. I place it at her disposal, in fact.

She can have everything she likes from me—except ready money. That is a commodity I notoriously lack!'

'Nay, *I'll* see her right for money,' said Dick at once, though his entire property was not worth one corner of Snape Foundry.

'She has money of her own, from Aunt Wilde,' Charlotte pointed out. 'Unless, of course, it is all invested in iron!'

'No, she was remarkably strong-minded on that score,' said William ruefully. 'Our friend Mr Hurst advised her against putting all her eggs in my basket. He regards me as a risky if highly profitable enterprise. So most of her small fortune is invested safely—which means that it brings in less than half the dividends she has been drawing from Belbrook and Snape!'

'Is that why you left Nicodemus's firm?' Charlotte asked curiously.

'Oh, not at all,' said William, imperturbably good-humoured. 'He has every right to advise his clients as he thinks fit. But Hurst and Hurst is only a small family firm, suitable for a market town. Potter and Shawcross of Preston suit me better, and work upon broader lines.'

'Well, I'd sooner be sure than sorry, speaking for myself,' said Dick frankly, 'and she's got nowt but her bit of brass, now Father's gone.'

'Anyway, let us return to the matter in hand,' Charlotte said wisely. 'I think Willie's solution is best. Are you to approach her, Willie?'

'Are you saying that I should, Dick?'

'Aye, you're the talker, Will. I'm no hand at saying owt.'

'Then shall we consult her now, at Quincey Place?' William asked. 'And tomorrow afternoon I can take her over to Upperton, and Ellis Field will come with us. Then we'll sup at Kit's Hill in the evening, Dick, and work out the plans.'

'Aye, right you are!' said Dick, astonished at the rapidity with which his problems were being solved. 'But suppose as she don't like the idea? I shouldn't want her to think as I were pushing her out. Father wouldn't have wanted that, neither.'

'Yes, do take care not to hurt her, Willie!' Charlotte cautioned.

'Oh, hurt her, fiddlesticks! The notion will fetch her alive again. And we have the summer before us. Let Mrs Dorcas but think that she will be in her own home by Christmas, and we shall see a new woman. Besides, I shall offer the welfare of the future villagers to her, as another bait!'

'But will Zelah not wish to take care of your people?' Charlotte asked.

'Why, Zelah will have her nursery to rule for the next ten years, by which time Mrs Dorcas should have had enough of Upperton's problems! Well, if you think not, then she shall discuss the village plans with Ellis Field.'

'But will Mr Field want that, Willie?'

'They will all work very well together,' he said cheerfully, but there was an obstinacy in his countenance which forbade further objections on her part. 'Come, Dick, unless you want to ride home in the dark!'

'Nay,' said Dick, leaving his sister's parlour with relief, 'you'll run ten mile afore I've set out, our Will! I've never knowed anybody like you, except our mother!'

He shook his head from side to side, and and chuckled, looking so like Ned for a moment that the other two were silenced, remembering.

'I thank you both heartily,' said Dick, shaking their hands. 'I can't frame what I feel, but I'm beholden to you. If ever I can do owt you've only to let me know. Me and Alice!' He was free. He said quietly, 'We could get wed come Christmas.'

William clapped him on the shoulder. Charlotte kissed his cheek and hugged him.

'I never asked how Zelah was, neither,' Dick reproached himself. 'Coming in full of trouble, and thinking nowt of other folks. How's the lass keeping?'

'Oh, she is great with child, and very well. Come and see her for yourself. We think it will be a son this time.'

'So long as she's safe,' said Dick, and silenced them again.

He turned his unfashionable hat round and round in his big hands.

'We planted 'taters in Sluther, and turnips in Breakneck!' he said, and paused again.

'Wilta do summat else for us?' he asked, shame-faced, shifting from foot to foot. 'Wilta tell Mother about Alice and me, our William?'

'I found, upon consulting the title-deeds, that your particular piece of land at Upperton was called *Bracelet*, Mrs Dorcas, said Ellis Field.

He was in full flight, taking this small project in his course, as it were, after an excellent supper.

'And *Bracelet* means "a broad meadow". Of course, we think of the word as an item of jewellery. What harm in that, we might well say? Shall the house not be a jewel when we have done with her? We shall knock down the out-buildings, of course. Build on a kitchen, to take away the four-square appearance, and give more space. Put a small conservatory at the side which faces south. Knock down the wall between the present parlour and kitchen and make one long living-room, and enlarge the windows at either end. Then you have a house large enough to accommodate a guest or two, as well as yourself and a small staff, Mrs Dorcas.

'With regard to the land around it, there is no need to call in our excellent Mr Stirling—our sterling Mr Stirling! Ha, ha!—no, no. Any labourer could dig and lay out a garden for you in a week or two. A handkerchief of lawn with a border of rose-trees at the front; a little kitchen garden sufficient for your wants at the back. You yourself have an artistic, an unerring eye for what is needed, ma'am. Shall we keep the trees on the far side? I think we shall! Noble plants, and such useful windbreaks in this wild country. Later, if you wish, we could lay a flagged path, make a pretty arched bower, put a small statue on a pedestal—something of that sort.

'And now we come to the name of the house. Upperton Lodge? Too heavy. Honeysuckle Cottage? Too sugary. Arbour Farm End? Nonsense! This is a new beginning, ma'am. Simply, we would suggest—*Bracelet!* . . .'

And he bowed very low, as to a very great lady.

'I've fetched your chocolate myself, Mrs Howarth, begging your pardon, because I wondered if I might have a word with you,' said Nellie, and closed the parlour door behind her.

'Sit down, my dear,' said Dorcas.

Her hair was whiter, her back thinner and more rigidly straight, but the quick keen way in which she looked over her spectacles indicated some degree of recovery.

'It's about you leaving, ma'am, and Mr Dick getting wed,' Nellie began.

Dorcas folded her hands and inclined her head.

'And it's about me and—Tom Cartwright!'

Dorcas's smile was delightfully questioning. Nellie's glance confirmed her hopes.

'Aye, well, I shall feel proper daft telling folks, after all this long while,' said Nellie, smiling, busy smoothing her immaculate apron, 'but Tom and me wanted you to be the first to know we're getting wed, Mrs Howarth. We're neither of us spring chickens. I'm nodding at fifty, and he's seen the last of sixty, but we suit each other, and if anybody wants to laugh they're welcome! We'st slip off, quiet-like, one morning, and parson'll do the rest.'

They were both so pleased with the news that they half laughed at one another.

'Oh, but we must think of your wedding, too, Nellie,' said Dorcas.

Half a dozen kindly little plans came to mind. Particularly as Dick's wedding-breakfast had nothing to do with her, but was being triumphantly hatched by Mary Braithwaite-Wharmby, up at Windygate.

'That weren't all I come to tell you, ma'am,' said Nellie, urgently heading her mistress away from the subject. 'Tom and me have both been at Kit's Hill longer than anybody. It's forty year come Michaelmas that Mr Ned rode down to Garth, and lifted me up to the saddle and fetched me back here as a kitchen-maid, to help my poor Mam as'd been left a widder wi' ten childer to feed. And he took Tom on as stable-lad long afore then, and trained him as a carter. . . . Mrs Howarth, we don't want to stop here when you've gone.'

Dorcas's face lost its radiance. Her plans faded.

'Oh,' she said, quite downcast, 'but I had thought you would take care of Dick and Kit's Hill for me.'

'Mrs Howarth, excuse me if I'm speaking out of turn, but Kit's Hill as you and me have knowed it is gone a'ready. It went wi' you and Mr Ned, ma'am. Now it belongs to Mr Dick and Miss Alice, and it's their turn, not ourn. I've got nowt agin Miss Alice. She's a grand lass in the dairy, and she'll make a grand wife. But I canna start all over again wi' a bit of a lass of eighteen as my mistress, and watch her change Kit's Hill to suit herself. I know she's planning to turn your parlour back into a store-room, for one thing! And I couldn't abide that! She'd be better off wi' Susan. They're much of an age, and they'll sort it out between them. But Tom and me, we're your servants, Mrs Howarth. Not theirs. Mrs Howarth, Tom and me want to come wi' you to Bracelet.'

So many expressions flitted across Dorcas's face that Nellie did not know which to count upon. Joy, doubt, astonishment, hope, concern, trouble, bewilderment.

'My dear Nellie,' she said slowly, shyly. 'I had not thought to take any of you with me. I would have trained up a girl from Garth, perhaps two girls. For then they would keep each other company.'

'If it's the wages, ma'am, we don't mind taking a cut. We'd be doing a lot less work, and we've both got a bit put by in us stockings.'

'No, no,' said Dorcas hurriedly, almost ashamed that Nellie should think her capable of cutting corners in this way. 'It is not the wages. I had not thought of setting up a proper establishment.'

'But who'd look after your horse and trap, ma'am?'

'Mr William said they would stable it, and bring it out to me whenever I sent word.'

'But who'd do your garden, ma'am, and mend things about the house?'

'Mr William said they would lend me a gardner and handyman whenever I needed one.'

'Well, a married couple only needs one bedroom, same as two maidservants,' said Nellie firmly. 'And though Mr William and Mrs Zelah grudge nobody nowt—there might come a time when you sent, and there wasn't somebody there. As my owd Mam once said, 'There comes the day when folks stops feeling sorry, and starts to think about themselves first, last and foremost!" Think on, ma'am. The three of us'd manage well enough without Kingswood Hall!'

For though she was proud to be connected to the great, she saw no reason why her mistress should go a-begging.

'I have no stable, you see, Nellie.'

'That Mr Field'd think up a stable in five minutes. I've heard him on about Bracelet, often enough,' said Nellie, not to be outdone.

She nodded her head up and down vigorously. She thought the architect a trifle too precious, but of his enthusiasm and ability she had no doubt.

'Nellie dear, give me time to think,' said Dorcas confused. 'It is not what I should have planned. Oh, I am so pleased for you and Tom. But would you not be better off at Kit's Hill?'

'Well, ma'am,' Nellie replied, rising, 'Tom and me is leaving Kit's Hill any road. We'll give Mr Dick and Miss Alice fair warning, and look elsewhere, if so be as you don't want us. But if you canna think what's right for you, Mrs Howarth, then think what Mr Ned would've said in the same place!'

With that Parthian shot, she bobbed a curtsey and left the room, head high, and mistress of the field for once.

But the architect will have to design and build a new stable now, and that will be further trouble and expense. And what should the three of us do at Bracelet, particularly with winter coming on, and the village unbuilt as yet? So isolated from Kit's Hill. It would be easier to manage on my own, with two girls who would talk together. Rather than have three lonely old people.

Three lonely old people? Don't talk so daft, Dorcas! Tom and Nellie'll be that taken up wi' each other you'll be lucky to get a cup of tea out of them. And there's a regular new household for you and Nellie to set up at Bracelet. And Tom's got enough on, wi' t'stables and t'garden and a new wife, at his age! Lonely? You won't have five minutes to turn round, you'll see. And our Will'll build up that village in no time. Now, if you were in poor Mattie Gregson's clogs, wi' no husband, no brass, no sense and six small childer, you'd have summat to grouse about! As it is, you'd best shift yourself, my lass, if you want to be in Bracelet afore Christmas!

Nellie and Tom had been installed at the new house a week previously, to make sure that the rooms were aired, the garden tidy, the stable ready, to receive their mistress and her horse and trap. This was in the nature of a honeymoon for them, and they exchanged many a smile across the scrubbed floors, and a hearty kiss or two as they folded the blankets.

Nicodemus Hurst had drawn up the documents, firmly separating Bracelet and its land from any connection with the rest of William's vast property. He regarded the young ironmaster as a social hazard, and acted accordingly, while preserving the utmost courtesy towards him. At any rate, Nicodemus reflected, Mrs Dorcas would have her own home when the crash came. And Mr William must look to himself! The firm of Hurst and Hurst had always been sound, and given sound advice. He must call upon Mrs Dorcas as soon as she was settled, and see how she did.

So on a raw November morning, almost a year from the time that Ned Howarth had taken his new shire-horses and his new plough up to that fatal field, Dorcas was helped into her little trap by her younger son. Dick's wedding would be held in a fortnight, and he had an air of rapt expectancy which both delighted and hurt her deeply. For so his father must have looked, almost four decades ago, awaiting the bride who had been Dorcas Wilde. And yet she was glad for Dick, and glad to go.

'Now, I'll be ahead wi' the wagon full of furniture, Mother,' said Dick, 'and don't you go trying to pass me on the road. I'm driving fast enough for anybody, and Father allus said as you licked the mare up when you was out of sight. . . .'

She listened to his scolding with nostalgia. No one would ever scold her again as lovingly as Ned did. She heard him in her head and in her dreams. She would have given all her world actually to hear his voice, and touch his coat or his face, this moment.

She held the whip resolutely. She must not cry. Fortunately, she thought she saw the long clock sway slightly in its corner of the wagon, and by the time they had wedged it afresh she had recovered her equilibrium. It was all there. The gilded looking-glass, which had seen her reflection turn from five-and-twenty to five-and-sixty, near enough. The Queen Anne clock in its walnut case, which had ticked her marriage-time away. The secretaire at which she had organised and run her household, kept in touch with her friends, and waged many a small domestic battle for improvement and progress. The sofa on which she had lain when great with child. The small oval table, beautifully inlaid, on which her breakfast was taken each morning of her life. The six dining chairs, whose legs Ned had suspected of being too slender for his weight. She really must have their seats re-furbished. The pattern was almost gone. The china: a few pieces missing. The glass: almost whole. The books: supplemented and in excellent condition.

So I came here, on the seventh day of February 1761, Dorcas thought. So I leave here, on the eleventh day of November, 1800. And then she recalled that Ned had written his offer of marriage on the eve of Martinmas 1760. The circle was complete.

'Are you right then?' Dick called from his perch.

'I am quite ready,' cried Dorcas.

Composedly, she clicked her tongue between her teeth. The wagon rumbled over the cobbles with its elegant load. The trap followed nimbly.

'When we reach that wide part of the road, towards Cold-cote,' Dorcas thought, 'I shall overtake him. There is no point in dawdling along!'

Part Three

Man of Straw
1802—1811

TWENTY

Straws in the Wind

When Dorcas Howarth was young, some forty years since, Millbridge had been a country market town with a population of twenty thousand souls, and most faces were familiar. Lord Kersall took care of everything, electing his brother James as the local Member of Parliament, seeing that a retired Kersall from the army was a magistrate for the district, and making sure that the town council had an overall majority of right-thinking men to put through his suggestions. This state of affairs had been accepted for so long that few thought about it, and everyone knew their place.

But gradually a change of mind and direction was becoming apparent. A rough and independent spirit was abroad. A new age brought forth new men to influence and lead it, and though some councillors would vote Tory because it suited their purposes, and others vote Whig and make a thorough nuisance of themselves, none of them were of Lord Kersall's kidney. He ruled now partly from habit, but mostly by means of his ability. While they insinuated themselves into social and public affairs, jostled each other for an honourable place and, since the aristocracy would have none of them, began to form their own society.

William Howarth was such a man, Ernest Harbottle such another, and yet there was a world of difference between them. Seen sitting together at a council meeting in the summer of 1802, in Millbridge's new Town Hall, they might have represented opposite elements: one self-possessed, the other as raw as the brawling city from whence he had come. Not for nothing did folk say. 'A Liverpool gentleman, and a Manchester man' when they looked on Mr Harbottle, who was loud-mouthed, square-built and red-faced.

Self-made, self-taught, and with an undoubted talent for business arithmetic, he had driven a bargain with Humphrey Kersall which pleased both sides. For he proved conclusively that a herd of cows in a pasture was a wasteful proposition, whereas a steam-driven cotton-mill would increase the value of the land a hundredfold. So Lord Kersall, keeping his distance, and occasionally putting a white handkerchief to his nose as though the Manchester man's presence were an affront, saw that as the lease ran out he could charge still more and thus benefit his heirs as well as himself.

Old names were acquiring new meanings. Millbridge itself had been so christened because of its ancient corn-mill and pack-horse bridge. The corn-mill wheel still dripped sunlit water, the pack-horse bridge sustained its weight of farmers' wagons, but the mill fields and mill bank were given over to bricks and mortar. Field Mill had opened soon after Belbrook, followed by Bank Mill. The third enterprise was built upon a hillock known locally as Babylon Brow, no one knew why. But the poetic side of Ernest Harbottle awakened to the name, and he christened his third-born Babylon Mill.

The time-honoured scheme of apprenticeships, as far as the cotton industry was concerned, was too unwieldy and old-fashioned to survive. The manufacturers put pressure upon the government to drop these legislations, piece by piece. When a man could make his fortune in a couple of years, who was going to wait seven while a lad was trained? Profit, as usual, won the day. But there were always those public philanthropists who would interfere with progress, and Ernest Harbottle had his problems—though his house was built high above the town, overlooking his three mills, and his wife could pay for her millinery upon the nail and wore finer hats than the Hon. Mrs Brigge of Brigge Hall, and his sons went to public schools and suffered for his success.

The Mayor of Millbridge wondered afresh whether he had been elected simply as a figurehead, for he seemed unable to control anyone. And he did not know which political party he detested more: from the extreme Toryism of Alderman Brigge to the extreme Whiggism of the Grammar School headmaster, each of whom had parti-coloured cohorts on the council. But on second thoughts he decided that Dr Matthew Standish was more trouble than all of them put together, for he voted Tory and acted Whig, and was an Independent as far as action went for they never knew which side he would come down upon.

Once retired from medical practice, though retaining his stewardship of the Millbridge Hospital, Dr Standish had turned his energy and honesty to public account, and was at present making them all feel extremely uncomfortable.

Tories sat upon one side of the long table, Whigs upon the other, interspersed with those who would be reckoned as the middle men, for whose council vote both sides fought bitterly. And altogether, the Mayor thought, looking round the chamber full of angry faces, there were some two dozen permanent or temporary headaches sitting at his mahogany board, and he wished he had declined the honour of acting as their chairman.

'Gentlemen! Gentlemen! If you please!' he cried, and hammered them pettishly to silence. We have a very detailed agenda. Pray, take your turns and do not argue upon every point. We shall never be done else.'

'Sir,' said Matthew Standish, 'these other gentlemen have their concerns, I do not doubt'—taking a lofty view of such frivolous matters as factories, ironworks, educational establishments, coal mines, printing presses and the like—'but my work deals in life and death—'

'Death, more like, judging from your outlandish notions!' muttered one councillor.

'. . . and my concern is with public health, and I beg to be heard first!'

Jack Ackroyd cried, 'Hear, hear!' but Ernest Harbottle drew out his watch and said, 'Time means money to me, Mr Mayor, and money'll fetch better health to this town than a mort of medical talk!'

Standish turned upon him, crying, 'Have you a close-stool in your fine new house, councillor?'

Reluctantly, Harbottle said, 'More than one, sir!' For he never knew where the doctor was going to have him.

'And where does your close-stool empty, councillor?'

'How should I know? Into the sewer, I dare say. I know it's the latest model, with a valve.'

'Into the sewer. Into the open sewer, gentlemen. That is my point. I have told you a dozen times, since Millbridge began to expand at such a rate, that more affluence means more effluence. There are now eighty thousand people in this town. Do you know why my hospital was built high up on the hillside? . . .'

'Because your wife paid for it!' Sotto voce.

'. . . because I wanted it as far as possible from a breeding-ground of the most virulent diseases. You, Mr Turner, and you, Mr Cape, are responsible for a great deal of shoddy building in this town. . . .'

'Mr Mayor, we protest!'

'An open sewer and countless cess-pools contribute not only to a vile stench but to a sick population. As Millbridge spills out into the countryside, and our small villages become towns, we are cramming poor people into ginnels and snickets and foetid courts which an animal would decline to live in!'

'Our poor,' said Alderman Brigge, in his role as a local squire, 'do not exist as you depict them, sir. I have a care for all my people. They want for nothing. My wife visits our sick. My daughters knit and sew garments for their offspring. We have an annual feast upon my small estate—'

'Balderdash!' cried Standish. 'I am not speaking of your estate, Squire Brigge, where you may do very well—but watch out, for these industrial foxes will be after your land and able to pay a great deal more for it than you can afford to refuse! . . .'

'Mr Mayor!' protested a dozen voices, who all had an interest in land.

'Order, order! If you please, Dr Standish, would you modify your language somewhat? You are needlessly offending members of the council.'

'Do they not pass water and squat upon their stools daily?' said the doctor, relishing this public debate. 'Do they not contribute to the stink? I am speaking of diseases which will not pass them by because they have made a fortune. They can writhe with cholera, lose their complexions and lives with smallpox, waste away with typhus and typhoid fevers whether they are rich or poor. Those damned cellars, which house ten persons in filthy spaces not ten feet square, will be all our deaths. . . .'

'I will make a note of it,' said the Town Clerk peaceably, 'if the council so wishes.'

'Well, do not lose it, as you did the last!' Matthew Standish warned. 'And I want more than a note. Mr Howarth, did not one of your famous colleagues cast pipes for the Paris Waterworks Company, some twenty years since?'

'Yes, sir,' William replied equably. 'It was the great John Wilkinson.'

'Well, whoever he was, he cast pipes. I dare say Mr Howarth and his partner would cast pipes for us, if we made a reasonable attempt to divide our water from our sewage. Would you not, Mr Howarth?'

'With the greatest of pleasure, sir.'

'And a damned great bill!' someone murmured cynically.

'Not so, sir,' William cried, cool but stern. 'We make fair profits, and only by charging fair prices!'

'Gentlemen, please!' called the Mayor. 'Is that all, Dr Standish?'

'No, it is damned well not, sir. I want a plan drawn up for a system of iron pipes to be laid underground throughout the town.'

'And how much will that cost?' cried several business members of the council at once.

'I have no idea,' said Matthew Standish. 'But when you have totted up the price of a few thousand lives, then set it by the side of your bill and see which is preferable. I have my hospital to attend to, Mr Mayor. I crave your indulgence,' he added, already on his way out.

He paused by the windows and smiled enigmatically.

'I leave my deadly enemy to persuade you into action!' he observed, and threw up the sashes one by one.

The day was fine and hot. The Old Town, as it was called, looked gracious still: a square mile of broad roads and fine houses. The Royal George only seemed to improve with age. The Market Square and Cross were famous for miles around, and visitors came to view St Mark's Church which was a particularly good example of the Late Perpendicular style. But behind this elegant façade sneaked a network of mean alleyways, seedy shops, cheap taverns, shabby tenements. And the wind was blowing in exactly the direction Dr Standish wished.

An unmentionable sweetness, like the stench of death beneath white lilies, entered the council chamber. Everyone put his handkerchief to his nose. Dr Standish gave his thin, dry smile and shut the door smartly behind him.

'Close them, Hawkins. Close them, if you please,' said the Mayor faintly. 'Now where were we?'

This was a mistake on his part because they all began to speak at once. William waited, since he had learned to outsit them before he made his point. Jack Ackroyd did the opposite, and fought until he was heard. William disliked him intensely, but Jack could never more than fume at the iron-master, for was he not Charlotte's brother? Nevertheless, though they did not quarrel openly, they did not agree either, except on broadly humane issues.

The Mayor looked nervously from face to face, and chose Jack.

'I thank you, Mr Mayor,' said the headmaster, with heavy sarcasm. 'Now before I speak on my own account I should like to sustain the motion put forward by Dr Standish—'

'On the close-stool?' muttered one wit, and there was a scatter of laughter among the councillors.

'. . . on the idea of better sanitation for Millbridge. Perhaps Mr Howarth here'—glancing at William—'would know how we go about it?' William inclined his head gravely. 'Then perhaps you would be good enough, sir, to look into the matter and give the council an estimate of costs? Is that agreed, Mr Mayor? Or will you throw it out before the idea has a fair hearing?'

'No, no, Mr Ackroyd.' Caught between hammer and anvil.

'Very good, sir. Shall we take it that better sanitation is first upon our agenda? I thank you. So now we have saved ourselves and the poor from death by disease, metaphorically speaking, do you think it possible that we might also save the poor from death by slow starvation?'

'I know what he's after,' said Ernest Harbottle to William, 'he wants that blessed poor-rate put up again!'

'Quite right, Mr Babylon,' Jack replied swiftly, and Harbottle reddened from neck to forehead. 'Workmen's wages are not rising as fast as prices. The war is not benefiting them as it benefits some members of this council! If I had my way you should all visit these inhuman dens, where your slaves are spawned, and know the extent of your iniquities. . . .'

The hubbub outdid any so far. Jack waved a sheaf of papers in the air, indicating that he possessed facts and figures they should hear. But they were too busy defending themselves.

'I would have you know, sir, that at both our ironworks the wages are above average and the men properly fed. They must be strong to work for me. . . .'

'A public benefactor, that's what I am. Taking paupers as apprentices. They're off the hands of the workhouses, which is off the public rates, and they make me take an idiot with every nineteen paupers. That means a loss of five per cent. . . .'

'You accused me, last week, sir, of withholding supplies of

corn that the price may be kept up. And I tell you, sir, damn your insinuations. . . .'

'We've got a lot of educated folk on this here council as has never earned bread by the sweat of their brow, and though they might mean well—mean well, I say—they're talking a lot o' rubbish. We put the poor-rate up in ninety-eight and ninety-nine, what with the bad winters and all. And we done it last year. I'm paying nearly four times as much poor-rate today as what I paid five years ago. And I say them as don't work shan't eat!'

'Aye, why pay an idle fellow to stay at home and get his wife with child?' cried Alderman Brigge. 'We have enough expense, keeping up the workhouses. It is all this industry that is causing poverty. Folk are coming into our valley that do not belong here, and when they cannot find work they come upon the parish for relief!'

'Not fair!' shouted Ernest Harbottle. 'Not fair, Squire Brigge, sir. I employ them young people in the workhouse, and give them a home second to none. Mr Howarth might not, but I do.'

'I have a *proper* system of apprenticeships, sir,' cried William, roused.

'Gentlemen, please,' said the Mayor. 'What of Mr Ackroyd's suggestion that we raise the poor-rate again?'

It was unanimously turned down.

'Was there anything else, Mr Ackroyd?' asked the Mayor.

'Yes, indeed,' said Jack between his teeth, 'though whether I am wasting my time in mentioning the matter I do not know. I should like the council to consider, once again, whether they could not allow the grammar school some money towards its evening classes for working people. Since we began these classes in a small way, some two or three years ago, they have grown to outstanding proportions. So far we have managed with voluntary help and donations, but our numbers are beyond our means.' He remembered what Charlotte had told him about losing his temper, and lowered his voice, saying peaceably, 'If the council would consider a modest sum of money per annum I should be pleased to render a full account of our expenditure, which is largely materials for the purpose of reading and writing.'

There was a bored silence as he sat down.

The Mayor said, 'Has anyone anything to say to Mr Ackroyd's proposal?'

'It's a dangerous business, educating poor folk,' said Alderman Brigge, as spokesman of the Tory party. 'It makes them forget their place, and start poking about in matters that don't concern them. I'm against it on principle.'

'Hear, hear,' said Ernest Harbottle. 'Reading and writing's for them that has time for it. I never learned much, and look where I am!'

Jack Ackroyd leaned forward and seized him, none too gently, by his left lapel.

'I have a third matter to mention that will concern you closely,' he muttered. 'You, and others like you, whose factories are a disgrace not only to this valley but to the whole human race!'

'Mr Ackroyd!' said the Mayor loudly. 'Would you be kind enough to wait until this motion is carried. How many for the proposal? How many against? Rejected, by a large majority.'

He recollected that William's sister ran a minor branch of the evening classes at her own expense, in her own house.

'We don't object to the classes,' he added magnanimously, 'and if folk want to help with them, or make a donation to them, that's their own affair. But the council regards an evening class for working people as purely charitable. It isn't public business, and therefore we can't contribute public money to it.'

Jack Ackroyd sat very pinched and pale, waiting to hurl the next missile.

'May I mention one thing more, Mr Mayor?' he asked as reasonably as he could. 'Should we not bring up the matter of Sir Robert Peel's Act concerning the care and protection of pauper apprentices in spinning-mills?'

The council was disturbed on many counts, depending upon whether Mr Harbottle was any use to them or not.

'Early days, I think, Mr Ackroyd,' the Mayor offered. 'The Act has only just been passed. We shall, of course, look into these matters and appoint inspectors, as required.'

'I hope you do, sir,' said Jack grimly, 'because if you do not then I shall approach the highest authorities. And if Sir Robert Peel thinks fit to disclose the abuses in our midst then he must have some about him who will listen to me!'

'Come, sir,' said Alderman Brigge, 'no one has said aught against the motion. You are too hasty.'

'Not hasty, rightly suspicious!' cried Jack, and now he was angry despite what Charlotte had said. 'I have seen too much swept under the carpet, gentlemen, to accept that this council will look seriously into the condition of certain mills in this valley. I have taken the trouble to fetch copies of the Act with me, in case any member has not read it. . . ,' and he began to distribute them.

'Oh, Lord!' said the Mayor, under his breath.

William hardly glanced at his copy. He did not care tuppence what happened to Harbottle, whom he despised, but he did not see why he should be dragged into open debate by Jack Ackroyd either.

'For instance,' Jack began, swaying to and fro on his heels, 'all mills must have proper ventilation and a sufficient number of windows. Walls and ceilings must be whitewashed twice a year, for sanitary reasons. Each apprentice should be given two new suits of clothes when employed, and a further suit of clothes every year. And!' Coming to the point he most relished. 'And, mark this, gentlemen. All apprentices must be taught to read and write at the owner's expense, and in time taken from their working hours, for the first four years!'

He looked round the table, nodding his head sarcastically at them.

'Sir Robert Peel evidently does not share your opinion as to education of the working class!' he observed.

'Mr Ackroyd,' said the Mayor, pained, 'I find your manner highly disagreeable. And I would remind you that you have a seat on this council purely because you are the headmaster of our grammar school. It is not your business to bring up matters which have nothing to do with education—'

Jack slammed his hand down upon the table in his temper.

'Show me a document which states that fact!' he cried.

'Order, order, gentlemen, please,' the Town Clerk begged.

'I'm not a-sitting at the same table with a man like that,' said Ernest Harbottle loudly.

His colour and voice were high, and he prepared to leave as though choked with rightful indignation. Jack Ackroyd lifted up his hands in a gesture of acceptance, and looked to William for a little justice.

'Mr Howarth,' he said quietly, 'I do not mind who takes up this cause, so long as it is won. *You* can have no interest in suppressing, evading or otherwise shuffling off this most excellent piece of legislation. Will you at least stand with me?'

'The next point concerns the roasting of a bullock in the market-place last October, to celebrate the end of the war with France,' said the Mayor loudly, over-riding him. 'The

263

farmer who supplied the beast says it hasn't yet been paid for....'

William lifted his eyebrows, and shrugged to show that the opportunity was past. Ernest Harbottle watched the pair of them with frightened eyes.

'Sir,' said William deliberately, 'I should be afraid to stand as your ally though your cause was the most merciful in the world. You have too great a knack of making enemies—and the worst of them is yourself.'

Jack sat as though all the wind had been knocked out of him.

'That's telling him, Mr Howarth,' said Harbottle, relieved.

'As for you, sir,' William continued, in the same deliberate manner, 'I would suggest that you clean your own doorstep. For an Act is an Act, and however long it takes to catch up with you, catch up it will.'

Then he caught the Mayor's eye.

'Mr Howarth?'

'Two very small matters, Mr Mayor. The first permission to build a Quaker meeting-house on private land....'

Very white, the headmaster collected up his papers. He heard Ernest Harbottle defending himself to his neighbour in a hurried undertone.

'. . . all them clothes, and the education, and only working twelve hour a day. Why, if I'd only worked twelve hour a day where would I be now? It means I'd have to shut the mills down at night, or part of them. That'd make a tidy hole in the profits. Then all that rubbish about male and female dormitories, and not sleeping more than two to the bed. Why, we can never let the beds get cold at our place. As one work-shift comes off to sleep t'other one goes on. And don't tell me as the poor ones haven't slept six and seven to the bed, brothers and sisters, at home! And then talk of fetching a doctor to them at the owner's expense. Oh yes, it's all at my expense, ain't it? I never heard of such a thing. Give the buggers a dose of worming powder and a kick up the backside is what I say....'

All that Jack wanted at the moment was to be able to walk into Charlotte's parlour and let her put him to rights again. William's rebuff had hurt him more than he would have believed possible. But he had seen that the ironmaster's horse was tethered outside Thornton House. So when the meeting finished he must go back to his rooms, and nurse his defeats alone. And he wished he possessed Dr Standish's temperament, which thrived on disappointments. For Jack had always strived to right matters. It was the right he wanted, not the battle.

The meeting was simmering to its close. William had been granted his requests. Harbottle brooded, sustained only by thought of his profits. The headmaster sat silent, head upon hand in a gesture of temporary defeat.

'Well, that seems to be all, gentlemen,' said the Mayor, relieved.

They rose in twos and threes, turning to chat and smile, to frown and growl.

Alderman Brigge said idly, 'We have not been plagued by our outlaw friends for a while, I notice. Of course, the weather is warmer and the nights lighter. They seem to venture abroad only in the cold and dark!'

'Aye, it is a curious business,' William replied, uninterested, for he had not been visited as other members had.

'They are very well organised, for sure. And we do not seem able to apprehend them.'

'That is hardly surprising, sir,' said William, more animated, 'for we have not the law-force in this valley that is necessary to keep order.'

'All law-abiding citizens,' the Mayor reminded him (for he did not want difficulties over the law-force as well as everything else), 'all good citizens, Mr Howarth, take their turn at patrolling. We cannot do more.'

And, lest William thought they could, he left the council chamber quickly.

'They are not violent, at least,' said Jack Ackroyd, recovering a little as he heard his society mentioned, 'and they do not steal, as such, nor harm anyone as far as I know.'

'But they are outlaws, nevertheless,' said Alderman Brigge, 'that you cannot deny, for all your nonsensical notions, sir!'

'Oh yes,' said Jack sombrely, surprising them by acquiescence, 'they are outlaws, sir, I grant you that. And I am sure they feels themselves to be such. Good-day to you, sirs!'

TWENTY-ONE

Jack Straw Riding By

The warehouse was fairly isolated on its black wharf just beyond Millbridge, lapped by black water. Once, small boys had sat on that bank when it was green and broad, and fished with home-made rods and lines, tempting the silver swimmers with a bit of bread impaled on a crooked pin. Now, bank and boys and fish were an old story, swept away by time and progress. Now, Joseph Dewsbury, Corn Merchant, had raised a brick and timber depot which was soon sullied by smoke, and stocked it full of grain. He was in no hurry to sell. The weather, as well as the war, was sending up the price. His sacks were making profit for him, even as they sat there. But human nature being what it was, and envy always ready to point a finger at him, Mr Dewsbury had taken care to purchase the stoutest locks and bolts and bars he could find; and he paid a couple of strong fellows to guard the place, and kept a fierce dog loose in the yard at night, to deter thieves.

The stars glittered in a black heaven, brilliant and cold. The moon shone like polished plate. Down below, a hard frost nipped flowers in the bud, froze meat in the larders of those who had it, killed new-born lambs. No one and nothing stirred in the glacial landscape. There were few signs that it had been a rural village some fifteen years ago, one of a necklace of such little places, linked by the winding river. The air smelled of sulphur. Tall chimneys, pit-head gear, cranes, etched strange shapes on the horizon. An orchestra of sounds, some near and some far off, played upon the ear; producing a mechanical composition of hums and roars, clanks and shrieks. From time to time the fires of Belbrook and Snape lit the sky for miles around. Mills gleamed like many-windowed palaces. And clustered round each factory a disorderly collection of houses, cramped and filthy and ill-smelling, swarmed with their human vermin.

Wagons were rolling along the Black Road as they always

did. That broad thoroughfare was as busy as any London street, day and night. Three or four which were covered with tarpaulin turned down towards Mill Wharf, and stopped a few hundred yards from Dewsbury's warehouse. One driver got down, swiftly and silently, and crept to within a stone's throw of the black yard. There, he appeared to throw a stone, though it made no sound in falling beyond the softest of flumps, and the brindled guard-dog slunk forward to examine it. In a minute or two the driver beckoned, and two men who had hidden beneath the tarpaulin joined him. This pair scaled the wall and were lost in the shadows. Only the faintest tinkle of glass betrayed their whereabouts. In another few minutes one of them was up on the wall again, signalling. The wagons rumbled forward. The doors of the yard were opened for them. More men emerged from the belly of the vehicles, running soundlessly into the warehouse. Presently they came out with sacks of grain and began to load the carts.

Inside, the watchmen lay bound and gagged, but would be none the worse for their fright in the morning, apart from the matter of sore heads. The guard-dog lay sprawled on the floor of the yard, and would not waken with them.

There was no furniture to speak of in the back room of No. 5 Babylon Street, unless you so described a broken-legged table and two crazy chairs. On a heap of rags in the corner lay four small children asleep. By the hearth a young-old woman huddled over a handful of dull coals, wrapped in a shawl. She had been waiting up for a long time now, listening for the quiet knock on her door. When it came she was ready, opening barely a slit in order to peep out, whispering, 'Who is it?' For everyone must be careful, on pain of death or transportation.

'All right, missis,' came the answering whisper. 'It's Jack Straw the baker. Let us in, wilta? Else the neighbourhood'll sniff us out!'

She opened the door hastily, but the summons of fresh-baked bread was there before him, waking the little lad of seven who had eaten rarely of it.

'How many in this house?' asked the messenger, hurriedly.

'Twelve room, twelve families, Jack Straw,' she replied. 'I've laid the paper on the floor over there.'

He was one of the men who had loaded the wagons with grain the other night. Since then it had been milled by three millers, free of charge they said; but nobody would blame them if they kept a sack, considering the risks involved. The same organisation had then transported the flour to sympathetic bakers, who probably took a similar fee, and from thence to the houses on the list.

'Quick!' the messenger whispered, and two other men, also muffled up to the eyes, began to pile loaves on the paper against the wall.

'Sign for No. 5 Babylon, missis,' he whispered hoarsely.

She made a cross on the paper, which trailed awkwardly.

'I shall be back tomorrow night at nine by Millbridge clock, missis. You're the shop-keeper for this house, so reckon up and have the money ready. Tuppence a loaf this time. A bit more, but the war's to blame for that, starting up again! Any road, you wouldn't get the same for a shilling if you had to buy from the shops. Now, *your* bread's free, along of being shopkeeper, that's five loaves. And here's a sixpence for the trouble, and the risk, and cutting into your night's sleep.'

As softly and rapidly as they had come, the three men disappeared into the night. The woman hid the coin in her bodice, looked longingly at the bread, and prepared to rest. This involved taking off the shawl and fustian gown which she then used as extra coverlets. The lad made room for her, and though their breath smoked on the air they contrived to warm each other.

'I heard Millbridge clock strike two not long since,' she said, 'and we've got to be at the mill at six. Get your sleep while you can. I don't want you falling into them machines while you're minding them.'

'What about you falling asleep then?' the boy whispered, for he had become both bread-winner and protector since his father was killed, falling from a high building at Snape twelve months ago. The money paid to them, in lieu of his death, had not replaced his earnings, and there was no follow-up.

'I'll manage. I'm older than thee. And it's worth the wait to get the bread and the sixpence.'

They lay with open eyes, staring into the bitter dark. But the scent of bread was as beautiful as a meadow full of clover. Tomorrow, today, they would eat of it before they went to work.

'Mam, why don't you bring our Betty along to Babylon

Mill with us? She's gone five years old. It'd fetch a bit more money in.'

'Aye, but who'd mind the other two while she were away? It'll be easier when Jennie's growed up.'

If we live that long, she thought, but did not say so.

'Mam, shall us have a corner of crust?'

She hesitated, feeling his hunger as well as her own, but resolved against such unorthodoxy.

'Not 'til morning, love.'

'I could eat all that, Mam.'

'So could I, love. We'st wait 'til morning.'

'Mam, who come to the door just now?'

'Oh, nobody we know. Nobody we must speak of. We'st have bread for breakfast, my lad. That's all we need to know.'

'It were Jack Straw, weren't it?' he whispered, trying to discern the expression on his mother's face.

He smiled, in answer to the glimmer of a smile on her mouth.

'Aye,' he whispered, turning over to sleep, 'that's who it were. Jack Straw. Jack Straw come riding by!'

The Town Clerk had received the usual letter in his morning's post. Though poorly spelled it was clean, well-printed and explicit.

TO THE TOWN OFFISERS OF MILLBRIDGE. A WERHOWSE ON MILL WORF BELONGIN TO JOS DEWSBURY WAS EMPTID OF GRANE LAST NITE WICH THE MERCHENT AS BIN SELLIN AT 127 SHILLINS A QWARTER. WE HAV LEFT A FARE PRISE OF 50 SHILLINS A QWARTER AND WIL RETERN THE SAKS! NO HURT WAS DONE TO THE WOTCHMEN. WE DAMAJED A SIDE WINDER FOR WICH WE LEEVE 2 SHILLINS TO REPARE IT. THE GRANE WIL BE GIVIN TO PORE PEEPUL HOO HAVE PADE THE FARE PRISE FOR IT.

It was signed simply JACK STRAW.

A week later, one of the nightwatchmen found the sacks, neatly folded, correct in number, in a back room which he had checked not more than an hour since. In spite of the fact that no one had wounded or attempted to kill him on the previous raid, he shivered at the thought of those eyes watching in the night.

And at the same time, further down the valley, a steam-powered flour-mill, one of Lord Kersall's enterprises, was being relieved of its contents. The Red Rose Society was working its way systematically down a long list of those who profited by other people's misfortunes.

The eccentric nature of these coups, the thought and planning invested in each foray, worried the authorities more than the events themselves. For who knew when the organisation might change its ways and methods? Human nature being what it was, as Alderman Brigge remarked, one of them might become over-ambitious, or a Jacobin agent could use them for his own purposes. But the town council never came to any satisfactory conclusion on the matter, and as the raids were sporadic and scattered throughout the breadth and length of Wyndendale, no one quite knew how to deal with them. It would be an admission of defeat, as Lord Kersall himself said, to put the matter before the Home Secretary. No, no, they would wash their own dirty linen! They did not want the government ferreting into their private affairs. And so, betwixt incompetence and difference of opinion, nothing was done.

The society's true name was known only among its peers, but the watchword, chosen on the spur of a moment, became its symbol and took on flesh and spirit. Children in the crowded dwellings, wakened perhaps at night by the muffled rumble of wheels, hearing whispers at the door, would be told sharply to 'Lay down again! Jack Straw's piking off!' And in their minds a giant, both great and good, rode the valley from Garth to Millbridge, distributing his bounty to such as themselves.

TWENTY-TWO

Charlotte's Children

1799—1805

Ambrose Longe was a copy-plate of his father, as if Toby had been aware of early death and sought to live on in his son. The lively little boy who wrote his own newspaper, in answer to the pompousness of *The Wyndendale Post*, became a lively scholar at Millbridge Grammar School; to which establishment he sallied forth daily, exchanging the loving solicitude of his mother for the discipline of his headmaster. And though he entertained Cicely and the kitchen staff with wicked imitations of Nobmaster Awkward, and twitted Charlotte to observe her reactions, Ambrose respected Jack Ackroyd. Their styles were different, but they learned to like each other very well.

Whether the boy had imbibed radicalism with his mother's milk or absorbed it from her associates was not certain. But he was a born Radical, even as he was a born journalist. Charlotte could always occupy herself at her desk, provided that her son had pen and paper as well. They would scratch away for hours together and in perfect amity, while Cicely sat in her own quiet world and sewed.

Ambrose was just fourteen when the Red Rose and the evening classes blossomed, and at that age when a lad is most curious and in need of adventure. The night-watch, as he called it, began as a private dare that he could hear what was going on without being discovered. Crouched in the shadows of hall or staircase, ready to scuttle silently away should he be disturbed, he played a game which gradually became shocking reality.

The classes were dull, predictable stuff, but the meetings afterwards provided him with more excitement than he had bargained for. Twice a week he took up his post, risking capture from the kitchen, the back parlour or a late arrival at the back door, and noted who came and went and what was said. His mental dossier grew, his eyes and mind were opened, he was enthralled and terrified. A new world was revealed, and he saw that it was good. He even drew a map of the valley to observe how the society was placing its leaders and parties. He knew which inns were friendly and would pass a message or give a warning. He hid the map carefully, under a loose floorboard in his room, and hugged his secret to his heart.

The first coup was brewing in the savage winter of '99. The men had been chosen, the place checked, times and movements worked out, and solemn oaths of secrecy taken. Then they produced the handbill which was to be sent to the authorities, and in this Ambrose found a fatal flaw.

He scurried upstairs as the parlour door opened, in a moral dilemma. Disclosure of his knowledge would bring retribution: he did not fear his mother, but the rest of the society were men and he knew that their justice would be of the rougher kind. And yet he knew that so much, and so many, should not be risked for the sake of his own young hide and safety. He resolved to sacrifice himself, though he shuddered at the prospect.

So Charlotte found him sitting on her bed, huddled in her coverlet, and shivering more than the cold night warranted.

'You are later than usual tonight, Mamma,' said Ambrose at once, resolving on a direct approach. 'Is Mr Ackroyd setting your class an examination already?'

Her heart leaped and sank at the sight of her son, and she silently thanked God that Jack had gone home that evening to nurse a cold, else they might have come in together.

'Why are you not asleep?' she said fiercely, softly. 'How dare you wait up like this. You are impertinent, sir, and not too old to escape punishment!'

They were both very white and scared, afraid of themselves and each other. Ambrose's brief heroism deserted him. He forgot the speech he had prepared and blurted out his boy's truth with a boy's desperation.

'Mamma, you mustn't send out that handbill as it is. They'll know who you are if you do. And they'll put you and Mr Ackroyd in prison, and Cissie and me will have to live at Bracelet with Grandmother, and they will close down the grammar school. And where will poor Polly and Sally go, and William Wilberforce as well? Oh, Mamma, don't send the handbill!'

And he cast himself upon her, and clutched her, and sobbed in spite of his resolution.

'There now, my son,' said Charlotte mechanically, stroking his head. 'There now, Brosey!'

Appalled by his knowledge of them. Chilled by their peril. She dismissed the questions she wanted to ask, the accusations she wanted to make. She drew him towards the fire in the hearth, sat him down on the rug, and questioned him forcefully, directly.

'What is wrong with the handbill?'

He wiped his eyes on the sleeve of his nightshirt, ashamed of his tears, collecting himself. He spoke rapidly, as though reciting a lesson.

'In the first place it is a professional handbill from an established society, which will challenge them to root you out. But in the second, it is obviously composed by a person of education who is a little too particular as to the spelling and grammar!'

He looked appealingly at her to see how she was taking this criticism. She motioned him, gravely, to continue.

'Mamma, Mr Ackroyd is known for his radical views, and folk guess at your own, and I have heard them speak of my father's doings in London and Paris. Surely, it will not be long before the local justices connect these things together and look for an educated Radical source?'

Her face was impassive. His courage wavered, for perhaps he was quite wrong and need not have spoken.

'All I think . . . from what I have heard of such matters . . . is that if the authorities receive an ordinary mis-spelled note, signed "Robin Hood"—or any similar name which hints at common insurrection. . . . I mean, Mamma, would it not be better that they thought the Red Rose was simply a group of cunning bumpkins?'

She sat, arms folded, feet on the fender, frowning in thought. Then her expression became clear again, even a little humorous.

She said, 'I once criticised Mr Ackroyd for a similar fault, and never thought to apply it to myself. It is the obvious that always escapes one.' Troubled, she asked, 'How much do you know of us, Spy Ambrose?'

'Pretty well all, Mamma,' he replied, and his heartbeat became less insistent. 'I was just spying for fun in the beginning. Not to know anything, if you understand me, just for the daring of it. I have a map of the valley under my floorboards, and you can see it if you want to. . . . I have told no one, Mamma. Not even Cissie.'

'Let that be a lesson to me,' she said, angry with him and herself. She now looked sternly on him. 'What is done cannot be undone,' she remarked, 'but you must take responsibility for it. Do you know the oath of life or death we make our supporters take, Ambrose? The need for absolute secrecy, absolute loyalty, absolute silence? The punishment that will be exacted for treachery?

'You wept easy tears a few minutes ago, my son, fearing my imprisonment and a change of home for you and your sister. My dear child, what an understatement of the consequences that would be!' And she cast up her hands momentarily, and clicked her tongue. 'They will hang a boy of seven for stealing a sheep, so why should they spare a woman who is guilty of sedition? As for your living at Bracelet, that would be the best you could expect in the midst of great misfortune. The two of you would be watched, suspected, from then on. And you, Ambrose, who have not yet learned how to govern your tongue or curiosity, what trouble you would be in. They would make sure that you held no honourable post, no responsible position, when you were a man. Do you understand me?'

He nodded, and his underlip quivered slightly. She saw that she had conveyed the gravity of their situation, and softened a little in her severity.

'So,' she said, touching his shoulder, 'you had courage enough to tell me, now use your courage to keep silence, and to keep away from our meetings and all talk and thought of them, henceforth. And I will have that map, sir, and burn it this moment upon this fire!'

He saw that he had been forgiven. He stretched out a bare foot to warm it.

'Was my father a spy, Mamma?' he asked, watching her face.

'I do not know,' she answered soberly. 'In this business no one—or only one!—knows everything. The less we know the less we can tell.'

'Mamma, I promise you you need fear nothing from me. But, Mamma. . . .'

'Ah! Toby's *but*,' she said wryly. '*But*, will you give me the world? What *but*, my son, have you to exact of me?'

'But please can I make up the name for your letter?'

She threw back her head and laughed quietly.

'Well, that depends, Ambrose. What name had you thought of, while you listened and plotted?

'We have been reading the Nun's Prologue by Chaucer,' he said comfortably, warming his foot, 'and learning the history of the Peasants' Revolt in thirteen eighty-six, and the same name cropped up in both, and caught my fancy. He was the leader of the revolt, you see, and his first name is the same as Mr Ackroyd's—but would they suspect him because of it?' he added, suddenly downcast at the thought.

'I doubt it. That is a little too obvious, and even his enemies cannot accuse him of vanity!'

'No. Of course it has another meaning nowadays. Thomas Nashe describes him in Nashe's Lenten Stuffe as a worthless sort of fellow. *Jack Straw!*'

'Jack Straw!' Charlotte mused. 'I do not see why not. But I must ask Mr Ackroyd. And I must tell him who supplied it, and why and how!'

Ambrose looked worried.

'Yes, it is always the way,' said Charlotte sadly. 'The mention of a man's displeasure instils respect and fear. The whole lifetime of a woman's misery may be dismissed in a few words of regret. Now, fetch me that map, Brosey!'

He scrambled up from the hearthrug, trailing his coverlet behind him. A boy playing king.

'Shall I tell you something secret about myself, Mamma?' he coaxed, part in truth and partly to extend this delicious adult confidence between them. 'Mamma, I shall never get married, and I shall have a proper newspaper of my very own!'

'Your father swore the same double oath, and doubly broke it!'

'No, you are not listening to me! Oh well then, I will change it a little. I shall not be married unless it is to a woman like you, Mamma, who thinks as I do! And even if I cannot have my own newspaper then I shall have a son, or a grandson who will. . . . Mamma, listen to me. Do not make me go to bed until I have told you the best of all! . . .'

'And what is the best of all?' she asked wryly, fondly, pushing the juvenile spy before her.

'Do you know, can you not guess, what the newspaper will be called? *The Northern Correspondent!* On my life, I swear it, Mamma. However long it takes. After you, you see. *The Northern Correspondent!*'

His accidental discovery of the Red Rose Society had sobered Ambrose somewhat. The Howarth common sense steadied the

Longe in him. He was more restrained now, more far-sighted. But his father lived on in his ability to enjoy the moment, to revel in the sheer exuberance of being, to survey the mass of humanity with infinite delight.

He knew that the most dangerous people in any household were its servants, however devoted, for they talked. So he began to make sure that they talked of safer matters. His portraits of Nobmaster Awkward, in the majesty of his calling, grew broader and more comical. He presented Jack as an eccentric scholar, full of wild ideals and harmless nonsense, who forgot more than his hat. He gently mocked Charlotte's spinsterish passion for teaching, the way she played Penelope to her three suitors, with the underlying hint that no man but Toby had ever interested her. For he knew how much Jack Ackroyd meant to his mother, and kept his own counsel out of delicacy to them both. And the three suitors, worthy men, were prime figures of fun in the kitchen. Indeed, Polly could scarcely forbear smiling when she opened the front door, and saw Proctor Stand-up on the threshold, or Solicitous Thirst, or Quaking Shoals. And when the High Street servants tended their morning doorsteps, or took the air as they pegged out clothes on the washing-lines, these caricatures were the heart of their conversation, and helped to protect the real people, as Ambrose intended.

Time assisted him. Millbridge was changing, but Thornton House seemed always to stay the same. Gossip can only be nourished by the new. As Charlotte weathered each small social crisis it became of no more interest than last week's *Wyndendale Post*. Folk even covered her behaviour with the respectable cloak of family faults.

'It's in the blood, my dear. Old Miss Wilde put up a tombstone to her dog, Walpole, you know, and often said she loved him better than any person, and she *would* have her own way! And though Dorcas is very proper these days she used to have a will and temper fit to match her aunt, and threw her bonnet over the windmill to marry that farmer in Garth! Mind you, old Mr Howarth was a very gentlemanly fellow, as are his two sons—and no one could do better than William Howarth, now could they? No, it is the female side that is a trifle odd. . . .'

So Ambrose picked up knowledge of those subjects which interested him, and neglected those which did not, and gradually lengthened into a handsome young fellow of medium height with a taste for fine clothes. They spoke of his going to

Cambridge, as Jack Ackroyd had done, and he did not gain-say them. Cambridge might do very well, and if it did not then he would find somewhere and something else to do. For himself, he rather fancied his chance in London, and whatever Ambrose fancied was likely to come his way. And he became a great hero among the younger pupils at the grammar school in his last year, and broke many budding female hearts along the High Street.

Cicely had always preferred the company of older people, and when Phoebe died she transferred her attentions to Dorcas. William, ever-generous, had given the young Longes a pony apiece, which they kept at the livery stables in Cornmarket Street. From there, Cicely would ride over to Upperton two or three times a week, and grandmother and grand-daughter would spend the day in perfect harmony: inspecting the small gardens at the back and front of Bracelet, compounding simple medicines and toiletries in Dorcas's still-room, drinking tea and conversing in the parlour. And as the girl grew older Dorcas would confide in her.

Apparently all was not well in the ironmaster's household, despite his increasing wealth and power. Every two years or so Zelah produced another daughter in her own image, and though William loved them in his fashion he no longer concealed his desire for the appearance of a son. By the time Ambrose went up to Cambridge in the autumn of 1803 there were four little girls gracing Kingswood Hall: Tabitha, Catherine, Anna and Olivia. William's absorption with Snape and Belbrook was becoming obsessive, and he entertained almost as lavishly, but not so exclusively, as Lord Kersall. Dorcas thought that Zelah looked too pale and worked too hard, in consequence. Also, she had never come to terms with the Church of England service, and now secluded herself for an hour each day, keeping a solitary Quaker silence in her private sitting-room. Besides that, women tended to spoil William—not that he noticed, of course, but still, it was not good for him. . . .

All this Cicely learned and kept to herself, though she would confirm Charlotte's opinion or doubts if the matters were raised. There was a slight shadow between mother and daughter, which did not exist between mother and son. It appeared to spring from an inner alienation, as though the girl distrusted Charlotte's way of life. And, just as Charlotte had preferred Millbridge to her own home at the age of sixteen, so Cicely was more at ease in Bracelet than Thornton House. On fine Sundays Dorcas drove into Millbridge in her new trap, meeting her grand-daughter for the morning service at St Mark's Church, and afterwards ate dinner with them. For Charlotte had long since given up church attendance, and though she would not have described herself as an atheist she seemed one.

'Cicely is so like my mother,' Dorcas remarked on one such occasion.

There was a hint of reproach in her tone, and Charlotte, who had hoped to do some work that afternoon, answered somewhat impatiently.

'So you have always said, Mamma.'

Then she felt sorry, because her mother looked hurt.

'I fear that repetition is one of the penances of old age,' said Dorcas, endeavouring to speak lightly.

But Charlotte came over and kissed her, and begged her pardon, so that was all right. And presently, Dorcas began again.

'My mother was a Beecham, you know, and closely related to four bishops, which they say is a mark of true aristocracy! Indeed, she was a great lady in the best sense of the word. But her family never quite forgave her for marrying my father, though he was a gentleman and a good churchman. You did please me so, Charlotte, by naming your children after them!' She was very bright all of a sudden, remembering. 'Cicely Beecham and Ambrose Wilde—ah well, that is an old love story. . . .'

Cicely sat, stitching and listening, shining head bent. She had heard all these tales countless times but did not tire of them. She liked to think of that gentle but tenacious Cicely Beecham, the ardent but impoverished Ambrose Wilde in his Gloucestershire parish, and their happiness together.

'Of course, their life was not easy,' said Dorcas in her reverie, 'for my mother bore seven children and only I survived. And her death was so cruel, and she died young. Well, young enough. How old are you, Charlotte?'

'Close on eight and thirty, Mamma,' her daughter replied drily, for she could not see the point of the conversation.

'Ah, she was scarcely that! Well, I must not run on. Where are my gloves, child?'

'Here, Grandmama, under your reticule.'

'I shall be going now, my dear ones. I have stayed longer than usual on account of the heat, Charlotte. Your father would not have liked me to drive home with the sun so hot! Oh, by the by, Mrs Graham made a point of speaking to us today after the service, and was most civil, was she not, Cicely? She asked us to drink tea with her at the Rectory next Sunday, and I thought how I should like to see the old place again. I have not been there since Phoebe's father died, above twenty years ago. And Phoebe and I were girls together at one time, Cicely, and used to sit by the fireside there and confide in each other as young girls do. . . .'

Charlotte's expression was doubtful.

'Surely, Mrs Graham does not want *me* to drink tea with her?'

'No, I am sure she does not,' said Dorcas crisply. 'She only mentioned you in passing, as a matter of common courtesy. Her invitation was extended to us, but since you are Cicely's mother it is only right that your permission is asked.'

'My permission is freely granted,' cried Charlotte, laughing at the quaintness of the request. 'Why, what a pair of oddities you are!' And she embraced them fondly. 'I do not mind if Cicely drinks tea there every day, if it makes her happy— only I should not like to do so myself.'

'Then we shall certainly go,' said Dorcas, with a curious look on her face. 'And if a friendship or special interest should develop between Cicely and Mrs Graham you would not mind?'

'I? Why should I?' said Charlotte, feeling a distance between them. 'I believe that everyone should do as they think best. I have friends and interests of my own which do not suit everybody,' she added a little bitterly, 'it is only right that they should have theirs.'

Grandmother and grand-daughter looked inscrutable, and said nothing.

'So Mrs Dorcas has been match-making all these months!' William cried, striding into Thornton House one blustering March morning in 1805. 'Are you dreadfully angry with her, Lottie?'

He was so very cheerful that Charlotte had to smile, though she was considerably put out.

'Come, offer me some of that excellent London coffee,' William coaxed, 'and you shall tell me everything. I can see you are bursting with things you must not say!'

Then she laughed ruefully, and prepared to confide in him.

'Oh, it is very well, really, Willie. Only I do wish the young

279

man were not Mrs Graham's nephew, and she is being very grand and distant with me, and very close with Mamma and Cicely. And I do feel left out, Willie!'

'But you like our Reverend Jarvis Pole nonetheless, I believe?'

'Oh, like and heartily approve of him. I am not such a fool as to let my aversion to his relative influence my opinion of him. And he is exactly right for Cicely, and his life will suit her perfectly. Mrs Dorcas has been both shrewd and wise—I wondered why she kept rambling on about her mother and father, and now I see all!'

'Ah! You brew better coffee than anyone I know, Lottie. Yes, the reverend young gentleman is a splendid fellow—though not half good enough for Cicely,' he added loudly, teasingly, as his niece came into the parlour. 'You grow prettier by the hour, miss. So give your uncle a kiss, for he has an idea that should please you mightily. Only we must ask your Mamma's permission.'

'Pray do not trouble yourself,' said Charlotte with desperate humour. 'The last time I gave Cicely permission she took gross advantage of it! No, no,' she cried, seeing Cicely's smile vanish, 'I think your Jarvis is a lovely man, and Mrs Dorcas has done well by you.'

'She was probably settling an old score,' said William slyly. 'Aunt Tib made your match, as I remember, and we did not even have the pleasure of your wedding. Do you know, Cicely, that I had to drop all my business and hurtle down to London in one of the first Royal Mail coaches to meet your father and see that all was well with your mother? So do not let her bully you, for she set us all back on our heels in her day!'

Cicely kissed his cheek and clung to his arm. The change in her was extraordinary, as Charlotte observed with a pang. For how hopelessly bored and wretched the girl must have been before, to look so radiant now. Her former reticence had gone. She sang about the house, confided small hopes and plans, smiled frequently and was anxious that everyone should share her happiness.

'Now when is this Jarvis Pole fellow intending to spirit you off to Wiltshire?' William asked. 'October? That gives us plenty of time. Lottie! Cicely! Zelah and I would like to offer you Kingswood Hall for the wedding reception. We promise we shall keep Mrs Dorcas in a glass case, lest she accidentally queen the occasion, and we shall sit in the butler's pantry and pretend that the house is yours, if so it please you.'

Charlotte tried to look grateful, but Cicely was enchanted.

'Then that is settled,' said William briskly. 'Let us have your wedding list, so that we know how many to cater for, and name your menu. We shall not disgrace you! Oh, and Zelah thinks we should give you your china and cutlery as a wedding gift, Cicely. For no doubt Charlotte will be giving the linen and so forth. Does that please you? Now I will not intrude further, for there will be comings and goings here all day. And we expect you all to dinner tomorrow. When does Jarvis return to Wiltshire?'

'On Thursday next, for he must preach the Sunday sermon.'

'Then give me another kiss—he shall not have all of them!—and God bless you both. I shall see myself out. . . .'

'And I am truly glad for Cicely,' said Charlotte to Jack that evening, 'and I know it is unreasonable in me to want to do most for her, and to come first with her, as I do with Ambrose—but I do grieve, Jack, I do grieve.'

He was not the awkward man he had been, and could comfort her.

'Well, we are a pair of dangerous revolutionaries,' he said, mocking her, taking her hands and squeezing them gently, 'and your family and Cicely are not. The girl is best to be out of the way, and to make a life of her own. I confess to worrying over her future more than once. And this Jarvis Pole is a good fellow, is he? In spite of being related to our righteous Mrs Graham?'

'Oh, there is another barb which I must suffer! Yes, he is an excellent young man with a beautifully plain face and a plain honest manner. But he finds me rather a terrifying obstacle, though he kindly invited me to stay at the vicarage whenever I would! Our Mrs Graham has lost no opportunity to tell him that I have outrageous notions and am not approved by Millbridge's politest circles. Oh, and William has swept us all off to Kingswood Hall, and is giving away the bride and giving the reception, and I do not know what else!'

'A Howarth occasion?' He was sombre, for the family did not like him, but he made an effort. 'Well, I shall give Cicely a present but do not feel you must invite me. I shall not be there. It is best that I embarrass no one. So what else troubles you?' As her face did not clear.

'Ambrose has met some fellow-student whose father owns a London newspaper, and apparently he has been very thick with them, and now he wishes to leave Cambridge for London and become a journalist.'

Jack consulted the knot of his hands. He would have liked Ambrose to become a teacher. Then he relaxed the knot and smiled at her.

'What troublesome creations children are! Aye, let him go, my love. He will only leave you else. Ambrose will find his own way.'

There were tears in her eyes, and she rose from her chair, turning away from him so that he should not see her crying.

'We are on our own now, my lass,' said Jack, understanding her. 'But the children are safe at least.'

Then she hugged him fiercely, and kissed him, and wept without shame.

News of Admiral Nelson's victory and death came through on the eve of Cicely's wedding, and St Mark's Church was thronged with thanksgivers as well as guests. Such a euphoria possessed Millbridge as had not been seen for many a day; and William, having toasted the newly married pair, now asked the company to raise their glasses a second time, to the hero of Trafalgar. They drank with pride and sorrow, for England had been at war with France, save that brief respite of 1802-3, for twelve long years. And at last the French seemed to be on the run. It was a double happy and tearful event, and, as Mrs Graham remarked afterwards, the Longes conducted themselves pretty well for once.

Ambrose came up from London, where he had taken lodgings not far from their old home at Lock-yard, and seemed to be as pleased with life as was his sister. Many old neighbours, and all the Howarths, attended the wedding, and Charlotte's three suitors were to be found mingling with the crowd. But Jack Ackroyd did not come.

He had watched at his study window that morning while the bride left for church, and saw her return in an open carriage and sweep down the High Street on her way to Kingswood Hall. Now, at four in the afternoon, he mounted guard again, since she would soon be passing with her new husband on their journey to Wiltshire.

He had known her since she was a little girl sewing her sampler, making a place for him at her side, taking him under her protection. He had endeavoured to understand her, and learned to love her. She had come closer to him than Ambrose, for whom he nourished an easy and amused affection. He supposed, in a way, she had been a daughter to him. And, though the religious ceremony and grand reception were not to his taste, he would have been grateful to look upon her happiness, to have some word with the bridegroom and find out for himself what sort of fellow he was, to wish them both well. But he must suffer the pains of a father without enjoying any of a father's privileges.

He could tell, by the sudden excitement in the High Street, that the bridal pair were approaching, and he pressed against the window, afraid to miss that last sight of her as she entered into her new life. Then, miraculously it seemed to him, the ironmaster's carriage slowed down as it came into view, Cicely had not forgotten, would not forget, anyone dear to her.

She rose up from her seat and smiled and waved: a slender brown-haired girl with Charlotte's eyes, in a velvet travelling-dress, a little posy in her hand. And the lanky young man by her side also looked up, with a smile on his pleasantly ugly face, and raised his tall hat in salute.

Stiffly, Jack brought one hand from behind him, and held it to the pane in acknowledgement. Then the driver whipped up his horses, for they were due to catch the Carlisle coach at Preston and must lose no time. But Cicely and Jarvis Pole looked round and waved and waved, until they were out of sight.

What had she said to that amicable new husband of hers about Jack Ackroyd? No matter. She had regarded him as important, as worthy of particular note. And that Pole fellow had lifted his hat. He did not seem a bad fellow.

The headmaster left his post by the window and sat heavily at his desk, feeling quite lost without her.

TWENTY-THREE

House of Straw

1807—1809

Cicely Pole's first child was born a year later and proudly christened Jarvis Tobias, a conjunction of names which amused and touched the Howarths. Toby Longe had never been one of them, but he continued to crop up in their lives. The greater event, for which they had hoped, did not take place. In 1807 Zelah gave birth to her sixth daughter, and was so ill in consequence that Dr Standish advised William to wait two years at least before resuming the marital relation. In itself, this would not have perturbed the iron-master, for he could always find other ladies to relieve his abstinence, but he was deeply wounded by his lack of dynasty. So the new baby was named Maria, after Zelah's ex-communicated aunt, received lovingly by her mother and ecstatically by her five sisters, and her father sought consolation elsewhere.

Millbridge's morals, though no better than anywhere else, were now being furbished to match the new age and its requirements. Excluding affairs of the heart, which are always irregular, respectable Millbridge men had so far made use of women from the poorer classes when their own wives were unable or unwilling to cohabit. For such people could be hushed up and paid off, and no one be any the wiser. But the influx of workers had elevated these women to a professional status, in which they were paid better wages than the mill could offer. And the influx of industrial adventurers had created a market for a better class of prostitute. Single ladies, all of whom appeared to have private incomes and a delicate upbringing, infiltrated the town at the turn of the century. They attended church assiduously, contributed to charity generously, and did not expect to be received socially. Everyone knew what they were but no one said so. They rented villas in a suburb of Millbridge, so that their clients should not be embarrassed by proximity. Those members of the council whom Jack Ackroyd had accused of shoddy building could not be faulted in this new development. They had helped to push the plans through, made a handsome job of the building, and let them very profitably. Many influential men, including William Howarth, found Flawnes Gardens a satisfactory arrangement, and any old-fashioned moralist on Millbridge Council would have been outnumbered at once had he dared to suggest that they gave the town a bad name.

At the moment, however, Millbridge was agog with quite another matter. Lord Kersall had recently astonished his people, his family, and probably himself, by marrying for a second time and very late in the day. It was not, as the town remarked over its teacups, that the noble gentleman needed an heir. He had a plethora of them: sons, grandsons, brothers, nephews, cousins. Nor that he required a resident hostess. His eldest daughter, the Honourable Miss Kersall, had filled that post to everyone's satisfaction since her mother's death fifteen years ago. And surely a man in his sixties was past lusting? The majority of Kersalls silently held the same opinion, but put up a gallant front, declaring themselves to be delighted with his lordship's happiness. Millbridge Council collected money for a silver loving-cup, in spite of Jack Ackroyd's tirade against wasting public funds; and the Kersall estate gave itself a celebratory banquet to which important local people were invited. William, being one of them, returned home flushed with wine and gossip to report on the festivities to Zelah.

'I should have thought him too old and cold a fish to be captured by such a hussy,' said William, laughing. 'But I dare say even the wisest man must make a fool of himself once in a lifetime. She was undoubtedly after his wealth, and the security of her position as his wife. It is a May and December match if ever I saw one.'

'Is she so much younger than he?' Zelah asked, out of duty.

She was resting on her day-couch, feeling indisposed for talk of any kind, but too conscious of failing William in a great matter to risk failing him in a small one.

'Some forty years at a guess! A little too old to be the freshest catch of the season, but far too young and prime for our Humphrey! Aye, a high-headed, high-minded, high-born lady, with a pair of bold black eyes and a bold black manner. He is besotted with her, though she looks at every man but her lawful wedded husband. I do wonder. . . .' But these thoughts were not for Zelah, and he went on another tack. 'Well, she will lead him a pretty dance before he is done. I would reckon her to be extravagant as well as wilful. She was wearing the late Lady Kersall's emeralds to great effect. You should have seen poor Miss Kersall's face—for she has had to give up both her mother's jewels and her position in the house for this bird of paradise!'

Still, he did not seem to condemn these faults in the new Lady Kersall. He straddled his hearth with a satisfied air, and jingled the silver in his pockets. His wife did not answer, and he did not notice her silence.

'Yes, old Humphrey is done for now. It is only a matter of time. She will fetch him to his grave one way or the other. So Master Ralph is beginning to creep into his own by means of the back door. Ambitious puppy!'

'Puppy?' cried Zelah, faintly amused. 'Why, he is of an age with thee, William!'

'He is a puppy in experience. His father first spoiled him, and then denied him access to the family business because he was spoiled. Fortunately for him he married Lady Caroline, and she made half a man of him—you would approve of her, Zelah!—and his two sons have sobered him down . . . ,' but this thought must not be pursued. 'At any rate, our Ralph turns out to be a true Kersall under the mask: cunning, tenacious, and anxious for power. So he is courting me, as being closest in business with his father, and I encourage him. Because, when Humphrey's dead I shall have to deal with Ralph. And it is better to treat with one you have formed a little! Besides'—lifting himself on his heels, jingling his change—'he will be an opening for us, socially. We can expect an invitation to Park House when you are stronger, Zelah. Though the one from Kersall Park will take a little more coaxing.'

She had withdrawn into a world less complex and more kind.

'But you are tired,' said William, noting her quietness at last, 'and I have business at Snape. I shall leave you to rest, my love.'

'Business at Snape at nine o'clock of a Saturday night, William?' she cried, roused by this news at least. 'Why, even my father, that was the busiest of men, made time for his family at the end of the week!'

'Your father, excellent man, had the good fortune to do his main business in one place,' said William, in that bullying, good-natured way which always silenced opposition. 'Mine, alas, is more varied and scattered all over England. When an agent journeys to see me from Bristol or Cornwall or London, I can hardly ask him to cool his heels until Monday morning.'

'But cannot this agent consult with thee here, and stay here?'

'Zelah,' said William indicating that he was at the end of his patience, 'Dr Standish has ordered you complete rest and quiet. And that is exactly why I am doing all business away from home!'

This could not be answered except by thanking him for his consideration, which she did.

In the race for wealth and honour among commoners, Millbridge would have been puzzled which way to bet, for William Howarth and Ernest Harbottle seemed to be running neck and neck. Power? Ernest was called King Cotton, and William the Iron King. Property? Kingswood Hall was in better taste, but no more opulent than Millside Towers; and each man had investments in places they would not have cared to live in. Business sense? Ernest was considered to be tougher, but William was cleverer: he stayed on the right side of the moral fence. Public spirit? Both were Aldermen and would be Mayor some fine day. Social graces? Ah, there lay a difference. William was more widely travelled nowadays, meeting great personages in London and elsewhere. He often said (as a joke, mind you!) that when peace cuts his profits in half he should make up the loss by trading with France. Whereas poor old Ernest could not make himself understood outside his native county, let alone endeavour to ingratiate himself abroad. And William's wife was a lovely lady. On the other hand, Margery Harbottle, though rougher than her diamonds would warrant, was far more friendly and ordinary than Zelah Howarth. As for William's own graces, well, handsome was as handsome did! Tales were being whispered, knowing glances exchanged. Perhaps, in the end, folk might prefer homely Ernest who never gave his wife cause for complaint—and frequently said so.

'Still, Howarth would be my choice as a Member of Parliament, if ever the Kersalls let go of the borough,' said one councillor. 'And that time may come sooner than we think.'

'What? You would choose him rather than a Clayton or a Brigge?'

'Oh, country gentry with no hard cash are out of the running these days, my good fellow. Neither noble nor rich! It takes a wealthy man to get to Westminster. And nowadays we want a man of the people to represent us. Yes, Howarth is the horse for my money.'

'He's a pretty runner, I grant you. But if you speak of such men then Harbottle might stay the course better. . . .'

From the terrace of Kersall Park, upon a clear day, thirteen mill chimneys could be counted, marching down the valley. Each lifted a wind-borne grey banner. Each was surrounded by a brood of cramped houses, whose domestic stacks smoked away in unison. A sense of order, a sense of space, had vanished in the sunburst of prosperity. But fortunate indeed is the entrepreneur with style and good manners who benefits from it. The ironmaster of Snape looked down on his part of this realm with supreme satisfaction.

Lord Kersall being unavoidably detained in London for a few days, William Howarth had called upon a matter of business. And stayed, merely out of courtesy, to talk with Lady Kersall a little longer. They were a fine-looking couple, and no doubt aware of the fact. Both handsome, dark and ruthless, knowing exactly what they wanted and how to get it. Clarissa Kersall's hair was as glossy as a raven's wing. Her eyes were black and brilliant. She moved well, showing off her fine plumage, her creamy flesh. Her gown was deceptively simple, pale and diaphanous, so that for one delicious moment a man could believe he was seeing more than the swell of breasts above the high waistline. The dress stopped short of a pair of narrow silken ankles. Her colour was rich, her mouth red and full. A dozen little gestures indicated that the ironmaster was to her taste, and that though her palate might be keen it was also discriminating. He felt exceedingly flattered.

Two matters faintly troubled him. The noble Humphrey had decided notions about his personal property, and there was the possibility of scandal in this closed community. But, these considerations set aside, he was as anxious as she to sate their appetites. Many times since Humphrey Kersall brought home the bride who was young enough to be his grand-daughter had these two lusty predators eyed each other across the social barriers. For his lordship's powers no longer resided in his loins, and the lady's birth and upbringing had never guarded her from hungers of the flesh.

'The wind is cold. Let us go in,' said Clarissa Kersall.

The ironmaster consulted his ancient silver watch.

'I fear I should be getting back, your ladyship.'

'Shall you not stay for luncheon? Oh, do stay. Millbridge is so dull after London. You are the only person I can talk to here. Of course you will stay! I shall fetch my companion to sit with us and then you will not be dull. I know you are half in love with her already. She is so entertaining!'

She spoke almost as rapidly as she thought, running from one sentence to another, from one topic to another, as though time itself were at her heels. She would throw a question into the air, answer it to her own satisfaction, lie openly and outrageously, smiling the while. She did not conduct or share a conversation so much as comment in passing.

'What time will luncheon be?' William asked, sensing the invitation within her invitation.

'Oh, when I tell them. Shall I tell them to serve it in half an hour? And we need not ask Beatrice to join us until then. In half an hour, shall we say? Can you bear my company so long?'

'I am charmed to bear your ladyship's company for any length of time, and in any way it might please you,' he replied, smiling.

She laughed, throwing back her head, exposing her strong white throat, showing her strong white teeth. Then she became Lady Kersall again for the benefit of the butler, to whom she gave orders with haughty correctness, while William turned the pages of an album.

What sons you might bear a man! he thought, looking covertly at Lady Kersall's full breasts and rounded limbs. But she did not belong to him.

'Well, sir?' she asked, smiling. 'How shall we entertain ourselves for this half-hour?'

And she let fall her stole, her yellow Spanish stole that was striped like a tiger, and ran her hands down her sides in anticipation. He had never experienced so cool and honest an advance before, and in such unlikely surroundings. His ladies were all flattered, lower in station than himself, and succumbed with sighs in hired rooms. For a moment, confronted by those purposeful black eyes, his confidence wavered. Surely she did not intend them to embrace here? In the sitting-room, where at any moment they might be disturbed?

Apparently she did. With a composure that he suspected was the result of practice, she began to disrobe herself. She seemed even more at ease without her clothes, and hummed softly to herself as she undid her satin garters. Then she straightened up and looked deliberately at his astounded face.

'The servants . . . your companion . . . callers!' said William.

The thought of them was horrific.

'They would not dare to interrupt. They have their orders,' she said superbly.

He could imagine her confronting them thus, even in her nakedness, and staring them down, staring them away. And what nakedness! Beneath the flimsy gauze gown she was unexpectedly sturdy: bell-breasted, narrow-waisted, her sooty triangle mounted between splendid thighs. It came to William as he started, weakly, to undo his black and white cravat, that he had never viewed a woman in this way before. Zelah was modest, suggested rather than seen. His girls squealed and giggled, daring him to tear their clothes (since he would also pay for them), or clutched the covers to their bosoms and swore they had never done such a monstrous thing previously. Hannah had been natural, unashamed, but gentle and womanly. Whereas this amazon stood there, giving him look for look, as though the shaft stood between her legs instead of his.

'Oh, how slow you are!' she cried, and stepped forward to help him, laughing as she proved to be a better valet than he, rubbing her belly against his to provoke him.

Then all the man and yeoman rose in him. He gave her a clout across the buttocks that left the mark of his fingers on her flesh, and thrust her down on the floor. She made so much noise over her pleasure that he prayed no one would hear, and he wished to God that he could spend all afternoon rutting on Lord Kersall's best Axminster carpet, for she gave as good as she got. They wrestled breathlessly, like adversaries, and without respect. But their appointed time must of necessity be brief, so he shot his bolt home and they lay in a muck sweat, drawing in air fast and short. He felt a little ashamed of himself as he got to his feet, but Clarissa looked better than ever, though somewhat blown and bruised in the contest.

'Pah, how we stink!' she said frankly. 'But Cousin Bea will not notice. She has never dropped her drawers for any man, poor devil. I often wonder if she knows what I am up to, but I doubt it.'

'You have distributed your favours elsewhere?' William asked carefully.

'Mind your business, ironmaster!' said Lady Kersall, but smiled the sting out of the rebuke.

His pride was piqued, but he liked her far too well to offend her. So Cousin Beatrice wandered downstairs, innocent spinster, to laugh at all their jokes and eat heartily and play chaperone. Her role in life was to guard the Kersall stable long after the mare had run loose, for which services his lordship gave her a home and a modest allowance. What else could the poor lady have done? She was plain, penniless and unmarriageable, though of good station. So she took care not to offend anybody, and they were all well satisfied.

Today Clarissa's colour was richer than usual, her conversation more delightful and impulsive, her appetite sharper. William did not linger over this light and fashionable meal. The purpose of his visit had been fulfilled. He had work to do. Nor would the lady grieve in his absence. Each had asked and received no more and no less than they desired, which was highly satisfactory.

Picking his way down Millbridge High Street on his white horse, the ironmaster thought to call upon his sister, partly from affection but mostly out of curiosity. He had not seen her in quite a while.

Behind her back the family had discussed Charlotte, as families are wont to do, and long since came to the conclusion that she would not re-marry until Ambrose and Cicely had left home. It was understandable, Dorcas had said, that Charlotte did not wish to disturb the children with yet another change of place and way of life. So they had let her be, as Ned advised. But Ambrose and Cicely had gone long since, and still Charlotte remained single. Her suitors continued to pay court, growing older and greyer and more pernickety and fixed in their ways. And she continued to receive them, and to give no encouragement, and obviously no discouragement either since they kept on visiting. The headmaster, it was once whispered, had joined this select little band of middle-aged bachelors. But as it became increasingly apparent that the interest between himself and Mrs Longe lay in educating the unfortunate, folk set romance aside. And when The Millbridge Society for the Furtherance of Literacy among the Working People was formed, and its meetings held alternately at Thornton House and the headmaster's rooms at Millbridge Grammar School, respectable ladies washed their hands of Charlotte altogether. True, the working people who attended twice weekly seemed to be of the decent sort, but it was not proper, it was not done, it all came of perversity and lack of respect for the class system. No wonder, folk said, that Mrs Longe did not re-marry, for who would risk such a misalliance? And if Quaker Scholes and Solicitor Hurst and young Dr Standish persisted in wooing this eccentric lady, well, only death is stronger than habit, and perhaps they felt safe with her, after such a long refusal.

But it was all very odd, and William could not understand it, so he called upon his sister as he was passing by, to see if he could solve in a few minutes the mystery which Millbridge tea-parties had been pondering for years. As he stood upon the scoured threshold of Thornton House, settling his chin into his cravat, Charlotte peered through the parlour curtains, irritated. She had been distracted by first one person and then another all morning. Some days were like that. On others she could work from breakfast to supper-time without interruption.

'It is my brother William, Polly!' she called down the hall, hastening to open the door. 'I will see him in. Pray fetch up the Madeira. It is too early for tea. And to what do I owe this honour, Willie?'

'Why, madam, I have come to be Improved by your Society,' he said impudently, 'for I am not half-learned enough!'

And he deposited his fawn beaver hat upon the hall table, and read the cards on the little silver salver, pursing his lips and raising his eyebrows.

'On that score I would agree with you,' said Charlotte coolly, 'but we only accept working men.'

'I am a working man,' he replied, walking into the parlour, rubbing his hands and standing over the fire, for there was a nip in the air on this fine afternoon. 'Indeed, I work a deuced sight harder than your precious labourers.'

'And are paid better, too,' she observed. 'Will you drink Madeira?'

'What? Let me look at the bottle first!'

'It is one of Grandfather Wilde's. You need not fear for your palate.'

'Why, it is better than mine,' he cried, tasting. 'How many bottles have you left?'

'I do not know. Not many, I think. I keep them for gentlemen callers.'

'Ah! Penelope and her suitors, as Ambrose used to say! Lottie, put us out of our uncertainty. When are you going to marry again? Surely you do not want to mope alone all your life? What do you do with yourself in this place all day?'

She folded her arms. She was already nettled, and saw that he intended to provoke her further.

'I am glad you asked,' she said sweetly. 'I had been wanting to consult you on the matter, Willie. How would you like Mr Ackroyd as a brother-in-law?' And laughed at the expression on his face. 'There you are!' she accused him, amused and annoyed at once. 'You dislike the idea intensely. What a thorn in your side he would be, diametrically opposed to everything you stand for. But let us not stop at him. How if I married Nicodemus Hurst?' She puffed out her lips in mock horror. 'No, of course not, for you have quarrelled with him already. What of Caleb? Oho! I am not so sure what reaction you might have to that Quaker piece upon your iron chessboard—though you would be bound to smile on him. So, would Hamish Standish please you?' Her brows lifted, she looked down her nose, crying, 'What? A piffling country doctor who attends my children when they have the measles? No, no, Willie. I am better not to embarrass you, my dear!'

Now she had annoyed him, and it was with some sharpness of tone that he said, 'Well, can you not do better for yourself than those four dummies, Lottie?'

'At three-and-forty a woman has no market value, Willie,' she said ironically. 'Even *you* could not buy me a husband worthy of you!'

She had picked her words carefully, as usual, and aimed each one at him for all her smiles and lightness. His temper rose.

'You take life too seriously, Lottie. Stewing over your books. Teaching sweaty bumpkins. Why cannot you enjoy yourself?'

'Perhaps your idea of enjoyment and mine are different,' she replied, colder now. 'I have a circle of good friends, who would not interest you. I have reasonable health. And I value my freedom.'

'Zelah says she never sees you!' he accused.

'No, *you* say that,' Charlotte replied, obdurate. 'Zelah and I meet as often as we can. She is mother to six children, hostess to Kingswood Hall, mentor of your industrial village, and wife to yourself. She is not seeking a fellow-gossip, and I have never had much time for gossip anyway.'

The colour ran into his cheeks until it was as high as Clarissa's after mating. But his eyes lit with fury rather than gratification.

'Has Zelah been complaining to you?' he asked.

Now Charlotte flushed in turn, lest she had compromised her sister-in-law.

'Of course she has not! What, Zelah complain? Zelah be disloyal to you? Dear God, I had thought we abolished slavery in this country two years since, but when I see how she works I realise that women were not included in the edict!'

'Oh, this is too much,' he cried. 'I did not come to be lectured. I shall take my leave of you!'

He set down his Madeira and rose, adjusting his waistcoat, and found one button undone. It must have been in that state since the morning's engagement. Hastily he set it aright, but it cooled his temper and when he next spoke his reply lacked edge, though he continued to make his way into the hall.

'I believe that rogue Toby set his mark on you for life, Lottie,' he said, 'you are still a-pamphleteering. But what times we had then!'

'Well, I must not preach,' said Charlotte penitently, 'only I am fond of Zelah, and how I wish she would trounce you now and then!'

He laughed good-humouredly, knowing she was right.

'You are like Mrs Dorcas,' he observed, 'teaching everyone their place.'

'And you, like God Almighty, expecting every place to be below your own!'

'You speak too sharp,' he said, displeased. 'There is something about this house which sours a woman. My mother always said that Thornton House was full of spinsters. You were as sweet as Zelah once, but now must argue. Well, I have work to do.'

Charlotte was silent for a moment, bearing the full weight of his personal disapproval, and that volume of public disapproval which seemed to hang about her. But the truth, as she knew it, was her only antidote.

'My dear Willie,' she said, as steadily as she could, 'you were out of humour with yourself when you arrived, and I am out of sorts today, so there's an end to it. Come, kiss me. Do not let us quarrel over nothing. But do not make game of what troubles me, neither.'

He put his arm about her waist and set his lips to her forehead.

'You are wrong about one matter at least,' he said, clapping the tall hat jauntily to one side of his head. 'I have never felt in a better humour than today!"

'I am glad of it. Give Mrs Dorcas my love.'

She stood on the doorstep, shivering, smiling, waving as he rode away, then went slowly into the house again, while he puzzled over her perception.

How had she known of his dissatisfaction, since he was only just aware of it himself? A profound displeasure stirred within him. He wanted to hit, to hurt, to perturb. And yet, God damn it, why should he feel like that?

He reined in at the smithy on Flawnes Green and sniffed the odours with a certain nostalgia. Stephen strode out to greet him, wiping his hands on his leather apron. A burly man in his late thirties. He spoke reverently to William, as became a blacksmith in the presence of an ironmaster. And Mrs Stephen, running into the dark shop after an escaping infant, managed to drop a curtsey while clutching her half-naked son to her bosom. William observed the baby's dimpled bottom and sturdy legs, the little tassel that proclaimed his father's immortality in however humble a capacity. He bowed gravely. He rode gloomily away.

Turning into the lane leading to Bracelet, seeking comfort, he remembered his sister's final remark. "Give Mrs Dorcas my love.'

'Now how the deuce did Lottie know I would visit my mother?' he asked himself.

William walked the length of Bracelet's parlour and peered irritably through the back window at the walled kitchen garden.

'Why do you not allow me to extend this cabbage-patch of yours?' he cried. 'Are you not weary of the same view?'

Dorcas sat very erect in her chair, hands folded. Her hair was quite white, but her eyes still sparked fire on occasion. She had not changed fashion, preferring to keep to her own style of full skirts and trim corsets, and so seemed part of time past but all the more reassuring for that. She had been reading when he came, but had put aside her book and was now taking off her spectacles.

'But it is not the same view,' she said reasonably. 'If I turn round I see the rose garden and the lane from my front window. From my bedroom I have a most excellent view up the hillside of Kingswood Hall. And when I walk about the house each vantage-point gives me a different picture.'

295

'Well, it is very small and pokey and would not do for me. And you have only to say what you want, Mamma, and I will see that it is done.'

'I have what I want, my dear,' she replied. 'Now what do you want of me?'

'I? I want nothing! I called because I thought you were somewhat lonely and would be glad of company.'

Dorcas's lips twitched with amusement.

'That was exceedingly, one might say unusually, thoughtful of you, William. But I am not in the least lonely, though always glad to see you, of course.'

'You are much alone, though,' he pointed out, feeling the situation slip away from him as it had done at Thornton House.

'Ah, that is a different matter. I am solitary, William, but not lonely. And I have always found a certain amount of solitude to be necessary to me. It was you who could never stay long in your own company. I remember that from your childhood.'

'Why, I spent hours, days alone. Making things, planning things . . .'

'Ah, yes. But if you were not involved in some new project then time hung upon your hands. You had always to be doing something new. You did not sit inside yourself, as Charlotte did, for instance.'

He drummed upon the window to startle the birds away.

'Oh, Charlotte is a blue-stocking!' he said, disgruntled. And then, 'I could build you a bigger house in a better position, if you wanted, Mamma.'

'My dear, you will find as you grow old that your wants are few. And I do not wish to move house again. I am content with Bracelet. Now go and buy yourself another copper-mine, or go into Parliament, if you are bored. But do not fret me, my dear. I am well enough!'

He strode the room, and she watched him prowl restlessly. He stopped by her, looking for something to grieve him.

'Is Dick's wife breeding again?' he asked abruptly.

'Not so soon after George's birth I should hope,' said Dorcas, still amiable. 'Do sit down, my dear.'

'How many have they now?' he asked, looming at her side.

'I must think for a moment! Why, there is Ned and Dickie and Willie and Mary—and little George.'

'Four sons!' said William bitterly, walking away again. 'Four sons!'

'And one daughter,' a little tartly. 'Is that what is troubling you?'

'Of course it troubles me!' he cried, and thrust his fists into his breeches pockets. 'It is as though life were determined to give me anything but that which I most desire!'

'That is a pity,' said Dorcas, in what Ned once called her Judgement Day voice.

'A pity? It is a damned tragedy. Here I am, having sweated myself into my forties to build up a business, and a great house, and more wealth and possessions than any man in this valley—save Humphrey Kersall—and all I can boast is six daughters, who will marry and leave me without caring tuppence for any of it! To whom shall I pass on Snape and Kingswood Hall? Tell me that!'

'I am sure you will think of some scheme. You always have,' Dorcas replied coldly. 'And do not shout and stamp about so, William. You will give me a headache.'

'Well, I am sorry,' he mumbled, feeling badly used.

There was a pause. She longed for him to go and leave her in peace. But he would brood by the window.

'You are exceedingly well dressed for this time on a week-day,' Dorcas observed of the cream pantaloons, the chocolate coloured coat with its velvet collar. 'That shade of brown suits you, William. I recollect you wore it on your wedding-day.'

'I had forgot,' said William sullenly.

The mention of his wedding-day, coupled with the thought of his chocolate coat lying where it had been dropped on Lord Kersall's carpet, made him uneasy.

'Zelah is young still, at four-and-thirty,' said Dorcas, attempting to console him. 'I was turned forty when Dick was born. There is time yet. Not that I advocate a woman bearing too many children, nor child-bearing too late in life.'

'Oh, Zelah is healthy enough.'

'You speak of your wife,' said Dorcas crisply, 'as though she were one of your brood mares.'

'It is the damnedest thing,' William burst out, 'that when I visit you and Lottie I get nothing but hard words for kind intentions!'

'So you have been teasing Charlotte, too, have you? At your time of life, William, a man is often plagued with his liver and spleen. You should try half a drachm of salt of camomile first thing in the morning, mixed with white wine!' Then, disconcertingly, she changed direction and said, 'Have you been doing business with Lord Kersall then, in your best clothes?'

'Why do you ask? Well then, yes, I have. Not exactly, for he is in London as it happens. I left a message. And came away directly.'

'I cannot think why men of that age make such gabies of themselves as to marry hearty young women,' she continued. 'It is obvious to all that Lady Kersall is only there for ornament. He can hardly be thought capable of getting her with child. And he has a number of grown children already.'

'Oh, I do not know,' said William uncomfortably. 'He is hale enough.'

'Let us hope so,' said Dorcas doubtfully, 'or she will make a fool of him in earnest. They have had trouble with her before'—glancing at his dark face—'and that is why she was so late marrying. An unsuitable elopement, I have heard. But caught in time. So they say.'

'Lady Kersall's behaviour has always been highly correct to my knowledge,' William lied, looking round for his beaver hat. 'Her air is somewhat haughty rather than frivolous.'

'Only with servants, I hear.'

'It is extraordinary to me how women will gossip!' he cried pettishly. 'I suppose it is because they sit moping by themselves with nothing to do. A man has more important matters on his mind.'

Dorcas put on her spectacles and looked directly at him.

'William,' she said very quietly and clearly, 'what you have done to offend Charlotte I do not know. But since you came here in a like mood I conjecture you made yourself thoroughly disagreeable!'

'No, no . . .' Stricken on the instant.

'Neither Charlotte nor I ask anything of you but your loving goodwill,' Dorcas went on inexorably. 'We make our lives as useful and pleasant as we can, and are no nuisance to you that I know of—certainly, we do not call on purpose to tease you. You have endeavoured in this half-hour to make me feel poor in myself and in my home, and that is despicable.'

'You do me wrong, Mamma. . . .'

'I have not yet finished, sir,' said Dorcas sternly, holding up her hand for his silence, as she used to when he was a small and disobedient boy. 'You do not hurt me in the least by comparing Bracelet with Kingswood Hall, and offering to move me to a place more suitable for *you*, because I am content here and should be wretched in a larger house. But to hold up the scarecrow of loneliness to me in my old age, knowing how I loved my husband, is the work of a coward, sir!'

'Madam, I swear I had no such intention,' he pleaded on a lower note.

'And what is more,' Dorcas continued, cutting in voice and argument, 'if your father had been alive and sitting there'—pointing at the empty chair opposite—'you would not so much as dare to throw your hat down as you did! Let alone to probe and needle me, and whine of your troubles—that are no troubles at all! And that, sir, brands you as a bully, too!'

No longer splendid, the ironmaster stood before her, holding the offending hat to his breast. An old spring of affection gushed forth and wet his eyes and flooded his heart, and he begged her pardon. But the little figure was unyielding, sitting very upright in her chair, and turned resolutely away from him.

'Forgive me, Mamma,' William begged.

She sighed, quick and short and sharp.

'Oh, I shall forgive you, I do not doubt,' she replied, weary of him, 'but not just now, William. Please to go away, my dear. And be good to Zelah.'

He gathered up all the courage that was in him, to embrace her, to kiss her cheek unbidden. For he could not leave her so. Her face was cold beneath his lips. She felt as small and frail as a bird. He saw that she was old and should not be troubled.

'It is your great spirit that misleads us,' he said gently, reproachfully, and drew her to him and kissed her again. 'You have cared for us all so long that we run to you like babes whenever we are bruised. We should protect you instead.'

Her mouth quivered, and held.

'Go now, Willie,' she said, and he rose forgiven. 'And Willie, remember this, never seek out another person's weakness to prove that you are strong.'

He swallowed that rebuke, even thought on it for a minute, and resolved to be good. He nodded.

Dorcas stood by her front window and watched him ride grandly off. Then she rang the bell.

'I think I shall rest in bed until supper-time, Nellie,' she said, as lightly as she was able. 'I find the weather somewhat tiring today.'

Nellie said nothing, but looked grim as she helped her mistress to undress. A homely guardian, she drew down the windows against the roar of Snape, she drew the curtains against the harsh light, she closed the door noiselessly behind her. But downstairs in the kitchen she spoke her mind to her husband.

'I tell you what, Tom. We did better than we knew, keeping Mrs Howarth free of Kingswood Hall. They'd have bled her like leeches, given half the chance!'

While Dorcas lay dumbly on her side of the bed, and wept the scarce and silent tears of the old to think that Ned would never again comfort her from the other.

'I am home!' cried William, restored, sweeping through the great hall like a storm. 'I am home, Zelah. I am home, children.'

They were drawn from schoolroom and nursery, from parlour and garden. They gathered like flowers about him. From shy and slender Tibby, close on womanhood, to plump and staggering Molly. And behind them was Zelah, in the dark gold of her maturity, relieved to see him in a loving mood.

'What a black bear I have been of late!' he challenged them, hungry for approval, thirsty for their denial of this statement.

And many times a bear before that, and very black indeed, and every time forgiven and excused.

They cried down this ridiculous notion at once, and swept him off to the family sitting-room to be soothed away from such a dark fancy. For was he not the best and kindest and handsomest and most generous of fathers and husbands? And was not every one of his virtues to be celebrated with a kiss? Did he not toil from morning to night, for nothing but their benefit and delight? And was there the smallest wish in the world that he would not grant?

He was undoubtedly a paragon at granting small wishes. It was the deep and necessary ones which eluded him, costing as they did so much time and thought and patience.

But at length they convinced him of his goodness, and he was able to think again about his work and his pleasure with a clear conscience.

TWENTY-FOUR

Justice

1810

William Howarth had moved ahead in the commoners' race. He had recently been appointed as Justice of the Peace, since the county gentry and professional men of the district considered him to be almost one of themselves. Rumour had it that Ernest Harbottle threw his dinner at his dining-room wall when he heard the news, and struck Mrs Harbottle. But rumour always exaggerates. Ernest simply knocked his plate to the carpet and called his wife a daft old bitch.

So now the ironmaster was in session with his peers, in the old Court House at the back of the Town Hall. He was a little pale after a heavy night, but looked all the better for it in his capacity as a magistrate. It made him seem stern and above reproach.

'Deuce take it!' he muttered, aghast at the length of the list. 'We shall be here 'til dinner-time!'

'Did I not say it would be so?' cried Squire Brigge. 'Crime is on the increase. Aye, and in leaps and bounds. It is all this industry that brings the rascals to town. They should transport and hang the lot of 'em.'

'Come, sir,' said William good-naturedly, 'you cannot blame industry for offences against the game laws.'

'No, Mr Howarth,' drawled Lord Kersall, 'you are in the right of it there. But though poaching and sabotage and sheep-stealing used to form the bulk of our offences in this valley, they are being outnumbered these days by the more sophisticated crimes. Pickpocketing, house-breaking, swindling, and every form of begging. Indeed, if violence increases at the same rate we shall soon be forced to ask for company on the way home, after nightfall, as Londoners do. And though I do not blame industry for this new state of affairs, the prosperity brought by industry certainly attracts villains.'

'Aye, well put, my lord,' said Brigge, 'and we must not be soft with 'em.'

'But we should be just,' said Humphrey Kersall.

He was a cool and arrogant man but a responsible one. As feudal overlord he still felt that the offenders were his people, and should be corrected rather than annihilated. Also he was well aware that occasional pardons, generally for first offences of small importance or cases which would not stick in court, did him no harm in the eyes of the community. He was not loved but they did respect him.

'Give 'em a touch of the branding-iron,' growled Brigge. 'Flog 'em.'

'Fetch up the first offender, Mr Hodgkiss,' said Lord Kersall grandly.

'Name of Smethurst, my lord. Occupation, collier at Swarthmoor. Caught deer-stealing in your lordship's park.'

'That's a hanging offence,' said the squire with great satisfaction.

'Weren't you the fellow brought before me for stealing coal last winter?' asked Lord Kersall sharply. 'And did I not give you a pardon on condition you behaved yourself in the future?'

'Yes, m'lord,' the man said, and bent his head before those glacial eyes, and twisted his battered hat. 'But we was froze to the marrow, m'lord.'

'And now you shoot at one of my deer. What were you going to do with it? Sell it?'

'No, m'lord. Sick wife and eight childer, m'lord. Eat it, m'lord.'

'Eat it?' cried Sir Francis Clayton. 'Good God, man. You don't eat venison because you're hungry. That's a gentleman's dish!'

'I been out of work, your honour. Accident in the mine. We was starving.'

'Who were your accomplices, eh?' Kersall demanded. 'My keeper said he saw two fellows running away. Who were they?'

The collier was doggedly silent, twisting his hat in his hands.

'We might be inclined to clemency if you told us,' purred the Reverend Robert Graham, leaning forward and coldly smiling.

'You simply cannot roam the countryside, stealing coal and shooting deer just because you are out of work, you know,' said Lord Kersall, being reasonable with him. 'If everyone did that where would we all be? And where did you get your gun from?'

The collier was indistinct upon this point.

'The rascals steal a gun and lend it to each other, that's my belief,' said Squire Brigge. 'Take it in turns to shoot our game they do.'

'Did we get the deer back safely, Mr Hodgkiss?' Kersall asked. 'Ah, good!'

They consulted together, Brigge leading the hanging faction, William tempering the wind with Humphrey Kersall.

'Now, as we got the deer back, and you have a large family and are out of work, we are inclined to be lenient with you,' said Kersall. 'But if this sort of thing happens again you'll be up before the Assizes. And you know how they would deal with you, don't you? You'd be lucky to get away with your life. And if you think that a little hunger and cold are bad things then you know nothing about transportation. You would soon change your mind, I can tell you!'

The collier clenched his hands and nodded, dumbly.

'A year's imprisonment and two hours in the pillory,' said Lord Kersall.

'What'll my wife do, and the childer?' the man cried. 'They canna eat as it is, m'lord.'

'Well, you should have thought of that before you started poaching on my preserves,' said Humphrey Kersall. 'Take him away, Mr Hodgkiss. Who is next?'

'Some thieving labourer helping himself to hares,' said Squire Brigge. 'The keeper found one stewing in his cooking pot.'

'Do you know,' said Francis Clayton conversationally, 'there was a fellow used to trap eighty hares a year on my land, and sell 'em for three shillings apiece in Millbridge market. He was making more money by poaching than by earning an honest living!'

The offenders were many, were diverse, and as Lord Kersall had remarked their crimes were becoming more sophisticated. A vision of Millbridge at the mercy of burglars, watch-stealers and gangs of trained thieves rose before them. The more temperate magistrates stiffened their penalties, the rabid ones became more insistent. They sent up offenders to the Assizes, handed out whippings as though they had been sweetmeats, inflicted the stocks and the pillory as afterthoughts. And then Mr Hodgkiss brought in the strange being who had written threatening letters to a property owner in Medlar, and set fire to his barn and stables.

He was under-nourished and under-sized. There was a terrible sense of inadequacy about him, a hunger for recognition. His eyes lit as he approached the majesty of Wyndendale's law, and he drew himself up as though his moment had come.

'Name of Low,' said Mr Hodgkiss. 'No fixed address. No occupation. Calls hisself a freeholder though he hasn't got no property. The letters is on your lordship's table.'

'Aye, and an uncommonly nasty pen he wields!' Francis Clayton remarked, reading them. 'Pah! What a rotten worm you are, you wretch.'

'We have all had such letters in our time,' said Humphrey Kersall carelessly. 'They are no better and no worse than most. Now, you, fellow. Low. You burned down a barnful of grain and—worse still!—a stableful of horses. What sort of murdering villain are you, to destroy innocent and valuable beasts?'

'Damned disgraceful,' said William sincerely, and had already condemned the man in his mind.

'Hang him,' said Squire Brigge, and the expression on the faces of all his colleagues echoed this sentiment.

'But it is extraordinary to me how they will *destroy* property,' said Francis Clayton. 'I can better understand *stealing* it.'

'Ah, envy!' the Reverend Robert declaimed, casting up his eyes to the ceiling. 'What a wicked and insidious vice thou art!'

'Come, you, fellow! What have you to say for yourself? Do you deny this charge?' cried Kersall, in cold disgust.

'I don't deny it,' said Obadiah Low, grinning. 'I'm glad of it. It's justice, that is. Justice, your honours.'

He had a peculiarly sibilant and unpleasant voice, and that total lack of fear that seems almost demonic. Clearly he was unbalanced, if not downright mad. Even in the security of the Court House the magistrates felt exposed. Even William, who could have crushed him like a nut, had a sensation akin to fear. Low chuckled, became confidential, garrulous.

'Wrigley stole my land,' said Obadiah Low, 'and thieves should be burned. It's a healing force is fire, your honours. I'd recommend it for almost anybody. But you got to watch and wait afore you burn down. Watch with your eyes, in the night. . . .'

'Is there any evidence of Squire Wrigley stealing land?' asked Lord Kershaw at large. 'No, I thought not.'

'Wrigley's turned many a poor family out,' said Low, 'ruined many a poor man in his time. And now he's come to justice by fire, your honours. It's a justice as'll be applied to all of you afore very long. I know more than you think, your honours. Far far more than you think!'

And he put a dirty finger to one side of his nose and smiled at them.

'Shut your mouth,' said Mr Hodgkiss, outraged.

And he picked the little fellow up and shook him as if he had been a marionette.

'Put him down, if you please,' Lord Kersall ordered. 'Do you confess to your abominable crime, Low?'

'I confess to that, and to more,' cried Low, safely on his feet again. 'I been the Saviour of the People, I have. I've given bread to the hungry and done justice by fire. . . .' He was hurrying to say all that he could, to make the most of his time before he was swept off to the hulks or the gallows. 'Fire! You'll see this valley a-fire from end to end when my people rise. There's more than you know, thousands more. All about you, working for you, watching you. All day and all night. They never sleep for watching and waiting. And when the Day comes they'll burn you in effigy, and burn your houses and mills, and last of all they'll burn you. And when you're swallowed up in fire, on earth, you'll roar in hell after. . . .'

He laughed with glee as he saw their faces, and hid his own in his hands. Then he peeped through his fingers, as a child peeps, and that was most horrible of all. Mr Hodgkiss did not touch him. The magistrates sat silent, listening.

'What do you know about the meetings in the fields at night?' Low whispered, and giggled to himself as he saw them strain to hear him. 'What do you know about the secret oaths, eh? Terrible oaths. Oaths that would make a man's flesh shrivel from his bones if he broke them. What do you know about the night-watchers and the silent thieves? I know them. Nobody sees or speaks of me. They keep their eyes closed, the little ones, hearing me ride by. Have you guessed who I am, your honours? Guess the riddle, do! I'll give a free pardon, when the Day comes, to any gentleman here who knows the answer.'

They sat, and Mr Hodgkiss stood, mesmerised. The little man's face expressed half a dozen emotions. He hoped, coaxed, teased, sought out, encouraged and was finally disappointed in them.

'Look!' he demanded. 'Who am I?'

And suddenly he flung out his arms and stiffened his legs, lolled his head to one side, like an effigy, like a scarecrow in a field, crucified.

'Jack Straw!' he shrieked, triumphant.

'Of course, I never thought he was Jack Straw at all,' said Lord Kersall, as they drank mulled claret to restore themselves, for the questioning had been hard and long and brutal. 'That was the wretch's way of claiming some beastly distinction for himself.'

'It was a plaguey rotten experience,' muttered Francis Clayton.

'They might only consign him to Bedlam,' said Brigge aghast.

'But he had seen something, at some time,' said the Reverend Robert.

'Yes, that was quite evident. But, like all the evidence of Jack Straw, it will not stand up in broad daylight.'

'I tell you one thing, gentlemen,' said William thoughtfully. 'This Jack Straw business is a running sore in our community. And though I am one of the novices here I cannot help wondering why we have not rooted him out in some—what? Ten years?'

Humphrey Kersall gave a short laugh, and helped himself to a biscuit.

'It is not for want of trying, Mr Howarth. We have employed informers and got nowhere. These poor people stick together, you know. He feeds them, clothes them, helps them. They will not give him away. And then you heard about the secret oaths? It is an organised conspiracy, but conducted in so many different places and at such different times, and so unexpectedly, that we find no pattern to it.'

'He will be quiet for months,' said Squire Brigge, 'and then, just as you think you will hear no more of him—poof! He's out again. And he never does the same thing twice together.'

'Then why do we not ask the Home Secretary for help?' William asked.

The other magistrates were deeply displeased.

'Mr Howarth,' said Humphrey Kersall, as spokesman, 'only Whigs, or men with some axe to grind who wish to be noticed, tell their troubles to the Home Secretary. We prefer to deal with our own problems, and so prevent interference from London. We do not want state assistance.'

'Then why not form a paid constabulary?' William suggested. 'Young, strong men who have nothing to do but hunt down, and deal with, criminals of every sort. When I see timid, middle-aged citizens creeping to do their turn at patrolling—or, which happens more often, paying someone to do it for them!—I am dismayed, gentlemen. We must fight crime, not hope that it will go away!'

'Mr Howarth,' said Lord Kersall again, even more displeased, 'to create a professional constabulary could lead to the sort of trouble they have had in France!'

'I do not see how, my lord. That was mob rule. This would be a private domestic army.'

'Exactly!' said Lord Kersall, very grandly indeed. 'The Englishman, Mr Howarth, whether he be high- or low-born, cherishes his freedom.'

'Still, my lord,' said the Reverend Robert Graham, after a suitable silence, 'I cannot help thinking that we should tighten our jurisdiction. Colonel Fletcher and the Reverend Thomas Bancroft of Bolton are zealous in their pursuit of conspirators. They employ informers, not as we do, but on a great scale. They rule Bolton with a rod of iron.'

'So I have heard,' said another magistrate, who was new to the business. 'But then, Bolton has the reputation of being the most insurrectionary centre in the country. You could hardly give that title to Wyndendale, sir! Indeed, I fear we should be laughed at if we admitted that our Jack Straw harms nobody, and leaves what he calls "fair payment" for his thefts!'

'Then we should bear with their amusement,' said William firmly. 'And, if there is some rooted objection to approaching the Home Secretary, can we not consult with some person or persons like these two gentlemen in Bolton? They will tell us how to deal with him, how to bring pressure to bear, how to infiltrate this organisation.'

Lord Kersall looked splendidly offended.

'The Deputy Constable of Manchester, Mr Joseph Nadin,' murmured Robert Graham, 'has a reputation for such matters. They call him ruthless, which I often discover to mean very efficient! And is there not an attorney in Stockport, who works in a somewhat unorthodox fashion, but has excellent results?'

'What do you mean by unorthodox, sir?' enquired Lord Kersall.

'Well, my lord,' said the Reverend Robert uneasily, 'he stretches his authority somewhat. He has been known to fetch Crown witnesses across the county borders, and to trade spies and information. He sets a thief to catch a thief, my lord.'

'Disgraceful!' said Lord Kersall, for he did not want to lose one jot of his entitlement to rule the valley.

'But the Home Secretary is particularly pleased to have such an efficient servant of the peace, my lord, and he turns a blind eye to these little irregularities.'

Humphrey Kersall gauged the feeling of the meeting, and tapped the table thoughtfully with his fingers.

'If we could track down Jack Straw. . . .' said Squire Brigge, hopefully.

'Very well, sir,' said Lord Kersall haughtily to the clergyman. 'If you care to enquire of these people I have no objection. But I shall not take orders, mind! We are our own government in Wyndendale. Remember that!'

He looked hard at all of them, and especially at William Howarth.

Like the poor man at the rich man's table, Dorcas Howarth picked up fine crumbs, and had thus come to the notice of the Hon. Mrs Brigge, Lady Clayton and Squire Wrigley's wife of Medlar. But it was with some surprise and anxiety that she now beheld Lord Kersall's middle-aged heir at her garden gate, looking for a stable-lad to take his horse. Still, she reflected that he must want a favour of her or he would not trouble himself. So she gave her orders with great dignity, and composed herself to receive him.

Ralph Kersall had many faults, but lack of style was not one of them. His dark riding coat, his glossy boots, his white pantaloons looked as though dust would never dare alight upon them. He entered Dorcas's parlour with a smile upon his face which did not reach his eyes. She curtseyed and he bowed.

He began by craving her pardon for his unwarrantable intrusion; complimented her upon Bracelet, but not too much or too effusively; paid flowery tribute to her influence upon her large family; hinted that the ironmaster would have got nowhere without her guidance; and arrived at the reason for his visit.

'I am come, madam, to throw myself upon your mercy and

ask your judgement, on a matter of considerable delicacy.'
He cleared his throat and consulted his nails. 'Madam, what I
have to say will be painful to both of us, and I am sorry for
that, but I believe we can set matters right between us. At
any rate, my wife thinks it best so.'

This latter gleam of honesty revived Dorcas, and she
smiled on him.

'Madam, I fear that my stepmother, Lady Kersall, and
your son, the ironmaster, are guilty of an indiscretion.'

Here he looked straight at her, and her momentary liking
vanished. He had the Kersall eyes of unwarmed blue, the
Kersall manner of staring through the person he was addressing. Of a sudden, Dorcas felt that she was being used. So
he thinks to overwhelm me with his high station and high
compliments, and give me my orders? she thought. And sat
very upright.

'Well, sir,' she said with some spirit, 'you are going a long
way about mending the matter. Why do you not speak with
Lady Kersall?'

He closed up his mouth in displeasure.

'That would not—for reasons with which I shall not trouble you—be possible,' he said, after a slight pause.

So they are not on speaking terms? thought Dorcas.

'But what do you imagine I can do, sir, which you cannot
do better?' she asked. 'You and my son are well acquainted.
Could you not talk to him?'

The interview was not going as he had expected.

'I would rather that he did not know the initiative came
from me, madam.'

'Sir, if we are to help each other at all you must be more
frank with me,' said Dorcas briskly. 'Did you hope I should
speak of this indiscretion with my son? That is rather too
much!'

He bent his head reflectively. And she knew that he would
tell her as little as he could, and she must conjecture the rest
for herself.

'I had hoped, perhaps, that you could break the news to
Mrs Howarth,' said Ralph, 'by putting it to the lady that
there were strong rumours, and you feared it might harm the
ironmaster.'

He looked at her again, and Dorcas saw that he meant
harm to William, however and whenever he could inflict it.

'You did not think to approach her first, sir?'

He hesitated, and then said, 'Mrs Howarth is a very

309

charming and charitable lady, but my wife thought it best that you should break the news to her.'

Then Dorcas understood that Zelah was a mystery to them. They had no yardstick by which to measure her.

'It would save a scandal, and my father's feelings, madam, for he knows nothing. And it will save your son a great deal of trouble!' He saw that she was not to be threatened, and added graciously, 'We should be so much obliged to you. We should be delighted to be of service to you in any way possible.'

'Very well, sir, it shall be as you wish,' said Dorcas, rising.

He bowed rather more deeply than he had done when he entered, and repeated that he was under an obligation to her.

'Then allow me to release you of it,' said Dorcas, smiling in a way that would have given any member of her family cause for reflection.

'Anything, madam. . . .' Apprehensively.

'I am forming a committee for charitable purposes, to raise funds for a School for Girls of Poor Families in Applegarth. It would assist me greatly if I had an illustrious lady as patron. There would be, of course, no work involved. Nothing but the lending of a name, and one personal appearance when the school is opened. Do you think that Lady Caroline would be so kind as to undertake this, sir?'

He paused only for a couple of seconds. There was nothing in the request which could offend in any way, but Caroline would probably be furious.

'I am sure my wife will be charmed, madam. I shall ask her to write to you!'

He bowed again, gave her his formal smile, which vanished when Nellie handed him his shining top-hat. They watched him ride away, immaculate in his riding clothes: cuffed boots as bright as mirrors. His horse, too, was very correct and noble, handsome and high-stepping. They made an exquisite partnership.

'He don't seem 'uman, somehow, does he, Mrs Howarth?' said Nellie, folding her apron round her hands, watching. 'But a very grand gentleman,' she added hastily, 'and his visit's done you a power of good, ma'am.'

'He called to tell me that Lady Caroline is to be patron of my school committee, Nellie. Is that not good news?' said Dorcas smoothly.

'Aye, that'll fetch the brass rolling in. There's nowt like a title to make folks come running! I dare say that's along of

310

Mr William being so famous these days, isn't it, Mrs Howarth?'

'Oh, yes,' said Dorcas drily. 'It is entirely because of William.'

It was difficult to find an aperture in the armour of Zelah's day. Like her mother she was up and dressed by six o'clock, to give the older girls their lessons before breakfast. She supervised her household, answered letters, listened to requests, made the rounds of the nursery and schoolroom, visited friends and relatives and dependants, and devoted herself to the two youngest children for an hour before supper. The evening was filled by family, visitors, and entertaining.

However, Dorcas had long been accustomed to domestic challenges, so she picked her hour nicely one wet afternoon, a few days after Ralph Kersall's visit. Warmly wrapped by Nellie, carefully driven by Tom, she set off for Kingswood Hall and was rewarded by finding Zelah sitting alone and writing her journal.

'I do beg your pardon for interrupting, my love,' said Dorcas sincerely, 'for we must all have some solitude. But I promise you I had good reason to call, and I shall be brief.'

Zelah's smile had lost its youthful humour but was still warm and sweet. She kissed Dorcas tenderly on both cheeks, and deplored the wet bonnet and cloak.

'Truly, Mrs Dorcas, I am astonished that those two kind dragons of servants allowed thee out in such weather!'

'My servants know when to be kind and when to be dragon,' Dorcas remarked.

For she would never let her five-and-seventy years dictate to her, nor allow them to make dictators out of anyone else. Zelah's smile was spontaneous this time, but she hid it and rang for tea.

'I have always endeavoured not to interfere,' Dorcas began, warming herself at the vast coal-fire on the hearth, 'and hope I have succeeded. But one never knows oneself well enough to be sure of that.'

'I count myself blessed in thee and my mother, who are the best and kindest of women,' said Zelah warmly.

'And we are blessed in you, and so is William,' Dorcas replied. 'Indeed, I never knew such a man for having his faults overlooked as William!'

'William is a great man,' said Zelah loyally, 'and hath a great man's little weaknesses.'

311

They drank tea, and reflected on their different worlds.

'Dearest child,' said Dorcas cautiously, 'I fear I have news to give you which implies some thoughtlessness on William's part. I do not place more importance upon the matter than that, but his actions could be misconstrued.'

She resolved to keep her tone light and her voice steady, though these days her emotions were as fragile as her bones, and as likely to break if she were not careful with herself.

Zelah turned pale and said, 'Hath he borrowed money of thee?'

'Indeed he has not'—crisply—'and I should not lend it to him if he asked, not however many per cent he promised me! Mr Hurst and I agreed long since that William's attitude towards money was not our own, though all very well for him. Old ladies on fixed incomes must be cautious. No, my love, it has nothing to do with me. It is a foolish matter which could be taken far too seriously, but should be nipped in the bud.' Here she laughed a little, to show how unimportant she considered it to be. 'There are rumours that he has been paying too many compliments to Lady Kersall, and if it came to his lordship's ears it could harm William. I should discount it, for I have no opinion of gossip, but William is a little too prominent, these days, to risk talk of this kind.'

Zelah set down her tea and mastered herself to speak.

'I thank thee for thy kindness to me, but I would prefer the truth. It cuts sharp, but it also cuts clean.'

Then Dorcas saw the rock beneath Zelah's sweetness.

'You give me no choice,' said Dorcas, after a moment's pause, 'but to say what I had rather not. Men of William's age, with William's amount of money and authority, often make fools of themselves over a young woman. And from what I have heard of Lady Kersall,' she added with some asperity, 'I should not be inclined to blame William entirely in the matter! Though he has undoubtedly done wrong to you. I do not excuse him on that account, my love.'

Zelah said sadly, 'I have sat a hundred times, as I do now, and wished I were a girl again and back at Somer Court. The thought of my home hath given me strength when naught else would have done.'

Forlorn, too stricken to find further excuse or to offer comfort, Dorcas put her hand upon Zelah's hand and two tears slipped down her face. She was too old to carry suffering as once she had done.

'Once, when Kitty was a baby,' Zelah continued, 'I wrote

to ask my father if he would send for us. But in the evening William came home and was sorry, and I tore up the letter to my father. And it hath been so many and many a time since.' She was conscious of Dorcas's distress, and stopped herself. 'I would not cause thee sorrow,' said Zelah gently. 'My mother and thee were loved faithfully and well, and so knoweth nothing of my helplessness. But though I have said the least, concerning William's behaviour, I have not felt the least.'

'I am ashamed,' cried Dorcas, and the tears slipped faster down her cheeks. 'I am ashamed that he should make you suffer.'

'I love thee, Mrs Dorcas. But I tell thee this. I have done all that I can, and it is to no avail either for him or for me. So we shall leave him.'

'I am very angry with William,' cried Dorcas, choking upon a sob. 'He need not come to me for comfort. I shall tell him what I think.'

'Poor William,' said Zelah, with the very ghost of a smile.

'Please to call Tom from the kitchen,' said Dorcas weeping bitterly, 'and have my bonnet and cloak fetched. I am not fit to see the children today. Oh, the children! You will all visit me before you go, will you not?'

'We shall besiege thee,' said Zelah, almost in her old fashion.

She had regained herself, could no longer be hurt, diverted or led.

'There is one thing thee can tell me, Mrs Dorcas,' she said in a different tone. 'I believe thee knew of Hannah Garside?'

I cannot support these scenes, thought Dorcas. I shall be abed all tomorrow, after this. And Nellie will be cross on my account.

But she answered resolutely, wiping away her tears, 'Who has spoken of Hannah Garside? She was William's house-keeper at Flawnes Green, but left there years before you were married.'

'Stephen's wife, at Flawnes Green, was one of Mrs Boulton's daughters, and she loved Hannah and spoke to me of her as of an old and trusted friend. And, though Hannah Garside left years before our marriage, she had been six years at the forge and left of a sudden and was not heard of after. We women are quick to scent out an attachment. Did thee act as confidante in that affair also, Mrs Dorcas?'

Dorcas hesitated, then threw up her hands in a gesture of resignation.

'I was her only confidante,' she said, 'and I kept her secret as she begged me to—except that I had to tell Ned, of course. Even William knows nothing. I gave her money to help her to leave the valley. She loved him, but she knew that he loved you. That was all about it. I have never heard from her since. That was her express wish.'

'Was she with child by him?' asked Zelah inexorably.

'Yes,' said Dorcas.

Enveloped in her cloak, she said tremulously, 'I should have liked to know when the child was born. If, indeed, it lived, it would be seventeen by now. And is a part of us after all.'

But this small and private sorrow was engulfed by remembrance of the greater sorrow to come.

Weeping afresh, Dorcas said, 'Oh, God bless and keep you, and do not forget me, Zelah.'

Helping her to her seat, Tom said grimly, 'Nellie's not half going to be vexed about this, Mrs Howarth!'

And that honest grumble gave her more comfort than any amount of sympathy.

The sound of William's arrival home always caused Zelah a degree of apprehension, which she used to conceal beneath her welcome. Today, she sent her daughters out and listened to him with formidable composure.

'You are very quiet,' said William, looking for faults. 'It is difficult enough, God knows, to bear with dull faces all day without finding them waiting for me at home!'

She said, kindly and firmly, 'Then thee must be delivered of them, William. Tomorrow we shall begin to pack for Somer Court. I am making the arrangements.'

He thought this statement over, without liking it very much but without feeling its full force.

'I was not told of this,' he accused her.

She saw the bully in his dark brows, and four generations of Quakers gathered within her to defeat him.

'I have not been told of anything but what thee chose to tell me for many years, William,' she said coolly, 'but I shall be franker than thee. I have loved thee with all that I was and could be. But thou hast cheated me and dishonoured our marriage, and now I am done with thee.'

He sat appalled at this sudden reversal of roles.

'Done with me?' he said, in quite a different tone. 'Done with me, Zelah?' Then he blustered in his pride and panic.

314

'What do you mean by this? If I offended you you should have said so! You know you have only to ask and you can have anything in the world!'

She smiled faintly, folded her hands and listened to him.

'Have I not worked for you, given you the greater part of myself? Did I not build this house for you? Finer and larger than Somer Court. Is it not enough?'

Her silence daunted him. He plunged deeper, more fatally, into explanation.

'I admit to one or two flirtations. Well then, some adventure. With light women. Who meant nothing to me, Zelah. I have not dishonoured our marriage, for my feeling for you remained untouched by these—frivolities. Not that I excuse myself. And, after all, I am tired of them. I shall be done with them from now on. We shall be as we were.' He thought of something else. 'Thee knoweth, love,' he said softly in his old fashion, 'that I must not get thee with child too often, lest thy health suffer.'

She watched him with compassion, waiting for him to be truthful.

'Thee should have told me thee wanted me, love,' he pleaded.

Charlotte would have damned him for a hypocrite, Dorcas exposed the flaws in his argument. Zelah listened, and let him hang himself.

'The ironworks, and all the other enterprises, have good managers,' he offered. 'I need not work as hard and as long as I did. I shall spend more time with thee and the children, Zelah.'

She saw that he could be intimidated into a semblance of consideration, and this more than anything else destroyed her faith in him.

'We speak in the same tongue,' she said, much as Catherine had once said to him. 'But no longer mean the same thing, William.'

'Thee should have a change and a rest,' he cried, putting the best face upon the matter. 'Thee must stay as long as needful, at Somer Court. And I shall visit thee there, love.'

She put her hands upon the arms of the chair and began to rise.

'No,' he cried, horrified into honesty at last. 'Do not leave me, Zelah. When will you come back?'

And he caught at her skirt as she passed him, like a child trying to detain her.

'I have not thought of coming back, only of going,' she said, immovable.

'But if I promise, Zelah, if I swear by all that is holy to me. . . .'

'What is thy promise or thine oath worth, William?' she asked ironically. 'Thee promised to love, honour and cherish me when we were joined together.'

'But have you no hope to give me? No direction?'

'Only in thy public world, William. There are those waiting to injure thee with Lord Kersall, so do not offend him. For that is all that is left to thee now.'

She was weary of people replenishing themselves through her, asking strength and favours of her. She left the room quietly, gracefully, but with finality. While William sat with his head in his hands and wondered how he should get her back again. For he had never envisaged life without her.

Zelah had triumphed after all, simply by being herself. She was the spirit of the law, the Word made flesh, the unwritten truth, the final and supreme counsellor of her family. Whereas William's vision was all fire and sword and must perish upon itself. Whereas, when day was done and voices were silent, he must start up in his sleep, asking why the wheels revolved. To be answered, 'For profit. For power.' But she had no need to puzzle herself as to the meaning or value of her life. What Zelah had accomplished was very simple and very difficult, and required no explanation.

TWENTY-FIVE

Bricks Without Straw

November 1811

Charlotte still held her evening classes and committee meetings in the back parlour: a large room overlooking the garden, which had spent most of its existence shrouded in dust-covers, and locked up between one spring-cleaning and the next. It was useful and private in a number of ways, having less obvious exits and entrances, and—as Sally said—saving the hall carpet from being trodden to death. Also, though this reason was felt by Charlotte alone, it separated the personal life of her front parlour from the political traumas of the back.

Tonight, though she was tired enough, God knew, the Red Rose must be convened for a special meeting. So Jim Ogden, the weaver, arrived early to rearrange the table and chairs. He had been a committee member for the past three years, highly recommended by the Manchester centre, from whence he had come after the weavers' strike and rebellion of 1808, and earned a bare living as an outworker for Ernest Harbottle at Babylon Mill just outside Millbridge. Self-taught, self-sufficient, a forcible character, an experienced trouble-maker, he was at once a jewel in the Red Rose's crown and a spur in its side. He had caused more difficulties on the committee than any other person, by representing the hand-loom weavers of the valley and voicing their opinions. In him, worthy and sincere though he was, Charlotte sensed a violence which was latent in this group, and she was finding it difficult to hold the society in check. Moreover, Jim Ogden disliked women, and Charlotte's position as secretary and as a member of the privileged and educated class. He did not especially like Jack, but at least they shared a common dedication to the Radical cause, and a common background of early childhood.

This evening, as Polly knocked at the door and asked if Charlotte wanted anything else, he answered for her. Deliberate. Impudent.

'That's all right, love. Get thee to bed. If we want owt we can get it for us-selves.'

Polly curled her lip at him and answered, 'I warn't talking to *you!*'

Charlotte turned her back on him, and said as though he had not spoken. 'Could you bring bread and cheese and ale in for the men, and tea for me, if you please, Polly? Then if you leave the back door unlocked they can let themselves in, and you can go to bed as soon as you wish.'

Polly gave Jim Ogden a significant look, and clicked the door shut behind her.

'There you are!' cried Ogden, aggrieved. 'No better nor me, and treats me like dirt!'

'She is a deal better mannered than you, Mr Ogden,' said Charlotte coldly, for she had long since given up any effort at friendship. 'And I'll thank you to allow me to conduct my own household. You are a guest here, not the master.'

317

He looked ugly then, crying, 'We'st wipe out masters and servants, tha knows. Then thee can get thy hands mucky, along wi' the rest of us!'

'Provided they can act as secretary still, that will not matter.'

No one questioned her value in the post, or her special knowledge, and so far she had proved irreplaceable. But that did not deter him.

'I've never heerd of a woman seckertary afore. Bloody daft idea!'

'There is a great deal you never heard of, Mr Ogden,' said Charlotte, like silk, 'and therefore I would always question your judgement on such matters. Ah, here is Mr Ackroyd!'

Her heart was sore that he should find her weary and quarrelsome, that they must greet each other formally and act the parts that were expected of them. He, too, was tired and apprehensive. The Red Rose had grown beyond their wildest expectations, and almost out of their jurisdiction. They had contacts with other and similar organisations throughout Lancashire and Yorkshire, and kept in touch with London movements through Ambrose. And since Jim Ogden had joined them they had corresponded with the highly secret union of weavers, which stretched from London to Nottingham and from Manchester to Carlisle. Ogden, as the expert at insurrection, was always pushing the society to act more forcibly. Sam Mellor, representing the valley's coal-miners, a man as truculent as the weaver, was usually opposed to him. Their hatred was mutual, and Mellor as a local man resented Ogden as an outsider. Then there were half a dozen or so representatives of various artisan trades: a baker, a shoemaker, a chandler, a carpenter, two printers. And finally the founders of the society: Jack Ackroyd the president and chairman, Charlotte as general amanuensis and pamphleteer, her two assistants Alfred Horsefield and Edwin Fletcher from the grammar school staff, Dr Wilkins from the Millbridge Hospital, and Jeremy Birtwhistle from Hurst's solicitors office as treasurer.

The others arrived in ones and twos, most having come on from their own classes along the valley. Each of them espoused a particular cause, aired a special grievance, brought personal problems and questions from his own group. Wrongs had multiplied and accumulated over the past years until Charlotte felt as though she were being pressed into the ground by injustice. And whatever they did, and they

318

never ceased trying, matters seemed to get worse rather than better. Each petition was shelved, evaded or rejected by the authorities. Each strike quelled more harshly, punished more severely. Piece by piece, the laws, which had since the time of Queen Elizabeth prevented masters from exploiting workers, were dismantled. The long struggle with France, resumed eight years ago, seemed as though it would never end. In answer to Britain blockading Napoleon, America had banned British trade and hit the cotton industry. Prices climbed, wages froze or were reduced. Finally, even the weather declared war upon them again, as it had done in the bitter winters of the '90s, and harvests failed.

'Not a very agreeable night, Mrs Longe,' said Jeremy Birtwhistle, very agreeably, as she mended the fire.

'It's a damned sight worse if you've got no coal!' Ogden remarked.

'Shall we sit down, friends?' Charlotte asked, taking her seat at the foot of the long table, with an assistant each side of her.

Jack sat at the head of the company. Ogden was on his right hand and Sam Mellor on his left. The others ranged themselves on either side, as they felt inclined, and Jack ran his hand through his hair and surveyed the paper before him. He was grey now, in the middle fifties, his face strongly lined. Thirteen years with Charlotte had softened his angularity, channelled his emotions, strengthened his purpose. Nowadays he held his tongue and thought before he spoke. He had learned to bank his fires and was more powerful in consequence, but they flared forth on occasion. He was in command, and Charlotte stood with him. Between them, even now when their energies and spirits were low, was the living bond. So she merely glanced at him, he raised his eyebrows, and each of them knew that the evening was going to prove rough.

'Since this is a special meeting, called on behalf of Jim Ogden who acted as our delegate recently at Manchester,' Jack began, 'we'll ask him to state his case, and then put it to discussion straightway. Pass the ale, Matt, and a slice of bread and cheese, will you? I've had naught to eat since dinner. We are ready when you are, Jim.'

Ogden stood up, planting his hands on the table, smiling aggressively at them all, as though he had found a nest of vipers instead of an assembly of friends. He cultivated the poor man's image, as the French revolutionaries had done, glorying in his lack of polish. Unlike Jack, who did not notice appearances and manners, Jim Ogden saw and deliberately flouted them. He began by blaming everybody.

'I told you when I come here from Manchester, above three year ago, and I've told you many a time since, that I'm fighting for the weavers and I don't give a bugger for the rest. So don't expect a lot of fancy talk wi' nowt behind it. I'm telling you now, once and for all, that there are close on half a million hand-loom weavers in this country as is facing destitution. Destitution!' And he hammered both fists on the table for emphasis. 'The price of wheat is already above a hundred shillings a quarter, and likely to reach a hundred and fifty by the summer. And while a weaver could reckon to make twenty shillings a week a few years since, he'd be lucky to get eight now. How do you feed a family on that?'

'State your case, Jim,' said Jack Ackroyd patiently. 'We know the facts and figures as well as you do.'

'Right! I'll state it bloody now. The weavers in this valley and elsewhere is fed up wi' signing petitions and stealing a sack of potatoes here, or a sack of flour there, to keep theirselves alive. And I'm fed up wi' this society being run by a lot of educated folk as has never gone clemmed and famished in their born days. We've decided to stop asking and start taking. If the manufacturers won't play fair wi' us then we'll make them smart. We'll hit them where it hurts most. We want marches and riots, and notes that puts the fear of God into them. Burn the bloody mills down, we say! And to hell wi' arsing about like you lot have done for the past twelve year. If you don't like that you know what you can do wi' it!'

Immediately the committee all began to talk at once, some directly to Jim Ogden in rebuke, some to each other, and none to any purpose. Charlotte held her tongue with difficulty, watching the struggle on Jack's face. Ogden had aimed for his belly reaction, but the headmaster was a thinking man. Finally he rapped the table for silence.

'Each member shall have his—or her—say, and then we shall put the matter to vote. But at the moment we are all a little too heated to come to any reasonable conclusion!' He turned to Ogden, who was slyly grinning to himself, like a dog who has fetched back a stick. 'I'll summarise your points, my friend, while we are thinking, and add a note or two of my own.

'There is more to the question of hand-loom weavers than you have stated. And it pertains to their way of life and their future, and was predicted by me—to them—when we burned down the first spinning-mill at Thornley, some thirty years ago. The mills are here to stay, and the power-loom is master. This is the age of machine-working not of handcrafting. However we help the weavers, whatever temporary reprieve they are granted, they are a doomed industry. So there is no question of breaking through some barrier, as you appear to suggest, and coming out the other side. The hand-loom weaver is finished as a money-making worker.'

'Not if we act instead of talking!' Ogden shouted. 'Break the bloody power-looms! Burn the bloody mills down!'

'Wait until I have finished,' Jack cried, and the edge in his voice silenced the weaver. 'The reason that the Red Rose still exists is because we have not openly provoked the authorities. I regret that you despise our education, for we should like everyone to be educated, and our ideals are the same as yours. But until we founded this society there was no organisation of workers in the valley. For the first time in the history of Wyndendale, working men and women have someone to whom they can complain, who will show them their rights, give them free schooling in a limited fashion, set up petitions and distribute political pamphlets. If we advocate violence we come out in the open, once and for all. The penalties risked will be extreme—and you have first-hand knowledge of how the Manchester Assizes deal with offenders! Wyndendale will be under martial low. We shall be hunted out and hunted down. And for what?

'Afterwards, the weavers will continue to starve, the government to ignore their condition, the manufacturers to prosper. And what might be called the weavers' only benefit society will have been wiped out.'

A murmur of approval made Jim Ogden look sullen, but his tongue was always ready to rebuke.

'Benefit society!' he jeered. 'Aye, that's about the long and short of it! A bowl of soup for the poor to keep them quiet and keep them under. Well, Mr Jack Straw Ackroyd, if you won't help us we'll break away. We'll have us own revolution. The Luddites have been breaking frames in Nottingham since March, drilling and arming theirselves, and if you want to see organisation you have a look in that direction! They can't hold them. Bloody troops, bloody magistrates, bloody nobody can't find them nor hold them. Masked and disguised. Working at night. And shall I tell you why the bloody government can't catch them? Because of the solidarity! Folk is solid behind them because they know summat's getting done. That's why. And if you wasn't feared of getting your feet wet you'd do the same for this valley. Nowt but a bloody laughing-stock you are! All piss and wind!'

'By Christ, Mr Ackroyd, but I've had enough,' roared Sam Mellor. 'Being spat on by a tuppenny foreigner that's all mouth! I'd fetch a pick-axe to thee——'

'Sam!' cried Jack, in the voice which could still a grammar school assembly. 'That will do. I said we should state our views objectively, reasonably. You shall be answered, Ogden.'

'Nay, I'm not wasting my time. You're either for Jack Straw or Ned Ludd! Let me know which, and I don't give a bugger either road. I'm off!'

And with that he snatched up his battered hat, pulled his jacket together against the cold, and departed into the dark. They sat smarting with defeat.

Then Matt Redfern said, clearing his throat apologetically, 'He used language as shouldn't be used afore a lady, and I'd like to say we're sorry about that, Mrs Longe.'

'It does not matter, Mr Redfern,' she replied. 'I do not listen to the language, but to what he says.'

'Mrs Longe takes the rough with the smooth, my friends,' Jack added, humorously and easily. 'Being the only woman on a male committee necessarily incurs certain social hazards, which will not be found in the tea-parlour. Well, what do we think of Jim Ogden's proposals?'

'He has a point,' said Jeremy Birtwhistle surprisingly, for he was the mildest of men. 'The Red Rose seems to be dragging its feet in the matter of action. We are not helping the weavers except in hand-to-mouth charity.'

'We can't help the weavers,' said Hal Middleton. 'Like Mr Ackroyd says, the weavers is finished.'

'Aye, but how do you tell a dying brother that you're going to leave him to die, while you save your own skin?' asked Matt Redfern.

'If we decided on Luddite-style action,' said Edwin Fletcher, 'is there any chance of our getting away with it?'

'Only upon one count,' said Jack. 'If the movement grows into a national one, and fetches all the radical organisations with it. Then we should be too powerful to touch.'

'Aye, it only took one mob at the Bastille to start off the French Revolution,' Hal Middleton observed.

'*Mob* is a word I do not care for,' said Dr Wilkins, who usually listened most of the time, and then brought up the point which had been worrying everybody. 'Mr Ogden was also talking about arming and drilling, and I like that even less. The thought of a crowd of untrained and angry men waving free muskets about is an anxious prospect. We stand as much chance of being shot by our own people as by the troops!'

'Yes, those who can use a gun mostly have one,' Alfred Horsefield remarked. 'We should be careful of handing out weapons.'

'I agree,' said Jack. 'A show of force always invites force, and too many innocent people get hurt. What do you think, Madam Secretary?'

'I abhor the notion of mob violence, and Mr Ogden takes too narrow a view. He thinks only of the weavers, whereas we work for all. I believe we should consult with other organisations, and make sure we are in control of our own people. It is not true, as Mr Ogden seemed to suggest, that the general opinion leans towards forcible action. The Manchester centre is divided in its councils, and so are others.'

'Aye, and Glasgow is determined to fight test cases in the courts,' said Jack. 'They pursue a peaceful—though no less onerous—course, and will not follow General Ludd. As he is called.'

'Does General Ludd exist?' asked Edwin Fletcher curiously.

'As Jack Straw does, I dare say,' Charlotte answered, smiling. 'He serves his purpose, whether man or legend.'

'And what if the weavers are vociferous enough to start a national movement?' Jack asked them. 'We must accept that they have strongholds throughout the country, and in Scotland and northern Ireland. Luddism could touch them all alight. Then, whether we like their methods or no, should we hang back still?'

Some looked reluctant, others dismayed. Then Charlotte, judging her committee from past experience, gave an answer which served for all of them.

'If we see that Luddism lays a foundation for a Radical society and political reform, we should declare ourselves for that society. But we must hold to peaceful principles, so far as we are able. Else shall we have the guillotine erected in the Strand, and thus exchange one tyranny for another.'

With this they agreed to watch, wait and hold themselves in readiness.

Charlotte and Jack lay in each other's arms, but neither made love nor slept.

He said quietly, 'I am too old and fearful, Lottie, to relish what is ahead of us. Five-and-fifty has not the stomach for a fight that five-and-twenty boasts. I have acquired a taste for peace and privacy. I should like nothing better, my lass, than to set up house with you at the grammar school, and later to retire together. We should do well enough, I think,' clasping her fingers and giving them a loving shake. 'We could read our books, and talk and write on politics. Some of my old pupils would come to visit us. And the Howarths might not mind so much. It is late in the day for all of us, Lottie. I cannot think that any would grudge us a modest happiness.'

'I wish we could tell the truth of ourselves,' she said with regret. 'I remember when Willie was a little boy and my father whipped him, not for stealing one of Betty's pies but for lying about it. And my mother said that the virtue she most admired was courage. But my father said no, it was truth. Above all else he held truthfulness to be the greatest virtue, and said it was strange that they did not include it in the seven virtues of mankind.'

'Truthfulness requires courage, Lottie. And, in our case, so does continual deception. There is another paradox for you!'

'But I am sick of paradox,' she said wearily.

'Aye, I know that, too. Well, when this last skirmish is over, we shall think of ourselves for a change, Lottie. Jim Ogden is not to your taste, I know, but he is the new kind of man that the Radical movement is producing. And he has a point about the society being conducted by intellectual rather than working people. Perhaps the Jim Ogdens will go one step further, do better than we can. We shall retire together, Lottie, anyway. What say you, my lass? I think sometimes what a firebrand I was, and know now that I am old-fashioned. We belong to the radical past, Lottie. Does that occur to you?'

He felt her smile against his cheek in the dark and tightened his embrace in answer.

'Shall I tell you what I have been thinking, in the past weeks?' she asked. 'I have been remembering how my parents raved over Toby's ideas and politics, and what a turbulent spirit he was in that quiet world of thirty years since. But when I look back now—poor Toby! Such a gentlemanly fellow, with his coffee-house speeches and his neat wig and laundered ruffles! How Jim Ogden would despise him! He belongs now, like us, to yesterday. And yet. . . .'

'He died for his beliefs,' Jack finished. 'Who can do more?'

'You are very gracious, Jack.'

'I must have learned it of you.'

They heard the long clock in the hall chime five. Charlotte sat up and fumbled for the tinder-box to light her candle. She shivered in the icy air, and Jack reached for her shawl. Then began, stiffly, to get out of bed.

'I must go before Polly and Sally wake up,' he said, pulling on his stockings. 'I have a touch of rheumatism—well, more than a touch!—in this leg.'

He was apologetic, for it does not become a lover to limp like an old man from his mistress's side.

'Oh, Lottie,' he said, smiling, sighing, 'my ambitions have shrunk to a sound night's sleep, an honest day's work, and peace of mind!'

'You shall have all three when the revolution is over! Jack, why do you not try the new remedy of cod liver oil? Old Dr Standish is a great believer in it, and you know how he suffers from rheumatism!' She was sitting up, wrapping her shawl about her. 'But I warn you, it stinks worse than any pig!'

'I will hold my nose while I take a dose. It can hurt no worse than my joints!'

'I shall not see you tomorrow, Jack. Shall you come on Sunday?'

'Aye, and pray that we have Sunday to ourselves for once, love. I should not care to make conversation with the ironmaster again—though he was very civil!'

'Well, you will not, for he has gone down to Somer Court this weekend, to woo his wife back!' Charlotte said, smiling. Then, bringing up the subject which had silently troubled her all night, 'You know that William extended his business a year or so ago, to produce small-arms and ammunition, as well as cannon? They would not break into Snape, would they, to avail themselves of weapons?'

He pulled on his coat, and shook his head at her question.

'I have observed of you, more than once, that you think like a man in council and talk like a woman in private! My dear love, you know as well as I do that they will avail themselves of any weapons they can find or steal, if they are let loose. The fact that the ironmaster is your brother means nothing—except to you. And doubtless he will defend his property stoutly! But I agree with Matt Redfern that artillery in untrained hands is a deadly danger, and I shall advise against our people being armed—oh, may the devil take my leg!'

'He has probably had a hand in your rheumatism already,' said Charlotte impishly. 'Do not tempt him further!'

'Well then,' he answered, slowly smiling, 'I will not. Shall you light me downstairs now? By God, this is raw weather, and speaks badly for the rest of the winter months! Put on your woollen gown, or you will catch cold. And watch that third stair. It cracks like a pistol-shot when you tread upon it! It is a good thing that your servants sleep at the top of the house.'

'Oh, I cannot think they do not know of us by this time,' Charlotte whispered, as she opened the door. 'Had they suspected nothing, we should have been discovered in *flagrante delicto* long since!'

TWENTY-SIX

Let There Be Light!

'I will say this for William,' Ironmaster Scholes remarked, 'that neither thy lack of welcome, nor thy rejections, nor the onset of winter doth deter him!'

He was standing at Catherine's parlour window as the postchaise spun briskly up the drive, and turned to smile upon his daughter, full of quiet humour.

'Oh, hath poor William arrived?' said Catherine, and hastened to put away her sewing. 'Ring the bell for me, wilt thou, Caleb, and Mary shall heat the soup. Poor fellow, he will be perished in this weather.'

She knew better than to ask Zelah to attend to his needs, and hurried out that William might find one warm welcome at least.

'Well, my child,' said Caleb, observing the obstinate white column of his daughter's neck, 'hath thy husband travelled all this way for nothing yet again?'

'I do not wish to see him, father,' she replied composedly,

biting off a thread, though she had lost her customary pallor and made two mistakes already in her stitching. 'And thee and my mother used not to trouble me over him!'

But sixteen months is a long siege, and though Caleb the ironmaster had refused to meet William on his first visit, and Catherine had been coolly correct with her son-in-law, they had come to admire his persistence. He had braved everything: no invitations, cold receptions, the briefest of letters in reply to his long pleas, a steely disregard for his suffering, and a resolute refusal to come back to him. He had promised her everything: no further philandering, more time for his family, a greater sharing of his life and himself with Zelah. He had offered her everything: even to selling up the ironworks at Snape, and leaving Kingswood Hall if she wished it, and the buying of whatever place she preferred instead. Still Zelah turned her face away from all his proposals, and stayed at Somer Court with her six daughters.

'He will not give in,' said Caleb thoughtfully. 'He hath made up his mind to thee, though it kill him!'

The girls were running down the stairs to greet their father. Zelah heard Catherine laughing at something he had said, heard his voice rise rich and cheerful despite the freezing journey, heard squeals of rejoicing as his customary gifts were opened, and the sound of much muffled kissing from Sophie and Molly.

'And though I would not advise thee to trade thy peace of mind for worldly promises,' Caleb continued, one ear cocked in the direction of the hall, 'he is not as we are, and in promising thee what he thinks is best—he means best. Heed not his words, daughter, but listen closely to the meaning beneath them.'

The voices were growing fainter. A crowd of footsteps strode and skipped into silence. Zelah lifted her head despite herself, wondering that he had not come to see her first as he had always done before. The ironmaster smiled, and hid the smile.

'Dost thee remember a conversation we had together, some seventeen years since, daughter? We weighed William in the scales, then, against thy religion and thine upbringing. Thee found him worthy of that sacrifice, and confounded me with mine own beliefs. He hath not changed, Zelah, except in the manner of successful men. Thee knew what he was, and made a life beside him. Thine only error was to believe him to be stronger than thee, and in no need of guidance. Now thou hast guided him, but will not walk with him. To what purpose, daughter?'

Then Zelah realised that Catherine had led William away so that Caleb might plead her husband's case. Anger, gladness and sorrow warred within her.

'Dost thee not want us to stay here with thee?' she asked directly.

But Caleb was too old and wise to be drawn in this way.

'Dost thee not want to live thine own life instead of ours?' he countered, smiling. 'Thou art too like thy mother to enjoy servitude, however loving and easy that yoke may be. And thou hast more to do with thy life than stitching regrets into a fire-screen!'

Zelah felt she was betrayed. Her lips quivered. She would not look at her father.

'Thou hast made thy point, daughter,' said Caleb kindly, 'and though it doth not behove us peaceful folk to speak in terms of war—still, war it hath been, and betwixt husband and wife. Now art thou victor, but victors should be merciful, not strip their erstwhile foe of dignity. William is a proud man, and a brave one. But he hath bent his pride before thee, and asked thy pardon, not once but many times. And thou hast not helped him, Zelah. Therefore I counsel thee, out of my love, to search thy heart as he hath done. For a new life could be found for thee both. Do not use thy victory to destroy thyself and him. He will listen to thee, for he doth more than love thee—he needs thee, and now he knows it.'

She remained silent, hands clasped loosely in her lap. Her bottom lip was stubborn.

'But thy home is here for thee and thy children, however long thee stay, my daughter,' said Caleb most lovingly.

He rested his hand for a moment, in caress, on her dark-gold crown of hair. Then left her to herself. She wept a little, but wiped her eyes fairly soon, and looked in the glass to see if the tears had stained her cheeks. The house seemed very quiet. She had thought they would send William to her, but the minutes passed, and she grew impatient to reject him. At last she ventured forth. Silence in the hall, Caleb alone in the library, Catherine upstairs with the children, a maid finishing the dusting in the great parlour. Zelah consulted her small watch, which told her it was time for Livvy to practise upon the harpsichord. She made her way there, and found William sitting secretly, as he had sat all those years since, in one corner of the room.

He had not changed his linen, and the shadow upon his jaw and cheeks spoke of long, fast travelling with no time to shave. He was tired but unconquered, bringing to bear on her that humble, hopeful gaze which had become his habit. Catherine had furnished him with a jug of mulled claret to keep out the cold, and he sipped his glass now and again, and rested his head against the back of the armchair.

'Livvy should be here to practise her music by now,' Zelah said, to account for her presence.

His black eyes were softened with weariness and wine. The last sixteen months had turned his hair quite grey. His frame was thickening as his father's had done, not with fat but with heavy muscle. She saw the yeoman in his face, in his strong body. Only the broadcloth suit proclaimed the gentleman.

'Dost thou remember how thee played to me, Zelah, upon thy gold and scarlet harpsichord?' said William, and his words were a little slurred because he needed sleep, but would go on. 'Thee wore a scarlet shawl embroidered with gold birds, and a white gown.'

'Dost thou remember what I played thee, William?' she answered ironically, giving nothing.

'An air by Handel.'

'True,' she said, surprised.

'But I cannot remember which air,' he admitted, which made her smile involuntarily.

He noticed the smile with hope, and it vanished immediately. But the man who will not admit defeat can never be defeated.

'I have thought what else I could do for thee, Zelah,' he continued hardily. 'I can have gas-light put into Kingswood Hall. We shall be the first house in the valley to have it.'

Her heart smote her, for he was still searching to please her through things that most pleased him.

'No gas-light,' said William, reading her countenance. His own was crestfallen.

She wandered over to the harpsichord and fingered the keys.

'Mrs Dorcas's school fund goes very well,' he offered.

'Oh, how is Mrs Dorcas?' she asked warmly, sadly.

'Growing old, I fear. I do indeed fear it,' said William honestly. 'For when she is dead I must face the foe alone. Until then she holds out her frail, defending arms.'

He spoke the truth through the wine. Zelah ceased to finger the keys, and listened intently. A tired man talking. Not finished, but running down.

'I was my mother's first living infant,' William said, in a reverie. 'The first fruit of that strange union to survive. They say a very young child has no memory, but I remember in the deepest part of me how it was then. Oh, they have told me stories of that time, and so would prove that I remembered those, but I know better. I was my mother's triumph, her seal upon a misliked marriage, her entry into a new life, her acceptance in my father's house. Betty said that Mrs Dorcas carried me everywhere in her arms, and spoke to me as though I could understand. We were one person for a little while. For a little while I was her world, and she was mine. Mrs Dorcas! That world is with me still. At certain seasons of the year, at certain times on the clock, it comes back to me as deep and sweet as ever it was then. Shafts of sunlight on a carpet, a fragrance blown in from the summer garden, the movement of a curtain in the breeze, a chime, an evening light upon the walls.'

He wiped his lips to steady them, and drank more wine.

'How my father loved her,' he continued, 'and how she must feel the lack of him. What a partnership that was! And I had thought it my right and my inheritance to have the same. As though it were nothing to be fought for, and to win day after day, in pain and in humility as well as in joy and contentment. I had thought'—and here he smiled at himself—'I could improve upon that match! For Mrs Dorcas was not the beloved daughter of a rich, established family like your own, Zelah. And my father, though a good and handsome fellow, was neither scholarly nor powerful. I thought to take what they had given me, and add your beauty and your family, and my ambition and skill and energy, and so achieve a human miracle of perfection. The perfect match.'

His hand lifted in salute to his parents, and dropped. He poured another measure of wine, but sat a long time over it, not drinking.

'How I am humbled and proved wrong,' he said quietly. 'With what mean bricks, with what lack of straw, did they build slowly and with difficulty their house of love. How dearly bought that heart's desire, and how ungrudged the payment. And I, who had thought to show them, in trumpets and splendour and fine gold, what love should be—I lie through the night alone, and travel in the cold, because I know nothing, and am nothing, and have achieved . . . nothing.'

He was looking inward upon his dark self and did not see the tenderness on Zelah's face.

'I had such visions,' said William, and his head fell back, his eyes closed. 'Such visions. I had thought that power would nourish love, but power is love's antithesis.'

She began quietly to play the Handelian air which had pleased him all those years ago, glancing at him now and again. The music wove a single gold thread through his night, and another and another, until the warp was set. Then came the weft, line by line by line, penetrating his thought until he heard and raised his head. She played on, not looking at him now, seemingly unconscious of his presence, of his hesitant and disbelieving joy. And when he was sure, and she turned to smile on him, he came clumsily over and knelt at her side and put his arms about her waist, and hid his head and wept at his homecoming.

All the Howarths and their kindred gathered together in Kingswood Hall on the last day of the year 1811. Even Cicely, nursing her third child, made the long journey from Wiltshire to spend three weeks with Charlotte and celebrate this particular occasion. And Ambrose travelled up from London by the Royal Mail, in return—as he said to his uncle—for a similar journey made on his behalf in the year of his birth, 1785.

'And a deuced long, hard journey it still is!' cried Ambrose, warming his hands before the fire in the great hall, and surveying the assembly.

'Long and hard?' cried Dorcas, who had only just arrived from Bracelet, and was being installed in the place of honour at the fireside. 'Why, what do any of you know about travelling these days? You young folk are all spoiled with speed and springs! You should have tried a four-day jolting in the old stage-coaches, Ambrose. Come, give me a kiss, you are looking quite handsome!'. .

'Aye, well, we are not made of the same stern stuff as yourself, my dear Grandmama,' he said charmingly, and raised his glass to her continued good health.

Dorcas was going slightly deaf, and so spoke more loudly and clearly these days, that she might hear what she was saying. Consequently, even her asides were audible. She beckoned Charlotte to her.

'You have done very well with Ambrose,' she said, to the amusement of the company. 'I had thought he was too like his father at one time, but he has improved out of all recognition. And how old is Tibby now?' As that slender maiden approached with a tray of Bohea tea for Dorcas's refreshment. 'Close on sixteen? Well, girls should not be married too young, but William and Zelah must be looking about them. I did Charlotte's duty for her with Cicely,' forgetting that her daughter stood by. 'Where is Cicely?' Ignoring the fact that her granddaughter sat opposite, nursing her infant. 'I wrote to her not long since. They have called their first daughter after me. Dorcas Pole. That is a pretty name. I have her letter somewhere. Tibby, look in my reticule, dearest child, and find Cicely's letter. I know that Toby would like to see it!' Turning to Ambrose, she said, 'You will be interested in Cicely's letter, will you not, Toby? And now I wish all the children to come up and tell me their names, for they are so many that I sometimes forget, nowadays.'

'Tibby dear,' said Zelah, 'wilt thee look to all our girls for me? I must enquire how the supper progresses. And, Alice dear, wilt thee introduce thy brood? And, Charlotte dear, thee had best introduce Cicely all over again, for Mrs Dorcas gets confused at times. But how thou wilt explain Cicely's children I know not! William, thy brother's tankard is empty, and Caleb would like more wine. Well, cannot thee help thyself, Caleb, after all these years? Here are thy grandchildren, Mrs Dorcas!' Speaking clearly that Dorcas might hear her.

'Gracious heaven!' Dorcas exclaimed, looking through her eye-glass at the battalion before her. 'Are these all ours, my dears?'

The two sets of Howarths were quite distinct, one from the other. Zelah had imprinted her likeness and her character upon the six golden girls. From tall silken Tabitha to plump velvet Maria, the daughters of Kingswood Hall stood smiling self-consciously, gracefully old-fashioned. One of them giggled, and was hushed. They basked in their brief importance, gravely aware, in spite of their sense of fun, that the party marked their reunion as a family.

But the crowd from Kit's Hill were a mixture of sexes and complexions, giving a general impression of sturdy limbs, rosy faces and curly heads. They had obviously never worried over anything more important than the next square meal in all their young lives. Always uncomfortable in her best clothes, Alice brought forward her offspring, scrubbed and dressed up. In her arms she held the youngest child, some ten months old.

'This 'un's Our Ned!' Wheat-haired and bashful. 'And Our Dicky!' Mischievous. 'And Our Willum!' Ready for his supper. 'And Our Mary!' Over-awed. 'And Our Little George!' Fat. 'And this here's Our Harriet!' Two round brown eyes staring over two round red cheeks. 'And you know me, I reckon!' With an embarrassed laugh.

'Very good indeed, Alice,' said Dorcas, inspecting the line through her eye-glass. 'The children are a credit to you.'

She was always especially kind to Alice, and it showed.

'And who are these?' As Cicely came up, infant in arms, two little fellows clutching at her skirts.

'These are my sons, Grandmama,' Cicely explained hopefully. 'Make your bows, Jarvis and Lucas, if you please, sirs! And this is my daughter.'

'Mamma,' said William loudly, seeing her utterly confounded, 'these are your *great*-grandchildren. *Charlotte's* grandchildren. . . .'

'Charlotte a grandmother?' Dorcas murmured, at a loss. 'Why, how can that be? A grandmother?'

'I am Cicely, Grandmama. Little Cicely!' cried the young woman.

They saw Dorcas visibly correct herself, give herself an admonitory shake of the memory, put herself back on the right course.

'Certainly!' she said briskly. 'It is Cicely, and she has fetched her children all the way from Wiltshire to see me. Come, give me a kiss, Cicely, for you were always a kind and thoughtful girl. And how is dear Jarvis keeping?' Then she was radiant with remembrance, touching the letter in her lap. 'I know that baby. Why, that is Dorcas Pole! The one I was telling you about, Ambrose!'

'Aye, there is my niece!' he cried affectionately.

'Have some more claret,' William advised, 'and let the relationships be. My mother's memory is not what it was!'

'Should you like to hold the baby?' Cicely asked, smiling.

'Oh, yes, if you please,' with childlike pleasure at the prospect. 'For we Dorcases must keep each other company. There are not so many of us, are there?' To the sleeping infant. 'Ambrose, please to slip a cushion under my left arm, so that I can support Dorcas Pole more easily. Ah, let me see her. Yes, I believe she is quite like, Cicely. Quite like!' Looking down at the anonymous little face, looking up with delight. Her glance was as quick and bright and dark as of old, now.

She recollected that she must not hurt anyone's feelings by seeming to have a favourite among them.

'But they are all beautiful, healthy children,' she cried, 'and so many!'

She saw that the youngest Howarths were becoming puzzled and restive.

'Let them go and play, Alice,' she said kindly. 'They have conducted themselves admirably, and I have enjoyed meeting them all at once. But let the children play.'

They were now divided into two groups, and marshalled together under the leadership of Tibby and Kitty, who were organising a game of hide-and-seek before the supper bell rang.

'And when shall *you* marry, Ambrose?' William asked genially. 'We may as well have a few more faces in the family!'

'Lord knows,' he answered, in his father's old manner. 'I love all the ladies, but can settle on none of them.'

'Oh, it is not we who settle such matters, in spite of the customary belief,' said William, only half-joking. 'It is the ladies who make up their minds to have us. We are not the hunters, Ambrose, but the quarry!'

'I am glad,' cried Charlotte, linking arms with her son, teasing her brother, 'that you realise the truth at last!'

The conversation arched above the heads of the oldest and youngest members of the company, who sat peacefully apart. The fire flung up its pink and amber banners, and Dorcas drew back a few inches, covering the infant's cheek with her shawl. Then she looked round and beckoned her granddaughter to her.

'Cicely! I am inclined to take a nap these days, without meaning to, and the fire is so hot—they will build it half way up the chimney-back in this house! So, if you should see me nodding off, my love, will you take the baby from me? I should not like her to fall. And, Cicely, I know very well who the baby is, though William will talk loud and make grimaces as though I do not! She is my first great-grand-daughter, and her name is Dorcas Pole.'

William squinted down the length of the blade, and sharpened his carving-knife as his father had done before him. But this was a token gesture, indicative of his position as head of the Howarth family, and his hospitable intentions. To carve generously for over twenty people would be a marathon exercise, resulting in more cold food than warm regard. So as the host's knife slithered through the first slice of roast sirloin, a man-servant was rapidly cutting a second sirloin at a side-table, while four maids handed hot plates and dishes of vegetables.

'That's a grand bit of beef, Will,' said Dick, with a professional glint of approval at the vast joint.

'Scotch beef, Dick. You advised me to buy Scotch.'

'I did right then,' said Dick, smiling shyly, and he gave Alice a nudge and a wink to sustain her.

'William,' called Zelah, from her end of the table, 'hast thee not a surprise for all to share? Hast thee forgotten, love?'

'No, I had not forgot. I was waiting until everyone had their supper and a glass of wine before them.'

They had, and all but the two infants would taste the claret, even if it were only a few drops to colour the water. William nodded to the butler. The butler snapped his fingers at the footmen. The footmen armed themselves with snuffers and formed into a stately procession. Then everyone saw for the first time that half a dozen curious iron brackets had been fitted into the walls of the dining-room.

'Douse the lights!' cried William, rubbing his hands in anticipation.

Cries of glee and pretended terror as the room dissolved into darkness. Then four fresh little flames shone through the gloom, as the four tall footmen supplied themselves with tapers. The butler stood portentously by the first iron bracket.

'Are you all ready?' William asked. 'Hush, children, if you please. Very well, Clarke!'

Into the silence came a strange sound of hissing, a faint pop, and then the most dazzling illumination. There was a concerted gasp of astonishment and delight. The butler moved sedately from one lamp to the next, turning up the gas, and each time one of the footmen stepped forward with his humble flame and touched the white glare to life. The company shielded their eyes against the blaze, and then, becoming used to it. smiled round in amazement.

Young Jarvis Pole said under his breath, 'And God said, "Let there be Light"!'

Everyone laughed. The tension was broken. The children shouted and clapped, and the Kit's Hill contingent yelled,

'Hip, hip, horray!' and banged the damask cloth with their silver spoons.

'By Gow,' said Dick, deeply impressed, 'it's as good as broad day, isn't it, Alice? I could do wi' summat like that in our cowshed of a winter's night.'

'It will come,' William prophesied confidently. 'There will not be a house, a shop, nor a business in the country which has not the benefit of gas-light sometime in the near future. But it will not be yet, Dick. It is a luxury, as yet.'

Then he was assaulted by a multitude of questions.

'Uncle William!' Hopefully. 'Might it blow up?' 'Why does it smell so nasty?' 'Does it make that hissing noise all the time?' 'Will it go out by itself?' 'Where does it come from?' 'Does it keep itself alight?' 'What's it made of?' 'Uncle William! Has King George got gas-light, too, or is it just you?'

'Nay, I cannot answer you all at once. We have the evening before us to tell you all about gas-light. And your Aunt Zelah thinks we should eat this good food while it is hot. So, everyone, I give you a toast to begin the meal!'

He stood at the head of his long table, a man splendid in his prime, and powerful. They were proud of him, proud to claim him as their own. William Wilde Howarth, Ironmaster of Wyndendale. 'A Man of His Time' the *Wyndendale Post* had called him, when he was appointed magistrate. Did he not know and rub shoulders with the famous men of his day, and entertain a number of them? Had not that hand, extended to them all in welcome only an hour or two ago, shaken the hand of the Prime Minister and the great Duke of Wellington? Was it not rumoured that he might go into Parliament, be offered a title, become heaven knows what? And yet was he not always available to any member of his family, ready to give or lend his money and time and name? So they applauded him, cheered him on.

'I shall be brief!' William promised, holding up one hand for silence. He came to the core of his speech. 'We are a goodly company here tonight. And every one of us, whether connected by blood or marriage—and I do not know which is closer by this time—'

'Hear, hear!' from Dick.

'. . . every one of us is here this evening because of a match made just over half a century ago. A marriage of heart and mind between Miss Dorcas Wilde of Millbridge, and Mr Edward Howarth of Garth Fells. I should like us to drink to them both. To a great lady!' Lifting his glass. And then, easily and deliberately, 'And to a great gentleman! And to all our ancestors. God bless and rest their bones! The Howarths of Kit's Hill!'

Dick flushed up with pleasure, and looked down at his plate confounded. Alice squeezed his fingers, and they smiled at each other. While their progeny, astonished to find themselves so elevated, glanced sideways at their cousins, and sat proudly in their seats: their meat for once forgotten.

Part Four

Man of Worth
1812

TWENTY-SEVEN

The Fuse and the Powder-Keg

January-June 1812

Several thousands of King George's redcoats were at present keeping peace in the Nottingham area, a Bill was passed in Parliament which added frame-breaking to the two hundred other capital offences, and the stockingers were rejoicing in a rise of two shillings a week: all brought about by Luddite action. This mixture of force, threat and fair play was supposed to halt further insurrection, but already the Yorkshire Luddites had fired a gig-mill in Leeds and were carrying out nightly forays against gig-mills and shearing-frames. Lancashire was slower to follow their lead, being divided in council and having a different campaign upon their hands; and this was reflected in the Wyndendale valley where Jim Ogden and his weavers opposed the general committee of the Red Rose Society.

The Millbridge ring-leaders, due to their social standing, were obliged to remain administrators and central advisers. It was their artisan colleagues who headed the groups of men along the valley, and held subsidiary meetings in lonely inns and farmhouses on the moors. So Jack Straw was a legend within the society as well as without, and the body of workers only knew the names of those who carried out orders and led them.

This had worked well until Jim Ogden came to them, for he was not a loyal follower and he had ambitions. Three years since he had taken command of the Whinfold section, four miles from Millbridge, and established The Spinning Yarn on Swarth Moors as his headquarters. Here, in a back room of the tavern, he held sway and held court. To him came weavers from all parts of Wyndendale, knowing he was one of them. They liked his style and the fact that he was pugnacious in their cause. When he reported back the verdict of the committee, and his reply, they cheered him roundly. And throughout the winter he kept them informed of Luddite

341

results and Luddite progress in other places, thus feeding and banking the fires of rebellion. The winter was hard and long, and they were desperate with hunger, but Jim was waiting for the right moment before he acted on his own initiative.

In the third week of March, Cheshire Luddites attacked a warehouse in Stockport, belonging to one of the first manufacturers to use power-looms. There was a pause of two weeks. Then the Church-and-King party called a public meeting at the Manchester Exchange, to congratulate the Prince Regent on changing his coat from Whig to Tory, and the crowd turned the meeting into a boisterous riot. Still Jim Ogden held his hand. Then, as though a wall had been breached, came riots a-plenty, all over Cheshire and Lancashire. Some said these actions were instigated by General Ludd, others that it was the Jacobins. But they were well-organised, armed and violent. The attacks were on a vast scale; threatening letters were followed by action. And yet the action was not of a high military standard.

'That's no bloody good,' said Jim Ogden, sitting with his chief cohorts in the back room of The Spinning Yarn. 'Throwing stones at a mill! Burning the owner's house down! And then getting killed and wounded into the bargain. What's a few muskets and bayonets and a mort of colliers' picks going to do agin the King's soldiers? They're not going to turn tail for the sight of a mob waving a red flag and carrying a man of straw at the head of them! We want plenty of arms, we do, and we want to strike while all's nice and quiet here, afore the soldiery arrive. We want an entry to Snape Ironworks, and we don't send no threatening letters. A burst of gunfire's the best message I know! Are you with me?'

'We're with you, Jim.'

'Mr Howarth,' said Jim Cartwright, 'can I have a word with you a minute, sir? It is important.'

William swung round to judge how important it was, finished giving his message and dismissed the messenger, and bade his foreman sit down.

'Mr Howarth,' said Jim Cartwright, 'I've had word that Snape Ironworks is to be robbed. Quiet-like, mind you, by some as has worked here and knows their way about. But they're after small-arms and ammunition. And it's summat to do with Jack Straw.'

William got up abruptly and strode his small office, ending

up by standing at the little window overlooking the entrance yard.

'Where did you hear this, Jim?'

'Dan Skelton told me, but we should keep that to us-selves. He's mortal feared, Mr Howarth. They come and asked him to let them in, and said as they'd pay him well for doing it.'

'How much?' asked William factually.

'A hundred gold guineas, Mr Howarth.'

'I'd do it myself for that much,' said William obliquely. 'Why has he come to us?'

'He don't believe them, Mr Howarth, and he's feared to be found out by either side.'

'I don't believe them either,' said William, facing his foreman, 'and it doesn't sound like our Jack Straw, who is a peaceful, cunning and housekeeping fellow. He would be more likely to leave me a trade price for my muskets!'

'Aye, but there's a whiff of Jack Straw about it, sir. Dan Skelton knows more than he dare say, and he told me that.'

'Does he know what they want firearms for?'

'He won't say that neither, sir.'

'We shall see,' said William, remembering how they had wrung the sorry truth from Obadiah Low.

'Sir,' said Jim Cartwright, 'I know my man, if you'll pardon my saying so. You press him and he'll panic. Then I don't know where we'll be, sir. Best deal with what he can tell us than lose all and make a muck of it. And if we play it cautious-like, you might catch Jack Straw.'

William considered this carefully, jingling the silver in his pockets.

'Very well, Jim. I'll take your word for it. Tell him to find out when he's to be door-keeper, to accept their offer, and to let them in. We'll be waiting for them. I was going to see him,' he added thoughtfully, 'but I'd better not. There may be others involved, who would notice. Let it remain between you and me, and you and him. Oh, and we'll give the fellow something for his trouble, but it won't be a hundred guineas! And Jim, thank you. I'll make sure you don't lose by your loyalty.'

'Mr Howarth, sir, loyalty don't need rewarding. You're more than welcome.'

A full belly and a fair wage makes for a contented workforce. William had no difficulty in assembling a body of men who could use a musket, and were prepared to fire upon any who entered Snape unlawfully. His own strength and courage, his ability to wield power and yet remain among the people he ruled, and his position of magistrate brought him respect. He had never planned a military resistance before, but he used his common sense and endeavoured to think out all the possible manoeuvres. And, as magistrate, he wielded the law in this part of the valley and did not have to ask anyone's permission or even to report upon what he was doing. The power of life and death was in his hands once he decided to defend his property, and the Crown would stand behind his decision afterwards, come what may.

Snape was never quiet, but the night-workers went about their business quietly as usual, unaware for the most part that the ironmaster and twenty picked men were hidden in and behind the little office at the entrance to the works. The great gates, a monument to Belbrook's artistic vision and fine craftsmanship, had been locked behind the night-force, and the watchman sat in his little sentry-box waiting.

As it grew dark the ironworks seemed to absent itself from the world: a priest performing sacred fire rituals. From time to time the sky was lit by flames from the cupola, and the regular in-drawing and out-going of breath from the iron bellows sounded like a valediction.

On the last stroke of eleven from Snape clock, Dan Skelton ran silently up to the watchman's box, apparently overcame him with a bludgeon, stole his keys and opened the gate, all in a matter of moments. The defenders kept mum and hidden. In another moment half a dozen men materialised from the shadows, so quickly and noiselessly that William jumped slightly. He was seeing the Red Rose in action for the first time. He signalled his cohorts to let them through, and those waiting behind the office captured them with hardly a scuffle. Then they all settled down again to see what happened. Ten, twenty minutes passed. Outside, the night was peaceful. Snape clock chimed the half-hour.

'Was that the lot, Mr Howarth?' Jim Cartwright whispered in his ear.

'Not unless Jack Straw is an utter fool,' William whispered back. 'In his place I should have provided a second attack, or at least a backing force.'

The attack came so swiftly that they were caught unawares. For Ogden the weaver had intended to rob Snape and proceed up the valley at once, and he had his army with him, and the foray had been timed.

The office was perhaps fifty yards from the gates, and, though their burglars had relied on secrecy and conspiracy to make their coup, the rest were armed after a fashion. The whispered word had spread, the men had gathered from building, field and hedgerow; and on a sudden the yard at Snape was full of insurrectionists brandishing forks and scythes, poles with spikes on top, old fowling-pieces and ancient muskets, with a pistol or two for emphasis. They were flooding round the office, looking for their comrades, unaware that they surrounded one small body of armed men and faced another.

Just too late, William shouted, 'Fire!'

The bullets crashed through the office windows and two men fell to the ground, shouting with pain. Almost simultaneously, the foremost rebels met William's second line of defence, who exchanged a few scattered shots and then ran.

'Christ, Mr Howarth,' cried Jim Cartwright, 'there must be close on two hundred of 'em!'

'Keep firing!' said William, seeing no other solution.

The rearguard of Ogden's army was falling back, for they were virtually without an answer to this hail of bullets. The middle of the force followed them as best they could, carrying those who were wounded. But the vanguard had broken up William's little fighting column, firing as they went, releasing their prisoners, and going on to the warehouse where the small-arms were kept.

Unable to move, lest he lose the few men with him, William ordered them to shoot anyone who passed the office. The vanguard were soon back again, for the shouting and shooting had penetrated even the ironworks' resounding clamour. Laden with guns and boxes of bullets Ogden's leaders scuttled past, anxious only to get away now, not returning fire. And as often as they could, the defenders in the office picked off one rebel or another, and kept up a sturdy resistance lest it be realised how few they were and how vulnerable in this mass of insurrectionists.

And when it was all over, and the yard deserted again, they went to count their victories and found them bitter fruit to eat. A brother turned over his brother's body, a father found a son, friend wept for friend—traitor though he had been, according to the law—and William, bending over a shabby figure, recognised the face of Willie Bawker of Garth, with whom he had played marbles in their childhood.

Now blood had been drawn in earnest, and wanted blood for answer. The magistrates sat in special session and agreed unanimously to call in the redcoats. Jack went down personally to Whinfold to demand an explanation of Jim Ogden, which he did not get and which would have been useless anyway. For the weavers were not alone in the Battle of Snape, as it was called. They had among them workmen of every class and kind: glaziers and joiners, bakers and shoemakers, farm labourers, out-workers and the unemployed. The whole of Wyndendale was involved, whether on one side or the other. And when the soldiers marched into Millbridge, to the sound of pipe and drum, they put the nine miles of valley under martial law and no man knew who his ally was, or who his enemy.

'So now we stand and fight, Jack Ackroyd,' said Jim Ogden the weaver, factually for once, 'or put the leg-irons on usselves. They say as Lancashire folk will be hanged for nowt, but I'm not like that. I'll take a few with me if I'm going. And them as cries "Peace!" now is against me and a thousand others!'

He was not alone in this opinion. From Cornwall to Carlisle, as though beacons had been lit upon the hilltops, hundreds of small and large Radical organisations expressed dissatisfaction with the governing bodies. Militia arms magazines were broken into and robbed. Women screamed in the market-places that they were General Ludd's wives, and took the food that was too dear to buy. And in Wyndendale, as elsewhere, the presence of the troops only sharpened wits without deterring the activists. Oath-taking upon the moors began again, and this time in the name of Ned Ludd. More arms were stolen, from farmhouses and private homes: the raiders coming in numbers so great that no one dared resist them. The Red Rose Society seemed to swell, then to change, and at last to become a core of the Luddite army. Now they were drilled, like soldiers, and whereas the name of Jack Straw had been revered it became a password for terror.

In Millbridge respectable citizens withdrew into the safety of their houses, and those who had men to guard them were thankful, and those who had not spent their time in terrified imaginings. No one would have dreamed of disobeying the orders given; indeed, they clutched at them gratefully as the only orders worth having. After curfew, the town was silent except for the sounds of military feet and voices, and the unbelieving cry of the watchman upon his rounds.

'Ten of the clock, and all's well.'

William had left a servant and a brace of pistols at Thornton House, for which Charlotte expressed troubled thanks. He also armed Tom at Bracelet, and every evening, just before curfew, a manservant with a musket walked down to Dorcas's house, to double her protection during the night. At Kit's Hill Dick kept the farmhouse like a fortress, and actually drove off one party of Luddites who called upon him after dark. Four of them were wounded by gunfire and carried away by their comrades. The kitchen windows were broken, and a bullet stuck fast in the back door. Otherwise, no one was harmed and Alice came from under the staircase with her brood, and mulled ale for the victors.

All along the valley nerves quivered, stretched, snapped under the strain. Paid informers found it easier to infiltrate the rebel ranks as numbers grew greater, and unpaid informers eyed the rewards offered and pondered how they could earn them. *The Wyndendale Post* brought no comfort to its readers, as force was answered with force. Notices appeared overnight, roughly chalked on walls and doors.

100 GINNY'S REWARD FOR HED OF PRINSE REJENT

The official notices betrayed their lack of knowledge, at least to the initiated. They were prepared to give fifty guineas for Information Concerning the Person and Whereabouts of one Jack Straw.

Then the real raids began, executed with an impudence and daring which were far more terrifying than the show of arms. The lessons of the Red Rose had been well learned. No one knew from what part of the valley the next attack would come, and sometimes the rebels would start one attack to draw the troops and then concentrate upon another further away. And they knew the terrain as the military did not. It was mild weather, and the rain hurt no one. Luddites appeared and disappeared like wraiths in the Pennine mists, and used the hills and fells to their own advantage. And many a lad, full of adventure, would lie chuckling in his rough eyrie, watching the redcoats stumble and lose their way on the moors.

At the former headquarters in Millbridge Charlotte and

Jack could only wait in sick surmise: swept aside now by the society they had formed and nursed for over a decade.

On a fine June night Garth was startled by the explosion of a rocket, which lit the countryside momentarily and dissolved into drops of golden dew: the familiar sign of an invading band. The majority of the troops had been garrisoned in Millbridge, and the few soldiers stationed in Garth considered themselves to be more in the nature of a deterrent than an instrument of war. Prudently, from the tower of St John the Divine, they scanned the territory and decided to stay where they were. And all the villagers doused their lights and barred their doors, knowing what to expect.

The Luddites were gathering in greater numbers that night than the redcoats had ever seen before: forming six abreast in a long column, flanked by guards with muskets, some bearing torches and all armed with stolen weapons of every description. At the front one tall fellow unfurled a red flag. Immediately behind him rose the effigy of Ned Ludd: a man made of straw. The leader gave words of command. They fell into line and began to march briskly through the village street, as precise and formidable as any of King George's men.

A child woke, hearing the measured tread of many feet, seeing the flare of many torches dancing on the walls, and cried out in terror.

'Mam! What is it, Mam?'

'Hush, my lad, hush. It's nobbut Jack Straw on the march.'

The footsteps passed into silence. Half an hour went by. Slightly ashamed, highly relieved, everyone reached for their tinder-boxes and tallow candles and consoled each other.

'It's not our turn tonight, seemingly!'

In Coldcote another rocket soared, and in Medlar, Childwell, Whinfold and Thornley. At each signal another group of Luddites formed into marching order, swelling the original number as they joined together. By the time they reached Flawnes Green an army of five thousand was marching on Millbridge, and as the local troops of redcoats surveyed the odds they drew back to consult with one another. Some suggested going back along the road to see how their comrades had fared, or to join up with them and follow the Luddites. But their ardour cooled again as they discovered that the valley was guarded all the way by riflemen, keeping a watch on the road. When they had been fired at once or twice, and helped a few wounded to safety, they changed their minds and stayed where they were: temporarily trapped behind Ogden's forces.

As the Luddites passed through each place, the inhabitants breathed more freely, and fastened themselves up close, and would not have ventured forth for a hatful of gold guineas. For the moment they were content that King George's soldiers should confront the forces of General Ludd, and let the contest come out how it might. Not a mouse stirred in the whole length of that dark valley. The flaming brands wound a golden trail to the town, unopposed, and as the Luddites marched they sang a doggerel verse which had caught their fancy, composed by a young weaver in their midst.

> We've come to get thee, Master,
> We've come to break thy loom!
> Our steps march faster, faster,
> They spell out words of doom.
> We'll take our vengeance on thee,
> We'll fire both house and mill.
> And tho' the world fought for thee
> We'd fight thee still.
> We've done wi' dirty dealing,
> We've done wi' being good,
> It's our lives tha'rt stealing,
> And spending our blood.
> But now we'll even up the score,
> So on thy knees, thou'lt rule no more!
> LUDD! LUDD! LUDD!

The last line ended in a great shout, and all who heard it thanked God that they were in no way involved.

The soldiers on guard, across the river in Millbridge, took only a moment to make up their minds that this was a direct confrontation. Then they acted. The town's citizens, hearing bugles blow and the cry 'To arms! To arms!' got out of their beds and hid under them. But they need not have feared for themselves. Jim Ogden, at the head of his army, was not at the moment concerned with peripheral sinners against the working classes. He was bent on the chief sinner, who was that instant peeping out of his bedroom window, in his grand house overlooking the town, quailing at the spectacle.

To Ernest Harbottle's left was the defending force, mobilising in the Market Square, apparently unaware that the Luddites' target was not Millbridge. To his right, preparing to assault his property, was the armed mob. In a nightmare, he heard faint shouts of command, saw the mass of men fan outwards to form into two horns and an attacking head. They were coming straight for the most notorious mill of all.

Their song had ceased. A chant took its place which sounded even more outlandish, more terrifying, as it gained rhythm and momentum.

Ba-by-lon. Ba-by-lon. BA-BY-LON!'

He wanted to cry out to the soldiers, 'Not there, you fools! Here! *Here!*'

But they formed ranks, and drilled, like toys in the Market Square, like dolls who were deaf and dumb and blind to reality. Then they took their posts, and waited, rifles cocked, for the invasion which would not come until Ernest Harbottle and all his possessions were in flames.

The mill was working full blast all night, in spite of Peel's Act which had been passed ten years before. Careful of its profit-makers, Millbridge had contrived to overlook a few broken rules, to wine and dine inspectors who knew which side their wheaten bread was buttered, and to make certain concessions which looked good when printed. Officially, the three mills were working on special orders for the King's forces, under strict supervision. This latter statement was perfectly correct. Their foremen were picked for discipline.

Jim Ogden, insurrectionist by conviction and profession, had fetched the Wyndendale valley to a pitch of comprehension unequalled in its working history. Rumour had run riot through the valley's mills for weeks. The Babylon workers, from stunted child to stunted man and drudging woman, knew what Ned Ludd was all about. They were attuned to this moment, this very moment, when a flicker of fear crossed the foreman's face, when they heard the shouts, when some dared to leave their looms and run to the window and look out, when they alerted their kind, when they shouted in unison with those outside.

'Ludd! Ludd! Ludd!'

Children with red eyes winding bobbins; children treading cotton in tubs; children yawning and falling asleep on their feet; children whose hands were bleeding from piecing the yarn; children being slapped to keep them awake; children crying out of despair and bewilderment; children who had never been children and might never be adults; children with no future, who had better not have been born. These children paused, wondering.

But their parents, and those older and wiser, seized the moment. One man, bigger than the rest, leaped upon the overseer and seized the leather strap he carried, and began to beat him in a kind of frenzy as though he could not stop. Young women, who had no trace of youth about them, picked up their suckling infants, kept by them in old boxes, and ran for the main door. The mills poured slaves, the cobbles echoed to the clatter of a thousand clogs, and as they ran to freedom, to help the rebels burn the place which had enslaved them, they joined in the shout of *'Luddl Luddl Luddl'*

Charlotte, in addition to her personal troubles, had been asked to house three officers, and was thus forced to watch the reversal of her former policies in company with the enemy. The requisitioning had come upon her so rapidly, and the situation had changed so fundamentally, that all her notes on the Red Rose Society—and enough evidence to hang several people—still lay in a locked box beneath the floorboards of Ambrose's old room. There Colonel Ryder slept, and so far she had not been able to prise up the boards and burn the papers. The last weeks had been torment to her. The news had swung first one way and then the other. William's account of the Battle of Snape had saddened her, for she recognised Willie Bowker as one of their people. The thought of Dorcas, old and resolute but privately afraid, concerned her. The story of Dick defending his family, and the house in which they had been born, caused her most grief, for suppose they had been hurt and Kit's Hill burned? Whichever way she turned, she could find no relief from the thought that she was responsible for this, though it had turned out other than she had planned. And then the officers, courteous to her and grateful for the hospitality and cooking at Thornton House, she could not help but like. They were brave men, and some had been wounded in the long fight with France. They were human beings, having wives and children, or sweethearts and families, who awaited them. The only difference lay in their beliefs, which were not hers.

Now, as the night sky lit with the fires of Belbrook down the valley, she came from her sleepless bed and looked through the window on to the Market Square. The noise of the bugle, the knocking at the front door, had roused her lodgers. They were buckling on their sabres, preparing to mount their horses kept at The Royal George—clattering down the stairs, waking Sally and Polly and herself. Charlotte put on her wrapper, and hurried after them, with her maids following. William's second footman had scrambled from his temporary bed in the kitchen, clutching his brace of pistols, ready to defend the house against a mad world.

'Ma'am!' said Colonel Ryder, saluting. 'Fear nothing, ma'am. We have had the defence of the town in the forefront of our minds for long enough. You may sleep sound, ma'am!'

A little selfconscious in their role as protectors, the officers ran down the steps and into the mêlée outside. Sally was crying. It was many years since she had left her family in Garth, and she only visited them to show off her new clothes nowadays, but in the hour of war they became dear to her.

'Oh, ma'am. Oh, Miss Charlotte!' she cried, terrified. 'Whatever will become of my poor mother?'

'We shall have tea,' Charlotte decided, as being the most comforting thing she could offer. 'We shall sit up until all is over, and drink tea.'

At the school the headmaster quietened his assembled boarders. Mind you, they were only half afraid. The other half longed for blood and slaughter, so long as it did not come too close to home. He gave them permission to stay up, provided there was no panic or noise. And he, and the other masters, patrolled the building, keeping order. It was some small comfort to Jack Ackroyd that two members of the original committee were with him. Charlotte was entirely alone. She sat at the window of her front parlour, hands clasped in her lap, and silently prayed for forgiveness.

By two o'clock in the morning, at Kingswood Hall, William heard that several thousand Luddites had marched up the valley, and left single riflemen behind them to hold the rear. He acted at once, departing for the ironworks with half a dozen armed servants, leaving enough men behind him to guard his household. He called at Bracelet on the way, and knocked them all up, insisting that Dorcas, Nellie and Tom leave at once for the safety of the Hall, and seeing them escorted thither before he continued his journey. That they were all three old, shaky, and frightened by his urgency did not occur to him. He would have been better to let them alone, but he could not, and they were too feeble to resist him.

By this time Ludd's army was well on the way to Mill-bridge, their guards at the rear were no longer upon their mettle, and the redcoats were sufficiently recovered to have thought of counter-attacking. Even as William reached Snape, the small local patrols were finding their way to each other, dodging through the trees and across the fields above the main road. Hearing nothing more, and being the braver for the silence, a number of male householders also reached for clubs, blunder-busses and the like, ready to be called into action should anyone think of doing so. William, now with small-arms and ammunition loaded into a wagon, his force augmented by a number of sturdy neighbours, began to follow the Luddites to Millbridge. At first there were exchanges of gunfire with solitary marksmen, but nothing very serious on either side. Then they met three or four groups of redcoats who had joined up together, which heartened them all. And, in his role as magistrate, William used Luddite methods to combat the Luddites, by knocking on doors and demanding men and muskets. But this time it was in the name of the King.

Sincerely determined, but experiencing a *frisson* of delight at the adventure and the hour, the ironmaster rode sternly at the head of his civilian column on a white horse. And in front of them, bullied back to their senses by a furiously moustached sergeant, the reunited soldiers now marched briskly, looked round them alertly for signs of rebels, and once more shouldered their rifles with bravado.

That spur of land which Ernest Harbottle had rented so reasonably from Lord Kersall, and built into a swarming township of his own, was now surrounded. For every Luddite who shouted his battle-cry there was a slave to echo him, an extra pair of hands to help him stack kindling round the mill. Some called for a battering-ram to break into the owner's villa, and began to saw down noble trees at the end of Ernest Harbottle's fine garden. Some picked up an iron bar or a wooden cudgel and prepared to avenge a private grievance, a personal injury. Many were the houses, that night in Wyndendale, which suffered professional visits from burglars who took advantage of the moment. Many were the little tyrants who recognised, under the mask of Luddism, a humble single enemy come to strike them down.

The Luddite army was being hindered by help. Ogden and his lieutenants called their forces together and bade them stay together, let the rest do what they would. Thirty years since, Jack Ackroyd and a mere fraction of these numbers had taken and burned down the first spinning-mill in the valley without loss of life, without a wound, without redress: quickly, quietly and efficiently. But this great mob screamed orders and countermanded them, fetched and carried away again, fought to be among the vanguard, snatched weapons even when they could not use them, and hampered those with cooler heads and more purposeful minds.

Not everyone was out of the Babylon mill. There were children sleeping head to tail in the crowded dormitories, overseers keeping feebler women back, men lying dazed where they had been knocked down and trampled in the rush for freedom. But there was no time for considering niceties such as these. The spearhead of Luddites thrust their way in, and the few defenders fled, hoping to be taken for rebels until they could creep away. Through the great clanking, clattering rooms ran the Luddites, yelling to everyone to get out of their way if they valued their lives. They had fetched barrels of gunpowder with them, oil and fuses, and they shouted that any who stayed would be blown and burned to hell. Still no one thought to clear the place completely before it was destroyed: the inmates because they were too stupid with excitement and terror, the Luddites because they had not time. So the majority of Babylon's workers tumbled and scuffled outside, leaving the helpless and uncomprehending behind them.

'Stand back!' roared Jim Ogden.

His men forced the crowd back. The fuses were lit. They stood almost hushed. Then a great cry rose, for there were faces of fear at the windows of the mill.

'Keep back, keep back!' Ogden shouted, 'Shoot down them as moves!'

The line of onlookers at the front swayed to and fro, curved, altered shape as they struggled to control those who had seen the victims call soundlessly for help. But one or two broke through the line and ran zig-zag, to avoid the gunfire, towards the doomed building. The fine trail of sparks ran faster, faster, gobbling up time.

'Back, back! Further back! Let them go if they wants!' yelled Ogden.

The gunfire ceased. The rescuers were almost at the entrance. The faces in the windows were all mouths crying. Then Babylon blew like one great cosmic powder-keg.

'Dunnot leave me!' cried Harbottle, clutching at the running servant.

'Nay, look after thyself!' muttered the man, and disappeared.

Mrs Harbottle and her daughters and their maids were all locked up in the servants' attic. But Ernest had felt safer in the midst of his men, until they saw the mill go, and the army form into its head and horns again and march for Millside Towers. Now he ran up the stairs and banged upon the attic door, shouting, 'Let me in! Let me in!' A chorus of screams was his only answer.

The Luddites had brought a battering-ram, and they now took up their positions and awaited the word of command. They had been drilled for this moment in the past weeks, and so far everything had gone according to plan. They were exultant as they lifted the mighty oak trunk and began to swing it rhythmically, and as the handsome door started to give their chant grew louder.

'Ba-by-lon. *Ba-by-lon*. BA-BY-LON.'

Halfway down his staircase, no longer able to move backwards or forwards, Ernest Harbottle sat down and wept like a frightened child, and rocked to and fro in his fear and grief.

Ogden took charge of him. He was too precious a hostage to lose. The weaver smiled at the spectacle the mill-owner made, in his crumpled nightshirt, tasselled cap over one eye. And he ordered his men to get everyone out of the villa and set fire to it, while Harbottle watched.

They smashed and broke and mutilated everything that they would burn, in a frenzy of hatred: grinding little precious things underfoot, shattering glass, beating elegant chairs to pieces against the fine papered walls. And when they had spent their rage they threw their torches into the midst of the kindling, and watched it roar.

Then Ogden once again brought his forces to order, though all around them was chaos. And he looked upon the destruction he had wrought, and the people he had roused, and reckoned that one last coup would see him sitting in the Town Hall as head of a Radical valley.

'We've had enough of him!' Ogden shouted into Harbottle's gaping face. 'We'll use thee instead!'

And he cast the man of straw into the flames, and told his men to strap the mill-owner to a pole. They set his nightcap rakishly over one eye, and slapped his quivering cheeks, and hoisted him up on to their shoulders. He perched there, slack-jawed and sawdust-limbed. They could not help but laugh when they looked at him.

'Now,' said Ogden, spreading his rough map upon a flat stone, and scanning it in the light from Babylon, 'there's three ways of getting into Millbridge from here. We can go scrambling up into the woods of Kersall's estate and come down into the town, but that's a hell of a long way round and we could easy get lost. So there's the straight way, over the river and through Millgate, or else right down as far as the turnpike road and up through the middle of the town. What we want to do is to make them think we're attacking head on, then they'll fetch most soldiers to defend Millgate. But only the spearhead'll be there. We'll send the rest down to the turnpike road, and rush them. There's nobbut five hundred redcoats in Millbridge, at the outside. There's nigh on five thousand of us!'

Hurrying along the road past Flawnes Green, the crowd of valley soldiers, mounted magistrates with civil guards, and armed citizens heard the explosion of gunpowder and saw the sky flame on the hillside.

'That's Babylon!' said Squire Brigge. 'What on earth are your fellows doing about it, sergeant? Why isn't Colonel Ryder there?'

'He will be holding Millbridge,' said William. 'He can hardly march out for every diversion!'

'Then, Mr Howarth, should we not engage with them?'

'I admire your spirit, Squire,' said William, smiling, 'but with our numbers we shall have to rely upon wit rather than courage. No, we should join Colonel Ryder. If the Luddites take Millbridge God knows where we shall be!'

'Colonel Ryder will be barricading the town north and south, sir,' said the sergeant. 'Those are the weak spots.'

'Then we'll join him at Millgate,' said Squire Brigge, riding forward again.

But as they rounded the final bend of the road they saw the insurrectionists preparing to cross the Wynden, and halted, seeing their way barred. From their vantage-point they watched Ogden divide his forces and send the greater part southwards.

'We dursen't come up on them from behind, sir,' said the sergeant to William.

'No, but we can get into Millbridge by a back entrance,' said the ironmaster, looking up to his left. 'I dare say Lord

Kersall would not mind our trespassing on his property for once, would he, Squire? And once there we can lend our support where it is most needed. For they look as though they intend to draw fire at Millgate but come up from the turnpike road!'

The going was awkward, particularly with the wagon, but they all scrambled breathlessly up through the woods, and terrified a gamekeeper on watch. The noble lord, though ill-equipped for modern warfare, had roused his household and disposed them round the estate. In the enigma of the night, William and the civil guard might have been shot before they could reveal themselves as friends, but the soldiers' bright uniforms were better than an introduction and they all arrived safely at the house.

'Tell me, Mr Howarth,' said Lord Kersall conversationally, as the ironmaster joined him on the terrace, 'do you think these damned things would fire? I have them trained in the right direction.'

And he pointed to a couple of ancient cannons and a pyramid of rusty roundshot.

'I doubt it, my lord, and if they did they might inflict more damage upon you than on the rebels. We are a little too late to fetch anything newer from Snape. Perhaps you would like to put in a personal order, in case of future trouble?'

'Are you serious, Mr Howarth?' Testily.

'Not entirely, my lord,' said William, unable to disguise his high spirits.

'This is hardly the occasion for merriment, sir!' Sternly.

'I beg your lordship's pardon,' William replied, courteous but unrepentant. 'If your lordship would excuse us, we are bound for the south of the town, where the rebels will make their heaviest assault. We plan to surprise them there. They will not be expecting reinforcements from our quarter!'

'Well done, well done,' said Lord Kersall, bidding his man-servants let the civil force go forward. 'You may cut down through the Park, Mr Howarth!'

Which was most kind of him. For the tread of horses and men, and the wheels of the wagon with its load of firearms, made a mire of his greensward which would take months to put right.

The Luddites halted in the shadowy road, at a safe distance from Millgate barricade, and paused to consider the situation.

'They'll be waiting behind there, ready to cut us to ribbons!' said one of Ogden's lieutenants.

'Nay, we've nobbut got to keep 'em occupied, and the lads'll come up from behind,' said Ogden. 'Here, let's try owd Harbottle, and see what their trigger-fingers is like!'

They brought the mill-owner down from their shoulders and untied him. He mouthed at them, helplessly. Some felt uneasy. They could shoot in the heat of the fray, mesmerised by the chants of their fellows, but the thought of sending a man to his death in cold blood disturbed them. Ogden was different.

'Here, Harbottle,' he said. 'Run over there. Run! Or I'll pick you off myself!' And he raised his rifle and pointed it at the man's heart.

Obediently, Harbottle bolted from the shadows. The defenders opened fire almost simultaneously. He gave one shrill scream which was cut off abruptly. He spun, rolled, kicked in the spitting bullets. Then turned on his side and lay still.

'Right,' said Ogden coolly, 'now keep 'em busy, and keep out of range.'

His lieutenants obeyed without answering, but their appetite for battle had been sated. They were weary with emotion and exhaustion. In their ranks were murmurs of doubt and discontent. They had burned Babylon, which was what they came for. A siege of Millbridge was too much. Besides, it would be getting light in an hour or so and they feared recognition. And the body of the mill-owner seemed pitiable now, lying in the road with its knees drawn up and its nightcap set awry.

Now a white flag was waved from behind the barricade, and a request to speak with the leader of the Luddites was bawled out. In the ensuing quiet Jim Ogden and two guards stepped forward, and were rewarded by the sight of Colonel Ryder coming up like some bemedalled puppet, flanked by two red-coats.

'I should warn you that you cannot win a fight with professional soldiers,' cried the colonel, 'and lives will be lost upon both sides needlessly, also the lives and property of innocent people endangered. We are expecting reinforcements at any time now, who will overwhelm you, but we can hold you for as long as you care to engage with us. Go back, and thank God for the chance I am giving you. You do not deserve it!' Grimly. 'And we shall continue to hunt you down! But, for the sake of Millbridge and its citizens, I ask you to disperse peacefully, and not a shot will be fired upon you as you withdraw.'

A murmur among the Luddites at the back seemed to indicate agreement, but Ogden was too near to total victory.

'Now I'll tell you summat!' he shouted at the colonel. 'You're on the losing side, my lad, not us. You've sent for reinforcements, have you? Where to? Bradford? They're too busy looking after our Yorkshire brothers there! Preston? They won't get here in time. You know as well as I do that this country's on the brink of civil war, and your lot's fighting the French as well as trying to hold us, and some of you'd come over to us for two pins! We know how many men you've got, and we've got ten times that, and ten times ten'll follow us when we've taken Millbridge. So look to your muskets, and watch that fancy moustache of yours—it might get blowed off!'

'I will give you two minutes to return to your ranks,' said Colonel Ryder, watch in hand, 'and then my men will open fire.'

'Bloody playing at it!' muttered Ogden in disgust, retreating. 'Right!' he ordered his army. 'Keep out of range, and keep popping at them.'

'Well done, sir!' said Captain Munnion, shaking William by the hand. 'I will give you your orders, if I may? The old Roman road cuts straight between the High Street and the turnpike road. There is too much territory to defend beyond it. So we are grouping all the way along the old road, and also guarding either end. The canal bank is covered, and the old town wall fully manned. I wish your people to stay at the back and form an inner shield of defence. And when I give the order to advance, sir, that only applies to my men, not to yours. You are to be the last hope for Millbridge's safety. But it should not come to that.'

He spoke factually, cheerfully. But William knew very well that if they had already decided to give up the turnpike road and all the ground between there and the old road, the number of troops was too small for comfort.

Several times in the last fortnight Charlotte had endeavoured to enter the colonel's room when he was out: only to be foiled by the presence of his batman, quietly brushing or polishing his master's uniform; or by hearing one of the other batmen, or another officer, in the rooms nearby. Now, as the

359

troops concentrated on the Luddites, she hurried up the stairs and softly into the deserted room.

The colonel had made himself comfortable, in an austere fashion. And the heavy clothes chest, which usually stood under the window, had been moved to the foot of his bed, directly over the floorboards she needed to raise.

Hours since, three army messengers had galloped along the turnpike road, headed for Bradford, Bolton and Preston, to beg for extra troops. Now reinforcements were coming, with more dash than their numbers warranted: the foot-soldiers at a trot, the cavalry at a swifter pace. But in the steady burst of rifle-fire the Luddites were losing their taste for battle. Their strength lay in the speed of a single raid with a single purpose. They were not trained for the long and arduous siege, and Jim Ogden had mistaken their enthusiasm for endurance. Once, twice, they rushed forward and inflicted some damage on the defending forces. Then they hung back. Their hesitation was noted and judged correctly by professional eyes; and William saw something which made him marvel—then, and when he was too old to do anything else but remember.

The redcoats formed into a double rank; one kneeling, one standing.

'Move the barricade!' Captain Munnion ordered briskly.

The Luddites, in astonishment, now saw the objective they had failed to achieve miraculously reached. There were the soldiers, few enough in all conscience, with a civilian group standing well to the back of them, and nothing between them and destruction.

With a whoop of victory they ran forward, rifles at the ready. And in that moment Captain Munnion cried, 'Fire!'

The redcoats had been trained to die in formation. Rank by rank, one kneeling, one standing, they moved forward: firing, turn by turn about. They came on in the manner of automatons, and even though some fell the others continued to advance. There was, at once, something so wonderful and so inhuman about them that nothing short of a machine would have withstood them. And their shots were thinning the Luddite ranks to such an extent that the rebels could no longer carry off their injured. The Luddite front-line made a convulsive movement, broke, and scattered. Their concerted run for safety was matched by a similar retreat at the other end of the town.

Still the redcoats fired and advanced, fired and advanced, until they were ordered to cease: when they immediately became ordinary men again, grinning in self-congratulation. And William and his force chased after the rebels.

'I did tell the fellow,' said Colonel Ryder, pulling his moustache in quiet satisfaction, 'that they could not win against professional soldiers! This hit-and-run business is all very well, but it takes a trained man to advance steadily under fire.'

They were bringing in the dead and wounded on both sides. The siege of Millbridge was over: a mere footnote in the history of Lancashire Luddism.

TWENTY-EIGHT

The Last Straw

July 1812

The ironmaster was a hero, and no doubt he felt that the honour was deserved. *The Wyndendale Post* spoke warmly of his services to the community, and ended with a diatribe on the offending Luddites.

'. . . their Leaders must be Rooted Out, their followers Hunted Down, their Hiding-places Discovered, and all connected with them, Man, Woman and Child, be Punished with the Utmost Severity of the Law. . . .'

Whereas Colonel Ryder was stern but just, some of his junior officers and most of the sergeants were interested only in obtaining results. Wounded and captured Luddites were interrogated without thought or care for their condition. Soldiers burst into suspected houses, roughly questioned suspected persons, and flung the smallest offender into prison. On the strength of a doubt, a hint, a careless word, all were in peril. Every scrap of information was ruthlessly followed up. Again, wrongs and grievances of a private nature were aired under guise of loyalty to the Crown, and many a lead ended in nothing more seditious than an old quarrel. But this was martial law with a vengeance, and Wyndendale groaned under a new oppressor. The army net was cast wide, and as they were not too particular as to the quantity of the catch, they were bound to haul in something of value sooner or later.

The first member of the Red Rose committee to be caught was Hal Middleton, the printer from Flawnes Green. His journeyman, in the years of apprenticeship, had been proud to run errands for Jack Straw. But, as an older man, he tended to hold his tongue and watch events. And after the siege of Millbridge he reckoned he had better save his own skin before he was arrested with his master. So Hal Middleton came up before Colonel Ryder, looking the worse for his arrest, but steadfast in his silence. He was shown an old Red Rose broadsheet which had been printed on his machine, several copies of Tom Paine's *Rights of Man*, printed extracts from Cobbett's *Political Register*, and a set of handbills ready to be distributed. He could not deny his offence, but he declined to implicate anyone else. So they threw him into the town jail, which had never been spacious and was now severely overcrowded. Then they fetched his journeyman in again, and combed his mind until he remembered events in which he had been involved long since. They offered him a King's Pardon, on the grounds that he had been young and foolish, and he dredged up everything he knew. And the links began to form a chain.

Circumstances had been too difficult, the atmosphere too tense, to continue evening classes at Thornton House and the grammar school; and the presence of Charlotte's lodgers kept Jack at a distance. But the demise of her Working People's Society, the importance of her army officers, and her brother's courage and initiative brought Charlotte back into favour with genteel Millbridgers.

The Misses Whitehead, now in their eighties, had always kept in touch. Mrs Matthew Standish had never cut Charlotte in the street. And Mrs Graham had been forced to acknowledge her because they were related via the Jarvis Poles' marriage. But now, in the lull after the Luddite storm, Thornton House began to seem a proper place to visit again, and ladies thought of leaving their cards.

That July Tuesday, uncertain whether to be wet or hot, managed to be both. Millbridge first drowned, then steamed, and all its noxious vapours rose to offend the nostrils. Charlotte had been sitting in the parlour, in a despair of mind and body, when Polly announced that they had run out of milk.

A longing for fresh air overcame her lassitude.

'I shall fetch the milk myself,' said Charlotte decidedly.

'But Boulton's farm is above a mile off, Mrs Longe!'

'I have walked more than a mile in my day, Polly. Give me the can. I have nothing else to do.'

So she set forth, feeling younger and more carefree than at any time in the past twelve years. She remembered London in the hot summer of '89, when she had walked through the crowded streets, knowing she had money in her pocket, a means of earning her living, and the desire to love Toby again. Today, Millbridge had just such an air of carelessness, born of excitement and uncertainty. Folk smiled when they learned her errand, though a month ago they would have looked askance. And Mrs Graham cried archly, across the High Street, 'Do not forget what day it is, Charlotte!'

But Charlotte simply waved and smiled, not taking in the meaning of the words, being grateful for the friendly tone of voice. She had been a pariah for a long time. It was nectar and ambrosia to be received again. If she had not promised to fetch back the milk, she thought, she would have walked the length of Wyndendale; calling in to see poor Caleb at Belbrook, taking luncheon with Dorcas at Bracelet, drinking tea at Kingswood Hall with Zelah and the girls, and coming to rest at last in Kit's Hill for supper. What an age it was since she last visited the house of her birth. On a day such as this, forty years since, she and William would have scrambled to the top of Scarth Nick and sat on the coarse grass and known the entire valley for their own. What a childhood theirs had been: loved and set free in the grey farmhouse, living within the circle of Ned and Dorcas, lying awake and unafraid as they listened to the wild wind scouring Garth Fells.

Strangers, seeing her coming towards them from a distance, swinging the milk-can in one hand, took her for a young girl on an errand. Her fair hair was pulled into a careless knot, her muslin gown was simple, her waist still narrow. Then as she came close they saw that time had claimed her. But still she walked and smiled as though she were sweet and twenty, and they thought how happy she must be to carry her years so lightly.

She popped her head round the door of the smithy at Flawnes Green, and asked for a mug of water. They made much of her. She dandled the latest infant and praised its health and beauty: passed on. The afternoon was magical. All would yet be well.

Mrs Boulton herself filled the copper can, and said as how they didn't know what the world was coming to, but England had allus been a good country to live in, and would be again, despite all.

With a pang of regret, she turned towards Millbridge. The journey was still beautiful, but sad now, for her family were in the opposite direction. She walked less eagerly, and the milk was heavy in her hand. By the time she reached Thornton House her idyll was over. Polly opened the door with an alacrity which presaged news of some sort.

'It's Mr Awkright, ma'am. He's been waiting and fretting for above an hour!'

He was grey with tiredness, and the lines on his face were deeply marked, but he endeavoured to smile and incline his head in greeting. As Polly closed the door he seized Charlotte's hands.

'I had to tell you myself, Lottie. They have arrested Dr Wilkins. He was attending a former member of the Red Rose, wounded in the Luddite rising at Babylon. The man is in agony with a shattered limb, but they dragged him out as well as the doctor. Charlotte, you have destroyed the papers, have you not?'

She shook her head, white to the lips.

'For God's sake, woman, why not?' he cried, and then dropped his voice lest they be heard. 'Why not?'

'I had no time, Jack. They have not left the house for a minute, except at the town siege. And there is a great chest pulled over the hiding-place, which would take two people at least to move. No! Do not look like that! Can you imagine how it has been, here? I am nearly out of my mind. . . .'

'But could you not say you must clean out the room, or some such excuse? Take Polly with you. Confide in her, since you must. She will be faithful.'

She pulled her hands away, crying, 'I will not implicate poor Polly. There are enough in danger as it is.'

He sat down and put his face in his hands, thinking. The long clock in the hall chimed thrice, calm and gracious in the hurly-burly. The door-knocker sounded very loud, and both of them jumped and looked at each other in terror.

'It is a woman's voice,' said Charlotte in relief. 'But who could that be? I am expecting no one.'

Before Polly could announce the visitor the knocker sounded again. A duet of female voices was augmented by yet another summons, yet another voice. The parlour door was opened in a hurry.

Flustered, Polly cried, 'Mrs Graman, Miss Frances Whitebred, and Mrs Sandwich, ma'am!'

The knocker was in brisk demand. Another lady's voice was heard, and then the deeper tones of a man. Charlotte and Jack rose together in mute astonishment.

Mrs Graham had stopped short at the sight of the headmaster, and then decided to let bygones be bygones for the afternoon. She extended her fingers to Charlotte.

'Why, we have caught you unawares,' she cried archly. 'But did you not hear me remind you, when we met in the High Street? It is Tuesday, my dear.'

'Tuesday?' Charlotte echoed, as in a nightmare.

'Your old calling day!' said Mrs Graham. 'We are all coming to call upon you. As of old, my dear.'

'But what a surprise!' cried Charlotte, trying to sound pleased.

Jack saw by her expression, and the way she took Polly hastily to one side to question her about the state of cake and biscuits, that a tea-party would be the final straw. He made up his mind to be distinctly agreeable and help her over it. So he sat down again, instead of departing in his usual flurry of coattails and cravat-ends, and addressed himself to Miss Frances Whitehead who was looking at him timidly.

'And how are you and your sister keeping, ma'am?' he enquired. 'Are you enjoying a well-earned retirement from the rigours of teaching? I confess, I look forward to my own retirement eventually.'

'. . . then run round to the bakehouse,' Charlotte whispered, 'there is no means of baking anything here, and no time to light the kitchen fire and warm the oven. And fetch tea, and the biscuits you have, immediately. . . .'

'And were your pupils very much afraid during the siege, Mr Ackroyd?'

'Just a minute, ma'am. There's the knocker again!' cried poor Polly, as bemused as her mistress with all this hospitality.

And Colonel Ryder, clanking down the stairs, immaculate as ever, was besieged as he passed the parlour. A chorus of ladies caused him to enter and bow and accept compliments.

'We shall miss you, Colonel, when you are gone,' said Mrs Graham, coyly fanning herself. 'We are greatly in your debt, sir.'

'Well, we are not yet gone,' he reminded her, smiling, 'but shall not be very long, I think. The worst of the rebellion is over, here and elsewhere.'

Sally, taking thought for the honour of the house, now sent the scullery-maid in with a tray of cups and saucers, to show them that tea was on the way.

'We are most grateful, sir,' said Miss Frances, and her frail head trembled in emphasis. 'We feel that you have protected more than our lives. It is because of these brave soldiers, I tell my sister, that we can be so pleasant together. Such a matter as taking tea with old friends may seem trivial to you, sir, but it means much to us.'

He bowed again, made some good-mannered comment, and turned to Charlotte.

'My batman tells me, Mrs Longe, that you have once or twice endeavoured to see my room set to rights. It is well enough for me, madam, but am I interrupting some household ritual?'

He spoke in the manner of a man who has been long married, and understands that there are matters of great importance to women which would not occur to him.

'Sir, you put me to shame before my friends!' Charlotte cried, so relieved at this opportunity that she could have laughed aloud. 'Now they will see me for the poor housekeeper that I am! There has been so much trouble of late that, with one and the other thing, you and your fellow-officers came upon me in the midst of our spring-cleaning, and your room was not yet done. That is all, sir. But if we had a day to ourselves we could easily set it right.'

'If that is your problem, madam,' he said courteously, 'I shall leave my room for the whole of tomorrow, at your entire disposal. I crave the pardon of yourself and your friends for introducing such a domestic issue!'

They all laughed, and Mrs Graham said afterwards that the party went quite merrily, and even the headmaster was most entertaining and amicable.

Then Polly came back from the bakehouse with a batch of fresh cakes and biscuits, and the kitchen staff made haste to put up a good show. So it was one of the strangest and nicest days Charlotte could remember.

Jack took care to leave with the rest, but he left last of all and managed a private word with her as he bent over her hand.

'It has not been so bad, Lottie! I believe we can face it out together. I shall see you shortly.'

They made a great palaver with mops and pails and hot soapy water the following morning, and asked the batmen to move the furniture out. Then, in the scrubbed expanse of bare boards covered with clean newspapers, Charlotte and Polly faced each other.

'You should've told me afore,' Polly whispered hoarsely, reproachfully. 'We've known each other long enough, I should think!'

'Oh, I could weep,' said Charlotte softly, 'but, Polly, swear to me that you will forget all this for your own sake. I beg you to know nothing. For your own sake, my dear.'

'Don't you fret, ma'am,' said Polly briskly. 'I can act as daft as a brush, if I want. They won't get nothink out of me.'

Together they lifted the boards which hid the box, and Charlotte got it safely out. Then, with Polly watching for signs of lodgers or servants, they conveyed it downstairs to the parlour, and hid it in a cupboard.

'We must light the fire,' said Charlotte. 'No, not now. That would seem suspicious, for the weather is hot. This evening. Late. Lay it for me, Polly, and then put the fire-screen back.'

In her new mood of confidence she helped her maids to finish off the colonel's room later that day. And even picked flowers from the garden, to put in a little silver vase upon his chest of drawers. Then she busied herself in the way which most calmed and ordered her mind, writing letters to those about her: one to Dorcas, promising that she should ride down to see her and would stay the night if she wished; one to Zelah, to say that she would be coming to Bracelet the following week and hoped to call on her, and asking after her sister-in-law's health, for Zelah was once again with child; a simple letter to Dick and Alice, saying that she would like to visit them when the harvest was over. Though she did not know this, she was setting herself aright by returning to her beginnings.

The hour drew close when all but herself were abed. Alone, serene, she lit the parlour fire and sat upon the hearth-rug watching it burn up bright. She fetched the box from the cupboard. She was standing with it in her hands when the door burst open and Colonel Ryder stood there, officers behind him.

'Do not touch those papers, madam,' he said commandingly. 'I believe them to be King's Evidence.'

His order halted her only for a second. In the instant that she realised she had been trapped, that they must have crept down and waited at the keyhole, hoping to catch her in the act, she flung back the lid and seized the papers at the top. The soldiers leaped to intercept her, but she threw the box at them and thrust the list which named both committee and leaders deep into the heart of the fire. She was conscious of pain, of crying out, and still she held the burning papers in the flame until they pinioned her arms behind her. Then she faced the colonel, victorious in this attempt at least, and sought to shield Jack Ackroyd. For he would live and learn from these events, and go on as she was not destined to do.

'I am guilty of forming, organising and directing the secret society of the Red Rose, known by its password, *Jack Straw*,' she said as steadily as she could, but her fingers were piercing her in their trouble. 'You have no need to look further, Colonel Ryder. You will find that I have knowledge of such societies in the past. My husband, Tobias Longe, was a well-known Radical and active member for parliamentary reform.'

'We have a considerable dossier on you, Mrs Longe,' said the colonel. 'You have been watched these past six months. But we could find no evidence against you, until you sought to burn those papers.'

As though she had sent him a message in her trouble, Jack rose from his desk where he was working late, and went to the window overlooking the High Street.

She was even now coming down the steps of Thornton House for the last time, wrapped in her old mantle, one hand bandaged, escorted by two officers. Behind them, Colonel Ryder carried the metal box of King's Evidence which could hang her by the neck until she was dead.

Unhurriedly, he reached for his own greatcoat. Though it was summer, the prisons were notoriously damp, and God knew how long it would be before they came to trial. He put all the money he had into a leather bag, and pushed it into his pocket. He looked round his room, engraving it upon his memory. He looked across the High Street at Charlotte's window. Then he ran down the stairs and caught up with the little group as it marched towards the jail.

Charlotte said instinctively, 'No, Jack!'

But he addressed himself to Colonel Ryder, briefly, almost peremptorily.

'Sir, I am Jack Straw!'

And put out his hand to touch her wounded one, so that she should know they were together even in this.

TWENTY-NINE

Speeches, Fear and Treason

In the royal duchy of Lancaster, late that summer, a man could not find a room for love or money. Every inn was bursting, every lodging-house crammed from attic to basement, and all charging the most monstrous prices. Solicitor Quirk, who booked accommodation for the four judges and their retinues, said he had never known anything like it. The Wyndendale Rising had fetched upon itself the full panoply of the law. A Special Commission was descending from London to conduct exemplary trials and order exemplary hangings, for the good of the nation; bringing with it five distinguished barristers for the prosecution, a flock of witnesses, and such necessary fleas as courtroom artists and journalists. For the defence, on the other hand, stood only three lawyers of fair repute who had demanded their fees before they went into court; and a mere handful of people who could testify to the former good character of some of the prisoners. Over a hundred honest men and true had been sifted to find twelve jurymen. And the sheriff's chaplain was busy polishing his sermon, which he had based upon the stricture 'Put the Evil away from the Midst of Thee' (*Deuteronomy 13:5*) and would preach in St Mary's Church before the trials began.

Though Lancaster's history was long and embattled it did not give the appearance of a medieval town, owing to the amount of building done in the reign of the three Georges. Penny's Hospital and the Quaker meeting-house were coming up to their century, but the Town Hall with its vast Tuscan portico, the majority of fine houses and Glasson Docks were no more than thirty years old. Even the castle, rising from its rock above the broad river, had been re-modelled to contain a Shire Hall and a jail within the last decade. So the first impression on the visitor was that of a stately modern place.

This graciousness would have delighted Dorcas Howarth at any other time, but now seemed like the face of cold indifference. Her journey to Lancaster was the conclusion to a bitter battle between mother and son. For, as head of the family, William preferred to take the protection and defence of Charlotte entirely upon himself. Within an hour of hearing the news from Lord Kersall, he had resigned his public offices, sought advice as to a sound lawyer, bribed the Millbridge jailer to make Charlotte more comfortable, sent in Dr Hamish Standish to dress her hand, and talked to her for a long while in the attempt to understand why she had behaved in such a fashion. All this he wanted to spare Dorcas, but she would not let him.

She had browbeaten Tom to drive her into Millbridge to visit Charlotte, and come home white and shaken from the ordeal. She had taken William's refusal to let her attend the Lancaster trial very badly, sending Tom back into Millbridge to book a seat upon the mail-coach, and weeping all afternoon when there was not one to be had. Whereupon Nellie wound her shawl round her head and shoulders and hurried to the Hall, to convince William and Zelah that Dorcas was prepared to walk to Lancaster and sleep out of doors sooner than give up the idea of going.

'Then thee must take her with thee, William,' said Zelah, understanding.

'But she could die of the effort, let alone the trouble!' he said, aghast.

'I'm feared she'll die if she stops here,' said Nellie, crying and wiping her eyes on the corner of her shawl. 'Best let her die the road she wants, Mr William.'

So on the appointed day William's coach was fetched round from the stables and packed with every comfort and delicacy. And at Bracelet Nellie and Tom helped up the indomitable Dorcas, complete with her case of home-made medicines and ointments, her Bible and prayer-book, and a small trunk of clean clothing. In sorry triumph she sat opposite her son, the ironmaster, who contemplated her with love and resignation. She soon fell asleep, and the coach rolled out of Millbridge on to the great turnpike road, and headed for the north. Its boot was filled with gifts for Charlotte from Kingswood Hall, Thornton House and Kit's Hill.

A traitor Charlotte might be in the eyes of the world, but to the Howarths she was still one of them, and the family closed ranks to protect her.

William and Dorcas made the sixty-mile journey in easy stages. She slept much and spoke little, conserving her energy for the trials ahead. But once, when they had dined and refreshed themselves at a particularly fine old hostelry, she said with a gleam of pleasure, 'Why, we have not had such an adventure together since we travelled to Birmingham!' Then she remembered the joy of that journey and the sorrow of this one, and her little satisfaction vanished.

A friend of William had offered them private lodgings in Church Street, where every member of the household strove to anticipate their wants and treat them with sympathetic kindness. But Dorcas sat long at her bedroom window that first night, gazing towards the ancient castle and picturing her daughter lying alone in darkness there.

Though William's money had provided her with all the amenities a prison could offer, prison could not be disguised. There was a dank odour in the cell which clung to Charlotte's clothes, tainted her flesh, pervaded the air; and it caused her lawyer to keep a scented handkerchief in his hand, and hold it now and again to his nose. Mr Pacey was a shrewd and agreeable fellow who would go far in his profession. He treated Charlotte with the courtesy due to a lady who has a rich and generous brother, but he was coming close to exasperation with the prisoner herself.

'Will you please to understand, madam, that you are confusing the issue with abstract notions of truth and justice,' he urged, 'and are like to lose your life if you insist upon this course! Pray let me plead for your gentle upbringing and gentler sex,' and here he cleared his throat and spoke in a mellifluous voice. 'A good wife is her husband's mirror, madam, reflecting his thoughts and moods, his aspirations and beliefs. She is an echo of his own ambition, his closest companion, his most trusted counsellor. Should we blame her, therefore, if her womanly tenderness is turned into channels she would not have followed, left to herself? If that charity for the unfortunate, so amiably displayed by other female members of her family, should become in her an abiding obsession? If, in a word, she were *misled*, should we hang her for it?'

He paused, head upon one side, bird-like in his contemplation of an invisible judge. His voice deepened.

'In every other respect, Mrs Longe, you have been exemplary. A devoted daughter, a loving mother, a loyal friend. I believe you to have been carried away by your own virtues. It is your virtues that shall plead for you, and the weakness—the natural weakness—of your sex!'

He became practical and brisk.

'Now, madam, Mr Ackroyd is quite properly pleading guilty and will take full responsibility for this Jack Straw business. I have spoke with him, and he is anxious to give you every advantage. He will modify his evidence so that the length of time you were together and your knowledge as to the complete workings of this secret society are somewhat smoothed over. You will seem more sinned against than sinning. If we present your case in the way I suggest, and throw ourselves upon the mercy of the court, I think we may be reasonably sure of a light sentence.'

She sat, hands manacled, head bent. She looked unutterably weary, possessed by a sadness which diminished her to a small grey woman on a hard chair.

'Will you consider these things carefully, Mrs Longe?' he asked.

Charlotte said quietly, 'Sir, I shall consider nothing but speaking the truth as I know it, and leaving my case to be decided as justice perceives it.'

Mr Pacey allowed himself a sigh of frustration. Charlotte lifted her head and regarded him with considerable irony.

'I do not wish Mr Ackroyd to distort his evidence, nor you to distort my character, sir, in the manner you have described to me. You may see it as a chivalrous gesture on your part, but I find it to be a vile calumny. I shall refute it utterly. Dear God, that you should make such a poor fool out of me! Why, how should I live after, having denied the very principles by which I lived at all?'

He said, as persuasively as he could, 'Then, madam, will you remain silent while I speak for you?'

'No, sir,' said Charlotte. 'I shall not.'

The interview seemed to have given her strength, for her voice now sounded resonant and she sat more upright. Mr Pacey shook his head, and bade her good-day.

But to William he said, 'Sir, your sister is too human to have the makings of a saint, but she may well become a martyr!'

'Then what do you propose, sir? For I expect you to do something for her.'

Mr Pacey judged his man accurately.

'Well, sir, we may roughly divide the trials into five sections. (Though I beg you to consider this as a reasonable guess rather than a definitive promise!) There are those whom they will hang: the male leaders of Jack Straw and Ned Ludd. They will be heard the first day. Then there are those who will be hanged or transported for life: such as used violence, are of poor character, or were seen to be in the thick of the trouble. That is the second day. On the third day there will be a mixture of good-hearted fools, and these will be sentenced to some years of transportation or imprisonment. The fourth day will see some imprisoned, and some pardoned. We shall save Mrs Longe to the last. She is the only woman, and for such a strong-minded woman she seems uncommonly gentle. If we could silence that articulate tongue, sir, meaning no offence, we might get her off entirely! However, she will appear when justice has been done and all are weary, and they wish to be merciful and go home again.

'I suggest, sir, that we leave her character to her witnesses: her personal maids, a friend or two, who will paint the picture we want. Then I shall say what she will allow me to say on her behalf, and hope she will not spoil my impression. And we shall be careful to keep away from dangerous ground as far as possible.'

'That does not sound much,' said William slowly, 'and there is much at stake!'

'It is all she will let me do, sir. If you can persuade her differently then pray do so!'

The newspapers were less charitable to Charlotte. The fact of her being the only woman on the committee gave rise to gross speculation as to her morals and intentions. Cartoons depicted her dressed as a French revolutionary, knitting at the foot of the guillotine, while heads flew into the air labelled, 'Democracy!' 'Freedom!' 'King!' 'Country!' 'Church!' and suchlike emotive words. In London, her past as a writer for the Radical press, her friendship with Mary Wollstonecraft, her marriage to Toby Longe were all dredged up and furbished to fit the present image. Stories circulated which people loved to read, and her family would have loved to deny, and grains of truth swelled up into full wheat-stalks of falsehood. The Tory press denounced her entirely.

In Wiltshire, the Jarvis Poles endured anonymous letters, knowing looks, and explicable coldness. They also discovered their true friends, and the strength which lies at the heart of a united family.

In London, Ambrose Longe and all those who belonged to a Radical press began to hammer home the opposite point of view.

The Wyndendale Post and its chief influence, Lord Kersall, had been neatly gored by a dilemma. Were they to be vindictive about the Red Rose Society they would increase the number of questions as to why it had gone on so long, and thereby hurt the valley's reputation. For was not the headmaster of its boasted and respected grammar school the leader of this society? Was not Charlotte sister to one of its richest and most powerful industrial magnates? Were there not a number of highly respected citizens on its committee? And yet, if they did not rant and rage and call upon heaven to witness their horror, would it not seem that they condoned these rebels? So they compromised: playing down the Red Rose Society and venting their spleen upon the weavers and Luddites.

'You will, of course, naturally deny that there was any immorality on your part, should the prosecution—most unfairly—take the attitude of the popular press, Mrs Longe?' said Mr Pacey in some anxiety.

'I shall certainly deny the general charge of immorality,' Charlotte replied. 'But if they specifically mention Mr Ackroyd I must witness to the heart's affection, sir.'

He would have liked to have hidden his face in his hands for a moment.

'With regard to other libels,' he said carefully. 'You would deny you were an atheist, for instance, I hope, madam?'

'I am not an atheist for I believe in God, and in the merciful salvation of God. But I have not been to church for a long while, so I dare say they would read that as being the mark of an unbeliever.'

'How would you read it, madam?' he asked sarcastically.

'That the preacher at my church was a hypocrite, and the members of the congregation more so, sir.'

She was, he saw with terror, improving in her spirits: more than capable of producing the speech that would damn her to perdition.

'Let us hope, Mrs Longe,' he said without hope, 'that these questions do not arise.'

Dorcas visited her daily, smuggling in comforts, seeming to gather strength from the sight of Charlotte eating a fine pear and wiping her fingers on her handkerchief, or wearing a clean gown. She did not ask for details of the personal or political past, accepting that it was alien to her and would remain so. That she could love her daughter so deeply as to put aside all question of morality amazed and puzzled Dorcas. And Charlotte was humble in the face of such devotion, contriving to speak cheerfully of small things, so that great ones should not bruise it.

Then, upon the eve of the trial, she found joy in another direction. For Ambrose arrived in Lancaster, with the sweetest and most steadfast of messages from Cicely and Jarvis and the children, and paid the jailer so handsomely that they were able to sup together. He had brought with him an artist who sketched for Ambrose's newspaper, and while they talked over a bottle of wine the lad drew that portrait of Charlotte which is best known: chin propped upon her manacled hands, her hair a little untidy, one slipper coming away from her foot as she sits with her face turned towards her son, but having such an air of grace and brightness about her that anyone who knew Charlotte would say, 'Ah! He has caught her admirably!'

The jailer must have lined his purse well that evening, for Ambrose visited his former headmaster also, and carried the first private message that Jack and Charlotte had been able to exchange since they were arrested. And as the young man tactfully contrived to make a great show of opening another bottle of claret Jack read the letter twice. Then Ambrose folded it carefully, and put it back in his coat pocket, and the artist was brought in again, and executed a remarkable likeness: strong and brooding. And shook his hand, and wished him well, and left headmaster and pupil together.

'Well then, my lad,' said Jack affectionately, 'how goes the world?'

'Oh, upside-down and inside-out, as usual, sir.'

'You can speak plain,' said Jack. 'I shall not come out of this alive, but we could save your mother—if she would let us.'

'I fear not, sir,' Ambrose replied. 'The charitable machinations of my uncle, the ironmaster, have gone somewhat awry.

I come as herald of news which will reach you officially to-morrow morning. You and my mother are to stand trial together, on the first day. Justice plans to begin, as it were, at the beginning, with Jack Straw. And to end with Jim Ogden and Ned Ludd. Thus bringing every insurrectionist into the net. They have more stomach for punishment than we had supposed. . . .'

The courtroom was already stuffy at eight o'clock in the morning, and many a lady would faint later on. Four judges sat in majesty, five counsel for the prosecution were ready to draw blood. The defence lawyers looked very collected. In the dock, decently separated, stood Jack Ackroyd and Charlotte Longe. Depicted in pencil by artists of the day they seem very human. He stands easily, with his hands chained behind the tails of his coat. She gracefully, with her hands chained before her. You cannot tell what age they are, except that youth has passed them by. They seem ageless, and although there is a space between them they stand together, the link is almost tangible.

'. . . in that the Accused, and a great number of False Traitors whose names are yet Unknown, did secretly Form an organisation known as the Red Rose Society, later called after its Password—*Jack Straw*. And over Many Years did unlawfully, viciously and seditiously Pursue. . . .'

Dorcas took out her smelling-bottle and contrived to sniff it without attracting William's attention. And though she was pleased to escape his notice she could not help thinking that Ned would never have missed that surreptitious dip into the velvet reticule. The courtroom was exceedingly noisy. Folk were walking about and eating oranges, chatting to their neighbours. A child cried and was hushed. A dog was chased out, but not before he had urinated against the door-post.

Counsel opening the case for the prosecution rose, giving the impression that he needed no evidence whatsoever and could convict on sight. Still, he must satisfy those who did not know as much as he did about politics and people.

He had decided to use Jack Ackroyd as a stick with which to beat social reform, and Charlotte as an example of the monstrous new woman. He would begin, he said, with the *man* known commonly as Jack Straw. The court would notice that he did not say *gentleman*, for gentility was foreign to such a person. Jack Straw had been the youngest son of a weaver, better to have remained in that station of life to which it had pleased God to call him. . . .

He then painted an idyllic portrait of Millbridge before the Fall, which those who had lived in lower stations would by no means have recognised as their own. He waxed eloquent upon that good but eccentric academic, Mr Henry Tucker, a *gentleman* who believed that by gorging the poor with education you improved them, helped them and changed them. Here he paused emphatically.

'Changed them?' he asked, upon a rising note. 'Does a snake change when it sheds its skin? Does a change of clothes make a difference in a man's nature? Does a smattering of grammar, or the ability to tot up a column of figures, or the acquisition of a few Latin tags alter a poor-born *villain?*'

The court was very much quieter now, and the Honourable Mr Runciman dropped his voice to a purr.

'Why do I say *villain?*' he enquired of them poignantly. 'Does low birth mean villainy? Not at all. There are those now tilling fields who will, in a better world than this, sit among the angels. Good men, honest men, better men than some of their masters, and poor men all. It is not of them I speak.'

Having made sure that the country would not suffer from lack of service, he whipped round to where Jack regarded him sombrely, and pointed his finger at the dock.

'But there stands a *villain!*' he announced. 'Was he grateful for that excellent scholar's charity? Did he thank God upon his knees each night? Did he labour to instil a proper sense of values into his pupils? Did he endeavour to serve his King and his Country? Did he, in any way whatsoever, show the smallest gratitude towards the society which had so graciously taken this *viper* to its bosom?'

Dorcas frowned slightly, and put her handkerchief to her lips. William sighed and crossed his legs. Mr Pacey smiled sarcastically. Charlotte and Jack stood in cold dignity. They had been warned to expect this, but it was more difficult to listen to than they had imagined.

'NO!' roared counsel for the prosecution, thus effectively silencing the last chatterer. 'He did not. This creature does not believe in God!' A gasp went round the courtroom. 'His morals are his own. He makes his own rules. Good and evil are not decided in Heaven Above!' His finger pointed up at the dirty ceiling. 'They are decided by a *worm* who does not know the difference between them! And he does not care for social order, nor King nor Country. He would change it to something'—here he fluttered his fingers to indicate that Jack had not quite made up his mind—'something more to his taste. Such as a place where honest men are robbed of the fruit of their labours, where property can be stolen or destroyed, where women and children can crouch shivering in their beds of a night, where weapons are stolen and used against one's own friends and kin, where the *Mob is King!*'

He had ended in a cry of horror, and horror ran round the room, echoed by the listening audience.

'But this is not enough,' said the Honourable Mr Runciman sorrowfully. 'He must also corrupt a lady who was hitherto of impeccable reputation!' Here all eyes were turned upon Charlotte, who looked proudly at the wall to avoid them. 'And not only does he get her to do his dirty work'—laughter from him and the crowd—'but he attempts to hide behind her skirts when the game is up!' Jeers and cheers. 'Oh, what a *gentleman* is this!'

I wonder how he is going to castigate me, Charlotte thought, having presented me as impeccable! She need not have concerned herself. Mr Runciman was as agile as his metaphors. Having set the scene, as it were, he now painted in the details with a fine brush: thus showing the depth and breadth of his researches. For diligence, Charlotte had to admire him. When he was done, Jack Straw was a villain indeed.

'And now let us consider his lady accomplice,' said Mr Runciman mildly, and the room gave a satisfied little sigh, and made themselves more comfortable on the wooden benches. 'Ah, what a different fortune was hers!'

Another idyll ensued, which was nearer the truth but unctuously delivered. He described Ned as 'an honest yeoman', Dorcas as 'gently born and highly principled', he gave William an accolade to keep him sweet. He even played down the deeds of Toby Longe, who came out much as Henry Tucker had done: very mistaken but well-intentioned.

'A lone widow,' said Mr Runciman deeply, 'with two small children to care for, what does she do, to whom does she turn? *To her family!*' Almost, they could hear the choirs of angels. 'She hides her head, she nurses her sorrow, in the fields of her childhood. The past is forgotten. That radical grafting has not taken. She is free to pursue the mild, pure path of her youth.' Their faces were solemn, their mouths hung slightly open in contemplation. 'But what have we

378

here?' cried the honourable gentleman, seeing the snake rear yet again in Eden. 'We have our Godless Friend, Mr Ackroyd. He has all the wickedness it takes to rouse discontent among working folk, but he lacks one vital ingredient in his Recipe for Revolution! He lacks the Yeast that makes it rise. Mrs Longe, in her involvement with her husband's business, has acquired all the skills of a secretary and pamphleteer. She knows that she has gone astray in the past. She wishes to right herself in the future. But—he—will—not—let—her!'

Here, counsel for the prosecution described Jack as 'a ravening wolf', juggled the dates to suit his convenience, started Charlotte's evening classes as a charity which became mere cover for adultery, and fetched Jack in with his underhand schemes for seduction and betrayal. He gave a description of purity defiled of corruption absolute, likened Charlotte to the lamb for slaughter, whetted their appetite, satisfied their desire for lechery, and then set himself right in the eyes of the law.

'. . . I do not bring in any evidence as to the intimate relationship between Jack Straw and Mrs Longe, for this does not concern the issue, which is entirely one of treason. We do not bring their morals into question. Their code of conduct *may* not *be our own!*' Fair-minded, he lifted his eyebrows to indicate that the law was great enough to live and let live. 'So we shall dismiss these things from our minds!' Which, of course, they could not and did not. 'But what was the effect upon Mrs Longe? Oh, grievous, grievous!'

Now it is indeed my turn, thought Charlotte, and felt naked before them all, for there was sufficient truth in the distortion to give her pause.

The honourable counsel evidently did not care for females unless, like most men, he could either pay them or discount them. Mary Wollstonecraft and her *Vindication of the Rights of Women* was well known to him in the past. He fetched up the old phrase 'hyenas in petticoats' to describe such creatures. He became possessed. Now Charlotte was brought down to the dust, crumbled: a broken statue of womanly virtue. He described the full extent of her fall from grace, told of books hidden in her private room, spat out the titles of the political ones, stopped with a shudder before mentioning others.

'I would not soil my lips, nor soil the minds of gentle females here,' he said gravely, 'with the vicious, bestial and filthy literature found in this woman's keeping. . . .'

He gathered himself for the final injunction.

'In a long, and I hope I may say *honourable*, career,' said Mr Runciman, giving the impression that he had wrestled with evil and was exhausted, 'I have not come across such monstrous joint depravity before. I have not been so— ashamed? Yes, that is how I should describe my feeling. But I leave the question of justice to you. The evidence is very clear. I do not doubt your conclusions.'

Whereupon he sat down and drank off a glass of wine which one of the court servants brought him, and seemed much refreshed by his exercise.

They had dredged up every witness who could have held a grudge against either of the prisoners. Most of them were poor, for even such prejudiced ladies as Mrs Graham would have declined to make a public spectacle of themselves. Also, as Charlotte noted with irony, William's money and power granted her a certain degree of protection. They did not care tuppence for her, but her brother was a different matter. But Jack Ackroyd took every sling and arrow that misfortune could aim at him, and even members of Millbridge Council bore witness to his temper—'fiendish bursts of rage'—his efforts to help the poor—'seditious suggestions'—his honesty— 'slander'—and his solitary nature—'secret plotting'.

The evidence for the prosecution rolled on like some ponderous wagon of destruction, and the hands of the clock crept past noon, and someone brought Charlotte a chair. Jack shifted his position to afford himself relief. His rheumatism had come on apace in prison. Folk went outside to drink and eat, and came back again wiping their mouths, or unwrapped the food they had brought and passed bottles between them. At one stage William escorted Dorcas into fresher air and they did not return for some time. And, like any audience at the theatre, the crowd reflected the quality of entertainment. If it flagged they yawned and talked among themselves. When it tickled their fancy they roared applause, groaned sanctimonious assent, sniggered at sly digs, hissed foul-play, and listened with hushed attention.

Now Mr Pacey was up to speak for the defence, and had evidently found the Honourable Mr Runciman a great jester. What a storm in a teacup he had raised! What mountains he had made from honest mole-hills! And piece by piece he stuck the statue of Charlotte Longe together again, laughing a little at 'these gross exaggerations' of her library and her character, but careful not to rouse his client's argumentative nature; depicting her somewhat as Ambrose had all those years ago, and for the same good reason—a learned, spinsterish lady with a strong sense of duty towards the less fortunate. He did very well indeed: not too much, not too little. And sat down again.

Jack's lawyer, Mr Hazard, was of a different kidney, being much like his client but clever enough to stay upon the right side of society and its laws. He was gaining a tremendous reputation for defending Luddites locally, and he did Jack proud. He swept away all notions of ravening wolves and rearing snakes as irrelevant rubbish. He went to the heart of the matter. He described the Society of the Red Rose as Charlotte and Jack had known and intended it. Perhaps he erred this side of softness, but it was well done. And he thrust the first wedge in the prosecution's argument, for they intended to mix and judge the whole boiling of prisoners together, whereas Mr Hazard wanted the activities of Charlotte and Jack and the Red Rose to be separate from the Wyndendale Rising. Again and again in the week of the trials, he brought the argument back to this point. Hal Middleton was saved by him, and so was Dr Wilkins: one to be transported for life, the other to a term of imprisonment: they would have been hanged else.

The day dragged on. The court recessed for necessary reasons. Charlotte and Jack could eat nothing, but they drank a little wine and water. The arguments went back and forth. And every time a counsel for the prosecution rose, Charlotte felt as though a hand had thrown mud into her face and on her clothes. She saw her mother wince and whiten, saw William's lips compress into a line of distaste, and heard Ambrose cry, 'Shame!' from the side of the court. She knew that all Wyndendale would read of this, and that any who had the least cause to envy the Howarths could now lambast them. The mud spread and spattered. Mr Pacey was up again, protesting, and suddenly Charlotte thought to herself, 'Why am I here?' She saw the Honourable Mr Runciman drinking his wine, unconcerned, viewing his colleague's performance with the appreciation one might bestow upon a particularly fine cock in a particularly vicious cock-fight. She saw the faces of the crowd, grinning, gaping. She saw the bitterness in Jack's eyes.

Charlotte cried, 'Stop!' and struck the top rail of the dock. 'Stop!' she cried, and struck the rail with her chained hands.

The audience gave her their hushed attention, obedient to drama. The counsel for the prosecution sat aghast. The judges all peered and frowned. Mr Pacey covered his eyes. But Dorcas sat very upright and willed her daughter to look in her direction, and nodded twice, thrice when she did.

'Order! Order in court!'

'Sit down, Mrs Longe!' said one of the judges.

'No, I will not. I will not. Take our lives if you must, prove that we have unwittingly been used for wrongful purposes, say if it pleases you that you abhor our ideals, detest our convictions. That would be fair enough. But, in the name of that justice which you represent, do not obscenely revile us like fish-wives in the street. . . .'

The courtroom now divided into two factions: players and spectators, the players bent on silencing Charlotte, and the spectators bent on hearing her.

'Order! Order! Order!'

'Let her have her say! You've been jawing long enough!'

'I shall clear the courtroom!'

'Oh, shurrup!' cried one big woman who was eating an apple, and she threw the rest of the fruit at the Honourable Mr Runciman and hit him on the chin, whereupon the whole audience fell about with laughter.

Still Charlotte spoke out, as loud and clear as she could, pushing away those who would try to silence her.

'There are human lives at stake and you play games among yourselves. What do you care for any of us more than your fees are worth? You should be humbler, truer, more compassionate in your great station. . . .'

'Lift her bodily, and remove her from the courtroom!' one judge ordered.

'You prate of morality!' she cried, above the heads of the crowd. 'Why, you have not the morality of swine at the trough. . . .'

'That's right, love, you give it to 'em!' shouted the big woman, and a constable pushed his way through the throng to reach her.

'You cannot try me or Jack Ackroyd! You are not fit to judge. You are not to fit to judge. . . .'

The crowd took up the chant and roared it at the bench.

'Not—fit—to—judge!'

'Clear the court!'

Mr Pacey removed his hand from his eyes. He turned round to William.

He said, 'She has done more harm than I should have supposed possible.'

William replied, tight-lipped, 'Yet she had a point there, Mr Pacey.'

'Yes, sir, but we are not concerned with truth and justice. We are trying criminal cases. Mrs Longe never seemed able to see the difference!'

An hour later the Honourable Mr Runciman rose in a subdued courtroom. Charlotte was back in the dock, and they had fastened leg-irons on her. Someone had brought Jack a chair, since he was in considerable pain with his rheumatic hip and knee. Now, late in the afternoon, he shuffled the chair a little nearer to Charlotte and endeavoured to comfort her with closeness.

'Well, well, well,' said Mr Runciman in dulcet tones. 'I feel we have had an excellent example of what Mrs Longe can do by way of raising a riot! Perhaps we should ask Mr Ackroyd to oblige us as well, and then we could take a verdict and go home to our suppers with a good conscience!'

The crowd laughed moderately. Not too much, because there was something about Mr Runciman that warned them to behave themselves, or perhaps they might find themselves in leg-irons with a bruised face, too. But Dorcas cried softly into her handkerchief, knowing that Charlotte could not be helped, and after a while William leaned forward and held a whispered conversation with Mr Pacey, who nodded. Then the ironmaster assisted his mother to rise, and they began as unobtrusively as possible to make their way out of the room. There was nothing more to stay for, except the verdicts, and those were almost certain. Someone was calling a witness back to the stand, there was a lull in the proceedings. As they passed the dock on Charlotte's side she looked down pitifully and they walked as slowly as they could.

'God bless you, love,' Dorcas whispered as they passed.

William nodded, and touched Charlotte's arm. Then he moved in front of his mother so that she should not see the leg-irons, and saw them very clearly himself, as though they were ten times life-size. On the thickest part of the ring was stamped the two-headed mark of Belbrook.

'Transportation for seven years,' said Mr Pacey, and did not know whether he would be praised or blamed for it. 'I feared a sentence of hanging, followed by a pardon, and commuted to transportation for life, myself!'

Dorcas was lying in the Church Street drawing-room upon a day-couch, and she looked to her son for an answer.

'Could we not plead against it, Mr Pacey?'

'My dear sir, after such an exhibition as we had today? Rather thank God for it. Seven years is not too bad. People do return.'

'But Charlotte was never robust,' said Dorcas faintly. 'We had to send her to Millbridge in the end. Because of her lungs.'

Neither man knew what to say.

'Shall we see her before she goes, sir?' Dorcas asked.

'Oh yes, madam. That can certainly be arranged.'

'And what of Mr Ackroyd?' William enquired, as he saw the lawyer to the door himself.

'Oh, to be hanged, of course. I never expected any other outcome.'

'When, sir?'

'It will take a month or so for the death-sentence to be confirmed. Shall you be coming up for it?' Conversationally.

Mother and daughter sat side by side, each grieving for the other.

Then Dorcas said, almost in her normal voice, 'Well, we have not all the time in the world, and there is much to be said. I have been thinking, Charlotte, about your voyage and so forth. . . .'

As though her daughter were about to take the boat for Calais.

'. . . of course, I know where Australia is on the globe, and you may find the climate trying at first. So I have fetched you my own medicine-chest. You and William may mock at me, but I have been proved right over and over again. . . .'

It was wonderful, William thought, how she donned this old self of hers to comfort Charlotte, when she had scarcely been able to rise from her couch the day before.

Charlotte laughed somewhat shakily. The leg-irons shamed her, made her move awkwardly. Her bruised cheek gave her a defenceless air. William's money could not assuage these things, but what he could do for her he would, right up to the moment of sailing.

'And, though you do not go to church as often as you did,' said Dorcas gently, 'I had thought that you would like to have my Bible and my prayer-book by you. For comfort.'

Then Charlotte began to cry silently and to hold out her chained hands as if to say, 'I cannot help it!' And Dorcas bent and cradled Charlotte's head against her shoulder, and hushed her as she used to do when Charlotte was a little girl, and spoke words of hope. While William suffered for them both.

'Now you will do very well. An end is always a new beginning. And you have great strength, Charlotte. Let us look upon the brighter side,' said Dorcas, wondering what side that might be. 'You will be needed there, my love. Do not tell me, after that *exhibition*'—she used Mr Pacey's word, but ascribed it to the opposition—'of so-called justice, that there are not others like you. Yes, I see it all,' she said very cheerfully. 'There is a purpose to everything. Even to our trouble of the moment.'

She stroked Charlotte's hair abstractedly. William saw that her strength was failing.

'Mamma,' he said softly, 'go and sit outside where it is quiet. For a few minutes. Just while I tell Charlotte our arrangements for her.'

He offered her his arm, and she rose and went with him like a sleep-walker, while Charlotte dried her eyes on her sleeve.

'She should not have come, Willie,' she said.

'No. But we could not dissuade her.'

Charlotte said, looking at her chains, 'I have enough upon my conscience, without her death.'

He replied awkwardly, 'It is not as bad as that.'

But Dorcas, sitting in the jailer's chair by the door, said to him, 'Her hair is grown quite grey. I believe I have had enough of trouble. We shall not see each other again. At least, not in this cruel world.'

THIRTY

Death of a Great Lady

William had kept the carriage windows closed as they came through Wyndendale, for Dorcas murmured that the smell of sulphur made her sick and faint. But as they drove through the gateway of Kingswood Hall the trees closed overhead, bringing a dark and spicy perfume to revive her, deadening the roar of Snape. The night was beautiful, warm from the garnered day, dense with dew. The ironmaster stepped out into a moonlit garden under a heaven of stars.

'We are home, Mamma,' said William gently, holding out his hand.

Then he saw by her face, small and white and scared, that she had not the strength to rise from her seat. So he half-carried her, and she felt no heavier than a child in his arms.

His household began to revolve around him. Servants fetched their baggage out, took the coach and horses to the stables, came unobtrusively to help their master. Zelah was by his side now: a noiseless step, a kiss upon his cheek. His daughters surrounded him, relieved to see the travellers returned, murmuring greetings, looking compassionately at his light burden.

'Thy room is prepared for thee, Mrs Dorcas,' said Zelah, and placed a warm white hand upon those two small cold ones. 'Thee needs a bowl of hot soup and a toast.'

'Where have you brought me?' Dorcas cried, agitated. 'I must go home, at once. Ned will be waiting all this while.'

'Bring her upstairs, love,' said Zelah. 'Tibby and Kitty, I shall need thee to help me with Grandmama. Nancy and Livvy, sit with thy father while he eats. Sophie and Molly, thee must go to bed now.'

'What a lot of children,' Dorcas whispered to herself. 'Where have they all come from?'

She let her hand trail on the banister, wondering. She did not know now who carried her, or the woman at his side.

'But they are being very kind to me,' said Dorcas. 'I shall

tell Ned that he need not have worried.' Then she remembered. 'No, no,' she cried, quite strongly. 'You must take me to Kit's Hill. Ned will be riding along the road, looking for me in the dark.'

'We shall send for him to come here,' said Zelah soothing her.

Dorcas began to cry weakly: a stranger in a strange place.

'Please to allow me to go home,' she begged. 'It is very late, and I have been away such a while.'

'God help me,' said William, from the bottom of his heart. 'I do not think I can bear more.'

'Nay, thee must,' Zelah answered sadly. 'Here, lay her down and go to thy supper, love. Then thee can come and see her later, when she is settled.'

'I do not know you,' Dorcas cried in terror. 'Where have you brought me?'

'Mrs Dorcas,' said Zelah, sitting by her, giving her hands a friendly little shake, 'it is thy daughter, Zelah. We have brought thee here to rest. Thou hast had a long, hard journey.'

'My daughter?' murmured Dorcas.

An image of Charlotte's ash-grey head lay against her shoulder. She stroked the hair softly, grieving over it. Then in a second, past and present and future merged. She received the full force of Charlotte's plight in one tremendous blow, and wailed like child who is utterly lost.

'Oh, I shall die,' cried Dorcas.

'I do not practise medicine these days,' said Matthew Standish truculently to William, 'but I have come with my nephew in a personal capacity. Miss Dorcas is an old friend of mine. Indeed she is the only friend. For we are both seven-and-seventy years of age, and all the rest are gone.'

So he took his rheumatism painfully up the wide staircase, making crooked progress with the aid of his stick. And his nephew followed him into the large light room where Dorcas lay upon a hill of pillows.

'Well, do your duty, sir!' he ordered Hamish, who was hanging courteously back. 'I shall not be here for ever, you know. You must learn to conduct your practice by yourself!'

Which Hamish would have been very glad to do, but could not say so. He examined Dorcas gently and carefully, which she allowed as being a necessary nuisance. Then he shrugged slightly, turning to his uncle for advice. But Matthew Standish did not trouble with the body. He came forward and looked into her eyes, to discern the temper of the spirit, and asked her how she was.

'I am pretty well this morning, sir,' Dorcas answered, 'but I do not wish to make an effort.'

'Why should you, ma'am?' said Matthew kindly. 'Rest as much as you can.'

'So you are not going to bleed me, nor set leeches on me, nor cauterise me, nor blister me, sir?' she asked anxiously.

'No, no. There is no need of that. No need of anything. A little wine. A light diet. A sleep when you feel tired.'

'I am glad of that,' said Dorcas to herself, smoothing the sheet beneath her fingers, 'for I have not the strength to endure it, and I should not like to die unseemly.'

Matthew Standish regarded her sombrely. His hands, folded upon the carved head of his stick, were cruelly knobbed.

Dorcas's attention wandered. She said, 'I should like to consult you as to Charlotte's health, sir. You was always concerned for her lungs. She is sailing to the other side of the world, you know.'

'Oh, then she is in the best possible case,' said the old doctor in a careless tone. 'A voyage to a warmer climate. Sea air and sunshine. I would recommend that above all things.'

Dorcas brightened. Matthew Standish bent his head.

'Your children will take care of themselves now, ma'am,' he said. 'You have done your duty!' And he lifted the hand which lay so lightly on the coverlet, and kissed it in a courtly fashion. 'Good-day to you, Miss Dorcas,' he said.

Dick Howarth and his family drove up in the farm wagon, since there was nothing else at Kit's Hill big enough to hold them all. And they trod softly along the corridor and stood outside her door with reverence.

The woeful face of the little maid who preceded them looked pleasantly familiar.

'Now you're a Bowker, if ever I saw one!' said Dick, heartened by this homely fact in the midst of splendour and death.

'Yes sir, please sir. Letty Bowker.'

So Dick gave her sixpence, and then wondered if he had done right.

There was a movement among the family as the Howarths entered. They came forward to press Dick's hand or kiss his cheek, to nod a welcome and whisper a condolence. They were all there: William and Zelah and the girls, Ambrose Longe, Cicely and Jarvis Pole and their brood. All there except Charlotte.

'We come as soon as you sent word,' Dick said hoarsely, 'but it's allus the same. Them as lives nearest gets there last.'

They were a handsome crowd of people, composed in manner, elegantly dressed. From the grave grandeur of the ironmaster to the small oval face of Dorcas Pole, they bore the marks of close relationship. Standing before them, his hat still clutched in his hands, Dick Howarth seemed a person apart: an honest yeoman, some seven-and-thirty years of age, sturdily built, his skin reddened by all weathers. He looked so simple, and yet he subtly perceived in Zelah the fatigue of long nursing.

They cleared a place for him by the bed, and suddenly all the faces and soft sounds receded, leaving only one face, one quiet drawing of breath.

Propped high against the white pillows, hands folded, eyes closed, Dorcas was dying as she had lived, in an orderly fashion. Zelah had brushed her hair and dressed it neatly under her best starched cap. There was lace on the cap, lace on the neck and cuffs of her best nightgown. But Dick noticed none of these fineries. He saw that she held her mouth as though it had been hurt, that there was a pucker of concern on her forehead, an air of loss, that now and again she gave the softest of moans as though she remembered something best forgotten.

'Come and sit by her, Dick,' said Zelah kindly. 'She will wake in a while. She talks quite freely and coherently. Then sleeps a little. Then talks again. It has been so for days. She will be glad to see thee.'

The children stood solemnly watching.

'Has she asked for me? I haven't been so lucky, the times I called,' said Dick, 'but you did tell her I come, didn't you?'

'Indeed we did, and she was glad of it, but she is something muddled as to people and time,' said the ironmaster, and he spoke lovingly of her. 'She had advised us all. And Mr Hurst has nearly slept here the last week! But her Will has become confused with that of Great-aunt Wilde, and the one my father wrote. So this morning she decided that you should inherit Kit's Hill, and I should have a thousand pounds to buy Belbrook!'

389

They sat together at their mother's side, and watched the coming and going of breath.

'And she has tied up my mother's annuity so that my father shall not draw the capital,' said Ambrose wryly.

He was very pale and looked far older than his years. There was in him a sternness of purpose, a depth of grief, which had never been called from Toby.

'Has she been very poorly-like?' Dick asked, nodding towards the composed face. 'She were weak when I saw her a-Wednesday, but not what I'd call poorly.'

'She is in no pain, thank heaven,' William answered, 'but sometimes restless and ill at ease, and exceedingly difficult to nurse.'

'Aye,' said Dick, understanding. 'She would be. She was allus fond of her own road! But do you mind how she nursed our Betty, all them years since? Day and night. Night and day. All through that summer and well into Martinmas.'

'Why, you could have been no more than five at the time!'

'Aye, but I remember all about it, our Will. You was away in Birmingham until the last. They sent our Charlotte to stay with Aunt Phoebe at the Rectory, and they parcelled me off to Windygate for a while. Then they fetched us back at the end. It were foggy and wet. I remember my father holding me up to say goodbye to Betty, and she said I'd been a good lad. . . .'

They sat together in harmony, as they had not sat since they were young, while Dorcas paused and trembled upon the final threshold. The pale forehead puckered, the lips moved, the breath came short and quick.

'She is fretting again,' said William, and stroked her hand. 'What is she saying?'

A dry sob shook Dorcas. She moved her head from side to side as if to escape from something.

'Eh, why must it be so hard for her?' said Dick, and he cupped Dorcas's fluttering fingers and stilled them in his warm clasp.

'Now then, now then,' he soothed, as he would comfort a child in a nightmare. 'What's to do, my lass?'

Her eyes opened at the sound of his voice. She was with them again. They felt her presence as a physical shock of recognition in the room. It was miraculous. To have been so poor, so harassed and bonded. Then, in a moment, to have put aside dying as though it were a garment she chose not to wear. Her voice was weary but distinct.

'Why have you been so long?' she asked the familiar face.

He answered as his father would have done, directly and to the point.

'It's a fair way between here and Kit's Hill, tha knows. I come as soon as I could.'

'And you will take me back there before dark, will you not?' she asked anxiously.

'Aye, never fear,' said Dick, smiling. 'I'll take thee home.'

Reassured, she looked upon the assembly. Children, grand-children, great-grandchildren and old servants. And they moved closer to make their farewells.

She strove to raise herself, saying, 'Fetch my cloak, Nellie, if you please!' Then smiled on Dick alone. 'Wait for me,' she said. 'I shall be with you in a moment.'

And was gone.

THIRTY-ONE

Epilogue

They stood together bare-headed in Garth churchyard, two middle-aged men at the head of their families, and watched the sexton begin to spade earth on to the coffin.

'I had thought, somehow, that she would never die,' said William, in sorrowful disbelief.

'Eh, she'd have lived to be a hundred if it weren't for our Charlotte's trouble,' Dick replied quietly.

They stood a few moments longer, before walking away. The funeral had been subdued because of circumstances, but full of a profound respect. Many who were prepared to cut William on account of his sister had pressed his hand in silent sympathy on account of his mother. Humbler mourners had walked from Snape to attend the service and express their sorrow, and Garth villagers wrapped their shawls about their heads or took off their hats in quiet reverence. William and Dick did not know all of them, but Dorcas had, and they would remember her.

There were to be no junketings, but the privacy of the event suited the Howarths better. They had suffered too much

391

to go through a burial banquet as well. It was enough that her family, all but one, were there. They could drink ale or tea together and eat Alice's honest currant cakes, and spread the summer's jam on homebaked bread and butter, and talk as they felt inclined. By tacit consent, the brothers, as chief mourners, were left alone and presently went outside to look round Kit's Hill. And William lapsed into the comfortable speech he had used with Ned. Picking up fragments of the past.

'Mother drove us to Millbridge in the trap, one time, our Charlotte and me. We'd been mewed up for a long while with that cattle disease, rinder-pest. Forty years, come last May, it would be. And the blossom was out. I broke a sprig off for our Lottie. "Sit down!" says Mother, in that quick short way she had. And I sat. I did as I was told!'

They smiled at each other, knowing.

'Her back was as straight and supple as a willow wand. Then she points her little whip down below there, and says, "Look, children. You can see the journey we are going to make, almost from start to finish!" Aye, and the valley was different then. And I have to admit to being one of them as altered it so much.'

He was silent a moment. How could he be sorry? And yet some part of him grieved for the shining river and the villages strung like daisies on its chain.

'But it's allus the same up here, Dick,' he went on cheerfully. 'Kit's Hill doesn't change so as you'd notice it. It's a fair while since I've been here, too. Too long, to tell thee the truth. So shall us stretch our legs a bit and you can show me round? I've got summat to ask thee, Dick.'

They began to mount the long hill up to Scarth Nick, overlooking the valley. Dick strode easily, as one who was accustomed to such exercise. But William had to stop now and again, for he was some years older and no countryman these days.

'I'm leaving Wyndendale for good, lad. Nay, don't look so startled. There's nowt for me here now, and you know it. I've done no wrong but they've got a big stick now to beat me with, and there's too many of them want to get hold of it! They'll see that I go no further here, bar making a profit, and I want more than that. So we're off!'

But, Will, you was born and bred here,' said Dick, aghast. 'It's thy roots and home and family and all.'

'Eh, I'm not piking away tomorrow, lad. Nor next month,

nor maybe next year. I shall take my time and look round and find somewhere else for us. And I shall sell Snape. The war won't last for ever! And it might not be worth as much in peacetime. But I wanted thee to be the first to know, after Zelah, what I had in mind.'

'If she has a lad this time,' said Dick, thinking, 'he'll born out of his rightful place.'

'Aye, I know. But the Williams never stop at home, Betty Ackroyd used to say. I'd sooner stop and king it here, if I had the choice. But if they won't let me be king I'll go some place as will!' He grinned at his younger brother. 'They call that being a great man!' he said drily. 'Well, I've learned a thing or two the past few years, and I can tell thee who the great men are. The quiet ones like thee and my father, and Caleb. The ones as don't need a brass band to march in front of them and tell folks they're coming. It won't alter me to know that, but at least I do know it. I'm a nowt, as Betty would say!'

He laughed at his brother's perturbed face, and clapped him on the back companionably.

'Now listen to me, Dick, because you're the Howarth as matters. And you're the Howarth as is stopping her. How are you off for money, lad? The truth, mind! Tell me t'truth.'

'Well, a bit short, our Will. But nowt as a good harvest wouldn't put right.'

'That harvest never comes,' said William humorously, honestly. 'You're behind the times, our Dick, and that's just where I want you to be. I don't want any clever bugger improving Kit's Hill and turning it into a cotton-mill—nor an ironworks, neither, come to that! Now, I'm selling Bracelet and Thornton House and putting the money in our Charlotte's name. If she doesn't come back then it goes to her children. That's how she and Mother wanted it, and that's how it will be done. Hurst is seeing to it all for me, and he was fond of our Charlotte—still is—so I know he'll do more than his best for her.

'I'm selling my share of Belbrook to Caleb, at a bit below the fair price, which is what he deserves. He'll be ironmaster in Wyndendale then. By Gow, though, he'll be on his own here. He's got nobody. Well, some have all the luck and t'others dursen't step over the threshold! Any road, what I get for Belbrook will be a tidy sum, and I want that money to go to you and yours as soon as I get it. Wait a bit! Wait a bit!' Holding up his hand. 'Don't go and chuck it in my face afore

I've done talking! Hear what I have to say. It's not just for thee, lad. It's summat I can do for all of us, wherever we are. Father used to say that there'd been a Howarth at Kit's Hill as long as the farm had been there. Well, I'm making sure of that as far as I can do. I want summat to be right, whatever sort of a bugger's muddle goes on anywhere else. So think on, our Dick, afore you say no!'

Then he laughed aloud, and said, 'By Gow, you do look like Father when you're being awkward and stiff-necked, our Dick!'

They smiled at each other then in complete understanding. Nothing needed to be argued or explained. So they strode on past Owd Barebones and the Ha'penny Field: judged a coming crop of Swedish turnips, talked of the drovers. The evening was sweet and mild about them.

'It seems a poor thing just to say thankee, Will. But I do thank thee. And from the bottom of my heart.'

'You're doing me a favour,' said William, content.

They reached Breakneck, and surveyed Wyndendale.

'Well, we've come full circle, I reckon,' said Dick. 'This is where he died, nigh on thirteen years since! Eh, look at that view, wilta? If that doesn't beat all!'

Kit's Hill lay small and perfect below them, with smoke curling from its kitchen chimney.

'How long is it since we first built her?' William asked.

'Nay, God alone knows that.'

'I'll get Ellis Field to find out for us. We may as well keep the record straight. Oh, and that's another thing. Ambrose is taking all our Charlotte's private papers—not the Jack Straw lot, that was King's Evidence—papers she's had for years, since she was a lass. Essays in Latin and Greek. Letters that she and Toby Longe wrote to one another. Grand stuff,' said William humbly. 'She was a right smart lass. It's a bloody shame. It went wrong somewhere for her. I don't know how nor why.'

They began to walk down from the Nick.

'So if it's all right with you, Dick, I'd like to give our mother's papers to Cicely. They were very close, those two. Closer than Cicely and Charlotte. And the littlest lass is called Dorcas Pole. What do you think to that?'

'Aye, it's all right by me,' said Dick readily. 'Cicely won't treasure them more than I would, but she'd understand them better. Is there owt else to divide up?'

'Charlotte's bits and pieces, and Aunt Wilde's furniture,

will go to the children sometime. But I'm flummoxed what to do with Mother's stuff! She thought the world of that roomful of furniture she fetched in and out of Kit's Hill. It belonged to *her* mother.'

'It's nowt in our line,' Dick said. 'But what about your girls?'

'Too far ahead to judge. I was thinking. Should Cicely not have it as well as the papers? She and Jarvis aren't rich, and they have that great parsonage to fill. Then Mrs Dorcas can go in one piece.'

'Aye,' said Dick, his face clearing. He chuckled.

'What's to do?' asked William, grinning.

'Eh, I shouldn't laugh, but I mean no harm by it. I couldn't help thinking on, our Will.'

'Well, don't keep the joke to thyself, lad!'

'I were thinking. If the life hereafter is owt like this one—she'll be sorting father up right now, for all that he's been there longer than she has!'

Then they burst into peals of laughter, clapping each other's shoulders.

'I'll race thee down the slope!' cried William, eyes glinting, for he must prove himself over and over again, always.

'Right! I'll give thee a start, seeing as tha'rt eleven years older than me!'

And they ran down the hill, arms wide, shouting and laughing. So that those who saw them coming from afar off thought they looked like boys together.

10 July 1978–7 July 1980

About the Author

Jean Stubbs was born in the Lancashire described in *By Our Beginnings* and *An Imperfect Joy*. She has written over fourteen critically acclaimed novels. Currently she lives in a 200-year-old cottage in Cornwall with her husband, and is working on the next in this series of novels, which charts the fortunes of the Howarth clan from 1760 to the present.